I0756159

Shenanigans
SERVING PARANORMALS
SINCE THE DARK AGES

Holidazed

HOLIDAZED

A SHENANIGANS ANTHOLOGY

PEPPER MCGRAW

Paperback Edition

Cover and inside images from Dreamstime:
Woman in Devil Costume © Jana Guothova
Glass Bottle with Love Potion © Dopingagen
Silhouette Cat Pet Animal © Christos Georghiou
A Glass of Beer © Leonora Adamchuk
Pink Poodle © Madartists
Dragon Silhouette © Elena Kozyreva
Illustrated Christmas Tree © Darmuji Darmuji
Georghiou Smoky Girl © Doodkoalex
Abstract Background © Olga Altunina
Spiral Energy of Movement © Inna Belavina
Woman Walking Pink Poodle © Madartists
Horizontal Snowflake Background © Shanna Cramer
The Snowflake © Shanna Cramer
Day in Winter Forest Landscape © Mast3r
Valentines Day hearts background © Stekloduv
Abstract heart pattern © Tatyana Martirosyan
Couple next to tree of hearts © Oleg Lytvynenko
Girl Leprechaun on Shamrock © Baken
Magic Clover Background © Stekloduv
Designs for St. Patrick's Day © Dip2000
Heart shamrock © Anker

ISBN 978-1-951247-06-5

Edited by J.L. Troughton
PMG Publishing

CONTENTS

SPOOKY SHENANIGANS

Chapter 1 5
Chapter 2 11
Chapter 3 19
Chapter 4 31
Chapter 5 41
Chapter 6 45
Chapter 7 53
Chapter 8 57
Chapter 9 69
Chapter 10 73
Chapter 11 83
Chapter 12 89
Chapter 13 99
Chapter 14 105
Chapter 15 119
Chapter 16 129
Chapter 17 135
Chapter 18 145

HOLIDAY SHENANIGANS

Chapter 1 155
Chapter 2 167
Chapter 3 175
Chapter 4 183
Chapter 5 191
Chapter 6 203
Chapter 7 217
Chapter 8 229
Chapter 9 239

VALENTINE SHENANIGANS

Chapter 1 249
Chapter 2 255
Chapter 3 263
Chapter 4 273
Chapter 5 283
Chapter 6 293
Chapter 7 301
Chapter 8 315
Chapter 9 331
Chapter 10 337
Chapter 11 351

LUCKY SHENANIGANS

Chapter 1 361
Chapter 2 373
Chapter 3 383
Chapter 4 395
Chapter 5 405
Chapter 6 413
Chapter 7 425
Chapter 8 435
Chapter 9 443
Chapter 10 455

Excerpt 461
Thank you for reading 465
Other Books by Pepper 467
Anthologies & Collections 469
About the Author 471

SPOOKY
Shenanegans

Edited by J.L. Troughton
PMG Publishing

1

KITTY SWEET KNEW that wasn't her name, but she couldn't quite remember what it should be, just like she couldn't remember her original form. She'd been so long in this one, she was beginning to feel like it was the only one she'd ever had.

She knew that wasn't true though.

She'd been something else at one time.

Some*one* else.

This form was so small and vulnerable, the world looked and felt entirely different while in it.

She especially liked it when the Dory woman cradled her and walked the floors with her, talking to her long into the night.

"I know you're not really a cat, Kitty Sweet," she'd say, "but for now, I appreciate the company. The traveling's been wonderful, but a bit lonely until you came along."

Then she'd stroke her hand along Kitty Sweet's back and scratch her head and under her chin and a rumble would rise in Kitty Sweet's throat.

The first time that happened, it had startled Kitty something fierce. It had taken her a moment to realize it was a happy sound.

Her first days in this form had been incredibly scary filled with terrifying sounds and scents. Everything had been so huge and scary.

Then Dory had found her, trembling and soaking wet, in the ruins.

Ruins of something.

Kitty couldn't quite remember anymore.

But Dory had swept her into her arms, dried her off, fed her and given her a home.

It wasn't such a bad deal after all.

Being a cat.

In fact, if Kitty had known how wonderful it was to be a cat, she might have actually wished to become one. Which made her wonder if that was how it had happened. Maybe a wish had come true.

Except it didn't feel like a wish.

It felt like something had gone terribly wrong, not right.

And even though Kitty enjoyed being a cat for the most part, now that she'd found Dory, she also felt as if something was missing.

Something quite large.

Vital even.

She was supposed to be doing something else.

Or *being* someone else.

Something.

Still, if figuring out what that something was meant leaving Dory behind, Kitty thought perhaps she would be fine as a cat.

Well, okay, maybe not *forever*.

That seemed an awfully long time to not be doing what she should be doing.

And there was *definitely* something else she should be doing.

Being.

Being and doing.

She tried not to think about it too much.

Instead, she focused on finding every patch of sunlight in the many different rooms they stayed in and chasing the prisms Dory's crystals cast across the floor, and in so doing, fell deeper into the joy of being a cat.

Then they went on a plane ride.

Kitty had to ride in an awful carrier in the bowels of the plane, which was a horrendous experience.

Loud and cold.

When the flight was finally over, to Kitty's horror, there was a second flight to endure, then a long car ride.

Finally, though, they walked into a hotel.

They had stayed in a lot of hotels in their travels, but this one felt different the moment they entered it.

Dory checked them into a large suite and Kitty had never been so relieved to finally be set loose from the carrier.

That sense of relief didn't last long.

Someone was in the suite with them.

Kitty could sense them.

Him.

Her.

It.

She didn't quite know what to call it, but it was definitely there, hovering, listening, watching.

And then Dory abandoned her.

She set out food and water, gave Kitty a quick stroke and

a scratch, then headed out the door to visit her nieces. "Be good, Kitty Sweet! I'll be back with some help before you know it!"

Help for what, Kitty didn't know.

Hopefully it would be someone who knew how to deal with this other being that shared the hotel suite with them.

Kitty spent the next several hours hunting the entity that refused to show itself. She'd sense it and pounce, only to have it disappear. Not that she ever saw it, but she definitely sensed when it was there and when it was gone.

Of course, it was never gone for long. A few moments would pass and then it would be back, making the fur on Kitty's back stand on end.

"Rawr!" Kitty swiped at the air, then tore around the room, trying to appear as large as she possibly could in this terribly small form. She leapt to the top of a desk and from there to the top of a bookcase.

The entity was gone again.

She glared around the room.

Any minute now, it would be back and she would be ready.

Kitty fell asleep waiting for the entity to return.

2

"SO WHEN'S YOUR aunt supposed to arrive again?" Cole asked Megan as she closed the shop.

"Any day now." Megan tested the door to make sure it was locked, then turned and hooked her arm in Cole's. "Come on. Lara and Jessica are probably already at the hotel waiting for us."

"Yes, because as usual, you insisted on closing the shop yourself."

"You know how they are. If I left them in charge, I'd have a mess in the mornings."

"Or maybe, *they'd* have a mess *they* could clean up themselves."

Megan huffed. His logic made no sense. Why he couldn't grasp the simple concept that it was just easier to do things herself, she had no idea, but she wasn't going to bother explaining again. It would be a colossal waste of time, seeing as they'd already had this conversation about ten thousand times in the last four months.

"I thought your aunt was dead."

Megan gasped and jerked to a stop. "Why on earth would you think that?"

"Well, for one, she's technically your great-aunt, plus she's old."

"You'd better not let *her* hear you say that!"

"And for another, she just disappeared."

"She didn't disappear." Megan started walking again. "If she'd died, don't you think there would have been a funeral? Don't you think we'd have been a little sad when we showed up here to take over her shop?"

"So, if she's not dead, where has she been all this time?"

"Traveling. She retired. It's a thing, you know."

"Traveling?"

"No, retiring. I know it seems rather weird to you, a cougar, that someone would actually work a job their entire lives and then retire from working to, you know, enjoy their twilight years."

"I don't even understand what you're saying right now."

"Right. Because you're a cat and cats are all about not working."

"I work! I work very hard, I'll have you know."

Megan pulled him to a stop and just stared at him.

He stared back.

They stood there on the sidewalk, just staring at each other for several long moments, each of them waiting for the other to break.

Finally, Cole grinned. "Fine. I *think* about working."

Megan rolled her eyes and started walking again. "Thinking doesn't count."

"I honestly don't understand this obsession with work."

"And I don't understand how you can be content to live in a cave!"

"Hey, I like my cave. It's perfect."

"It has no electricity. Or plumbing!"

"I'm a cougar. What do I need plumbing for?"

Megan let out a huff of exasperation. She honestly had no idea if he was messing with her or not, but if he was, it was the longest practical joke in history.

He'd taken her to his "cave" back when they first mated and she'd put her foot down right away. She was *not* moving into a cave. Not even for her true mate.

So he'd moved into her apartment above the store.

Sort of.

He'd only moved in some clothes and shoes and not much of either of those. When she'd asked when he was going to move in the rest of his stuff, he'd insisted he didn't have much and what was left belonged in the man-cave.

Whatever that meant.

She'd decided long ago, she absolutely did not want to know.

So whatever.

He kept his man-stuff in his man-cave and slept with her in the apartment, and as far as she was concerned, that was good enough for her.

During the day while she was working, he went off to do whatever it was cougars did, which she suspected involved a lot of sleeping and not a lot of work.

After all, caves didn't exactly cost a whole lot to maintain, and since Megan and her sisters owned the store and the apartment above it outright and the store more than covered their basic living expenses, she really didn't need him to contribute.

So fine.

She figured it was more than fair since he'd given up sleeping in a cave for her.

Or so he said.

Besides, as she was the one insisting on having a roof over her head, it made sense that she (and her sisters) would pay the utilities for said roof.

He contributed groceries, which led her to suspect he might just be messing with her.

How could he afford food if he never worked?

It was a big mystery and one she wasn't going to solve anytime soon.

In the meantime, she kept him around for the amazing sex and because she kind of loved the big, lazy bastard.

And because, despite all his faults, he could be really sweet.

Case in point: as they arrived at the hotel, he swept an arm around her shoulders, opened the door for her and ushered her inside.

~

Lara and Jessica were excitedly catching up with their aunt, hearing all about her travels on the other side of the world, when Megan arrived.

"Well, it's about time," Lara exclaimed. "Look who's here."

Megan let out a joyful cry and hurried to hug their aunt.

"You look wonderful, Aunt Dory!"

Lara had said the exact same thing to Dory, who looked as if the traveling had done her a world of good.

"Oh, you!" Dory waved her hand as if to dismiss the very idea.

"So what brings you home so soon?" Megan asked.

Dory smiled. "Well, I actually have two reasons for visiting. First, I can't believe you girls got mated and didn't invite me!"

"Oh, dear. Aunt Dory—"

Jessica snickered and Lara grinned.

They'd both fallen for Dory's sad face too.

Dory burst into laughter. "Oh, don't mind me, darling. I'm just teasing. Believe me, I know a shifter doesn't wait for anyone when his mate is in his sights."

Megan giggled. "Have you met my Cole?" She reached back to catch his hand and pulled him forward to meet Dory.

"I certainly have," Dory said.

Cole looked surprised.

"Don't think you fool me. Not for one instant, mister!" Dory shook her finger at Cole. "You and that other one, always coming around and stealing my pumpkins."

Lara, Megan and Jessica all burst into laughter at the deer-in-the-headlights look on Cole's face.

"Oh. Um. Sorry."

"Well, where is your partner in crime anyway?"

"Hold on. Are you talking about Dan?" Jessica demanded.

"Um." Cole looked like he wanted to be anywhere but where he was.

"You two used to steal from our aunt?" Jessica asked.

"Wait a minute," Megan said. "Are you the reason our zucchinis keep disappearing?"

"And our watermelons?" Lara demanded.

"Okay, now you can't blame the watermelons on us. That's Karl's deal."

"Are you kidding me right now?" Lara asked. "My own mate's been stealing my watermelons?" It all made sense now. There were never any seeds or pits or rinds left behind and now she knew why. Their thieves were of the two-legged variety!

"So all the groceries you've been bringing in are from our own garden?" Megan exclaimed.

"Well, not *all* of them," Cole said. "I have to pay for the canned goods and the bread."

Megan narrowed her eyes. "What about the milk and eggs?"

Cole looked a bit sheepish. "Well, see the wolves are real good at stealing eggs from the chickens. They run right away the minute Karl slinks into the hen house, so—"

Lara gasped. "Karl's been stealing from our neighbors?"

"I don't think he considers it stealing. More like reallocating. I'm sure they don't mind. Or they wouldn't, if they knew it was us. And if they knew shifters existed."

"That's a great way to get shot!" Megan shouted exactly what Lara was thinking. "We do not need your stolen goods, especially not if they come at the price of your life."

Cole grinned. "Aw, darling. I knew you cared." He swept her into his arms and kissed her.

At that moment, Dan and Karl walked into the hotel.

The minute Jessica saw her mate, she started raging, "You should be ashamed of yourself, Daniel!"

"And you!" Lara exclaimed as the two of them stormed toward their startled-looking mates. "What were you thinking, Karl?"

"Uh." Dan threw a wild look at Karl, who shook his head, appearing completely mystified.

At that moment, while their mates were clearly a bit panicked trying to figure out what they were in trouble for, five older women walked into the hotel and right past where they were standing.

Lara and Jessica both spun around and watched as the five women called Dory's name, causing her to squeal and race toward them. They met in the center of the lobby in a flurry of hugs and exclamations and demands for all the details of Dory's adventures away.

Lara was utterly horrified, and by the look on Jessica's face, as well as Megan's as she hurried to join them, her sisters were as well.

"This is *not* a positive development," Jessica muttered.

"I had no idea Aunt Dory knew our mates' mothers," Megan said.

"We're never going to escape them now," Lara groaned.

3

BEFORE THEY KNEW it, Megan and her sisters had been surrounded by their aunt and her friends, three of whom just happened to be their mothers-in-law.

Megan tried to grab hold of Cole to force him to stay with her, but discovered he was no longer at her side. The big bastard had probably bolted, Dan and Karl at his heels, the minute he saw his mother.

"Now where did that boy of mine go?" Evie, Dan's mom, scowled as she scanned the lobby.

"Fled his mama," Jessica muttered. "Pathetic."

Megan dug an elbow into her side.

"I could have sworn I saw Cole around here somewhere," Chloe said.

Jessica scowled at Megan.

"Just play it cool," Megan muttered, then said earnestly to Chloe. "He was right by my side a minute ago. I can't imagine where he went." She tried out a devastated expression. She'd been practicing it for just such an opportunity, given Cole's penchant for abandoning her the minute his mother appeared.

The look on Chloe's face said that it was working.

Megan could barely contain her glee.

Catching on, Lara said, "I can't believe they left without saying anything. Karl was here too, and I barely had a chance to say hello."

Yeah, she was too busy yelling at him.

Jessica let out a giant sigh. "I suppose it's our own fault. We're probably being too clingy."

Megan had to turn away. She was afraid she might burst into laughter at her sister's mournful tone.

~

For a moment there, Lara was afraid they'd overplayed their hand, but then Dory stepped up.

Of course, Lara was certain their aunt knew exactly what they were up to, but that's what had always made Dory their favorite aunt. She'd encouraged and even participated in many of their escapades growing up.

"Oh, darling." Dory slung an arm around Jessica's shoulders, sympathy oozing from her tone. "Don't be ridiculous. Of course, you should expect your mate to stand with you at all times."

"Exactly!" Evie sidled up to Jessica's other side. "Shifters are a different breed. You have to be firm with them."

Francine, Karl's mom, and Agatha, Adam's mom, came up to either side of Lara and looped their arms in hers.

"Come along, dear," Francine said. "We can see you three need a bit of guidance."

Lara threw a wide-eyed look over her shoulder at Megan. They really had gone overboard on this one if it meant they were going to be stuck getting advice from their mothers-in-law.

Unfortunately, Megan appeared to be rather busy dealing with Max's mom, Betina, and of course, Chloe, to be able to help Lara.

Within minutes, the three sisters found themselves conscripted into joining the women for their daily "meeting," whatever that meant.

"Ugh," Lara muttered to Megan and Jessica as they pulled several tables together in the lobby. "The price of revenge is surprisingly steep."

Megan didn't answer. Probably too busy cursing Cole in her head. This was all their mates' fault!

"I didn't know you guys were friends," Jessica said to Dory as everyone got settled.

"I've lived in this town my entire life, grew up with these women."

"That's right," Francine said. "We've been friends for decades."

Chloe nodded. "Yep, we've celebrated birthdays, matings—"

"Harumph," Agatha snorted. "Don't rub it in."

Chloe winced.

"I'm sure it's only a matter of time," Evelyn assured Agatha.

"Yes, just be patient and—"

"Are you seriously advocating patience, Betina?" Agatha snapped. "I seem to remember you lecturing Max on a daily basis about how shifters don't wait patiently once they've found their mate."

Betina giggled. "Okay, true. Sorry. He was driving me crazy though! Moping around, mooning over his bear, but never actually making a move."

"Well, at least he found his mate! Adam hardly ever leaves pack lands, so how is he ever going to meet his mate, I ask you?"

Lara couldn't even begin to describe her relief as the other women started to throw around ideas about how to get Adam off pack lands to search for his mate. As long as they were focused on the alpha wolf, she and her sisters were safe from the nagging.

"You know what we need?" Dory asked suddenly.

Agatha stopped mid-rant to focus on Lara's aunt. "What?"

"Babies," Dory stated emphatically, completely throwing her nieces under the bus.

Jessica gasped, Megan let out a growl and Lara glowered at Dory who just grinned unrepentantly.

"I've been saying that for years!" Francine exclaimed. "And now that my Karl's finally mated, I want to know what the holdup is."

The women all stared at Lara, which was a truly horrifying development. She opened her mouth to protest, to change the subject, to claim that Karl was impotent, to say *anything* to get their attention away from her. The only problem was she couldn't seem to find her voice. What could she possibly say to convince these highly traditional shifter ladies that children were not necessary in this day and age?

"It appears she's speechless," Jessica said dryly.

"You do realize that Lara has no plans to have children ever," Megan said in her hideously blunt way, causing all the shifters at the table to gasp in horror and Dory to press her lips together as if by doing so, she could somehow contain her laughter. Dory's shoulders appeared to be shaking from the effort.

Lara stiffened. How could Megan just blurt it out like that? She glared down at her sister, who just shrugged back at her.

"Why on earth would you be against having babies?" Francine exclaimed in a shrill voice. "Babies are our future." And thus began a new rant as all the women focused their efforts on convincing Lara that babies were the answer to the world's ills.

~

"I can't believe you did that." Jessica took advantage of Evie moving closer to the argument by sliding into her suddenly vacated chair.

"I did her a favor," Megan said. "She keeps avoiding the question rather than just taking the bull by the horns."

"Yes, but look at her."

Megan tilted her head to stare at Lara, who was slouched in her chair, chin to chest as she listened to the women ranting.

"She's not even defending herself." Jessica shook her head. "If that girl doesn't find her voice, she's going to end up pushing out wolf cubs every year for the rest of her life. Either that or witchy babies." Jessica thought about that for a moment. "Witchy wolf cubs," she decided with an emphatic nod. "Has a nice ring to it."

Megan snickered.

"Don't laugh," Jessica said. "I'm terrified at the thought.

Lara might lose her mind!" Seriously, their sister would *lose her mind.* She had to stick up for herself or they would never hear the end of it.

"A valid point," Megan said. "But I'm not about to wade in to save her."

"Well, don't look at me!"

"I'm not. You're the one who suggested it."

Jessica groaned. "Seriously? You're not going to help her at all? You're supposed to be the sensible one."

"Not when helping her out means the grandbaby mission might shift my way!"

"Having fun, ladies?" Dory stood above them, hands on hips, giving them her sternest look. "You two just abandoned your sister. It's shameful."

"Us?" Megan demanded. "You're the one who mentioned babies in the first place!"

Dory grinned. "Yes, I did. And it was quite funny. But now it's time for you to step up and save your sister."

Megan groaned. "Fine." She made a fist and knocked it against the table. "Ladies, ladies." She raised her voice to be heard over the ranting. "Why don't you just *ask* Lara why she doesn't want babies."

Silence.

No one spoke for a long moment, then Francine finally said, "All right. Lara, why don't you want children?"

Lara sent a wild look down the table toward her sisters.

Jessica nodded encouragingly back. Out of the corner of her eye, she saw Dory and Megan doing the same.

Lara let out a huge breath of hair, then said, "The world is already terribly overpopulated. There aren't enough resources to support the paranormals and humans already on this planet. So, no, I don't want to add to that problem."

"But you do want children?" Francine asked.

Lara shrugged. "I mean, I'm not opposed to kids. I like kids. But it's up to all of us to save the planet."

Jessica was so proud of Lara in that moment. She'd actually managed to express her beliefs to a bunch of very traditional shifter women. She just hoped they wouldn't crush her spirit.

There was a long moment of silence as Francine and the other women pondered Lara's position.

Finally, Betina said tentatively, "Well, there *are* an awful lot of unwanted paranormal children in the world."

"That's true," Agatha said.

Silence fell again as everyone waited for Francine's verdict. She seemed a bit stunned at first, but after a few moments, took in a deep breath and said, "Adoption is certainly a valid life choice. And as Betina said, there are many children in need of a good home." She smiled at Lara. "I'll still be a grandmother and I can live with that."

Lara smiled back. "Really?"

"Absolutely, my dear. Now let's talk about when. You and Karl aren't getting any younger."

Lara rolled her eyes and Jessica and Megan giggled.

After a few moments of what Jessica could only term as negotiation between Lara and Francine, they both came to an agreement that Lara would speak with Karl and they would make a plan for when and as soon as they knew, they would inform Francine.

Jessica and Megan sent each other wide-eyed looks. Jessica knew Megan was hoping the same thing she was, that they managed to "overhear" the conversation between the wolf and their sister, something that was entirely possible, given they were all sharing an apartment together.

"All right, then," Chloe said. "Enough chitchat. It's time for us to get down to important business. This meeting of the Alpha Six is now called to order."

"The Alpha Six?" Megan asked.

"Yes. It really is too bad your names aren't exactly in the right order. You need a K."

"What?" Jessica asked.

"Jessica, Lara, Megan. J-L-M. Where's the K? It doesn't work, you see," Agatha said. "So you can't be the Alpha Trio. Nor can you join our group and make us the Alpha Nine because you're all out of order."

"We're the first six letters, you see," Dory pointed at each of the women as she listed their names. "Agatha, Betina, Chloe, Dorothy, Evelyn, Francine."

"That's brilliant," Lara said. "Did your mothers do that on purpose?"

Chloe burst into laughter. "Not at all. It was just coincidence. But oh, how much fun we had, proclaiming to everyone we knew that we were the Alpha Six."

"The alphas didn't exactly appreciate it," Evie giggled.

"Not even a tiny bit," Betina said.

"They especially didn't like it when Dory cast that spell."

Dory burst into laughter. "Don't tell my nieces that story! You'll give them ideas!"

Megan leaned forward. "What spell?"

"Dory cast the water tower," Chloe said. "Every night at midnight exactly, the words "Alpha Six" would appear on the tower."

"They glowed in the dark," Francine said, "and lasted until dawn."

"But in the light of day, no one could find the words to wash them away," Agatha said.

"That's a pretty powerful casting," Megan said.

"How old were you, Aunt Dory?"

Dory shrugged.

"Oh, don't be so modest, Dory. She cast it for the first time at age ten," Agatha said.

"The first time?" Jessica asked.

Chloe nodded. "When was the last time, Dory? Maybe a year ago?"

Jessica and her sisters all burst out laughing.

Dory grinned. "Well, I don't like to brag. These days, I only cast for a single night, you know. Just to prove I've still got it."

"Oh, you've definitely still got it," Betina said.

"True, but honestly, whatever bit of magic I have—"

"Bit of magic?" Chloe repeated incredulously.

Dory rolled her eyes. "Anyway, as I was saying, whatever bit of magic I have, it's a drop in the bucket compared to my nieces. Their power is simply incredible. Which reminds me, I was hoping you ladies might be willing to come meet my cat."

"You have a cat?" Jessica exclaimed.

"I do. I found her in Greece almost a year ago now. Or maybe I should say, she found me, and we've been traveling together ever since. The thing is, I'm pretty certain she's not just a cat, though I have no idea what she really is. It's why I came for a visit, hoping my amazing nieces could help."

"Is she a shifter?" Lara asked.

"I don't think so."

"Interesting," Jessica said. "A mystery."

"Maybe she's jut an ordinary cat. Did you ever think of that, Dory?"

"I think I'd recognize an ordinary cat, Betina, and she is definitely not that."

"Well, we'd be happy to check out your cat." Jessica started to stand, in the hopes this would bring an end to their impromptu get-together.

"Oh, no." Dory waved her hand. "We have time for some dominoes first."

As if this was a signal to all the other women, they each pulled a tin of dominoes out of their bags.

Jessica's eyes widened. That was a lot of dominoes. She glared at Dory, but settled back into her chair.

Dory just grinned. "Now then, let's get the boneyard set up, shall we?"

Three hours of dominoes played in two different teams, endless questions about when Jessica and Megan planned to have their first cubs ("And don't try to convince me you're going to save the earth by adopting!" Evie admonished Jessica), followed by lectures about not letting their mates walk all over them, culminated in a raging headache for Jessica.

She was pretty sure Megan was suffering alongside her. She wasn't so sure about Lara. After all, she'd come to an agreement with Francine and seemed much more relaxed as a result.

It wasn't the lectures, the game or even the demands for grandchildren. It was the constant raging need to strangle her mate, all while keeping a smile on her face for her mother-in-law, that did Jessica in.

She was going to *kill* that mangy cougar the next time she saw him!

Which turned out to be approximately two minutes later when Dan, Cole and Karl all made the mistake of entering the hotel again, clearly headed for the bar.

Deer-in-the-headlights didn't even begin to describe the looks on their faces when they realized their mates and their mothers were still in the lobby *and* had apparently been socializing since they'd abandoned them hours before.

This was going to be worth literal decades of torture for her mate and Jessica was looking forward to every minute of it.

4

"IS EVERYONE READY to meet my cat?" Dory asked as soon as they'd finished packing away the dominoes.

Megan and her sisters replied in the affirmative, but Agatha made a face.

"I'm not really in the mood to meet a cat, Dory," Agatha said. "Truthfully, I'll probably never be in the mood."

Betina nodded. "Yes, they're really rather obnoxious creatures aren't they?"

Dory huffed. "Don't even start. If Chloe and Evelyn were still here, they'd be appalled."

Chloe, Evelyn and Francine had dragged their sons out of the hotel moments before, clearly intending to lecture them on the proper treatment of their mates, signaling the end to their dominoes game.

"Fine," Agatha grumbled.

"I stand by my statement," Betina said. "And Chloe and Evelyn would be the first to admit that cats are excellent at being obnoxious."

"Pretentious too," Agatha said.

"Well, Kitty Sweet is neither of those things. She's a sweetheart is what she is," Dory proclaimed as she led the way to the elevator.

The sisters hung back a bit as they followed the three friends, who continued their good-natured arguing.

"Did you see the look on the men's faces when they realized we were still in the lobby?" Megan asked.

"I did." Jessica grinned. "Serves them right."

"The price of vengeance was well worth it," Lara said.

"Yep," Jessica agreed. "I'm sure they're getting an earful right about now."

"Is this the cat who's not a cat?" Betina was asking as they reached the elevator where the older women were waiting. Before Dory could answer, she continued, "Because I can't imagine why you would name it Kitty if it isn't one."

"I named her Kitty Sweet, not just Kitty, and just because she's not a cat doesn't mean she isn't excellent at pretending!" Dory led the way into the elevator and pushed the third floor button.

"You think she's pretending?" Megan asked.

"Well, no, I think she's probably stuck."

"So if she's not a cat, what is she?" Jessica asked.

"I'm not sure, but she's surrounded by some pretty powerful magic."

"You haven't been able to break the spell?" Agatha asked.

"Unfortunately, no," Dory said.

This was surprising. Dory had a lot of power, no matter how much she liked to downplay it or insist her nieces had more. If Dory couldn't break the spell, there was only one reason she'd come to her nieces for help.

"We might have to combine our powers," Dory said as she

led them out onto the third floor. “It would be better if we had a fifth witch, but I suppose four will do.”

Megan was shocked to hear this. Four witches wouldn’t be enough?

“This doesn’t sound good,” Jessica muttered.

“It must be a truly powerful spell,” Lara said.

Megan just nodded, trying to think through all the pitfalls.

“Something that powerful—” Jessica stopped and shook her head.

Megan knew exactly what she was thinking. Perhaps the spell wasn’t something that should be tampered with at all. What if whatever was inside the cat needed to stay contained? What if they released it only to discover they’d unleashed something truly dark upon the world?

“I know what you’re thinking,” Dory said as she stopped at room three hundred thirteen. “You’ll see there’s nothing to worry about when you meet Miss Kitty Sweet. She shines with innocence.” She pushed open the door and they all walked inside.

A small black cat launched itself from a bookcase in the living room and Dory laughed as she caught her in her arms.

“Well, hello, my darling.”

From where Megan stood, she could hear the cat purring.

“Oh, she’s so cute.” Lara instantly melted, which was totally predictable. Lara absolutely loved animals. “Can I hold her?”

Dory passed Kitty Sweet into Lara’s arms and right before their eyes, both kitty and witch fell in love.

Lara cuddled the cat under her chin and the sound of purring got even louder, though that didn’t really seem possible.

"Oh, you're right, Aunt Dory, she *is* sweet. Can I adopt her?"

Megan burst into laughter.

Dory looked shocked. "First of all, absolutely not. Kitty Sweet's *my* companion. Besides, she's not really a cat. You can't keep a non-cat for a pet."

Lara held the kitten out in front of her and stared into her eyes. She then pulled her close and cuddled her some more. After a long moment, she sighed and said, "I suppose you're right. There's definitely a lot of power keeping this kitty's spirit contained. I can sense it, but I'm not exactly sure what she is. If we can't figure it out, can I adopt her then?"

"No!" Dory exclaimed. "Find your own kitty to adopt."

Lara grinned. "What a fabulous idea! I'm going to the shelter as soon as possible."

Megan and Jessica started giggling.

"What's so funny about that?" Lara demanded.

"I just can't wait to see Karl's face when he realizes his mate has adopted a kitten," Megan said, a huge grin on her face as she imagined the wolf's reaction.

Agatha and Betina both laughed as well.

Lara scrunched up her face for a moment, then grinned. "Well, he'll just have to get over it."

"This I have got to see," Agatha said.

"I can't wait to tell Francine. She'll be beside herself. This is the perfect revenge, ladies," Betina said.

"Oooh, I hadn't considered that angle," Megan said. "I've never had a cat before, which now that I think about it is just wrong. We're witches. We should at least follow some of the stereotypes."

"True," Jessica said. "And since we don't fly on brooms, a black cat would definitely be the next best thing."

Lara eyed her sisters. “So we’re thinking three black cats. Right?”

Megan grinned. Revenge aside, she’d always loved cats. Their apartment above the store was quite large. They’d even renovated the attic to increase the living space since they’d all mated. The idea of three cats running around the apartment, playing with each other when they were out, and aggravating a couple cougars and a wolf when they were in, was quite a lovely one.

“Definitely!” Jessica exclaimed, clearly of the same mind as Megan and Lara.

“That all sounds fabulous,” Dory said. “But before you three run off to the shelter, could you please help me figure out what’s going on with *this* kitty?”

“Here, you hold her.” Lara passed Kitty Sweet to Megan. “You have the most power of us all. What do you think?”

Megan accepted the cat and instantly knew what had caught Dory’s attention and what had captured Lara’s adoration.

The cat was adorably soft and cuddly, but there was also unimaginable power rippling around her, forming an invisible aura, one that could almost be felt, it was so strong.

“What on earth has happened to you, sweet darling?” Megan lifted the cat as Lara had and stared into her bright green eyes.

Dory was right.

This was no ordinary cat.

“All right then. I suppose we need a spell of revelation.” Megan cuddled the cat close. “What have you got here, Dory?”

“Everything I thought might help.” Dory opened a small

bag sitting on the coffee table and began to lay out a variety of herbs. "Basil, eucalyptus—"

"Uh-oh. Better not let the koala catch us burning eucalyptus," Jessica muttered.

"Hyssop, peppermint." Dory continued laying out the ingredients she had gathered. "Rosemary, sage, witch hazel, wormwood, orange, lemongrass, marjoram, parsley, thyme, a bit of bee balm, and some matcha." She set out a tiny container of the green tea powder.

"Why the bee balm?" Megan asked.

Dory shrugged. "I'm not sure. I just got a really good feeling when I was choosing ingredients. I felt it had to be included."

Megan took that to mean the fairies had a role to play.

Perhaps not though. Perhaps there was some other use to the bee balm. Attracting fairies was probably just a side effect.

She wasn't a big fan of using ingredients for the first time on a spell that impacted a living being, but she did trust Dory and her instincts. The rest of the ingredients made total sense, so probably this one did too.

"Ready then?" Dory asked.

"Are you going to cast a spell right now?" Agatha exclaimed.

"No time like the present," Dory said.

"Oh, but, don't you think you should maybe practice first on something that's not alive?" Betina asked.

"Are you suggesting that my magic might harm a living creature?" Dory demanded.

"Oh, of course not," Agatha said, though she looked quite spooked.

"You don't have to stick around, of course," Megan said.

"Right, then, we'll see you ladies later." Agatha headed for the door, Betina on her heels.

Seeing the look of disappointment on Dory's face, Megan realized her aunt had probably greatly missed her friends, and quickly added, "Though, you know, Lara and Jessica are quite the experts at love spells."

Agatha froze on her way to the door and turned back.

Betina sighed and turned back as well.

"What do you mean?" Agatha asked.

"They cast a spell to bring my true mate to my side and within hours, I met Cole," Megan said. Never mind that her sisters had screwed up the spell quite magnificently, impacting all the humans in town as well.

"We can't make someone fall in love," Lara cautioned.

"Or even make them recognize their mate when they find each other," Jessica said.

Agatha shook her head. "Adam's too darn stubborn. Even a spell wouldn't get him to go in search of his mate."

"Oh, but that's the beauty of their spell," Dory said quickly. "If he won't leave pack lands, it might ensure his mate enters them."

"Exactly. That's the sort of spell we cast for Megan," Lara said.

"What have you got to lose?" Betina asked. "Things are looking pretty grim right now."

Agatha waved a hand as if to dismiss their comments. "Yes, yes. I'll consider it. If I get desperate."

Betina raised an eyebrow at her.

Agatha let out a chuckle. "Okay, fine. I'm already there. But first, I believe you ladies have a cat to—" She stopped, a perplexed look on her face. "What exactly are you planning again?"

"A spell of revelation." Lara rubbed her hands together. "This is going to be so much fun!"

5

AN HOUR LATER, Megan decided Lara had chosen the wrong F word.

Frustrating perhaps.

Two hours after that, she'd moved on to frightening. A spell this strong was utterly terrifying.

It was during hour five when they finally had their breakthrough, but by that time, Megan had graduated her thoughts to the supreme F word of all time.

If it weren't for the flicker of a woman they saw for about half a second during hour two and once again toward the end of hour four, she would have given up long before.

It was that woman, though, that kept them going.

Some poor woman was trapped inside the cat!

Perhaps a shifter, who'd been trapped in her cat form due to some dark magic. Assuming there was such a thing as a house cat shifter.

After contemplating that for a moment, Megan had sent a text to Cole to ask. After all, he was a cougar shifter. He should know, right?

All she'd gotten back were a bunch of laughing emojis.

Bastard.

So this tiny woman with pitch black hair, who wasn't a house cat shifter, was trapped and Megan was determined to pull her out.

At the end of hour four, they'd taken a break to visit their shop and their garden to gather more ingredients and some crystals.

Lara had suggested if this didn't work, they might have to reach out to their cousins.

Dory had made a face at the suggestion.

Their cousins weren't bad witches. They just weren't good ones either. But sometimes, a neither-bad-nor-good witch was better than no witch at all.

Of course, sometimes it was much, much worse.

Probably, in this situation, it would be worse.

As it turned out, though, they didn't need to reach out to their cousins because the final casting did it.

Or perhaps, the final casting, with a fairy along for help, was what actually did it.

Lily had caught them on their way back up to the third floor and had tagged along, wanting to get a sense of this mystery kitty.

And so four witches, two shifters (who by that time, were mostly sleeping) and a fairy managed some quite powerful magic that fifth and final hour.

6

KARL FINALLY MADE it away from his mother. Lord, that woman could nag something fierce. He headed back to the hotel, plotting exactly how he was going to make his mate pay for this unexpected turn of events, when he ran into Cole and Dan. "So you managed to escape the wrath of motherhood as well, huh?"

Dan scowled. "Barely. I thought she'd never stop her ranting."

"Eh, it wasn't that bad." Cole grinned.

Karl and Dan both stopped and stared at Cole, who grinned at the looks of shock on their faces. "What? I got cookies out of the deal, didn't I?"

Dan chuckled. "Okay, yeah, the cake did make up a bit for the endless lecture."

"Seriously? Your mothers baked for you?" Karl demanded. What craziness was this?

"Well, not for me specifically," Cole said, "But yeah, the cookies were there, so I took some obviously."

"And when my mother gets angry, she bakes," Dan said.

"Which meant she was pretty much baking the entire time she was ranting. So of course, I stuck around for the rewards."

"And she didn't stop you from pilfering the goods?" Karl demanded.

"Of course not," Cole exclaimed. "No cougar mother would fail to feed her children when they were hungry!"

"Exactly!" Dan laughed. "Even though my mom was baking out of pure fury, that didn't stop her from serving me both brownies *and* cake as soon as they came out of the oven."

Karl shook his head in disbelief.

Cougars and their mamas. They wouldn't have survived five minutes in a wolf den.

And now he had a hankering for cake, dammit!

He was still grumbling when they reached the doors to the hotel. He came to an abrupt stop.

Dan and Cole paused as well.

"What's up?" Cole asked.

"What if they're still in there?" Karl wasn't exactly afraid of Lara, but still. She had a mean right hook when riled up.

"Well, one of us is going to have to look," Dan said.

They both looked at Cole, who rolled his eyes. "Fine. You two are such wusses." He stalked up to the door and peered inside. "They're not in the lobby," he reported.

"Are you sure?" Karl wouldn't put it past his mate to ambush them.

"Positive. Come on, you two. I need a drink." Cole stalked inside the hotel.

Karl glanced at Dan, who shrugged and led the way inside.

A few moments later, the three were seated at the hotel bar with drinks in front of them.

"Don't you find it a little strange that our mates are nowhere to be found?" Dan asked. "I was sure they'd be lying in wait for us."

Cole nodded. "Strange isn't quite the right word for it."

"Disturbing," Dan suggested. "Probably means they're off somewhere plotting."

"Okay, that's a terrifying thought," Karl muttered. "And frankly, it's not right. After all, they're the ones who set *us* up!"

"How do you figure that?" Cole asked.

"They waited in the lobby until we came back, didn't they? All so they could watch our mothers light into us." Karl scowled at the memory of the satisfaction on Lara's face as his mother had dragged him from the hotel as if he were a mere cub. "Rude is what that is!"

"Yeah," Cole drawled out the word. "I'm pretty sure our mates weren't exactly dying to play dominoes with their mothers-in-law."

Karl thought about that for a moment. The cougar had a point, dammit! "Okay, fine. But I want to blame them anyway."

Cole let out a bark of laughter. "I'm pretty sure they're doing the same."

"What do you mean?" Dan asked.

"Well, unless our mates have suddenly transformed into some other, much more forgiving, versions of themselves, I'm pretty sure they're going to blame *us* for abandoning *them*, considering it resulted in their having to play dominoes with *our* mothers all evening."

Karl groaned. Unfortunately, this was very true, and if Karl knew his mate, she would be sure to make him pay.

At that moment, Harry, the hotel manager, walked up. "Have you guys seen Lily? I've been looking for her everywhere."

"No idea," Karl said glumly. "She's probably with our mates, plotting their revenge."

Harry looked alarmed at this bit of news. "Revenge? I haven't done anything to rile Lily up today!"

"Not you," Dan said. "Us."

"Oh, that's all right then." Harry beamed with relief.

Karl couldn't blame him. After all, though it hardly seemed possible, witches had nothing on fairies when it came to vengeance.

"Well, I hate to tell you this," Harry said cheerfully, "but if your mates have recruited Lily for their revenge plot, y'all are doomed."

"This is so unfair!" Karl exclaimed. "What did we do to deserve this?"

"Well, we did abandon them with our mothers," Dan said.

"Yeah, but they could have come with us!" Karl exclaimed. "We didn't so much abandon *them* as flee our mothers. They could have come along!"

"Be sure to use that excuse with Lara," Cole said.

"Yes," Dan agreed. "Then let us know if it worked."

Karl groaned. "You guys suck."

"Eh, cheer up," Cole said. "We're at Shenanigans, and for once, the ladies aren't here to drink us under the table!"

Karl perked up at that. This was a very good point.

"Drinks all around," Dan called out.

A cheer went up and the party was on.

Harry disappeared for a while, probably trying to get

someone to cover the front desk, and when he returned, he brought Logan with him.

"Logan!" the dragons, who had joined the shifters in their drinking, shouted in unison.

Logan sauntered over and settled into a chair between Liel and Zee. "Where are all the women?" He scanned the table.

"Ashlynn and Cassie are working." Zee waved a hand toward the bar where Markos was flirting with his mate, Cassie, and Zee's mate, Ashlynn, was picking up a tray of drinks for their table.

"Lily still hasn't shown up?" Harry demanded.

"Nope." Dan grinned. "Neither have our mates either." He waved a drunken arm in the air, indicating Karl and Cole, who were sprawled in chairs on the other side of the table. "And we're thinking that's a good thing. After all, they're plotting against us!"

Logan lifted an eyebrow. "Is Lily in on this plotting?"

"Probably so," Karl said, enunciating carefully.

Logan shook his head. "Well, it's been nice knowing you lot. I'd wish you luck, but I'm afraid what you actually need is a miracle. Witches *and* a female fairy plotting against you? You're doomed."

"That's what I told them," Harry announced.

Karl groaned and slammed his head down on the table. "Just shoot me," he muttered to Cole. "It's a much more humane way to die."

Cole chuckled. "Cheer up, man. Surely, the aftermath will make it all worthwhile."

Karl thought about that a moment, then nodded. He supposed there was that to look forward to. "I'll distract her with kisses," he announced.

It sometimes worked.

About half the time.

Well, maybe more like twenty-five percent of the time, but even when it didn't work right away—

He grinned.

All that really meant was more kisses were in order.

"Yes," he said emphatically. "Kisses are definitely the way to go."

7

KITTY SWEET, WHO had looked progressively sadder as the night progressed, suddenly perked up and did something.

It wasn't really a shift.

They were all familiar with what a shift looked like and this wasn't it.

It was more of a glitch.

As if the cat herself phased in and out of existence, and in the tiny spec of time between the in and the out, became a human.

This wasn't much to get excited about though.

They'd seen this glitch twice before, barely a glimpse in a fraction of a second.

This time, though, the glitching stabilized so that when the cat phased out and the woman appeared, she flickered for a few moments, then stayed.

She was curled up on the couch, in the same position the cat had been in, but as soon as she realized she was human, she was on her feet.

Eyes wide, she opened her mouth to speak, and it happened again.

She phased in and out, glitching at a rapid rate, so that her woman form flickered in and out at first, then phased to cat, then to her woman-form again.

Back and forth to the point Megan worried they'd made things worse. At least before she'd been one or the other.

Now, though—

The glitching stopped.

And she was a cat again.

"Well, pooh," Dory said.

"This is okay," Megan said. "We're on the right track. It just means we need more ingredients and maybe some stronger magic."

"Stronger magic than four witches and a fairy?" Lily asked.

"Do you think Logan would help?" Jessica asked.

It was a great question. The twin fairies had incredible power. It hummed in the air around them, but Logan's power was off the charts. Every time she was around him, Megan could feel the energy of the universe responding to him.

It was as if the fairy attracted and then reflected all the energies around him, manifesting them into an aura of such power Megan was stunned silent every time she felt it.

"That's a great idea!" Lara exclaimed.

At that moment, there came a knock at the suite's door.

8

LOGAN HAD DECIDED the shifters were crazy.

He'd decided this months before when he first met them, and nothing had changed his mind since.

Truthfully, it was a toss-up as to which of the shifters were the most insane.

The wolves, with their obsession with the full moon and their penchant for howling at the most ridiculous of moments.

The cougars, who thought nothing of shifting into their cat forms in the middle of a bar and taking impromptu naps under the table.

Or the dragons, who were just plain mad.

He was leaning toward the cougars, if only because two of their kind had been crazy enough to mate with witches, who were almost as terrifying as female fairies when it came to potential mates.

Logan hated to admit it, but he was rather relieved he'd never met a fairy who roused his mating instincts.

He'd seen both the wonder and the horror of two fairies mating and he just wasn't sure that was the life he wanted for himself.

He already had enough responsibilities, what with running the fairy side of the hotel and, well, everything else, without adding a fairy mate to the mix.

All he had to do was spend a few moments with his sister, Lily, and her traveler mate, Harry, to know he needed what Lily had found.

Harry was laidback and calm and brought a sense of peace to Lily's life that she desperately needed.

Of course, he also took great joy in riling her up, which was why Logan thoroughly approved of the mating.

Harry understood what Lily needed to be happy.

Peace.

But also an outlet for her crazy.

Logan desperately wanted the same for himself.

He was afraid, though, that he would end up with all the crazy and none of the peace, or perhaps neither at all.

He was beginning to lean toward the latter. The more time that passed, the less likely it seemed he would just stumble across his mate.

And so, he'd resigned himself to being alone.

Which he supposed was why he found himself visiting Shenanigans on the human side of the hotel more and more frequently.

The shifters were quite entertaining, and much to his surprise, he found himself enjoying their company.

Which was why when he entered Shenanigans that night, with his brother-in-law, Harry, at his side, and the dragons shouted his name in welcome, he grinned and joined them without a single hesitation.

They didn't exactly bring him peace, but it was the closest to it he'd ever found.

And so, he passed the many hours of the evening, drinking with his friends, the dragons and wolves and cougars, and trying ever so hard not to feel the lack of a mate as many of them spoke of theirs.

"You know what we need?" Dan exclaimed drunkenly, demonstrating once again that cougars (and wolves, for that matter) had no tolerance for the alcohol of the realms.

The dragons and Logan were drinking them under the table.

The only surprise was that neither Dan nor Cole had actually crawled there yet.

Karl let out a wolf howl from the end of the table, and the sound echoed through the room as wolves in every corner joined him in his ridiculous display.

"No, not that!" Dan shouted over all the howling. "No one needs to hear that, Karl. Knock it off."

"Well, what then?" Karl asked.

"We need to deal with that." He waved his arm in the air.

"Deal with what?" Cole asked.

"The betting board! No one's found room thirteen yet and that just makes the whole thing rather boring."

"Huh. That's a good point." Karl leaned forward to stare at the board. "I think we're going to have get more involved if we want to solve this mystery and close out those bets."

"Exactly!" Dan said. "We need to have ourselves a good old-fashioned ghost hunt."

Logan perked up. As far as he was concerned, this was excellent news. His sister and her mate were endlessly entertaining when together, plus he was rather curious about this room thirteen himself. Well, not really the room so much as what Lily claimed was inside it.

He'd never actually met a poltergeist before and was quite looking forward to the experience.

"So what's the verdict, Harry? Any clues where we should start our hunt?" Cole asked.

Harry looked surprised. "You heard Lily. She refused to tell me where room thirteen is. Frankly, I doubt its existence. She probably invented it just to make me crazy."

Logan had to admit that was definitely something Lily would do.

Of course, if there was such a thing as a poltergeist, Lily was also the sort of person to hide it in a revolving room, for that very same reason—to make her mate crazy.

"Well, let's go demand she tell us." Dan stood and swayed before catching his balance. "We can't leave the bet like this. There's money to be won, shifters!"

The dragons all let out a cheer.

Logan rolled his eyes. As if the dragons needed money.

"We still don't know where Lily is," Harry reminded them.

"Of course, we know where she is," Cole said.

"Yeah, you just need to tell us the room number," Karl said.

Harry looked about as confused as Logan was. "What room number?"

"The room number where their aunt Dory is staying," Cole.

"Whose aunt Dory?"

"Our mates," Dan exclaimed.

"I'm so confused," Harry muttered.

"Join the club," Logan muttered back.

"Come on, man," Karl stumbled over to where Harry was, grabbed his arm and dragged him toward the door of the bar, Dan on Harry's other side.

"Don't mind me," Cole called. "I'll just settle the tab, then."

Logan chuckled and followed his brother-in-law and the shifters out the door.

Fifteen minutes later, they were all on the elevator, heading up to the third floor, where apparently the witches' aunt had a room she'd checked into twenty-four hours before.

"Where'd the dragons go?" Dan asked, swaying in place.

"They said to text them if there really was a room thirteen," Cole said. "Otherwise, they're going to keep drinking."

"Well, that's not right!" Dan exclaimed. "Don't they want to win?"

Logan rolled his eyes. He was pretty sure the dragons knew, just as he did, that this was going to be a waste of time. There was no way Lily was ever going to take them on a tour of room thirteen as long as her doubting mate was along. She probably intended to torture Harry for the rest of their lives about this possible room thirteen that no one had ever actually seen.

"Are you sure Lily will be in here?" Harry asked, stopping at a door midway down the hall.

"Where else would she be?" Cole demanded.

Harry glared at him. "You'd better be right. I will not be happy if I wake up one of my guests for nothing."

"If this is Dory's room, I have no doubt our witchy mates will be inside. They're Dory's nieces and a more devious trio I've never met. I have no doubt they've dragged Lily into whatever they're up to."

Harry drew in a deep breath, nodded, then knocked.

A moment later, the door opened and an older woman stood there waiting.

"So sorry to barge in so late, I was just wondering if you've seen—Lily!" Harry stepped into the room and hurried to his mate's side while Cole, Dan and Karl made beelines for their own witchy mates.

Feeling a bit like a fifth wing, Logan followed behind.

The moment he stepped inside, an adorable black cat launched herself across the room and landed in his arms.

Logan froze for a moment in astonishment as an incredible feeling of peace washed over him. "Well, hello, darling, aren't you a sweetheart?" Though pets were quite common throughout the realms, he'd never really understood their appeal until now.

He began to pet the cat and was rewarded with a loud rumbling purr. He smiled, completely charmed, and was contemplating kidnapping the darling when the woman who'd let them in said, "She *is* a sweetheart, isn't she? In fact, her current name is Kitty Sweet."

Current seemed an odd way to describe one's name. He wondered if cats often switched their names, and if so, what her name had been in the past, and what it would be next.

"Logan, this is our great-aunt Dory," Lara said.

"Nice to meet you," Logan said. "Does Kitty Sweet belong to you then?"

"Of course not," Dory said. "She's a living being. One cannot *own* them."

This was wonderful news to Logan. He'd always thought pets were a form of ownership and it had been one of the reasons he couldn't understand the appeal. He was quite gratified to learn he was wrong and gave a short bow in

Dory's direction. "Quite right. My apologies. To whom is Kitty Sweet companion then?"

Dory gave a huge smile. "For now, she is my companion, though I do not expect that to last long. Especially not given how she's attached herself to you. She's never taken so quickly to someone before."

"Yes, I think she likes you even more than me." Lara pouted. "I'm not sure I like this development."

Karl snickered and slung an arm around his mate's shoulders. "Come now, darling. She's just a cat."

Kitty Sweet froze for a moment in Logan's arms then spat a hiss in Karl's general direction.

Cole let out a bark of laughter.

"She's never done that before," Dory said in surprise.

"It's almost like she knew what I was saying," Karl said.

Megan laughed. "Oh, I'm pretty sure that's not up for debate."

Logan had to agree. The cat had definitely understood what the wolf had said. It made her all the more interesting.

"Exactly." Lara slammed her fist in her mate's midsection, making him grunt, and slipped out from under his arm. She glared at him. "You hurt her feelings. Apologize to her!"

Karl looked stunned. "If you think I'm apologizing to a cat, you're crazy!"

Lara growled and spun so her back was to her mate.

"So, Logan," Megan said. "Are you sensing anything from Kitty Sweet?"

Logan froze in the act of petting the cat and glanced around the room. "Am I supposed to?" That wasn't to say he didn't, but it was what he sensed from every living being.

Was there something more to this cat who understood the conversations of those around her?

"Well, yes," Megan said. "Can't you sense her power?"

Ah. Logan hesitated, uncertain how to explain that he did, but he also didn't.

Luckily for him, Lily jumped right in. "Logan senses power differently from the rest of us. He—I want to use the word absorb, but that's not right because he's not a vampire or a succubus—but his power does sort of draw the energies in from all the living beings around him and then it kind of reflects those powers back, creating a sort of bubble, if you will. An aura, you might say, that reflects the power around him."

"I don't even know what that means," Karl said.

Lara let out a scoffing sound. "I'm so not surprised."

"Hey!" Karl scowled at his mate, but she still had her back to him so didn't notice.

"Yes, but that means his power should be reflecting hers," Megan said. "Which means he should be able to sense it, right? So why isn't he?"

"Oh, he is," Lily said. "It just feels the same as everyone else's power."

"That doesn't even make sense," Jessica exclaimed.

"Yeah, not everyone has the same amount of power so they couldn't possibly feel the same," Lara said.

Logan waited for Lily to say something, but when she didn't respond, he felt compelled to clarify. "Power untapped is power nonetheless."

Silence fell in the aftermath of that statement.

"Okay," Megan said. "But, for example, a normal cat doesn't have power." She looked around the room. "Right?"

Everyone nodded except for Lily and Logan.

"Perhaps you should explain it another way," Lily said.

Logan glared at her.

She just grinned back.

She was doing it on purpose! Forcing him to talk when she *knew* how much he hated that. He tried to wait her out, but she just stared him down.

Logan scowled. "Fine. Power unrecognized is still power."

"So you're saying that even cats have power," Karl said, then snickered.

Logan could tell by the look on the wolf's face that he believed Logan was having them on.

He sighed.

Shifters.

Especially earth ones.

So arrogant.

So insular.

"No," Logan said slowly. "I'm saying that all living creatures have power."

"But not equal power," Jessica said. "That's just not possible, right?"

"The universe is quite synchronous and full of patterns everywhere," Lily said. It was about time she started contributing to this conversation again. "Do you truly believe that in a universe filled with both simplicity *and* complexity that equality is impossible?"

"But humans." Lara said it as a statement, as if they were proof that equality could not exist in such a universe.

"Again," Logan said. "Power untapped is power nonetheless."

"So, you're saying that not only cats have power, but humans do too?" Dan asked.

"Of course, they do," Logan said. "Look at what they've

accomplished. Imagine the good they can and will do when they break through their own barriers and tap into their true power."

"Imagine the evil," Jessica muttered.

Logan glared at his sister again. This was all her fault!

She just smiled back at him.

He let out a huff of exasperation, then said, "There are good and bad witches, good and bad fairies, good and bad trolls. It's the nature of being alive. There are even, I imagine, good and bad cats. It is what we do with our lives, our energies, our powers, that define us. So, yes." He stroked a hand down Kitty Sweet's back. "Power *is* distributed equally, which means that when my power recognizes another's—" He broke off, uncertain how to explain.

"It all feels the same," Lily said. "Logan cannot differentiate between great power and weak power because the potential for all power is the same and that is what he senses."

"Huh," Megan said. "Well, that's not very helpful."

"Do you not sense anything when you pet Kitty Sweet?" Dory asked, watching him closely.

What exactly was she expecting him to say?

"She brings me peace." It wasn't really what he intended to say, but it was what came out. It was also the truth.

Lily jerked around to stare at him. "Really?"

He nodded.

"That's never happened before, has it?"

Logan shook his head, even as he continued petting Kitty Sweet.

"Let's try the ritual again," Megan said abruptly.

Logan froze. "What ritual?"

"We're trying to reveal her true form," Lara said.

"She's not a cat?"

"Not at all," Lily said.

"Cat shifter?" he asked.

Cole made a scoffing sound. "Have you ever heard of a house cat being a shifter?"

Logan shrugged. "I don't pretend to know the vastness of the universe. I'm sure it's possible somewhere."

"Well, it's not here on earth," Dan said emphatically.

"Right," Jessica said. "Just like it's not possible for witches to exist here either."

"Or fairies," Lily said.

"Or dragons or phoenixes," Lara said.

"Whatever." Dan rolled his eyes. "I'm a cougar. You'd think I'd know if there were such thing as house cat shifters."

"You didn't know about the koala," Jessica said.

Dan waved a hand. "A koala is not a cat shifter. And she's from Australia originally. Of course, I'd never encountered one before."

Jessica rolled her eyes.

9

KITTY WAS INCREDIBLY content to sit in this man-who-wasn't-a-man's arms.

She'd started to become something else earlier.

Several times.

But she couldn't quite remember what.

Then the man-who-wasn't-a-man arrived and she'd known he was hers.

She'd bolted toward him, landed in his arms and he'd instantly made her purr.

He pet like a dream.

And she knew she was right.

They belonged together.

She wasn't sure how she knew, but she did.

But then he seemed surprised to hear that Kitty was not just a cat.

He kept on petting her, which felt amazing, but she had to wonder. Was he petting her because he felt as compelled toward her as she felt toward him or was it just because he thought she was a pet?

Then the entity came back.

She felt it slide right in, right over, right around them all.

It was there, everywhere around them, sliding closer and closer.

Creeping across the floor, down the walls, sliding toward the man-who-wasn't-a-man.

The man who had wings hiding inside him.

She didn't know why he hid such glorious wings, but he did.

And she saw them, which had to mean something, right?

She could see his true form.

Except he didn't see her the way she saw him, so it probably meant nothing at all.

And then she couldn't think anymore because the entity was right there.

Right.

THERE!

10

LOGAN COULDN'T BELIEVE the shifters and the witches. They were all as bad as his sister. They could literally argue about anything *and* nothing all at the same time.

"All right, enough," Megan said, clearly of the same mind as him. "Let's get this done, shall we?"

That was when Kitty Sweet lost her mind.

She leapt from Logan's arms, claws out, hissing fiercely, and landed on the back of the couch. She stood on her hind feet and swatted the air above the couch.

That was when Logan noticed Agatha and Betina were in the room as well. Agatha, the mother of the local wolf alpha, was sleeping on the couch.

Logan winced. Wolves weren't entirely fond of—

Agatha opened her eyes, let out a startled shriek and fell off the couch.

The cat launched herself over the woman and landed on the coffee table, scattering papers and ingredients everywhere.

She then let out a soft growl and pounced again.

On nothing.

"Huh," Dory said.

Logan narrowed his eyes. Was there something there, getting the poor cat all riled up?

Kitty Sweet swung around in a circle two times, then darted down the hall, disappeared into the bedroom at the end of it, then came barreling out the next moment.

She raced back into the living room, leapt onto the back of the chair where Betina was napping and let out a loud yowl, making everyone in the room jump.

"What on earth—" Betina woke with a start.

"Your cat's gone psycho, Aunt Dory," Jessica observed.

"She's not psycho!" Lara exclaimed. "She's just upset. It's probably Karl's fault."

"My fault!" Karl exclaimed. "I didn't do anything."

Logan had to agree.

Kitty Sweet's bizarre behavior had nothing to do with the wolf. He glanced around the room. And yet he wasn't sensing anything else in here. Just shifters and witches. Plus his sister and the cat, of course.

"You're a wolf aren't you?" Lara said. "That's reason enough. Cats are very sensitive creatures, you know."

Karl rolled his eyes. "Whatever."

Logan slipped around the arguing couple and approached the cat who watched him warily.

She crouched low, fur bristling, but didn't move as he approached.

He held out his hand and crooned, "It's all right, love." When she didn't swat at him, he settled his hand on her back and slowly pet her fur down. After a few moments, she relaxed enough to allow him to pick her up, though this time she did not purr in response to his gentle handling.

She might have settled down a bit, but she was still quite unhappy.

Logan was sorry he was unable to transfer that sense of peace she'd given him back to her. He continued petting her gently, wondering what was going on with this adorable cat who had the witches convinced she wasn't a cat at all.

He didn't necessarily agree. He just couldn't see it.

Still, he was quite intrigued.

Megan sighed. "It's getting pretty late. I'm thinking maybe we should try this again tomorrow. Kitty Sweet's clearly upset or tired or something. Besides, we're running low on ingredients. I'm also thinking we maybe need to consider adding something for longevity."

"Oooh, good idea," Lara said.

Logan raised an eyebrow. What in the great realms were these witches up to?

Dory nodded. "All right, dears. That sounds like an excellent plan. We'll try again tomorrow." She approached Logan with her arms out, clearly ready to take back her companion-cat.

Logan hesitated. He wasn't quite ready to give her up yet, but he supposed he had no choice. She wasn't his companion, after all.

He went to hand her over, but Kitty Sweet stiffened her body in resistance.

"Oh, my," Dory said. "Are you wanting to stay with Logan, then, my darling?" She reached out a hand and scratched Kitty Sweet under the chin. "Very well, then. Off you go."

"I'm sorry. I didn't mean to—"

"No, no. Just bring her back tomorrow, so we can get on with it, understood?" She gave him a very stern look.

Logan nodded. He wanted to ask exactly what they were going to get on with, but decided he probably didn't want to know.

He followed his sister to the door, murmuring to the cat along the way. "Well, my sweet darling, looks like you're my companion for the night, and it's grateful I am too, for the company."

Logan had every intention of heading straight home with Kitty Sweet, but the moment he stepped into the hallway with her, the shifters started in on Lily, wanting her to take them on a tour of room thirteen.

Logan grinned, already shifting his plans in his head because there was no way he was missing this.

"Sorry, guys," Lily said. "A tour's not possible at the moment."

"Right. Because once again, you're just messing with us," Harry snapped. "Just admit that there *is no room thirteen.*"

Of course, that set off a whole new argument between Lily and Harry. Or rather a continuation of the same, old one, with Lily insisting the room did exist and Harry demanding proof of that.

"Oh, don't worry, darling," Logan murmured to Kitty Sweet, when she let out a tiny hiss of surprise at the snapping couple. "This is entertainment for them."

"Well, I can't prove it since I don't know where it is anymore, now can I?" Lily glared at Harry.

"How could you not know?" Harry demanded.

"Because it moved. That's how all rooms thirteen work!"

"So it could be anywhere?"

"Well, not just anywhere. It won't take over a room

that's already inhabited. And obviously, it can't move outside the hotel. It's around here somewhere, I'm sure of it."

"You said you knew where it was!"

"Well, I did! Last week. It moves around an awful lot, you know."

"So, all we have to do," Karl said, "is visit every uninhabited room to find it?"

Lily shrugged. "I suppose. Assuming the idiot here hasn't checked someone into it."

"Checked someone in?" Harry exclaimed. "I thought you had that room contained!"

"Wherever did you get that idea? What part of 'it moves' do you not understand?"

Harry whirled on Logan. "You told me she would have it contained."

Logan winced. "No, I said, she *might* have it contained." He'd also said if it *had* been contained, he wouldn't be surprised if his sister let it loose again, on sheer principle, just to aggravate her doubting mate. Though now that he thought about it, he might have only mentioned that possibility to the dragons.

Oh, well, no sense in bringing it up now.

"So you *don't* have it contained?" Harry asked Lily.

"Again. It moves around." Lily spoke through clenched teeth. "There is no containing a thirteen."

Logan happened to be looking at the witches at that very moment and caught the look of distress on Jessica's face as well as the smirk on Lara's.

Yeah.

He was pretty sure the room *had* been contained, at least at one time. Too bad Harry had a fairy for a mate. And an insane one at that. Everyone knew fairies got their vengeance one way or another.

Lily had probably paid the witches to contain the room, and later, when Harry pissed her off, had probably paid them again to release it.

And now the thirteen was on the loose in the hotel.

With a poltergeist in residence.

And if Logan knew his sister, she probably felt no remorse at all.

Ah well, at least it wasn't on *his* side of the hotel.

"If we don't know where it is, Lily, and you don't have it contained, how can I possibly protect my guests from it?" Harry demanded.

Lily rolled her eyes. "It's not like a room thirteen is that dangerous."

Harry looked at Logan and he nodded. "She's right. They're more of a nuisance than anything."

"Exactly," Lily said. "What you should really be worrying about is the poltergeist in the room, rather than the room itself." And with that statement, she popped herself away.

Logan bit back a grin. So she was back to that, was she? For a while there, Lily had taken to dragging her mate with her whenever she disappeared.

The fact that she hadn't this time, probably meant she wasn't truly gone.

Logan glanced at Harry, who looked as aggravated as he'd ever seen him, and wondered if he should warn his brother-in-law that Lily might still be lurking.

Before he could decide, Agatha demanded, "Is there seriously a room thirteen in this hotel?"

Logan had completely forgotten about Agatha and Betina. They'd accompanied them into the hallway, presumably planning to head home themselves, but then had stayed for the entertainment, much as they all had.

"I'm sorry, ladies," Harry said to them. "It's awfully late. Were you wanting your own rooms?"

"Not if there's a room thirteen in this hotel," Betina said. "I thought those were just a myth. The number thirteen's terrible bad luck, you know."

Harry sighed and hung his head. "Yes, I know. I've been trying to convince someone to get rid of the thirteen, but she's really quite stubborn." The way he said that last word told Logan Harry was well aware his mate was probably still in the vicinity and was taking the opportunity to provoke her.

It worked, of course.

Lily reappeared right in front of Harry, wings fluttering like mad, and raged at him, "How dare you? That room thirteen has every right to exist, just like every other room in this hotel. More even, considering it's rather sentient. You can't just snap your fingers and wish it away!"

Harry shook his head. "You're a fruitcake."

Logan winced in anticipation of the explosion he knew was coming, but then Agatha headed it off by saying, "Well, I for one, think a room thirteen sounds like quite an adventure."

"Agatha," Betina gasped.

"No, really. If you discover where it is, Lily, I hope you'll let me know. I would love to check into a room thirteen. It sounds like a simply marvelous experience, especially if it includes a poltergeist."

Lily smiled. "See there, Harry? Not everyone has hysterics when they hear about the thirteen. In fact, I do believe we should add it to our marketing literature. Imagine the adventurous souls who would pop in for a stay, just for a chance at possibly checking into a room thirteen." She hooked arms with Agatha and Betina and said, "Come along, ladies. Let's discuss this in detail." And she led them down the hall toward the elevator.

Harry let out a huge sigh and shook his head. "Now she's going to be completely unbearable."

11

LOGAN WAS STILL chuckling about the look on Harry's face fifteen minutes later as he walked through the fairy side of the hotel.

Still cradling Kitty Sweet in his arms, he murmured to her as he reached the door to his suite of rooms, "That traveler's in way over his head with Lily, isn't he, darling?"

He let himself inside and stood in the entryway, listening to the silence.

Once upon a time, he and Lily had shared this suite together, but since she'd mated and moved to the human side, he had the large suite of rooms to himself.

"I guess it's just you and me," he murmured to Kitty Sweet as he set her down in the living room. "Are you hungry, love?"

She stood on her hind legs and set her paws against his knees.

Logan grinned. He wasn't sure exactly what that meant, but he had an idea. "Are you wanting me to carry you some more, Kitty darling?"

She meowed softly at him, which he took for a yes and leaning down, picked her back up. This time he set her up on his shoulder and she instantly started kneading him with her paws. After a moment, she rubbed her head against his cheek and settled so that she was sitting on one shoulder with her tail draped around his neck to fall off the other.

He headed into the kitchen and set to fixing dinner with her perched there the entire time. As he cooked, he fed her tiny bits of food and chatted with her about his day.

It was perhaps the most relaxing evening he'd spent in a very long while.

~

In the middle of the night, Kitty woke and stretched her body quite a bit further than she'd been able to stretch it in a very long time.

As she took stock, she realized she was in her other form.

The larger one.

The one with arms and only two legs.

Human.

Yes. She was human again.

She stretched her neck and opened her mouth to speak, but only a soft meow came out.

She slapped a hand over her mouth and in that moment, realized she was not alone.

The entity was back.

Sort of.

She could feel it hovering, not quite there yet.

But someplace close.

Waiting.

She'd just about decided to go hunting for it, when she realized she was in bed with a man.

Just like that, all thoughts of the entity were obliterated in favor of this unexpected development.

It was the man with the hidden wings.

Only they weren't hiding anymore.

He'd brought her home with him, she remembered, fed her dinner, then pet her until she'd fallen asleep purring.

And now they were in bed together.

Only she wasn't a cat anymore and he wasn't wearing a shirt.

He was lying on his stomach and his wings were draped across the bed to either side of him.

They were gorgeous, black and dark gray.

As she watched, they fluttered a little, and she wanted to play with them. She was reaching out to bat at them when she noticed her hand.

She hesitated because hands weren't for batting at toys. They were for—

Other things.

She pulled her hand back, clenched it in a fist and stared at the man some more.

Logan.

He was utterly scrumptious.

Plus he had the most delicious voice and smelled like catnip to her kitty side.

She wanted to rub her body all over him.

Just like she'd done as a cat.

Only now, she wanted to do it as a human.

She leaned over and stared into his face.

Still sleeping.

She had a sudden urge to wake him by licking his cheek.

It probably wouldn't be a very nice way to greet the man who had been so kind to her.

But oh, how she so wanted to.

It was then that the man, Logan, opened his eyes.

~

It was the most delicious dream Logan had ever had.

A beautiful, naked woman crouched above him, watching him from stunning, green eyes.

So perfect.

He rolled slightly to the side, leaned up on one arm, hooked her around the waist, and toppled her to the bed beside him.

She let out a soft sound of surprise and he kissed her.

She threw her arms around his neck and kissed him back.

And oh, what a kiss.

He lost all sense of time and place, all sense of himself in that endless, exquisite kiss.

They rolled across the bed together, their passion raging out of control.

He pulled away to ask her name, but somehow the bed disappeared from beneath them and they were falling.

He flung out a hand to break their fall and tried to cuddle her close, but right before they hit, she was gone and he woke with a raging hard-on and a cat sitting two feet from his head, staring at him curiously.

Logan let out a bark of laughter. "Well, that was some dream, wasn't it, Kitty Sweet?" He pushed himself up, scooped the cat into his arms and crawled back onto the bed with her. "I can't imagine where that came from." He settled

Kitty Sweet on his chest. “My subconscious must be really anxious for me to find a mate.” He sighed. “It’s just too bad, really. No woman could possibly be that perfect.”

“Meow.”

He grinned at Kitty Sweet.”Well, except for you, my love. You’re perfection personified.” He stroked his hand down her back and fell asleep thinking about the beautiful woman with bright green eyes and curly, blonde hair, whose kiss was perfection itself.

12

LOGAN WOKE THE next morning thinking about the woman from his dreams the night before.

It was really quite depressing, to realize he'd become so lonely, his subconscious mind was now creating imaginary mates for him.

Pathetic, really.

Kitty Sweet followed him from room to room as he showered and got ready for the day.

Like the night before, Logan fed her tiny bits of his own breakfast, before heading out with her perched on his shoulder.

"Well, what do you think, Kitty Sweet? Shall we check in downstairs first? Make sure there are no crises demanding my attention?"

She meowed, and without pausing to think about it, he replied. "Yes, then we'll head over to the human realm to see the witches. I'm sure by then, they'll have figured things out, whatever it is they're up to."

And so Logan and Kitty Sweet spent the morning

together, working the fairy side of the hotel. "Fairy management can be quite challenging," Logan murmured to her as they set about soothing a troll who had somehow stubbed its toe on one of the many trees growing everywhere.

Once the troll had moved on, soothed with the promise of a spa mud bath to make up for its trouble, Kitty Sweet claimed the offending tree as her own. She ran up its trunk, raced across its branches, peeked through its leaves at him and then played a vigorous game of hide-and-seek, which only ended when she pounced on his head, making him laugh.

From that point on, anytime they passed a tree (which was quite often), Kitty Sweet would leap from his shoulder to one of its branches. She would play in the tree for a few moments before eventually hopping back down onto his shoulder or sometimes pouncing on his head.

He shouldn't be surprised.

After all, cats of all kinds were excellent climbers.

What was a surprise was how very much he'd come to adore this cat in such a short amount of time.

"Dory was right," he told her. "You're the sweetest thing ever. I don't know how I'm going to give you back." Just thinking about it made him grumpy.

More than grumpy.

It made him sad.

He should probably return her immediately. Before he got even more attached.

Instead, he found more and more reasons to delay their return to the human realm. An issue with a room here, an employee concern there, and before he knew it, lunch time had come and gone.

"Well, Kitty Sweet. I suppose we can't put it off any

longer. After all, I promised Dory I'd bring you back today. So off we go."

After checking in one last time with his front desk manager, Logan set off for the elevators that led to the other realms.

As he stepped out of the elevator into the lobby on the human side, he tried not to think about saying goodbye.

~

Kitty Sweet was falling in love.

It was ridiculous really.

She was a cat, for goodness sake.

And he was a man-fairy.

Still, she couldn't help how she felt.

And that kiss had just sealed the deal.

It was really too bad about the bed.

Imagine what might have happened if it hadn't spontaneously moved on its own, dumping the two of them on the floor.

The fall had startled her so badly, she'd landed in her cat form and that was the end of the kissing.

Of course, Logan had no idea she was the woman he'd kissed. He actually thought he'd been dreaming!

Which was just another reason in a long line of them for why he probably wasn't meant to be hers after all.

She wanted him to be, of course, but his inability to see her true self was not a good sign.

She knew how true mates were supposed to work because Dory had explained it all to her.

Dory's nieces had emailed her regularly and Dory had read the stories of their matings to Kitty.

She'd especially loved the story of Cole and Megan and how he'd seen right through Megan's glamour when she'd tried to prove she was a witch by casting a spell of invisibility upon herself.

"True mates can always see through any glamour to the true essence of their love," Dory had explained, which was why when Logan had walked into the suite of rooms and Kitty had instantly been drawn to him, she'd been sure that he would see her true essence, proving he was her mate.

Except when she'd leapt into his arms, he'd not seen anything in her but cat.

And later, when he'd seen her human form and then kissed her, he'd dismissed the entire thing as a dream.

Kitty was also starting to remember bits and pieces about being human, including the fact that they didn't *have* mates. Oh, they got married, but just as regularly, they got divorced.

As far as she could remember, there was nothing about fated mates in their culture at all.

Except for fairy tales, of course, and true love's kiss.

That hadn't worked out either, though, because their kiss had only resulted in her returning to her cat form and him denying she existed at all, which meant either the power of true love's kiss was highly overrated or he wasn't her true love after all.

What a terrible thought that was.

~

By the time Logan knocked on Dory's door, it was rather late in the afternoon and no one answered.

He hadn't planned it that way, but his heart definitely wasn't broken.

He went downstairs and checked in with Harry, who told him Dory's nieces had picked her up about an hour before. "I'm not sure where they were headed, but they were laughing and excited."

Interesting.

"Were the shifters with them?"

"Nope."

"Huh. Okay, well, when they get back, let them know I was here with Kitty Sweet, will you? I'm heading back over to the fairy side."

"You got it."

Logan headed for the elevator.

"Logan, hold up!"

He stopped to smile at his sister. "What's up, Lilybelle?"

She threw her arms around him in her usual exuberant greeting, then scooped Kitty Sweet into her arms. "Hello, darling. Aren't you just adorable? When are you going to come out and visit again?"

"Um, are you talking to the cat?"

"Of course, I'm talking to the cat! Or really the woman. I wonder what her name is. Have you seen her yet? Did she tell you?"

Logan froze. "What woman?"

"The one everyone's been talking about! The one the witches have been trying so hard to reveal. We need your help, by the way. I promised I would recruit you if I saw you before then. We forgot to ask last night."

"Recruit me for what? What's going on, Lily?"

"We're going to help Miss Kitty Sweet here return to her natural form, of course."

There it was again. "Why are the witches so convinced she's not a cat?"

"Weren't you listening at all last night?"

"Of course I was. I just never heard anything to convince me she's anything more than a cat." He leaned over to look into Kitty Sweet's eyes and said directly to her, "And there's nothing wrong with being a cat. In fact, I quite like you as you are." He stood back up and glared at his sister. "Now give me back my cat."

Lily raised an eyebrow at him. "Your cat, is it? Does Dory know you've claimed her companion for your own?"

"She's my companion until Dory says otherwise, so for now, hand her over."

Lily smirked and passed Kitty Sweet back to Logan.

He promptly set her down on the lobby floor and they both watched as she ran around the lobby, sniffing everything. "See that? She's acting like a cat, nothing more."

"I know what I saw, Logan! And that cat has a woman inside her."

"Okay, tell me about this woman. What does she look like?" Logan tried not to get his hopes up. Lily was probably just messing with him again. She quite enjoyed torturing her victims and wouldn't hesitate to bring witches into her plotting.

"Wouldn't you like to know?" Lily snapped, then whirled and flew away.

Logan let out a huff of exasperation. "Come along, Kitty Sweet. That, right there, my darling, is why I never wanted a fairy for a mate. Can you imagine? All the crazy. None of the peace." He headed for the elevator, Kitty Sweet on his heels.

Kitty followed Logan into the elevator, expecting the doors to reopen at the fairy hotel. Instead, they landed somewhere else, a magical place with even more trees than the hotel!

She darted forward and leapt onto a branch.

She looked down at Logan who smiled back at her and gave her a nod, and so she took off, racing from one branch to the other, always peeking out to make sure she hadn't left him too far behind.

As she darted from branch to branch, Logan followed a similar path below, walking across bridges and down walkways that meandered in and out and around the trees.

This was truly an enchanting place.

Kitty Sweet ran and played, batting at vines and branches, peeking through the leaves at Logan and sneaking around to pounce on his head when he was looking in the wrong direction.

He never got upset with her, but instead just laughed and congratulated her on her sneakiness.

He really was the perfect man.

Fairy.

Mate.

It was just too bad she was stuck as a cat and he had no idea—or refused to believe—that she was also a woman.

Eventually, they returned to the hotel and found Lily waiting for them.

"Dory wanted me to tell you they won't be ready for the ritual for another week or so," she informed Logan. She then leaned over and said quite seriously to Kitty, "Don't worry, darling. They just had to order in a few herbs for longevity.

As soon as they arrive, we'll have you all fixed up. In the meantime, you get to stay with Logan. Isn't that lovely?"

It really was.

And yet, it wasn't.

The longer she stayed with Logan, the more enamored of him she became.

What if he didn't like her as a human?

What if *she* didn't like *being* a human? She'd never actually considered that before.

She *liked* being a cat. She especially liked having Logan stroke her back and tickle her under her chin.

The life of a cat was quite enjoyable, in fact. She was pretty certain her life as a human had probably been quite a bit more stressful.

Not that she really remembered it, but she did know, deep down inside, that she'd never been so content as these days she'd been trapped as a cat, those first few days notwithstanding, of course.

Once Dory had found her and once she'd settled into being a cat, she'd found it to be quite freeing.

She would miss the cat once she had her other form back.

She would miss it a lot.

Oh, well.

If these were going to be her final days in this cat form, she would enjoy them as much as she could.

And so over the next few days, Kitty played with Logan, running all over the fairy hotel and the shopping gallery attached to it.

They visited a pet shop, where Kitty met a variety of pets and was astounded to realize Logan was right. They all had an aura of power.

Though as far as she could tell, none of them had humans trapped inside like she did.

Logan bought her a jeweled collar that she absolutely adored and some delicious fishy treats. She thought she might have found them disgusting as a human, but as a cat, they were simply divine.

As they wandered through the mall, she would dart from tree to tree, then race back to Logan and nudge his hand. He would scratch her head, then feed her a treat, and she'd be off again.

It was the best game ever.

And he was the best man-fairy-companion she could have ever imagined.

Now, if only he would turn into a cat.

She decided that would be amazing. Her man-fairy-companion-cat.

Only that seemed a bit much to hope for, so instead, she was relying on the witches to work their magic.

And of course, on Logan, to not reject her, even though she wasn't his mate, even though she wasn't really a cat.

13

THE REST OF that week, as they waited for the witches' herbs to arrive, was simply wonderful.

The days were full of fun and games. Even though Logan had to go to work every day, he took Kitty Sweet with him everywhere and always found time to play games with her and to make the work fun.

While the days were wonderful, the nights were even better.

Kitty would fall asleep in her cat form and at some point in the night, would wake up human. Sometimes Logan woke with her and sometimes she would wake him herself.

Always, when he realized she was there, he would kiss her and the passion would rage between them.

Every night, Kitty fell a little deeper in love with her man-fairy-companion.

Unfortunately, each night of passion ended in frustration.

Their second night together, the blankets got all tangled up and somehow yanked Logan from the bed. He laughed and called himself clumsy, but Kitty didn't really believe that at all.

The next night, the curtain rod fell off the wall and crashed into the bed, narrowly missing Logan's head.

The fourth night, the sprinkler right above them, went crazy and started shooting water everywhere.

The fifth night, the bed collapsed.

At that point, Logan was fuming. He was sure something was wrong in his suite. He'd called in repairman after repairman and no one could figure out what was wrong.

The curtain rod had been installed correctly and never should have fallen.

There was no reason for the sprinkler to go off and they couldn't find a single fault in the system.

The bed was in perfect condition. It was brand new, in fact, barely a year old.

Their sixth night together, Kitty was determined to catch whatever entity was torturing them. So instead of falling asleep like usual, she sat on the bed, glaring across the room, tail twitching, ready to defend her man-fairy if she had to.

Logan had long since fallen asleep.

He was relaxed behind her, adorably exhausted and she was determined to protect him.

The hours passed and nothing happened.

Kitty was just beginning to think maybe she should give up and go to sleep herself when a ball came rolling across the floor.

She leapt from the bed, pounced on the ball, rolled and kicked it up with her legs, then batted it back into the shadows.

It came rolling back in the next instant, making her fur stand on end.

She faced the shadowy corner of the room and hissed.

Something was trying to play with her.

That was Logan's job, not this scary entity that refused to show itself.

She stalked back to the bed, leapt onto it and settled back into her defensive stance.

"It's okay, darling," Logan murmured, stroking a hand down her back without opening his eyes.

The ball rolled across the floor again.

Kitty hissed at it.

Then she hissed again.

Because how dare this entity try to get her to play with it after ruining all those kissing sessions?

Just thinking about every kiss it had interrupted made her angry all over again.

She growled low in her throat.

~

Logan woke to the sound of Kitty growling softly.

He was disappointed and disturbed. Usually when he woke in the middle of the night, it was because he'd been dreaming.

This time, though, he was pretty sure he wasn't dreaming.

Kitty sounded agitated.

He opened his eyes just in time to see something come flying through the air at them.

Logan let out a roar and leapt to his feet on the bed, startling Kitty Sweet.

She jumped to the floor, hissed at the shadows in the corner, then leapt back onto the bed.

Logan sent a bolt of energy around the room, lighting it up so there were no shadows.

There was nothing there.

The light died down, so he flicked a hand again, turning on the lights throughout the room.

Still nothing.

Then suddenly out of nowhere a hail of cat toys—small stuffed animals, jingly balls, toy mice—came flying at them.

With a snarl, Logan scooped Kitty Sweet in his arms and leapt for the door to the bedroom, which snapped closed right before he reached it. He turned, protecting Kitty Sweet, as he slammed into the wood.

He scowled around the room.

What was going on?

Kitty Sweet let out a soft hiss and snarl.

"It's okay, darling. Everything's going to be fine." He stroked her gently and coaxed her up onto his shoulder so that his hands would be free.

Her claws were out and pricked at his shoulder as she settled there.

He wished for one of his ancestors' swords, which were all displayed in museums around the realm.

Probably for the best.

He couldn't even see his enemy to fight him and would probably chop off his own leg if he tried.

He reached behind him to try the doorknob.

Locked.

This door didn't even have a lock so he didn't know how that was even possible.

Another toy came flying across the room.

Kitty let out a hiss and swatted it back as if she were one of those ball-players from earth.

"Look," Logan said to whatever was tossing the toys around the room. "It's time for bed now. You need to settle down." He used his sternest voice.

For a long moment, there was no response.

Just as he'd begun to think he'd convinced whatever it was to let them alone for the evening, a barrage of cat toys came flying at them again.

Logan turned into the door, so that Kitty was protected from the flying toys, some of which hurt, thank you very much.

When the pelting finally stopped, Logan whirled around and snapped, "Kitty would love to play with you. Tomorrow. Now go to sleep!"

A bit of wind rushed through the room, almost as if whatever was there had let out a giant huff of exasperation, then silence.

In the silence, there came an audible click from behind them.

Logan reached back again and tried the doorknob.

This time it turned.

He pulled open the door and stepped into the hallway. He listened, but heard nothing. "Right. I think we should try sleeping in the living room tonight, what do you say, Kitty Sweet?"

She rubbed her face against his, which he took as a yes.

He headed down the hall to the couch, where he stretched out with Kitty Sweet curled up on his chest.

It was while he was resting, listening to Kitty's Sweet's purr, that he realized exactly what had invaded his suite.

If Kitty Sweet hadn't been sleeping on his chest at that moment, he would have leapt to his feet and stormed the human side of the hotel.

Never mind that his sister and Harry were probably sleeping at this very moment.

His sister's ridiculous antics had caused this!

And to think he'd been looking forward to meeting the poltergeist. Well, not in his own suite, he hadn't! He couldn't believe his sister. What had she been thinking?

He was lying there fuming when it happened.

The soft weight of Kitty Sweet became heavier and quite different.

He opened his eyes and found his dream woman staring down at him.

For the first time, he realized her eyes were the same bright green as Kitty's were, and for a moment, he allowed himself to believe.

She leaned down and pressed her lips to his.

He wrapped his arms around her and turned so they lay side-by-side on the couch.

He brushed a blonde curl away from her eyes and murmured, "You're her, aren't you?" He wanted to see Kitty Sweet in the human, but he couldn't. Just as he couldn't ever see the human in the cat. Still he desperately wanted to believe.

Not only that they were one and the same, but that she—the woman and the cat—were his.

His mate.

His everything.

He wanted to talk to her, to ask what her name was, to ask why she stayed in her cat form and only ever came out at night, but even as he opened his mouth, she leaned forward and kissed him again.

Every thought disappeared as he sank into the bliss and the beauty of her kiss.

14

THE NEXT MORNING, while Logan was cooking breakfast, Kitty Sweet batted a toy ball across the kitchen floor and waited for it to come back.

She wasn't thrilled Logan had promised she'd play with this scary entity, but since he wasn't leaving her side, and the entity was only tossing one ball at a time this morning, she played along. Mostly because she was in a pretty good mood.

After they'd fallen asleep on the couch, she'd woken a couple hours later in her human form, plastered on top of Logan. The minute he'd opened his eyes, she'd been unable to resist temptation and had kissed him. They'd spent hours on the couch, cuddling, then kissing some more before eventually drifting off to sleep, still kissing.

When she woke this morning, she was back in her cat form, but a lot more relaxed.

All things considered, ghostly entity aside, it had been a pretty good night.

This morning, however, Logan was pretty agitated.

"I blame Lily," he said to Kitty Sweet. "She let that poltergeist out. I know she did and now it's somehow haunting my own apartment. I'm not sure how she did it, but she won't get away with it, I promise you that."

Kitty was a bit worried he might hurt his sister's feelings, he was so angry. On the other hand, it really wasn't nice of Lily to send her pet poltergeist their way.

How would she like it if she and Harry woke in the middle of the night to a bunch of pens being tossed at them or whatever else they had hanging around their apartment?

Kitty focused on trying to cheer Logan up as they went about their regular morning. She played in the trees and pounced on him and generally managed to lighten his mood by the time lunch time came around.

She thought he might head over to the human side of the hotel at that point, but instead, he took her to a restaurant in the fairy mall where they enjoyed a delicious lunch of tuna melts and fruit salad.

Logan set her up right on the table so that she could eat with him.

A number of people stopped by to chat with him and to meet Kitty Sweet. By that time, apparently everyone had heard about the cat with whom Logan was keeping company.

Kitty had met everyone he worked with by that time, of course, but now she was getting to meet many of his friends and even some of his family members.

"So, I finally get to meet your Kitty Sweet." A beautiful, older fairy stopped by just as they were nearing the end of their lunch.

"Mother." Logan stood and kissed her on the cheek, then

gestured to a chair across from him. "Would you like anything?"

"Perhaps a glass of water."

Logan motioned to the waiter, who immediately stepped up with a tumbler and pitcher of water.

Once they were alone again, Logan's mother held her hand out to Kitty Sweet.

Kitty, wanting to make friends with the woman who had made the man-fairy-companion she loved, stepped right up and rubbed her head against the woman's fingers.

"Oh!" The woman giggled and gently stroked Kitty's head. "She's very soft, isn't she? I've never pet a cat before."

Logan grinned. "I hadn't either. Lily's pretty convinced she's not really a cat."

Logan's mother peered into Kitty Sweet's eyes. "Yes, I can see why she thinks that. My name is Iris, Kitty Sweet. It's quite lovely to meet you. I've heard all about you from Lily and we're all pinning our hopes on you. We really are."

Kitty Sweet wasn't sure what she meant by that, but she took it to mean that she'd been accepted by this woman and that was fantastic news. She let out a soft meow and nudged Iris' hand, prompting another soft, tinkling laugh.

"Well, Logan, my darling. It appears you've found the best of companions in Kitty Sweet."

"Indeed, I have. I'm afraid I'll be giving her back soon, though."

Kitty Sweet froze, as did Iris' hand on her back.

"Whatever do you mean, giving her back?"

"The witches are planning some sort of ritual tomorrow. She's not really my companion, you know. She's Dory's."

"Dory?"

"The witches' aunt."

"Oh, of course. I wouldn't worry about that, my son. From what I gather from Lily, the witches have all accepted that Miss Kitty Sweet belongs with you."

"Even Dory?"

"Of course, even Dory. In fact, I believe the ritual they're planning is to ensure it. Well, I'd better get on with my day." Iris stood. "Kitty Sweet, it was excellent to meet you. I hope we meet again. In fact, I look forward to it and to many conversations in the future." She leaned into Logan, who had stood when she had, and pressed a kiss to his cheek, then popped away before he could offer to accompany her home.

Shaking his head, Logan sat again. "Like mother, like daughter," he told Kitty Sweet. "Now you see where Lily gets that ridiculous habit of hers."

~

Logan had intended not to return to the human side of the realms until the next day, when they were scheduled to join the witches for the ritual they were planning.

Unfortunately, at the end of a long work day (a work day spent playing as much as working, a new development he was quite enjoying, mind you, especially because it meant he could finally pay his sister back for all those times she'd disappeared with her mate in the middle of a work day), when they stepped into their rooms, the poltergeist pelted them with cat toys, clearly demanding they play some more.

"And to think I actually wanted to meet you," Logan muttered. He pacified it by tossing a few balls in its direction, then scooped Kitty Sweet into his arms, and escaped into the hallway with her.

"I guess we have no choice but to confront my sister. This is her fault, after all." He scowled. Even though he owned the hotel and could just check into a different room, he considered that to be giving in, something he wasn't about to do. Not when the poltergeist was holding his own quarters hostage.

And it was all his sister's fault. She'd literally made his sanctuary intolerable.

And he was going to tell her that very thing!

As soon as he managed to find her.

It took quite a bit of searching—she wasn't on the fairy side at all nor was she in her quarters on the human side—but he finally tracked her down to Shenanigans.

The bar, not the hotel.

The one inside the hotel, not the one in the woods.

It was really rather confusing, actually.

All those Shenanigans.

They should come up with a new name.

The one time he'd suggested it, though, the earth residents had all gasped in horror. It wasn't like he was suggesting they give up the Shenanigans brand. Just add to it, so things weren't so confusing all the time. Unfortunately, no one else agreed.

Logan entered Shenanigans (the bar) and carefully set Kitty Sweet on the floor. "Go ahead, now, darling, explore to your heart's content. I'm afraid I must deal with my sister now."

Kitty Sweet stared up at him a moment, almost as if she'd understood. Almost as if she wasn't sure she should abandon him or not.

"I'll be fine, darling," he said to her. "Go make friends."

Kitty Sweet darted away and Logan set his sights on the table where Lily was sitting. It was a rather large table. She was at the center of it, surrounded by shifters and witches, and was laughing and drinking and generally appearing as if she didn't have a care in all the realms.

Well, he'd see about that.

~

"You really adopted three kittens?" Lily grinned at the disgruntled look on Karl's face. The wolf was clearly put out by this turn of events.

"Actually, we adopted five," Dory said.

"Five?" Dan, Cole and Karl exclaimed in unison.

"I only saw three," Karl said suspiciously.

"The shelter had a family of five orphaned kittens," Dory explained.

"We couldn't possibly leave any of them behind," Megan said.

"Exactly," Dory said. "And with Kitty Sweet moving on—whether because we manage to counteract the spell or simply because she settles into life as a cat with Logan—I knew one kitten wouldn't be enough to make up for her loss. So I adopted two."

"Plus she fell in love with them," Lara teased.

"And you didn't?"

"Oh, no, I definitely did."

"So what are their names?" Lily asked, delighted at the thought of five adorable, playful kittens. "And what do they look like? And when can I come and visit?"

The witches all laughed. "You can visit anytime," Megan

said. "And they're all black, except for mine has a tiny white spot on its nose."

"And mine has a bit of white on the tip of its tail," Lara said.

"Mine's pitch black," Jessica said. "Even its whiskers are black!"

"Wow," Lily breathed. "What about yours, Dory?"

"They're both black, one with white paws and one with a white toe. I'm going to name them Puss and Boots."

Harry chuckled. "Puss 'n Boots. That's adorable."

"I'm so excited to meet them," Lily said. "I've decided I love cats. We may need to get one for the hotel, Harry. A hotel kitty!"

Harry grinned. "Whatever you want, darling."

"That's what I like to hear!" Lily cheered.

Karl groaned. "More cats? What is wrong with you people? If you must adopt a pet, why not go for a nice big Husky?"

"Dogs are smelly," Lara informed him.

"And litter boxes aren't?" he demanded.

She grinned. "That, my love, is what you are for."

Karl looked horrified and everyone burst into laughter.

It was at that moment that Logan arrived, looking as aggravated as Lily had ever seen him.

~

Logan glared at his sister. "I thought you said you'd contained that poltergeist."

The table fell silent and everyone looked at him, then back at Lily, who appeared quite startled. "Well, of course, I did. It's in room thirteen."

"Not anymore, it's not. Now it's in my personal suite on the fairy side of this hotel. So tell me, how exactly did that happen?"

"That's just not possible, Logan. Jessica cast a spell on the poltergeist, tying it to room thirteen. If the poltergeist is in your suite right now, then so is the thirteen and *that* room is attached to *this* hotel, not the fairy one."

"Well, technically, the two hotels are connected by the elevator," Lara said, "so couldn't they be considered the same hotel, in that case?"

The twins stared at her.

"Surely not," Lily exclaimed. "But even if they were, Logan's rooms are inhabited. Rooms thirteen aren't able to take over a room that's already got a resident in it!"

"Well." Megan hesitated.

"Well what?" Lily asked.

"Spells can be very powerful things," Megan said. "And a poltergeist itself has its own reservoir of power. As far as I know, it doesn't have any limitations as to what rooms it might choose to enter—or haunt, as the case may be."

"Ohhhh," Lara said. "That makes total sense."

"What? I don't understand," Lily said.

"Neither do I." This conversation was getting rather convoluted, as far as Logan was concerned. He just wanted the poltergeist gone!

"It's because I cast the room," Jessica said, "and tied it to the poltergeist."

"Exactly," Megan said. "So when the poltergeist, having no limits on where it might travel, decided to follow Logan to the fairy side of the hotel—"

"The thirteen went with it?" Lily's voice got higher at the end.

"You did have us tie them together," Lara said.

"Yes, to keep the ghost contained!" Lily exclaimed. "It was a perfect plan! How could this have happened?"

"Well," Megan said. "Like I said before, spells are quite powerful things. One must never cast them lightly."

"Hold on a minute!" Logan exclaimed, horrified as his brain finally caught up to what he was hearing. "Are you saying that I not only have the poltergeist living in my quarters, but I'm also hosting the thirteen?"

"Unfortunately," Jessica said, "yes. The spell was really quite powerful, you see. Lily wanted to make sure the poltergeist could never escape the room."

"And good news," Lara said brightly. "It worked!"

Logan glared at his sister. "Lily, if you don't fix this situation—"

"Yes, yes." Lily waved her hand. "Here's what I don't understand. How on earth did the poltergeist even attach itself to Logan in the first place? He would have had to have entered room thirteen at some point!"

"The only hotel room on this side that I've visited is Dory's," Logan said.

Everyone turned to stare at her.

Dory's eyes widened. "You think I checked into room thirteen?"

"Well, no. I think you checked into room three hundred thirteen, which just so happened to be housing room thirteen at the time." Lily looked aggravated. "What were you thinking, Harry?"

"Me? I kept asking where room thirteen was and you kept refusing to tell me! How was I supposed to know I needed to avoid checking anyone into a specific room if I didn't know what room it was?"

"Well, perhaps you should have stayed away from all rooms thirteen!"

"You never told me it was more likely to inhabit a different version of thirteen."

Lily paused at that. "Well. That's probably coincidence. I've never known a thirteen to show specific preference for any number. But still. Of all the rooms in this hotel, you just had to pick the one housing the thirteen, didn't you?"

"And how would you have proposed that I avoid doing such a thing when I had no idea where it was, and given its penchant, as you put it, for moving around?"

Lily grinned. "Well, all I can say about that is, this hotel's never boring."

Harry let out a huff. "So, the good news is the thirteen has moved on?"

"Yes, to my side of the hotel," Logan snarled, "and more specifically, to my own suite of rooms. This is all your fault!" He glared at Lily.

She shook her head. "Actually, now that I think about it, I'm pretty sure it's the cat's fault."

Kitty Sweet, who had been busy exploring every nook and cranny of the bar, froze and turned to glare at Lily, then expressed her displeasure with a loud yowl.

Lily jumped.

Logan held out a hand to Kitty Sweet and she raced for him, leaping into his arms in one long bound.

"Wow," Megan said, eyes wide.

Kitty Sweet climbed onto his shoulder, nuzzled Logan's cheek, then turned her back and twitched her tail at Lily.

Harry let out a bark of laughter. "Guess she doesn't appreciate being blamed for something that's not her fault. Not that I can relate to that or anything."

Lily rolled her eyes at Harry. "Oh, please, stop being so dramatic." She stood and walked around the table to stand next to her brother. "My apologies, sweet kitty. I used the wrong term. It's not your fault that you're so sweet even a poltergeist would fall in love with you."

Kitty looked over her shoulder at Lily, appearing for all the world as if she were listening intently.

No wonder Logan was finding it easier and easier to believe she and his dream woman might be the same.

"What do you mean the poltergeist fell in love with her?" Megan asked.

"Well, at first, I thought the poltergeist had attached itself to Logan, but that really doesn't make any sense. I mean, look at him." She waved a hand at her brother.

Everyone stared at him, then back at Lily.

Logan wasn't sure whether to be insulted or amused.

"I mean, he's so serious all the time. He's kind of a downer actually."

Logan rolled his eyes.

"Poltergeists, on the other hand, are playful and a bit rowdy. They usually prefer to haunt children. Why? Because they're fun and they like to play, of course. And who's the most playful among us?"

Karl opened his mouth and Lara snapped, "You're not playful. You're just immature."

Lily giggled. "Kitty Sweet, of course. So my guess is the poltergeist attached itself to her and when she left with Logan, it followed, dragging the thirteen with it."

Logan groaned. "Great. Does that mean we're stuck with the poltergeist AND the thirteen?" Because no way was he giving up Kitty Sweet, no matter what he had to put up with to keep her.

"Not at all." Lily grinned. "We'll just have to do what I did to get the poltergeist contained in the first place."

"And what's that?" Harry asked.

"Convince it to move elsewhere."

"Yes!" Dan exclaimed. "Finally, the ghost hunt we've all been waiting for!"

15

"WELL, KITTY SWEET, what do you think? Will we be stuck with a poltergeist for a roommate forever?" Logan set her down on the kitchen table and smiled at her.

Kitty Sweet nudged his hand with her head, so he started petting her again.

"Yes, I know Lily promised to bring the witches here as soon as they have what they need for the spell, but who knows how long that will take? I think it's entirely possible Lily will leave me to suffer! Of course, you being here is a definite plus. She wouldn't want to torture an innocent kitty, so there may be hope after all."

At that moment, the lights flickered, then plunged them into darkness.

Logan let out a huff of exasperation. "Listen, you." He sent a glare around the room. "I don't know what your problem is, but we need to be able to see if you want us to play with you."

Long moments ticked by, then the lights came back on just as one of Kitty Sweet's toys came flying at them.

Logan caught it just before it would have hit poor Kitty in the face. "Be nice!" he snapped at the poltergeist. "That could have hurt her! Then who would play with you? Not me, that's for sure!"

Another toy came flying at them, this time aimed right at Logan's head.

He batted it away, picked Kitty Sweet up in his arms and stalked into the living room. "We should have gone with the witches," he muttered to her. "Don't know why I didn't think of it." He picked up a couple toys along the way, settled on the couch and started tossing the balls randomly around the room.

No matter where he tossed them, they invariably came flying straight back at him and Kitty Sweet. He caught one of them and bopped it to the couch beside them.

Kitty Sweet instantly pounced on it.

Another ball came flying at them. He caught it and sent it sailing back.

He hoped the witches would be quick. This could get old fast.

An hour later, just as his aggravation and annoyance hit an all-time high, a knock came at the door.

Logan surged to his feet. "About damn time." He stalked to the door and flung it open. "Took you long enough. Do you know how annoying it is trying to keep a poltergeist entertained?"

Lily and Harry stepped inside, followed by the witches and their mates.

"Sorry we're late," Jessica said. "Lily just had to play with the kittens and well, so did we. They're really quite adorable."

"Who cares about the kittens?" Karl demanded. "I want to know where the poltergeist is." He rubbed his hands together. "This is the most excitement we've had in quite a while!"

Before Logan could explain that even though the poltergeist couldn't be seen, it was definitely in the room with them, a cat toy flew through the air and hit Karl in the head.

Lara burst into laughter. "You should see your face!"

"Did Kitty Sweet do that?" Karl asked, looking stunned.

"No," Logan said. "That was the resident poltergeist. It likes to play fetch. Or something like that."

"See?" Karl exclaimed. "This is what I was talking about! We should have brought a dog, not cats!"

"But we didn't have a dog, Karl. We've already talked about this." Lara looked exasperated.

"I'm just saying! This situation right here with the poltergeist is why you should have adopted a dog."

"But the poltergeist attached itself to a cat, not a dog," Megan said.

"Only because there wasn't a dog around!" Karl exclaimed. "If there had been, I guarantee the dog would have won the playful contest. Cats only want to play when *they* want to play, not necessarily when a poltergeist does."

"Which is why we brought all five of them," Jessica said.

"Wait. You brought your cats here?" Logan asked.

"Well, replicas anyway." Megan set on the coffee table a box Logan now realized was an animal carrier. "Trust us. These kittens are pivotal to our plan."

Tiny meows came from the animal carrier, startling Kitty Sweet, who leapt from the couch to the top of the carrier. She leaned over the front of it and peered inside. A moment later she jerked back, looked up at Logan and let out a plaintive meow.

"Oh, now, look. You've upset Kitty Sweet." Logan picked her up and cuddled her close. "Don't worry, darling. These kittens are not here to stay."

"Hold on a minute," Lily said. "Are you sure this won't hurt the kittens?"

Megan rolled her eyes. "Lily. We've already discussed this."

"I know, I know, but they look so real."

"That's because we modeled them after the real thing," Megan said.

"It's also why they're going to work like a charm," Dory said. "So let's get started, shall we? Nobody touch the kittens once they're loose. Play with them, but don't touch them."

Megan opened the carrier door and five adorable kittens came tumbling out. They immediately leapt to the floor and started pouncing on all the cat toys the poltergeist had scattered around the room.

Lara handed out sticks with feathers and strings and everyone started to play with the kittens. Before long, the poltergeist got involved. Balls were rolling across the floor and strings were dancing, all without any help from the witches, the shifters, the fairies or Harry.

Logan thought Kitty Sweet might be a problem, that she'd start playing with the kittens, possibly touch them and destroy the illusion the witches had created, but instead, she stayed perched on top of the animal carrier and watched with an almost regal air as the cats and poltergeist played.

Eventually, Lily took one of the wooden rods with a string and feathers and began backing slowly toward the door.

One of the kittens followed.

Dory, Megan, Jessica and Lara all did the same, each of them leading a kitten out the door and down the hall.

Harry hurried along ahead of them and unlocked a room at the end of the hall that Logan happened to know was uninhabited at the moment.

Though apparently not for long.

Lily and the witches entered the room, each with a cat trailing behind.

Logan paused in the doorway and glanced down when something brushed against him.

It was Kitty Sweet. She stood at his side and watched as Lily and the witches played with the kittens.

Lily opened a bag and started tossing cat toys around the room—mice, long stuffed animals perfect for kittens to hug and kick, balls of yarn, balls that jingled and so forth.

The kittens pounced as soon as the toys were in the air and then they were racing around the room, tumbling over each other as they played.

For a moment, Logan didn't believe it had worked.

The kittens were playing, yes, but there was no sign of the poltergeist.

Then it happened.

A ball came rolling across the floor from a shadowed corner, where no kittens crouched. Two kittens tried to pounce on it, but ended up running into each other instead and tumbled across the floor, wrestling.

A third kitten pounced on the ball and sent it skittering back toward the corner.

A moment later, it rolled back, along with two other balls.

While the kittens and the poltergeist played, the witches set up their casting. They burned the herbs they had prepared, smudged the entire suite of rooms and whispered words of power to set their casting in stone.

Logan felt it when the magic went live. It was like the room suddenly became ringed in an aura of power.

Kitty Sweet must have felt it too because she leapt straight up into his arms. "It's okay, darling." He started petting her as he pondered what he'd just witnessed.

The witches were incredibly powerful, which made him worry they were wrong about Kitty Sweet, after all, for surely no magic could resist their combined powers.

After gathering up their supplies, the witches took one last look around the room, nodded to Lily and followed her out.

Harry closed the door behind them and locked it. "I can't believe that worked."

Jessica smiled. "You just have to know how to tempt a poltergeist. Magic kittens, built from smoke and illusion, who will never get tired of playing? It's the perfect poltergeist lure."

"And since we tied the kittens to that room specifically," Megan said, "and since the poltergeist has now bonded with the kittens, well, I'd say you have a permanent resident poltergeist in there."

"And the thirteen?" Logan asked.

"That's a bit more tricky," Lara said. "It should have followed the poltergeist since they're tied together. The problem is I don't know if it will *stay* with the poltergeist."

"Well, why not?"

"Because the poltergeist has now bonded with the kittens, which could theoretically, weaken the prior casting that tied it to the room."

Logan groaned. "This is terrible. Not only do I now have

a room that I can't rent out because it houses a poltergeist, not to mention an entire family of imaginary kittens, but I also potentially have a thirteen on the loose!"

Lily grinned. "I'm sure Jessica will be happy to contain the thirteen for you."

"Hold on a minute!" Harry exclaimed. "You said rooms thirteen couldn't *be* contained!"

"I don't know what you're talking about, Harry. Of course, they can be contained."

Megan shook her head at Logan. "It really can't be contained," she whispered. "All we can do is cast certain spells that make it less likely to cause havoc in the hotel. For example, we can cast the entire hotel so that anytime the thirteen inhabits a room, that room instantly because unavailable in your system."

"Let's do that," Logan said.

"Oh, please," Lily said. "I highly doubt that's going to be necessary."

"And why is that?" Logan asked.

"Well, it all depends on whether or not the poltergeist and kittens count as residents, but if they do, then technically, the thirteen should be stuck there now too."

"How do you figure?"

"If a thirteen takes over an uninhabited room, but has the misfortune of not moving along before the room *becomes* inhabited, well, it ends up stuck there until the residents move out. It's why thirteens prefer hotels. Because the residents tend to move on fairly quickly."

Logan had never heard this before, but trust Lily to know all the details of the bane of every hotelier's existence—rooms thirteen. "Do you mean to tell me I might have had to *move* to get rid of the thirteen?"

"Afraid so. Luckily, it came with a poltergeist and poltergeists are often easily swayed. Aren't you happy you have me to problem-solve these things for you?"

"No!" Logan couldn't believe she'd asked that question in all seriousness. Sometimes his sister's insanity reached unparalleled heights. "Honestly, Lily, if it weren't for you, I wouldn't have these problems in the first place."

Lily grinned at him.

Logan rolled his eyes and slung an arm around her shoulders, hugging her close. "On the other hand, life wouldn't be anywhere near as exciting without you around either, that's for certain."

16

IT WAS PERHAPS to be Kitty's final night as a cat and yet she found herself hoping she would be able to spend it mostly in her human form so that she might kiss her man-fairy-companion a thousand times before morning.

Before the truth came out.

By this time tomorrow, Logan would know that his dream-companion was not his mate, and that his cat-companion was not a cat at all.

With these revelations, she could lose everything.

And so, when Kitty Sweet woke in her human form that night, she didn't hesitate to wake Logan too.

They spent the wee hours of the morning indulging their passion for one other until just before dawn when sleep finally pulled them under.

~

When Logan woke later that morning, he was utterly convinced his dream woman was not a dream at all.

Nothing that felt that real could possibly be a dream.

Unfortunately, he had to be willing to risk losing Kitty Sweet, at least in her adorable cat form, to discover the truth.

"Well, Kitty, my darling. Today's the day." With that statement, he got up to face what was coming. He showered, dressed and prepared breakfast for them as usual. They sat at the table together, Logan feeding Kitty tiny morsels from his own plate, enjoying the quiet of the morning.

"Can you believe it's our first morning without that damn poltergeist and it may be our last morning together, at least with you in this form?" Logan was thoroughly depressed thinking about it. Oh, he wanted his woman to be more than just a dream in the middle of the night, but he didn't want to give up his sweet kitty either.

Maybe the witches had the right idea. They might have to adopt a kitten or two, to round out their family. He thought about that word. Family. He was really counting on the witches to bring out his dream woman and he was counting on her to want to stay.

"You won't leave me, will you, Kitty Sweet?"

She nudged his hand, so he fed her another tidbit, then gently pet her from the top of her head all the way down her back. He repeated that stroke over and over again until the room was filled with the sound of her purring. "Aw, my sweet love, I will miss this if the witches are successful."

He'd be shocked if they weren't.

Magic the likes of the kind the witches had didn't come

along too often. He was actually shocked their efforts hadn't worked sooner.

He examined Kitty, staring closely to see if he'd missed anything in the many times he'd tried before.

He still couldn't see it.

Shouldn't he be able to sense her true form if they were mates?

This was the question that kept him up at nights.

How on earth could his dream woman, the one whose kisses lit up his nights, be his mate, if no matter how closely he looked, he could never see her in Kitty Sweet?

Mates were supposed to see each other, know each other, from the moment they met.

That Kitty Sweet seemed only a cat to him was evidence enough, he supposed, that if there were a woman inside, she couldn't be his mate.

He'd been thinking about that a lot and he'd come to the conclusion that he just didn't care. If there was a woman inside Kitty Sweet and she was as sweet as her cat, he wasn't giving her up, not for anything, not even for the possibility of one day finding his true mate.

If she even existed, something he very much doubted, she would simply have to resign herself to living without her true mate.

Because he had gone and committed himself to a cat.

Who might be a woman.

How ridiculous.

How cliched.

How very Hollywood, as the earth shifters would say.

Though he wanted to delay and avoid what was coming, he forced himself to leave the apartment on time, with Kitty Sweet perched on his shoulder as usual.

He went to his office and completed the paperwork that had to be done, then checked in at the front desk to make sure there were no crises demanding his attention.

Once those tasks were done, he headed for the elevator that would take him to the earth realm.

The entire time, he spoiled Kitty Sweet—feeding her treats, stopping to allow her to play hide-and-seek in the trees, and of course, stroking her into a blissful, happy, purring state.

No matter how slowly he moved though, eventually, they stood outside Dory's room, his hand raised, poised to knock.

17

INSIDE DORY'S SUITE, they found organized chaos.

The witches were all bustling around, setting up their herbs, candles and crystals, positioning things just right when they arrived.

They instantly arranged Kitty Sweet and him at the center of the main room, seated in a circle of protection.

Kitty Sweet was right in front of him, sitting quite calmly, licking a paw, and he was looking right at her, when Megan clapped her hands together, just once, and magic rolled through the room.

Kitty Sweet, for one incredible moment, was his beautiful, dream woman.

Logan was stunned speechless.

Before he could get his wits about him, she morphed back into her cat form.

"She really is my dream woman!" he exclaimed.

"Of course, she is," Lily said. "Haven't we been saying that all along?"

"I don't understand this," Megan said. "No matter how powerful our magic, or the ritual, whatever power is keeping her contained is always greater."

"You know what we have to do," Lara said.

"And you know that I hate calling upon the goddesses," Megan protested. "It's never a good idea."

"It may be the only way we can help Kitty maintain her human form," Jessica said.

"They're right," Dory said. "I've never seen magic quite like this. It's so strong, so powerful. I'm beginning to think only a god or goddess could possibly reverse it."

Megan had a thoughtful look on her face. "Is it possible it *is* god magic?"

"Why on earth would a god bother to trap a woman inside a cat's body?" Dory demanded.

"Why do the gods do any of the things they do?" Lara asked.

"Wouldn't Logan have been able to sense *that?"* Lily asked.

It was a very good point. Sure, the universe distributed power fairly evenly among living beings, but the gods and goddesses were something else entirely.

They were as old as the universe itself. Some even said they were simply different manifestations of it, entire planets, even galaxies contained within their forms.

"How about Athena?" Jessica suggested.

"Athena? The goddess of war? Are you mad?" Megan looked horrified.

"She's also the goddess of knowledge and of wisdom," Lara said. "If anyone can help us, it would be her."

"I'm not liking this plan," Megan said.

"They're right though," Dory said. "We need more help than we've got at the moment."

Megan sighed. “Fine. I’ll get us set up.”

So that was how, an hour later, from his position on the floor, Logan ended up being confronted by one of the few beings in all the realms who had more power than him.

“I *am* a goddess, you know,” Athena snapped, glaring down at him. “And as such, I most certainly do not have the time to leap to the beck and call of some random fairy—” She caught sight of Kitty Sweet and her eyes widened. “What’s this now? Come here, love.”

Kitty Sweet jumped right up into the goddess’ arms.

Athena lifted Kitty Sweet and peered into her eyes, much the same way each of them had done when they first met her. “Now, how in Zeus’ name did you get trapped in there? Does Artemis know where you are? Of course, she doesn’t. She’s been looking for you for ages, storming around, demanding to know who stole her handmaiden.” Athena cuddled Kitty Sweet close and swept the room with her arctic gaze.

She paused to stare at every witch and every shifter, on Harry and on Lily, and finally on Logan, clearly cataloguing exactly who had summoned her.

“So. Which one of you had the audacity to steal a handmaiden from the gods?”

Dory cleared her throat and stepped forward. “I don’t know anything about handmaidens. I found poor Kitty Sweet shivering in the rain outside Athens a year ago.”

“A year? Has it really been a year?” Athena seemed to think about that a moment. “Well, no wonder Artemis is so put out. It’s all Hera’s fault. She was the one showing off that day.” She huffed. “Well, then. I suppose we’d better get on with it. I hate this part.” She closed her eyes and said quite softly, “Hera, Aphrodite, you are summoned.”

A moment later, a second goddess arrived, looking quite

as furious as Athena had. “How dare you call me to your side, Athena, as if I were your mere servant?”

Before Athena could even reply, a third goddess arrived. Rather than berating Athena, she first examined the room they were in and made a face. “Where are we, Athena? This is —” she paused, then shook her head. “—not good.”

“Not good? Is that all you can come up with, Hera?”

“Aphrodite.” Hera grimaced. “It’s not been anywhere near long enough for us to already be back in each other’s presence. Unless—have you found the handmaiden, Athena?”

“I have. And she’s a cat.”

“A cat?” Hera exclaimed. “But—no.”

“Oh, yes. Yes, Hera,” Athena said. “As it turns out, when you were showing off that day, tossing about your goddess powers, well, you turned Artemis’ handmaiden into a cat.”

“That cat?” Aphrodite pointed at Kitty Sweet.

“Yes. This cat.”

“But that’s the cat we saw at the ruins!” Hera said.

“Exactly. In other words, if you two hadn’t been shouting at each other, we might have actually noticed what happened to the handmaiden, reversed the effects of your god magic and sent her home to Artemis with no one the wiser. Now your power has set in her bones and Artemis is on the warpath and has been for a year. Do you know how difficult it’s going to be to reverse the workings of your powers now? And Artemis. She will never forgive any of us.”

Aphrodite blanched. “I’m not fond of Artemis’ ideas of vengeance. Really, I’m not. I vote we fix this without involving her.”

“And how do you suggest that?”

“Well. She’s lived without her handmaiden this long,” Aphrodite said.

"Yes, good point. So, how about if we just leave the cat here," Hera suggested. "Where is here anyway? Are we still in Europe?"

"I'm afraid not." Megan spoke for the first time. "You're on the other side of the ocean now."

"The Americas? How very uncivilized," Athena said.

"Right. Well, here's the thing," Megan said. "Our friend, Kitty Sweet there, we'd really like her to be given back her human form now, if that's all right."

"No. No." Hera shook her head. "That's really not a good idea."

"Yes, I think perhaps she should stay in this form," Aphrodite said.

"Absolutely not," Athena said. "We're going to have to fix this. Poor sweet Katie." She lifted the cat and stared into her eyes again. "You know, there's only going to be so much we can do at this late stage in the game."

"Here." Hera reached out. "Let me see what I can sense."

Athena passed Kitty Sweet to Hera, who closed her eyes and ran her hands gently down Kitty Sweet's back and sides. "You're right." Hera's eyes opened. "The power's set. The only thing I can really do at this point is smooth it down, even out the rough edges, so that it's not smothering her human side. She'll be able to shift back and forth between the two forms. It's the best I can do."

"That would be wonderful," Logan said. "Will she be able to control it? The shift, I mean?"

"As much as any shifter in this realm can," Hera replied. She closed her eyes, ran her hands down Kitty Sweet's back again, then opened her eyes once more. "That should do it." She set Kitty Sweet on the floor and stepped back.

"That's it?" Lara asked. "We've been trying to undo that spell for days."

Hera laughed a tinkling laugh. "Well, that was your problem, wasn't it? It wasn't a spell keeping her in her cat form. It was god power. Well, go on then, Kitty Sweet. You can transform now."

When nothing happened, Cole stepped forward. "Just think of your human form, Kitty Sweet. Hold it steady in your mind's eye and let go."

Long moments passed, then suddenly, in as seamless a shift as Logan had ever seen, Kitty Sweet went from cat to naked human.

Logan stood, grabbed a blanket from the couch, wrapped it around her and helped her to her feet. "Can you speak, Kitty, darling?"

Kitty opened her mouth and a soft mew escaped. She lifted her hand and held it against her lips.

"Oh, yes, the larynx, the pharynx, the vocal cords." Hera waved a hand and Kitty let out a soft cough. "Humans. So very complex in form, yet rather simplistic in thought."

"Hera!"

"What? Am I not right, Athena?"

"It's still rude."

"The real question now is what are we going to tell Artemis," Aphrodite said.

"The truth," Athena said. She closed her eyes and softly said, "Artemis—"

"No!" Hera and Aphrodite cried out at the same time.

"You are summoned."

"Now why did you do that?" Hera demanded. "She'll never forgive us!"

Athena smiled. "Just let me do all the talking."

"It's getting rather crowded in here," Logan muttered as Artemis arrived with a gust of wind.

"What in Olympus' name is everyone doing *here*?" Artemis looked around the very crowded hotel room. "With all these earth people-things?"

"We found your handmaiden, Artemis," Athena said.

"You found Katie?" She looked around. "Where?" She froze as she caught sight of Kitty Sweet, sitting on the couch, wrapped in a blanket. "Katie?" She stepped forward and knelt in front of Kitty. "Are you all right?"

Kitty nodded, opened her mouth, but said nothing.

Artemis looked at Logan who had his arm around Kitty.

"She just got back the power of speech," he explained to the goddess, who looked startled and then confused.

"What?"

"Artemis," Kitty spoke softly.

Logan froze at the sound of her voce. So soft, so beautiful.

"I missed you. I'm sorry. Something happened and I—" she shook her head. "I forgot. But I've been ever so happy. Dory took care of me. And then Logan."

"I'm sensing a very complicated story here." Artemis looked up and speared each of the other goddesses with her piercing gaze. "And I'm guessing you three are right at the center of it."

Athena cleared her throat. "Yes, well, you see. It appears our god powers work in ways even we do not always anticipate. If you'll look at sweet Katie there and at the fairy holding her so close, they've clearly fallen in love." Her brow wrinkled. "Despite the odd circumstances."

"My maidens aren't allowed earthly love." Artemis glared

at Logan. "She is pure, untouched, a maiden of the gods. And you think to take her from me?"

Logan tightened his arm around Kitty Sweet—Katie—and drew in a deep breath. He'd realized what she was the moment she'd transformed. He could see her clearly now, without the god power obscuring her true form, hiding her light from him.

But this goddess was someone who could take his mate from him and there'd be nothing he could do. "We're true mates," he said to Artemis. "And I adore her, in whatever form she takes."

He sensed Katie looking at him, but he kept his eyes on Artemis, willing her to see his sincerity.

Artemis nodded and transferred her gaze back to Katie. "And you, my sweet handmaiden. Does this fairy make you happy?"

Katie smiled. "Oh, yes, Artemis. He is everything I never knew I could have."

Artemis nodded. "Very well, then. I wish upon you both all the happiness in the realms." She stood and turned to face her fellow goddesses. "As for you three, I believe you owe me a story *and* a handmaiden." She lifted her hands and snapped her fingers on both hands, and just like that, all four goddesses were gone.

"We're true mates?" Katie asked Logan.

Logan smiled down at her. "We are. Though it really doesn't matter, does it? True mates or not, we belong together."

Katie smiled and threw herself in Logan's arms.

He chuckled and hugged her close. He then made sure she was fully wrapped in the blanket and stood with her in his arms.

"My thanks to all of you." He nodded to Dory and her nieces. "We are forever in your debt, but now, I'm afraid my mate and I need some time, just the two of us. So, if you'll excuse us." Then, for the first time since he was a very young child, he borrowed a trick from his sister's playbook, pictured his bedroom in his mind's eye and popped them straight there.

"Well, my love." He laid her down on the bed and stroked her cheek. "You are truly the most exquisite gift I have ever been given. I am so blessed, my darling Kitty-Katie Sweet."

He kissed her and she clutched his shoulders and kissed him back.

As their passions ignited and they loved the night away, neither noticed when Artemis popped into their home to deliver her favorite handmaiden's clothing and personal effects, including a painting of Artemis and Katie on Mount Olympus.

18

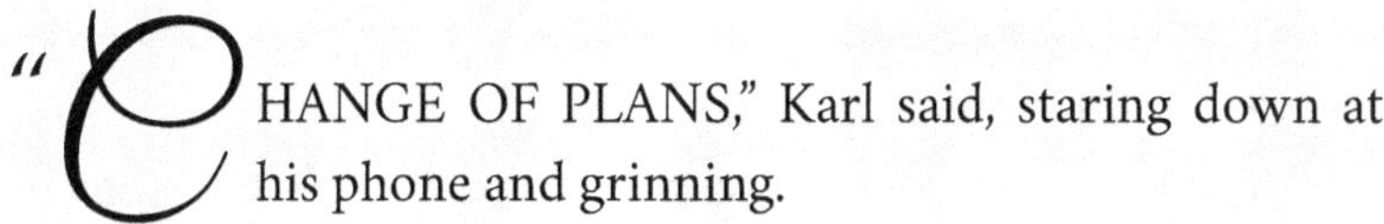

“CHANGE OF PLANS,” Karl said, staring down at his phone and grinning.

“What’s up?” Cole asked.

“Max just texted. Adam’s at Shenanigans I getting drunk.” This was something Karl absolutely had to see.

“Alpha wolf Adam?” Lara asked incredulously.

“Yep.”

“Workaholic Adam is off pack lands and in a bar?” Dan asked.

“To drink?” Cole said.

“Apparently so,” Karl said. “And according to Max, it’s an event not to be missed.”

“Wait a minute,” Megan said. “Are you guys talking about Agatha’s son, Adam?”

“Yes. Why?” Karl asked.

“You didn’t tell us he was the alpha wolf, Lara!” Megan exclaimed.

“How could you not know?” Lara asked.

"Because we've never met him before." Jessica said.

"And we're not mated to wolves," Megan said.

"Exactly," Cole said. "You're mated to cougars so why do you care if Adam's *their* alpha?"

"Oh, no reason at all," Megan said innocently. "But you should have told us, Lara!"

"Would that have changed anything?"

"I don't know. Maybe."

Lara rolled her eyes. "You know it wouldn't have, so don't pretend."

"Well, it would have at least been nice to know who exactly we were—" Jessica broke off.

"Who you were what?" Dan asked.

"Oh, nothing," Jessica said.

"You three are up to something and I don't like that it somehow involves my alpha," Karl said, staring at Lara sternly.

She just smiled back at him and said, "We'd best be off if you want to catch Adam at the bar. If he's truly a workaholic like you say, he might stop drinking any minute to go back to work."

This was unfortunately true, so Karl gave up trying to figure out what the witches were up to and instead focused on getting them out of the store and on their way through the woods to the bar.

When they arrived, it was packed, which wasn't necessarily unusual for the weekend, but Karl noted there were a lot more wolves in attendance than usual. Many, in fact, who rarely if ever came to the bar to hang out.

And there, at a table off to the side, were Adam, Max, Pete and Jenny.

Karl led the way to their table and with Dan and Cole's help, wrangled some extra chairs and another table to extend the one they were at.

Once they were settled, Max said, "Just in time, my friends. Adam was about to explain why he's here."

Adam scowled into his empty shot glass and raised a hand to signal for another. "Can't a man just come out for a drink with his buddies and not be subjected to an inquisition?"

"Not when the man is you," Max said cheerfully.

"Exactly!" Pete said. "I don't think I've ever seen you here at Shenanigans. And I've definitely never seen you drinking."

"I drink," Adam said belligerently. He grinned at Phoenix when she showed up with a tray full of shots plus a bottle of Witches' Brew. "Excellent!" He grabbed four shots, two in each hand, and said, "A toast! To vacations!"

"Vacations? You never take vacations, Adam," Karl exclaimed. "You always claim there's too much to do to take time off."

"Yes, well, I'm taking one now, aren't I? Leaving tomorrow I am."

"You're leaving pack lands?"

"Not just pack lands. I'm leaving Jamesville! I'll be gone for a week."

"But. Why?" Max asked.

Adam downed one shot, then the other, slammed the glasses to the table and glared at Max. "My mother."

Max looked surprised. "Agatha? What has she done?"

"Nagged me incessantly, she did! For more than a year, she's been nagging. I finally couldn't take it anymore, so I told her I'd take a vacation if she'd just stop whining about me finding a mate."

Karl snickered. That definitely sounded like Agatha.

"I tried to just take a vacation at Hotel Shenanigans. It would have been the perfect location, close enough to pack lands to be here if I'm needed, but I'd be staying in a hotel, and everyone knows you're on vacation when you stay in a hotel, right?"

"That's true," Pete said.

Adam threw back a third shot, pointed at Pete and said, "Damn right, it's true. But the truth apparently doesn't matter to my mother because she nixed that idea right away. I didn't even mention it. She just said I couldn't vacation within a hundred miles of pack lands. Can you imagine? My own mother, forcing me to leave the area."

"You're the alpha wolf," Max exclaimed. "Just tell her no!"

Adam just looked at Max. "Have you met my mother?"

"Okay," Max said. "Valid point. Still, I'm not sure I'd trust that bargain she made. I mean, I can't imagine Agatha not harping about you needing a mate."

"She probably thinks if he goes on vacation, he'll find his mate wherever he goes, so she won't have to keep her word," Jessica predicted.

Adam pointed at her. "Exactly! That's exactly what she thinks. Well, I've got news for her. There's no mate out there for me and no vacation's going to change that."

"Now you've done it," Karl said.

"What's that supposed to mean?" Adam asked.

"All I'm saying is, you really shouldn't tempt fate like that," Karl said.

"He's right," Lara said. "After all, we're all on the gods' radar now."

"What?" Adam looked horrified. "What are you talking about? What gods?"

Lara just grinned at him, then started pouring out drinks of Witches Brew.

Karl shook his head at the smirk on her face. If he knew his mate and her sisters at all, Adam's days as a single wolf were numbered.

~

HOLIDAY
Shenanegans

Edited by J.L. Troughton
PMG Publishing

1

GIGI WAS NOT happy.

Which was why she was inside the Furry in Pink salon at that very moment, on her day off, mind you. She'd walked in, not as the owner of the salon, but as a client, determined to cheer herself up with a bit of color.

JoJo went along, of course, because Furry in Pink wasn't just any salon.

No, they were a shifter one. Which meant they were well-versed in color techniques for both the human and the animal side of a shifter.

Of course, JoJo was a poodle, not a shifter, but that just made her all the more popular at the salon.

JoJo was the salon's mascot. She was even featured on their marketing materials, so clients expected to see her when they came in. This, of course, meant that JoJo was used to going in to work with Gigi, and as a result, to being pampered by all the ladies working there.

This was different though. Today they were clients, which meant a whole new level of pampering.

After contemplating the many color choices and consulting with JoJo of course, Gigi landed on pink.

She knew a lot of women who eschewed pink, feeling it was too girly, but the truth was, Gigi was a girly-girl and she took pride in it.

Well, girly shifter.

Girly snow leopard to be exact.

And now she was going pink. And JoJo was going there with her.

This was going to be awesome. And a definite requirement due to her special circumstances of extreme rage and sorrow.

Damn that wolf.

"Pink? Really?" Lexi asked with a big smile. She had lots to smile about after all. As one of the women who specialized in working on shifted forms, she would be the one working with JoJo.

Personally, Gigi preferred working with shifters when they were in their human forms. So much easier to control. Some shifters, in particular, were a complete nuisance when shifted.

Wolves were a perfect example.

Always howling and chasing their tails.

It was really quite ridiculous that she'd fallen for one.

She'd thought he was her perfect man though! She'd even believed they might be mates.

She'd woken after their weekend together, heart full from the memory of the most incredible hours she'd ever spent, loving a man who made her heart thunder and her body burn, only to find he'd deserted her.

Just left.

Without a word of goodbye, let alone a see you next time.

When she realized he'd skipped out, she'd actually cried.

The wolf had made her, a snow leopard, cry!

Her kind was known for being solitary, for not living in packs, for not even mating, really. The problem was Gigi wasn't a normal snow leopard. She craved bonds and none more than the mate bond.

She'd dated a number of humans and shifters through the years, but none had interested her snow leopard at all.

The leopard was the true epitome of a cat. Standoffish, snobbish, uninterested in pretty much anyone around her.

Until the wolf. That damn wolf.

He'd caught her leopard's attention, making her sit up and take notice. They'd talked for hours in that bar and she'd liked him. Really liked him.

He'd taken her back to his hotel room and they'd set the world on fire with their passion. They'd spent an entire weekend in bed and when she woke Monday morning, it was to a note that simply said, "Thanks for a lovely weekend. The room is paid for. Checkout is at noon."

That was it.

No phone number.

No request for a future date.

Her perfect man had walked out the door and left his potential mate behind.

She'd cried for a week, then she'd gotten mad, thrown herself into her work and tried to forget about a certain wolf who'd turned her world upside down.

Then she woke yesterday, a month after their liaison and discovered everything had changed.

She'd spent the day crying and binging on ice cream. Eventually, she'd called the salon in tears and Jeanette had booked her an emergency all-day workup the next day.

And so here she was.

The minute she'd walked into the salon, everyone's eyes had come her way.

They'd all inhaled, their eyes had widened and everyone in the salon, employees and clients, had frozen for one long moment.

Then Lexi had unstuck herself, rushed over to hug Gigi and led her to their collection of hair dyes.

Slowly, the sound of voices picked back up and everyone got back to work.

Now Lexi had her hands full of pink dye and was leading JoJo and Gigi to the back area, where they worked on shifters in their animal forms.

Gigi quickly stripped and transformed.

She shook out her fur and walked with JoJo into the large shower room where they frolicked and played in the sudsy water.

By the time they had been thoroughly cleaned, brushed, massaged, dyed, rinsed and dried off, Gigi felt like a limp noodle. She stood in front of the long mirror and stared at herself. She was a snow leopard who would *not* be blending into a snowy, rocky environment anytime soon.

She shook out her fur and gave a happy chirp as JoJo did the same.

They were spectacular!

After one last shake, she transformed back to her human form.

A tinge of the pink followed her back, but it wasn't enough to last even a day.

That was okay, though.

After many years of trial and error, Gigi and her employees had learned the sequence of dyeing a shifter's fur and hair for the best and longest results. The fur had to be dyed first, then the hair. Then perhaps a second round, depending on how well the first round of dye took.

They were the best salon in the city, as a result, which is why they were able to charge such outrageous prices, and why her employees were the best-paid salon workers in the state.

What followed was nothing less than bliss.

Carrie took over for Lexi, washing Gigi's shoulder-length hair and then dyeing it.

While the color was setting, Carrie finally asked what Gigi was sure everyone was wondering.

"What are you going to do, Gigi?"

Gigi sighed. "I have no idea."

All the women knew her story. She'd come back after that long weekend away and had shared everything. How she'd thought he was the one, but instead he'd ended up being the one who broke her heart.

The women in the salon might be her employees, but they were also her friends, and they'd been infuriated on her behalf.

"How can he not realize how lucky he is to have someone like you as a mate?" they'd demanded.

Of course, their outrage had gone a long way toward soothing the edges of Gigi's sorrow and she'd done her best to forget the bastard even existed.

Only that was an impossibility now.

"Are you going to tell him?" Lexi asked from where she was giving JoJo a pedicure.

"Why should I? He doesn't deserve to know!" Gigi huffed. "Besides, I don't even know how to find him. He told me nothing about his life."

She'd thought about that later, how there had been so many clues he wasn't planning to allow her into his life on a permanent basis. She'd just assumed their passion was so fierce, he hadn't gotten around to sharing anything specific.

Except later, she'd realized that wasn't true. They'd spent hours in the bar talking about their lives. Or she had talked about hers. She'd told him about the salon, about JoJo, about what it was like to be a snow leopard who craved connections and roots when most snow leopards were disconnected wanderers.

As for Adam, he'd shared his love of movies, how his favorite season was winter (hers was too—she'd thought that was another sign they belonged together) and that his mother was driving him crazy (which she'd taken as a sign he was sharing as much about his personal life as she was).

Only later had she realized that wasn't true at all.

She didn't even know his full name or where he lived. All she knew was it was somewhere with four seasons.

"Are you sure you don't have any clues at all?" Carrie asked as she led Gigi to the sinks.

"I know his mother was driving him crazy and that he agreed to travel no less than a hundred miles away for vacation, just to get her off his back."

"A hundred miles?" Lexi asked.

"Yes."

"Well, there aren't that many wolf packs within a hundred miles radius of here, you know," she said.

"He might be a lone wolf," Carrie pointed out.

"And he could have gone further than a hundred miles. Who knows how far he really went?" Gigi said, but she was thinking about how annoyed he'd been at having to be so far from pack lands, which now that she thought about it was a clue right there. Chances were, he'd only traveled as far as required and no more.

"What are you thinking?" Carrie asked.

"That he mentioned pack lands, so he can't be a lone wolf."

"Oooh, that's good," Lexi exclaimed. "Do you know what his position is in the pack?"

Gigi snorted. "Given the number of times he looked at his phone in the bar and remarked how shocked he was that no one had needed him in the five days he'd been gone so far, I'd say he's pretty high up."

Carrie froze in the act of rinsing out Gigi's hair. "Like alpha high?"

Gigi thought about that a moment. "I mean, he was pretty dominant in bed." She shivered at the memory while all the other women sighed. She smirked. "Yeah. It was truly spectacular, and frankly, another reason I was certain we were meant to be together."

"Well, I'd say you were right," Lexi said.

"How do you figure?"

"Hello. The asshole knocked you up!" Lexi exclaimed. "That doesn't happen with just any old shifter."

Gigi had been trying not to think about that part.

It had been so much easier when she'd thought she was wrong, that he wasn't her mate after all. She'd had a glimpse into what it might be like, bonded with a wolf, who had all these bonds himself. For one moment, she'd allowed herself to dream.

To believe that a snow leopard could find herself a pack.

And then he'd crushed that dream.

She'd tried to convince herself that she could still have

the dream, because the man she'd thought was her mate clearly wasn't.

Except his superhero sperm had left an unexpected gift behind.

Merry Christmas to her.

So now she knew.

Her mate had rejected her and she'd never have that pack life she'd been dreaming of.

Except.

"We'll be our own little pack," she whispered to the little one nestled inside.

"What's that?" Lexi asked.

Gigi shook her head. "Nothing. I don't know what to do. I should track him down, I guess. He doesn't deserve this cub, but my cub deserves a father, so I'll do what I can to try to find him."

"His name was Adam, right?" Jeanette, having just finished with a client, was now staring at her phone.

"Yep."

"I think I found him."

"You did?" everyone in the salon exclaimed at once.

"I mean, I think so. There's a small town called Jamesville exactly a hundred and one miles away. They have a wolf pack and a cougar settlement, plus a hotel Shenanigans and two bar Shenanigans."

"Seriously?" Lexi exclaimed.

"All in one small town?" Carrie asked.

"It looks like the hotel is a kind of crossroads of sorts. Run by a traveler and some fairies."

"What's a traveler?" Lexi asked.

Jeanette shrugged. "I don't know, but I feel like we should have known about this town long before now."

"So you found Adam?" Gigi cut to the chase. She didn't care about Shenanigans or crossroads or whatever a traveler was. She didn't even care about fairies—though the girly-girl inside might disagree at some point.

"Well, there's no picture, so there's really no way to be certain, but according to the Shenanigans website, the local wolf pack alpha is named Adam."

"You found that on a Shenanigans board?" Carrie asked.

"No, not the boards, the website. They have a whole section dedicated to the different paranormal organizations in the country. Probably even the world. So I did a search for wolf packs within a hundred miles of our location and it gave me three. But only one of those has an alpha named Adam."

"It might not be him," Gigi said.

"You're right," Jeanette said. "But it's a place to start. If you want to tell him."

"Want to? No. Need to? Yes."

"Well, there's a snowstorm scheduled to arrive early next week," Lexi said. "So if you're going to go, I'd suggest leaving tomorrow."

"It's the busiest weekend of the season. I have clients scheduled all day tomorrow *and* Sunday, plus—"

"We'll cover your clients," Lexi interrupted.

"Not just this weekend, but next week too," Carrie said. "You need to take the time to find him and work things out. He's your mate, for heaven's sake."

"You know he's not going to want to see me and the fact that I'm pregnant isn't going to change that reality." It hurt to say those words out loud, but Gigi knew they were true.

"His loss," Carrie said fiercely. "Do you want us to come with you? We can close the salon for a couple days."

"Take them up on that offer, honey," Mrs. Aggers said from where she was getting her hair styled. "A woman needs her girlfriends around at a time like this."

Gigi blinked back tears at the show of support. "I appreciate it, I really do, but I think I need to do this part on my own. Once I'm back after he rejects me, though—"

"We've got your back," Lexi said.

"We'll bring the chocolate and the ice cream," Carrie said.

"The pedicure and manicure tools," Jeanette said.

"The essential oils, candles, mud baths, facial creams and all the works," Lexi said.

"You guys are truly the best." Gigi sniffed and brushed a tear away.

"So," Carrie said brightly. "What do you think?" She spun Gigi's chair to face the mirror.

Gigi beamed at the bright pink hair Carrie had styled into a sassy bob. "It's wonderful, Carrie!"

"When that alpha gets a good look at you, he'll swallow his tongue," Lexi predicted.

"Now don't forget," Jeanette said. "Fashion is everything when making a statement."

"Exactly!" Carrie exclaimed. "Adam needs to see in perfect detail exactly what he gave up when he walked out on the fabulousness that is you."

2

THE DRIVE TO Jamesville took a lot longer than expected, mostly because of the snow. The predicted snowstorm landed early and made the trip a little more treacherous than expected.

Gigi stopped at Hotel Shenanigans first, checked into a room, and remembering the girls' advice, spent a good amount of time showering and dressing in her sassiest outfit.

Once she was ready, she and JoJo headed to the front desk so she could ask where she might find the alpha wolf, Adam.

The man at the counter looked extremely surprised at the question. "From what I understand, he rarely leaves pack lands," he said.

"And where exactly *are* pack lands?" she asked.

"Not a clue," he said cheerfully. "Somewhere in the woods, no doubt."

Great.

"You might ask at Shenanigans. The bar, I mean."

"The hotel bar?"

"No, that's Shenanigans 2. You'll have better luck at Shenanigans 1. It's out in the woods and from what I understand, it's a favorite gathering place for the pack."

"And how do I get there?"

"Now that's a little tricky." In the end, he drew her a map, which actually was quite helpful, since she was pretty sure, she would never have found the turnoff otherwise.

It was kind of creepy, driving into the woods, but eventually, the road opened up into a small parking lot, which was also rather creepy, given it was surrounded by woods, but it had a walkway that led right up to the bar, so she really couldn't complain.

Okay, yes, she could.

By this time, the snow was coming down pretty heavily, which made walking in her bright pink, spiked heels a bit of a challenge, but she managed it, thanks to years and years of practice.

JoJo pranced at her side as they headed for the entrance.

Gigi drew in a deep breath for courage—"All right, JoJo, here goes nothing"—and opened the door.

~

It was the hush that spread across the bar that Max noticed first.

A woman was standing right inside the door, a flurry of snow at her back.

The door closed behind her and Max got his first good look at her.

In the middle of a snowstorm, she was dressed in a short pink skirt, a sheer white blouse over a bright pink bra and—were those heels?

"What kind of crazy shifter goes out dressed like that in a snowstorm?" Pete asked.

"Maybe she's a polar bear," Cole suggested.

Glory rolled her eyes. "There's no chance on earth that little bitty thing is any kind of bear."

"What about a sun bear?" Max challenged, just to mess with his mate, something he was exceptionally good at, if he did say so himself.

Glory huffed. "Fine, maybe a sun bear. But I doubt she'd be loving the snow, in that case."

"She's not even covered in it," Pete said. "I would have expected her to fall in those heels in this snow at least a dozen times before she made it to the door."

Max had to agree. And if the look on Phoenix's face as she rushed by was anything to go by, she was about to offer the woman an entire wardrobe of winter wear.

"My goodness, aren't you cold?" Phoenix exclaimed. Before the woman could answer, Phoenix let out a squeal and disappeared.

Max quickly stood to see if she was okay, only to realize Phoenix had dropped to her knees on purpose to embrace a fancy-looking, pink *dog*. A dog whose fur matched its owner's hair.

He couldn't believe it. Her hair matched her skirt, her shoes, her bra *and* her dog.

"Who *is* this nutcase?" Dan muttered.

That's what Max wanted to know.

"He's adorable!" Phoenix exclaimed, loving all over the dog. "What's his name?"

"He's a she," the woman answered, "and her name is JoJo."

"Oh, that's so cute. Hello, JoJo, baby. Aren't you adorable?"

Max looked toward the bar, expecting any moment for Travis to demand the dog stay outside, but Travis had his elbows on the bar, chin on his fists and a giant grin on his face as he watched his mate fawn all over the dog.

The *pink* dog.

It bore repeating!

Who dyed their dog pink?

"There's a dog in the bar, Travis," Dan complained. "Do something!"

Not surprising that Dan would be the first one to complain. He *was* a cougar, after all.

Travis shrugged. "Sorry, Dan. If Phoenix loves the pooch, it gets to stay."

Phoenix dragged the woman further into the bar, which caused every wolf in the place to sit up straight, eyes wide. They'd finally caught her scent.

Dan looked even more disgusted.

"She's a cat," Cole muttered.

"A cat with a dog," Dan agreed.

Pete looked surprised. "She smells like a wolf to me."

Cole groaned. "Not another chameleon."

Glory grinned. "Actually, I'm pretty sure you're both right. And she's *not* a chameleon."

She was right. Max had finally caught the woman's full scent. He couldn't believe it. He stepped away from their table to join Phoenix and the pink duo.

"Hey, Max. This is Gigi and this precious baby is JoJo."

Max curled his lip at the dog, who completely ignored him. What kind of dog was so stupid it didn't know when it was in the presence of a fierce predator? "So. Why do you smell like—"

"I'm looking for Adam," Gigi interrupted him. "Assuming

your Adam is the one I'm looking for. He's a wolf shifter, got me into this predicament, left without so much as a goodbye, see you later, that was fun, and fine, so it was a one-weekend stand and I agreed it would only be for one weekend, but that doesn't mean he can just skulk away in the middle of the night without a single by-your leave, especially when he left behind a Christmas present I never ordered." She paused and took a deep breath.

Max was impressed she'd managed to say all of that in one go. Before he could respond, though, she was taking off again.

"So even though he doesn't deserve me tracking his ass down, he can tell me to my face if he doesn't want anything to do with me or his little bun in the oven."

The second hush of the night rolled through the bar, but she didn't even notice.

"So that's why I'm here. Just tell me where he is and I'll listen to his rejection one more time, this time to my face, and then I can go back to civilization and my manicures and pedicures and fancy salon."

Max grinned. This was wonderful! "Adam actually unbent enough to have some fun on his vacation a while back?"

"Some orgasmic fun?" Pete had wandered over, followed by Sam and several other wolves.

Pete leaned closer and sniffed at Gigi. "Yep. You're preggers all right. And they're definitely Adam's."

Gigi scowled. "Of course, they are. Wait a minute. What do you mean *they*?"

"Smelling at least two, possibly three different scents," Pete said. "You're carrying a wolf litter, all right."

"Are you serious right now? That bastard not only slithered out in the middle of the night after knocking me up, he also managed to leave me with multiples?"

Pete grinned. "We wolves are a prolific lot."

"So I'm guessing you'd like us to take you to Adam," Max said.

"Of course, I want you to take me to him. Do you think I'd come out here into the middle of nowhere and traipse through these woods just for the fun of it? There's not even a shopping mall anywhere nearby!"

Phoenix grinned. "Oh, honey. I promise you, when you're ready for a shopping excursion, I'm your gal. You'd be surprised at the shopping you can find around here."

Gigi looked confused. "Okay. If you say so. Look, I just need to find Adam, so I can do my due diligence, tell him he's going to be a dad and give him a chance to say he's not interested. Then I'll be on my way and that'll be that."

"Where is she?" The bar door slammed open and two women came hurrying in, a flurry of snowflakes following them. "Is this her? Max, is this her?"

Max sighed and whirled around toward the back of the bar. "All right. Who called the mothers in?"

Not a single wolf confessed. Imagine that.

"Darling, how wonderful to meet you. My name is Agatha." She grabbed hold of Gigi's hands and squeezed them tight. "I'm Adam's mother and this is Betina."

"I'm Adam's auntie. We were starting to think he'd never choose a mate, but look at you. So darling, with an amazing fashion sense!" She leaned in and kissed both of Gigi's cheeks.

"And who on earth is this?" Agatha asked as she leaned over and stroked JoJo's head. "Such an adorable —" She snapped her fingers a couple times. "What do we call these animals again?"

"It's a dog, Aunt Agatha. You know that," Max growled.

"No, no, no. It's a special kind of dog and pink! I had no idea they came in this color."

Gigi giggled. "She's a poodle and they don't. It was just a little pick-me-up. I was feeling a little lonely and depressed after—well, anyway—so I thought I'd treat us to a day at the salon. I mean, I should be able to take advantage of being the owner, every once in a while, right?"

Phoenix gasped. "You own a salon? Really?"

"I do. And one of the best perks of owning a salon is having access to all the beauty things. So this time, we decided to go pink, didn't we, JoJo?"

JoJo looked up at Gigi with adoring eyes and let out a little bark.

"Oh, my gosh, she's so cute!" Betina said.

"Wait. Lonely and depressed?" Agatha repeated. "Sweetheart, that's no good at the holidays. Where's your family?"

Gigi shrugged. "My kind—we're mostly loners. We don't really live in packs."

"Well, that just won't do at all," Agatha declared. "You're coming home with us and that's that."

"Oh, but, I really don't think that's necessary," Gigi said. "I just need to speak with Adam for a brief moment and then I'll be on my way—"

"Oh, no, no, no," Betina said. "Not at the holidays you won't. You're family now and you're coming home with us."

"Oh, but—"

"Come along, dear." Agatha took her by the arm and led her to the door. "You're going to love living in a pack!"

3

GIGI HAD NO idea how it happened.

One moment, she had a plan to swoop in, deliver her news, take the rejection she knew was coming with a stoic attitude, then drive home to fall apart with her girlfriends.

Only somehow that plan got blown to smithereens.

When she called the salon the next day to explain what had happened and why she wouldn't be returning as soon as expected, Jeanette laughed, then put her on speaker and had her explain all over again to everyone in the salon. For some reason, they all found the story to be hilarious.

"Oh, Gigi," Lexi said. "You've just run up against one of the fiercest creatures on earth."

"She's right," Carrie said. "You've been adopted by an alpha wolf's mama. I don't expect we'll ever see you again. Don't worry, though, we'll take good care of the salon."

The salon had a lot of clients scheduled that day, which had to be why the laughter in the background was so loud in that moment.

Gigi had to wait for it to die down to ask, “But what should I *do*? I haven’t even seen Adam yet. If I didn’t know any better, I’d think his mother is hiding me from him.”

Carrie snickered. “Oh, she probably is. She wants you well and truly adopted by the pack before he finds out what she’s up to. Just go with the flow, Gigi. You’ll be mated before Adam has a clue you’ve even arrived.”

Gigi giggled. “I doubt that, but okay. I do really like it here so far.”

“Then have fun, and keep us posted,” Lexi exclaimed.

So that was how Gigi ended up taking a very long, extended break from the salon to live with a bunch of wolves in the woods.

It sounded like the start of a horror novel, but much to Gigi’s surprise, she loved it. She’d always considered herself to be a city girl, but she’d never experienced winter in a cabin surrounded by trees.

She especially loved the snow.

It was so beautiful.

It blanketed the world and created a kind of hush that resonated.

Even better, it was blissfully, blessedly *cold*.

Instead of dealing with morning sickness, Gigi was boiling from the inside out. She didn’t exactly consider it to be an improvement. She might have preferred the vomiting.

The heat was utterly unbearable and she blamed the wolf.

Even though it was the middle of winter and snow was everywhere, the cubs had raised her core temperature by about ten thousand degrees. Thank goodness she’d brought all her flirty skirts and tank tops. Without them, she might actually spontaneously combust.

The wolves thought she was crazy, of course. The women

kept fussing over her and offering her sweaters and blankets. She had to keep explaining that it was too hot for anything but tiny skirts, flip flops (yes, she'd retired the heels in favor of more sensible footwear) and tank tops.

She'd started taking afternoon naps outside in the middle of the day when the sun was highest in the sky and she felt like her blood was beginning to boil.

Most of the time she'd stretch out on a snow-covered tree limb in her snow leopard form, but every once in a while, she'd just lie down on the ground in human form. The snow felt so good against her sizzling skin. It was about the only time she didn't think she might burst into flame, she was so unbearably hot.

"Oh, dear."

Gigi looked up to see Agatha, Betina and their friend, Francine, peering down at her.

"What on earth are you doing down there, Gigi?" Betina exclaimed.

"You didn't fall, did you?" Agatha asked anxiously.

"Oh, no. I'm just cooling off a bit, that's all."

JoJo barked from the porch of the cabin where they were staying.

Gigi sighed. "All right, all right, I'm coming." She climbed to her feet.

"What's wrong with JoJo?" Francine asked.

"She doesn't like that she has to stay on the porch. She wants to join me down here, but it's really too cold for her."

They headed for the porch, where JoJo was waiting.

"Oh, look at her boots and jacket!" Betina cried. "She's so cute. She can't come out even with those on?"

"She's already been down here playing with me quite a bit today. Even with the boots and jacket, it's too cold for her to be out here long. At least the porch is covered and out of the wind and I've got her set up on a heated bed." Gigi waved the ladies to the rockers on the porch and settled on the top step next to JoJo. "So what brings you ladies over here?"

"Oh, well, we were hoping to, that is—" Agatha hesitated.

"Yes?"

"We thought we'd give you some advice on how to deal with Adam," Betina blurted.

"Not just with Adam. All male wolves are the same, you know," Francine said.

"Exactly," Betina agreed. "Alpha or not, at their hearts, they're all— " she hesitated.

"Dogs," Agatha said.

"Dogs," Francine and Betina agreed.

Gigi laughed. "Okay. Well, I haven't even seen Adam, so I'm not sure how much help this advice is going to be. But obviously, I like dogs, so I don't think that will be a problem." She ruffled JoJo's fur.

"Oh, no, dear," Betina said. "You don't understand."

"They're not dogs like JoJo," Agatha said.

"They're more like Cujo," Francine said.

"That's a terrible analogy," Betina said. "They don't go around attacking people!"

Francine waggled her eyebrows.

"Well, not in that way," Betina amended with a girlish giggle.

Gigi's eyes widened. Were they insinuating what she thought they were?

Agatha laughed. "It's true, I do enjoy a good mate-mauling, but let's not get off track here."

Gigi buried her face in JoJo's fur to muffle the sound she

made in the back of her throat. Dear god, they *were* talking about what she thought they were.

"Oh, look, Agatha, you've embarrassed the poor dear," Betina said.

"No, no." Gigi lifted her head and smiled at the women. "I was just imagining torturing Adam with this story later."

"Now, you've got it!" Agatha exclaimed. "That is exactly how you deal with an alpha wolf."

"Well, any wolf really," Francine said.

"But an alpha wolf most definitely," Betina said.

"What do you mean?"

"You must be stern with them," Betina said. "Don't allow them to walk all over you."

"And if they try," Agatha advised. "Revenge. It's the healthy choice."

Oh dear.

"Now we don't mean anything drastic like lopping off important bits," Francine said.

Agatha shook her head. "I was sure that woman had to be a demon or denizen from hell. Turns out she was human."

"*Humans*." Francine shuddered.

"Scariest beings on the planet," Betina said.

"Anyway. That's neither here nor there." Agatha waved her hand in the air. "The point is you need to ensure your mate absolutely dreads your fury."

"Exactly!" Betina said. "It's the only way to control a wolf. His dread will ensure he treats you right."

"I'm really not exactly sure what it is you're trying to tell me," Gigi admitted. Surely they weren't advising her to make Adam miserable? He was Agatha's son and Betina's nephew!

"Okay, it's like this," Agatha said. "At a certain point, you're going to see my son for the first time since he left you.

And he's going to figure out right quick that you're pregnant with his cubs."

"Which means, he'll expect you to move in with him," Betina said.

Gigi highly doubted that. She was pretty certain the wolf would reject her, just as he did by leaving the last time. Were they actually saying he'd want her to stay?

"He's an alpha wolf, honey." Agatha leaned forward. "He's going to consider you his as soon as he realizes you're his mate."

"You can't give in right away," Francine said.

"You must make him grovel," Betina said.

"Make him work for your forgiveness," Agatha said.

Well, this was unexpected. Gigi wasn't sure what to say in response. The truth was she desperately wanted Adam to want her. And now that she'd experienced living in the woods, being part of a pack, she wanted that too.

Because some tiny part of her still harbored hope, she'd known coming here would open herself up to more heartbreak, but she'd come anyway because it was the right thing to do. Now these women were telling her that she really could have it all.

The surge of joy she felt in that moment brought home exactly what they were cautioning her against.

What happened between her and Adam next would define their relationship moving forward. Because she wanted it so deeply, she ran the risk of not making him work for it, and of ending up with a mate who took her for granted.

"Your job when you see Adam again," Betina said, "is to make him pay for leaving you."

"And then, he must work to earn back your love and respect," Francine said.

"Until he has proven his ability to be a good mate for you, to make your life better, to enrich it in some way, he does *not* deserve you," Agatha said.

"But he's your son!" Gigi exclaimed. "Shouldn't you be, I don't know—"

"Convincing you to forgive him?" Agatha asked.

"Yes!"

"I want my son to be happy," she said. "And a half-mating, where he walks all over the woman he should cherish would not make him even one tiny bit happy."

"Exactly," Betina said. "So give him hell and make him work for it."

4

TWO DAYS LATER, Gigi was still thinking about that conversation with the women and how difficult it was to implement their sound advice when Adam refused to cooperate.

When she'd pointed out that she couldn't exactly give Adam hell if he didn't even know she was there, Agatha had promptly invited her to a family dinner that evening.

Though Gigi had cringed at the idea of confronting Adam in front of his family, she'd accepted.

The only problem was Adam didn't show up.

Apparently, someone had tipped him off that his mother was mate-matching, and he'd run away like the coward he was.

Two days later, she still hadn't seen the bastard so when the knock came at her door, she felt a quick burst of hope.

She opened it to a male pack member she hadn't met before.

He handed her a note and walked away.

Gigi closed the door behind him and opened the note.

All it said was, "Get off my lands."

Gigi crumpled the note in her fist and slowly sank to the floor. She'd *known* this would be his reaction and yet it still hurt. She rocked forward a bit and suddenly JoJo was there, crowding into her space, loving on her.

Gigi buried her face in JoJo's fur and concentrated on pushing back the tears that burned. She'd done more than enough crying over that damn wolf.

Dragging in a deep breath, she pulled back and said to JoJo, "Well, I guess we'd better start packing."

She headed for the bedroom, texting Agatha along the way. She wouldn't leave without at least saying goodbye first.

She'd just pulled out her bright pink suitcase when Agatha and a bunch of female wolves arrived in a flurry of movement.

"You can't leave!"

"He doesn't want me to stay, Agatha." Gigi blinked back tears as she grabbed an armful of tank tops and dropped them into her suitcase.

"Did he tell you that himself?"

"No, he sent a note." Gigi waved an arm toward the outer room where she'd dropped the note and continued packing.

"So he has no idea you're pregnant."

"I'm sure someone told him!"

"Ah, but did they tell him you're pregnant with *his* children?"

Gigi paused for a moment, then shook her head and stormed into the bathroom, where she pulled a bag out from under the sink and began tossing hair and body products into it.

JoJo followed and plastered herself to Gigi's side again.

Something her mate should have been doing. Drying her tears. Hugging her. Holding her close.

Instead, he just kept breaking her heart.

Gigi paused in the packing to crouch down and hug JoJo. "You're a much better mate than he could ever be," she whispered to the dog. "If only I were into girls and you were a shifter, we'd be so happy together, sweet JoJo."

"Now, Gigi." Agatha stood in the doorway and shook her head at the two of them. "You know you would never be happy with anyone but Adam. We just have to make sure he knows those cubs are his."

"Who cares if he knows, Agatha? I don't want a mate who only wants me because of the cubs I'm carrying!"

"Sweetheart, Adam's stubborn. He's a wolf. Even worse, an alpha wolf. Remember what we talked about. You have to play hard to get, but not so hard you're not even here for him to win over."

"How is he going to do that when he doesn't even want to see me, let alone win me over?"

"Well, he doesn't have a choice, now does he?" Agatha pulled Gigi to her feet, cupped her cheeks and gently brushed away a tear. "You can't give up, my dear. He's your mate."

"I can find another one. It's been done before. It's not like it has to be him."

Agatha just looked at her.

"I don't want a mate who doesn't want me in return," Gigi whispered. Her heart was breaking all over again, and the worst part was the women had given her hope.

"I know this is hard, but you can't give up. Besides, if you leave, I'll have to follow you and I'm not cut out to be a city wolf."

"What do you mean?"

"You don't really think I'd let you go off with my grand-cubs and not follow, do you? Your babies are going to need their grandmama and if my son is too stupid to realize what he has in you, he'll end up losing me as well."

Gigi burst into tears.

"Oh, dear. Come along, sweetheart." Agatha led her out of the bathroom and into the living room where the two of them settled on the couch with the women of the pack on all sides.

It took a few moments for Gigi to stop crying.

The moment she did though, the women started introducing themselves.

"My name's Jenny," a young wolf said, settling to her right. "I'm mated to Pete. I think you met him at the bar."

Gigi nodded. "The wolf who told me I was carrying more than one cub. I'd just barely gotten used to the idea of having one."

"Yep. That sounds like Pete," Jenny said. "No filter at all."

"I'm Glory," another shifter said. "I own the bar with my brother, Travis, and I'm mated to Max."

Gigi looked toward Betina, who nodded. "Adam's cousin and beta and my son."

"You're not a wolf," Gigi said to Glory.

"No, I most definitely am not. I'm a bear, a black bear to be precise. And let me just tell you, speaking as someone who is not a wolf, but is mated to one, you can't let them dictate how your relationship will be. They're stubborn and quite idiotic and if not for the women in their lives, they'd probably make a muck out of everything."

"That's the truth," another woman muttered.

"So, whatever that idiot said to you in his note, just ignore it and remind yourself, he's an idiot. He probably wasn't communicating well."

Gigi raised an eyebrow. "Oh, I think he communicated his demand quite well."

"Demand?" Agatha and Betina repeated together.

"What did my boy demand of you?" Agatha asked.

"Here." Francine passed a crumpled piece of paper over to Betina. "Found it on the floor."

Agatha stood and walked over to Betina's side.

"I had no idea our alpha could be such a dick."

"Francine!" an older woman Gigi hadn't met yet exclaimed. Gigi was pretty sure she wasn't a wolf, but some kind of cat.

"Well, it's true, and you'd think so too if you'd read that note, Evelyn!"

Gigi leaned forward. "Are you a feline?"

Evelyn smiled. "Yes. Me and Chloe." She indicated the woman at her side. "We're both cougars."

"And I'm Dory."

Gigi cocked her head. "Human?"

"Witch," everyone chorused.

"You have such interesting friends, Agatha." Gigi smiled, then froze at the look on Agatha's face.

"My son sent this note to you?"

"I-I mean, it's not signed. Maybe it was someone else."

"No one else would refer to these lands as theirs," Betina said.

"Wait until I get my hands on that boy." Agatha crumpled the note in her fist.

"Oh, now, Agatha—"

"You're not leaving. Do you hear me?" Agatha walked back to the couch, and touched her hand to Gigi's cheek.

"You deserve a mate who adores you and I'm going to make sure you get one. If my son doesn't step up to the plate, I'm sure there are plenty of other wolves in this pack who would adore you in his place."

"Oh, um, I don't think—"

"Now you stay here and get to know some of these women. Trust me, they have plenty of advice for how to survive being mated to a dick. I mean a wolf." She stormed toward the door.

"Um. Maybe I should go with her," Betina said.

"Yes, I think this definitely calls for the Alpha Six," Dory said. "You know, in case we have to rein her in."

Betina, Chloe, Dory, Evelyn and Francine all hurried after Agatha, calling goodbyes as they went.

"Now, you be here when we get back." Evelyn stuck her head back in to admonish. "We won't like having to travel to the city to find you. Got it?" Without waiting for a response, she quickly retreated.

"Well." A young woman let out a nervous giggle. "I have to say I'm awfully glad Francine is my mother-in-law and not Agatha. I'm Lara by the way. I'm a witch too."

"It's nice to meet you, Lara, but Agatha's really quite wonderful," Gigi said. "So kind and sweet."

"Oh, I know," Lara said. "She's just—"

"Intense," Glory offered.

"Well, she is the mate of an alpha, not to mention the mother of another one." A young woman plopped down at Gigi's side, right where Agatha had been sitting. "I'm Vicki."

"Nice to meet you," Gigi said.

"And who is this adorable puppy?" She leaned over to pet JoJo, who was sitting on top of Gigi's feet, once more plastered to her legs.

"Her name's JoJo."

"Is she normally pink?" Vicki asked.

"Not usually, no. But I had to do something to cheer us up. So I had my ladies pinkify us both."

"Well, I love it," Lara exclaimed.

"What ladies?" Glory asked.

"I own a beauty salon back in the city. We specialize in shifters. So we're used to dyeing hair and fur and all the things."

"Do you dye your hair every day?" Jenny asked.

"Not at all. I do add a bit of pink to my conditioner, but it's really not necessary to keep dyeing it. This dye job will last about a month, maybe even six weeks if I'm lucky."

"How is that even possible?" Vicki asked. "I always lose the color when I shift."

"Me too!" Several other women exclaimed.

"The trick is you have to dye your hair *and* your fur."

"Wait, what?"

"No way!"

The women all started talking at once.

As Gigi answered their questions and shared some of the beauty tips she'd collected over the years, she found herself falling in love all over again. First, Adam. Then his mother and his aunt. Then the pack lands. Now these women.

And that's when she knew.

Agatha was right.

Gigi deserved this and she was going to *fight* to keep it all.

The friendships.

The land.

The pack.

And most of all, that bastard, Adam.

Her mate.

5

ADAM WAS WORKING in his office when he heard the shouting.

"Where is he? Where is that worthless son of mine?"

For howl's sake, that was his mother's voice and she was searching for him.

He leapt to his feet and hurried into the hall, planning to escape out the back, but it was already too late.

He found himself surrounded, not just by his mother, but by the entire Alpha Six.

What had he done to deserve this?

"How could you treat your mate in such a cruel fashion?" his mother shouted.

Mate? "What are you talking about?"

"I can't believe you would send such a cruel and harsh note. I am so ashamed of you right now, Adam, I can't even stand it!"

"She's claiming she's my *mate*?" Adam couldn't believe the nerve of that woman. Okay, so the sex was spectacular and he'd had a hard time forgetting her, but he didn't have time for distractions, especially not the kind that came from getting involved with some fancified, city cat. "I told her to leave, not to manipulate my own mother!"

"Manipulate? How dare you? As if I'm some child to be manipulated by a perfectly lovely woman."

"Lovely woman? She came here without an invitation, invading my lands, and for what? So that she can get her claws into the alpha and the power that comes with the alpha mate position? Forget it!"

"Power?" Aunt Betina laughed. "What power? We're a pack not a monarchy!"

"She still doesn't belong. She's a cat, for heaven's sake!"

Francine gasped. "How dare you?"

Great. Now the cougar mamas were up in arms too. "Look, no offense, but if I'm going to choose a mate, it's going to be a wolf. If I wanted a cat, I would have chosen one of the cougars. At least they're local. She's a city cat."

"She's a snow leopard. How city can they get?" his mother demanded.

"Have you even met her? A more high-maintenance shifter I couldn't possibly imagine. She'd never fit in here and you know it."

"You don't even know her," Agatha snapped. "You're not even giving her a chance."

"I know her quite well, thank you very much. I learned all about her salon and her crazy dog when we first met—I cannot believe she had the audacity to bring a dog onto wolf lands!"

"You're impossible," his mother said.

"All I'm saying is I got to know her quite well, and she's *not* my mate."

"I had no idea I'd raised such a judgmental child," she replied.

"I'm not judgmental. I'm realistic."

"Well, you're going to have to figure things out," she said, "because your mate is pregnant and needs your support."

"What? She's also claiming I got her *pregnant*?" Adam could literally feel his blood pressure rising. "So the real father walked out and now she's trying to blame *me*?"

"Are you serious right now? *That's* the conclusion you've drawn?" Betina demanded.

His mother seemed speechless, but he couldn't be bothered to wonder why. He was too angry.

The audacity of Gigi, coming onto pack lands to snare him while pregnant with another man's child. He ignored the feeling of intense jealousy that swept over him at the thought of her with another man and fanned the flames of his rage instead.

"What is wrong with you?" his mother finally recovered enough to ask.

"*She's* what's wrong with me," Adam growled and stormed for the door. He'd throw her off his lands himself if he had to.

"Do you think we should go after him?" Betina asked.

"Not at all," Agatha said. "He's finally going to see his mate and no matter how angry he is, there's no way he'll be able to miss the fact that it's his children she's carrying."

"I hope you're right, Agatha," Francine said. "He seemed a bit—"

"Unreasonable," Evelyn suggested.

"Agitated," Dory said.

"More like infuriated," Chloe said.

"Yes, and I believe that's the perfect combination of emotions to ensure Gigi won't be giving in at first sight of him."

"You riled him up deliberately," Dory accused.

"Of course I did. We can't have her falling into his arms the minute he shows up, now can we?"

Betina chuckled. "You're my hero, Agatha. Always have been. Always will be."

"Aw, that's so sweet. Now let's go play dominoes, shall we?"

~

Adam stormed out of the main pack house, exploded into his wolf form, shredding his clothes in the process and took off through the woods, racing down the path that would lead him to the cabin his mother had given Gigi.

He couldn't believe his own mother had fallen for her story, had even moved her into a cabin on pack lands!

When he arrived at the cabin, he skidded to a halt, lunged up the stairs and landed on the porch in his human form.

Stark naked, he strode to the door.

~

One moment the women were laughing and chatting about hair colors, and the next, they were silenced by a fierce pounding.

The women all jumped in surprise.

JoJo lunged to her feet and started barking at the door.

Gigi giggled and patted her. "It's okay, girl."

"Gigi, open this door!"

"Oh, boy," Jenny whispered.

Gigi groaned and headed for the door, JoJo at her side.

The hammering started again and they both froze for a second, but then JoJo went back to barking furiously, clearly agitated at the noise.

"It's okay, JoJo. It's okay." Gigi dropped a hand to the top of JoJo's head and stroked her gently.

"Do you want me to get it?" Glory asked.

That was when Gigi realized the women had followed her and now stood at her back, all of them staring at the door that might seriously fly off its hinges if Adam didn't stop abusing it soon.

"No, it's all right. I can get it." Shaking off her paralysis, Gigi took the last steps to the door and flung it open.

Damn.

Adam in all his glory stood on the porch, glaring at her.

He was a mouth-watering sight and it took Gigi a moment to recover, but she did it. No way was she falling for his blatant attempt to beguile her with his naked body.

"What is your problem?" She yelled at him, which honestly was a bad choice on her part because it set off JoJo, who lunged at the wolf, teeth bared, growling fiercely.

~

dam was stunned speechless at his first sight of Gigi. Her honey-gold hair was now a brilliant pink

and at her side was the dog everyone was talking about. His wolves were right. The damn thing really was the same pink as her hair. Had she seriously turned her dog into an accessory?

She shouted at him, but before he could even respond, her ridiculous dog lunged at him, barking and snarling.

Startled, Adam took a step back, but the dog plowed into his chest, sending the two of them flying back and off the porch.

Adam landed in the snow with the snapping and snarling dog on his chest.

"JoJo!" Gigi rushed down the stairs and scooped the pink monster into her arms. "Are you okay, baby? Did you get hurt?"

"Seriously? Your dog attacked me and you're worried about *her*?"

Gigi turned her back and continued petting and crooning to her ridiculous mutt, ignoring Adam as he struggled to sit up in the snow.

That's when he noticed the women on the porch, all lined up and grinning at him.

Great.

Just what he needed.

An audience to his fall from grace. At the hands of a non-shifting dog.

He should be given a medal for not biting the pink monstrosity's nose off.

He scrambled to his feet and glared at Gigi, who was still ignoring him as she walked back up the stairs.

That's when he noticed what she was wearing.

Was she crazy?

She was in a tiny blue and yellow polka dotted skirt and a bright yellow tank top. Her arms, legs *and* feet were completely bare. Not to mention, her toenails were painted pink to match her hair and dog.

Seriously. The woman was too much.

"Gigi, this had gone far enough," he barked at her.

She froze, one step down from the porch, then slowly turned to face him. "Excuse me?"

Somewhere in the back of his brain was the thought that perhaps this wasn't the best way to handle things, but he was fed up and she'd already taken too much of his time this morning. "I said this has gone far enough. You know we're not mates, so stop with this nonsense and move on."

Gigi narrowed her eyes at him, then still cuddling that ridiculous dog in her arms, she stepped down one stair and then another until she stood right in front of him.

And that was when he caught her scent for the first time.

Only it wasn't just her scent.

It was his too.

And—

Seriously?

"You're pregnant with my child?" he roared at her.

"No, you moron!" She shouted back. "I'm pregnant with your *three* cubs, something you would know if you'd ever allowed me to talk to you for two seconds!"

This shut him up because he knew she was right. Before he could think of what to say in response, she stormed back up the stairs and into the house, slamming the door behind her.

Gritting his teeth, Adam started to follow her, but Glory stepped to the top of the stairs and blocked his path.

The damn bear pointed at him and said, "Don't even try

it. Go home. Figure out a different approach. Because that one, right there, wasn't the way any shifter goes about earning himself a mate." She turned and followed Gigi into the house, the rest of the women right behind her.

~

Adam was still fuming when he stalked into Shenanigans an hour later.

He'd returned to the pack house, but had been unable to concentrate on a damn thing.

He still couldn't believe he'd gotten the snow leopard pregnant. He wanted to think it wasn't true, that it was just some kind of trick, but there was no way to imitate the twining scent of two mated shifters and the cubs they'd produced.

Once he'd gotten the full effect, his wolf had gone wild, pressing to the front, wanting to play with his leopard right then, right that minute.

When she'd locked them out, the wolf had gone berserk, howling for its mate. Thankfully, Adam had retained enough control to lock those howls inside, though it had been touch and go there for a minute.

Once he was sure he wouldn't lose control, he'd walked away, and the wolf had been sulking ever since.

Not Adam, though. Adam was furious.

How dare she deny him?

Never mind that he'd been a bit of an ass.

She'd obviously come here to claim her mate. Well, he was right there and what did she do? Walked into the cabin and shut the door in his face. Rude!

Walking inside Shenanigans, Adam headed straight for

the bar, ignoring the silence that spread in his wake. So what if this was only the second time he'd ever visited, the first time being just two months ago, when his mother had insisted he take a vacation.

Now that he thought about it, this was all *her* fault! If she hadn't insisted he travel a hundred miles out, he'd never have met Gigi and his life wouldn't be in turmoil right now.

And once he got drunk enough, he'd be sure to tell his mother exactly that!

"Hey, Adam. Don't see you in here very often." Travis grinned at him. "What can I get you?"

Good question. He was tempted to go right for the shots he'd drank last time. They'd been super effective, but considering he wasn't looking to pass out quite this early, he'd probably better start off with something lighter. What was that brew Pete had been drinking the last time he was here?

Oh, right. "I'll have a bottle of Be Were."

"You got it." Travis stepped away to grab a bottle, popped the top, poured half into a tumbler and set both in front of Adam.

"Thanks," Adam muttered. He grabbed the mug and took a giant swallow. "Just keep them coming."

An hour later, three Be Weres down, Adam was no more relaxed than when he'd started. He was still stuck on cubs. He couldn't believe she'd gotten pregnant. And with multiples! What exactly did she expect him to do—become a *dad*? How ridiculous.

He picked up the latest bottle of Be Were and glared at it. Alcohol was supposed to relax him, dammit! Or at least get him plastered.

And what kind of name was that anyway? Be Were. Whoever made this brew should be ashamed, playing on human superstitions like that. He glared at the wolf logo. No self-respecting shifter would ever go out in public like that. It looked completely deranged!

Adam set the bottle back down and pushed it away. Maybe it was time to get serious about his alcohol consumption.

6

MAX AND GLORY were holding hands, flat on their backs, gasping for breath, staring at the snow-covered branches above them, when Travis called.

"Your brother's getting on my last nerve," Max muttered.

Glory grinned and sat up. "Well, he *could* have called fifteen minutes ago. That would have been way worse timing." She waggled her brows at him.

He grinned, then lunged upward, taking her to the ground beneath him.

Her laughter changed to a squeal and then a soft moan of pleasure and it was another thirty minutes before she finally managed to answer one of Travis' barrage of phone calls.

By that time, he was calling and texting them both.

Unwilling to walk as is into a bar full of shifters who would know exactly how they'd spent the last two hours, Max and Glory took the time to walk down to the river bank, where, in their wolf and bear forms, they washed in the partially frozen water.

It wasn't exactly a wonderful experience, but Max figured the pleasure that came before had been well worth it.

By the time they walked into the bar two hours after Travis had called the first time, things had clearly progressed to a point where they'd gotten completely out of hand.

"Unbelievable," Glory said as they entered the bar and stared around them. "Did we forget a full moon?"

Max had no idea what she was talking about, or at least he wasn't going to admit it. "Seriously? First of all, the full moon's not for another couple weeks. Secondly, it doesn't affect us this way."

Glory sent him an incredulous look, but he did his best to radiate confused innocence in return. "I mean, look at them, Glory. They're acting like a bunch of cubs."

"Exactly. Just like they do anytime there's a full moon."

Max made a scoffing sound. "Please. Adult wolves are some of the most rational and mature shifters around. The full moon doesn't change that." And he quickly walked away, leaving Glory sputtering behind him. Seriously, one more minute in her presence and he wouldn't be able to contain the laughter.

"It's about time you got here." Travis glared at him. "You need to get your alpha under control." He pointed to the area of the bar where Max and his friends usually hung out and that's when Max saw him.

Adam, the most serious wolf in the pack, the one who actually *was* the epitome of rational and mature, not because he was their alpha so much as because he was a stick-in-the-mud, was currently in his wolf form, chasing his tail.

And the rest of the bar was urging him on.

Many were in wolf form too, some of them chasing their own tails while others were simply chasing each other.

And was that—Max shook his head as Pete, in wolf form, lunged past, bringing his mate, Jenny, to the floor beneath him.

Oh, howl no.

If they went at it right there, in the middle of the bar, the bears would never let the pack back inside. And Glory would never forgive Max.

But no—after catching Jenny, biting her nape and then licking at the bite, Pete lunged away and took off running, Jenny on his tail.

"Watch out!" Travis shouted as they weaved in and out of chairs and tables.

Glory was right. It really did look like a scene from one of their full moon parties.

The only difference was Travis always had every employee in the bar working those nights to ensure things didn't get quite as thoroughly out of hand as they were right now.

Before Max could decide what to do, Glory let out a roar, the likes of which he never, *ever* wanted to hear directed at him.

Everyone in the bar froze.

Max slowly turned his head and stared.

For howl's sake, she had made that horrendous sound while still in human form.

And he was mated to the woman.

Sometimes he marveled at his own brass balls.

"Get yourselves under control right now, wolves!"

Out of the corner of his eye, Max noticed that even Adam had frozen in his tail chasing.

For about two seconds.

Then he shook out his fur and stretched up into his

human form.

Max had always been a little envious of how easily and seamlessly Adam flowed from human to wolf and back again. In a split second, less, he went from one form to the other. And then he was standing there naked.

Wonderful.

Phoenix suddenly appeared at his side and passed him a pile of clothes, which caused Travis to roar, a sound that made everyone who had just begun to recover from their previous paralysis, freeze again.

Except for Phoenix, who simply walked calmly away from Adam, back toward her mate, and Adam himself, who began to calmly dress right in the middle of the bar.

Too bad he'd obviously had too much to drink because he was having difficulty with the entire process, what with all the swaying and such.

Glory stomped over to Max and said to him, "I hold you responsible."

"*Me?*"

"He's *your* alpha and as long as he's out of control, the rest of this riffraff will be as well. So rein him in."

Great.

~

"Surprised to see you here, Adam."

Adam glared at Max, hoping to hold off the inquisition, even knowing there would be no stopping his beta and cousin from butting his nosy self into things that were none of his business.

"That's what I said!" Pete joined Max in righting tables and chairs, Jenny at his side. Adam was surprised to see they were still with them, what with all the chasing they'd had going on.

As everyone got settled around the tables, Adam raised an eyebrow at Jenny, who blushed.

He'd been horrified to see her walk into the bar with Pete earlier that evening. He'd been hoping all the women would stay with Gigi and far away from the bar while he was there.

No such luck though.

Not only had Jenny joined them—it was *date night,* whatever the hell that meant—but now Glory was in the bar too.

Both of whom had the inside scoop on all the drama that had happened earlier that day. Which meant, if they'd shared, Max and Pete might have it as well.

Adam scowled at them both.

"Hey, no offense," Pete said. "It's just you always like to say—" He broke off and shook his head. "No, no, Jenny, you do it much better than me. What does Adam always say?"

Jenny looked horrified to be put on the spot. "Um, I'm not sure—"

"Come on, please!" Pete put on his most ridiculous, sappiest expression and Jenny caved.

"Okay, fine." She cleared her throat, straightened her shoulders, lifted her chin and announced in a low, growly voice, "No time for frivolous games, everyone. There's important work to be done."

Adam scowled. He didn't sound like that.

Did he?

Everyone else laughed.

Rude!

"Exactly," Max said. "So tell us, Adam. Why are you here, drinking? Again?"

Adam just shook his head and waved his hand to catch

Phoenix's attention. He was going to need more shots if he had to endure an inquisition.

"Perhaps he's in need of some advice," Jenny suggested with a grin.

Oh, thank all the alpha gods, Phoenix arrived just in time to thwart that line of conversation.

"So what are you thinking this time, Adam?" Phoenix grinned at him. For some reason, she was vastly entertained by his determination to sample as many of his own species' concoctions as possible in one night. "So far you've tried Be Were, The Howler, Howlers' Paradise *and* a Howling Orgasm, not to mention The Beast Within, which is how everyone ended up furry. So what's next?"

Good question.

"Flaming Moonrises!" Jenny exclaimed. "You haven't tried a Flaming Moonrise yet!"

She was the reason he'd tried the Howling Orgasm in the first place and Pete had been the one to suggest The Beast Within.

Adam was starting to think there was a conspiracy afoot. Oh, well. He shrugged."Sounds good to me."

"Everyone want a round or—"

"Might as well," Max said.

"So, what's this about advice?" Pete asked as soon as Phoenix walked away.

Adam knew it had been too good to be true. He glared at Pete, who just grinned back at him.

"Oh, Adam really screwed the pooch with his mate this afternoon," Jenny explained.

"What the hell does that even mean?" Adam demanded. "Screwed the pooch. Who would want to do such a thing?"

"Exactly," Jenny said. "No one wants to screw the pooch, but you sure did."

"I'm confused," Max said. "Are you suggesting JoJo is Adam's mate?"

Adam blanched. The pink monstrosity?

Jenny burst into laughter. "No. It's just a saying. Phoenix taught it to me."

"What saying?" Phoenix was back, no shots in hand though.

Adam glared at her.

She shrugged. "Travis is working on them."

"Screwed the pooch," Jenny said. "You said it means someone screwed up real bad, right?"

"That's right."

"Well, Adam did just that this afternoon. I'd be surprised if Gigi ever speaks to him again."

"Oh, dear." Phoenix got a concerned look on her face, pulled out a chair and sat down. "What happened, Adam?"

Adam scowled. "Don't you need to be serving drinks or something?"

"Oh, don't worry. Travis'll call if he needs me. So what happened? Did you really screw things up that badly?"

"Me? Why is it always me? Why can't it be her? She has a lot of nerve, prancing onto pack lands with her pink dog, trying to win over the pack, just because she's—" He stopped, not really ready to admit anything.

"What? Just because she's pregnant with your litter?" Max asked.

Adam froze and glared at him. "You knew?"

"'Course, I knew, man. She showed up here in the bar, looking for you. If you'd ever come here with us, you might have been here that night."

"She was quite a sight," Karl said.

"Who was?" Cole walked up, Dan at his side, and within seconds the two were seated at the table with them.

Great.

Now not only would the wolves get to hear all about his humiliating afternoon, but so would the cougars.

Of course, their mothers had been witness to *his* mother chewing him out, so he supposed it wasn't much of a secret at this point.

In fact, now that Max had pointed out that Gigi arrived at the bar first, Adam was starting to realize he was perhaps the very last one to know that Gigi was his mate and that he'd somehow gotten her pregnant.

Unbelievable.

"Gigi," Karl said. "The night she arrived at the bar."

"Oh, yeah," Dan agreed. "Tiny pink skirt, pink high heels, silly pink dog. Not to mention that shirt. Can you believe she walked through the snow like that?"

"Oh, that's nothing," Jenny said. "She likes to stretch out on tree limbs in her snow leopard form and sleep that way. You should see her, all fluffy and pink. She really stands out against the snow."

"Seriously?" Adam exclaimed. What kind of shifter dyed their animal form pink?

"Yep. She's so cute! Plus once I saw her walking in the woods barefoot. She says it's too hot. Can you believe that?"

"It's twenty degrees outside!" Pete exclaimed.

"I know. It's crazy."

Adam let out a low growl. Gigi was climbing trees while carrying his cubs inside her *and* walking around barefoot on purpose? What was wrong with that woman? Clearly someone needed to take her in hand.

“Not sure that’s the best approach either,” Glory snapped from where she’d suddenly appeared on his right.

“Huh?” Adam shook his head, confused.

She glared at him.

What had he done?

“I told you to figure out a way to earn your mate and the best you can come up with is ‘taking her in hand’?” She made air quotes around the last phrase.

Damn. He couldn’t believe he’d said that out loud. “Look, the woman’s crazy. Clearly you can see that.”

“You don’t even know her, Adam,” Jenny said.

“I do. I spent an entire evening talking to her before we got busy, if you know what I mean.” He smirked.

Jenny blushed, but then demanded with surprising temerity, “So you thought she was crazy after chatting with her all night, but you still took her to bed with you?”

Damn. Now what was he supposed to say to that? Though he wanted to say yes, it wasn’t exactly true. He hadn’t found Gigi to be crazy at all. Instead, he’d really liked her.

She was sweet and passionate and different from every other female shifter he’d ever met. And his wolf had been as taken with her as he was. It was why he’d taken her to bed, why he’d spent the entire final weekend of his vacation burning up the sheets with her.

The problem was he had too many responsibilities and she was a city leopard with her own business. Their lives just didn’t mesh, and so, even though he’d liked her, he’d left her behind because it was the right thing to do. He couldn’t leave his pack and it wouldn’t be right to ask her to give up her business and life for him.

“Well?” Jenny demanded.

Adam sighed. Might as well get the torture over with, but before he could say anything, Travis arrived with a tray full of Moonrise shots. They weren't flaming yet, but Adam had no doubt Travis would take care of that soon enough.

Phoenix helped Travis distribute the shots, ensuring that everyone got one, and then Travis set about lighting them up. Once he finished the rounds, everyone carefully grabbed a shot glass and held it up high.

Adam and his wolves all threw back their heads and howled, then everyone blew out the flames and downed their shots.

Shit, that was good stuff.

Adam stared into the empty shot glass, stunned.

He wasn't sure what was more surprising.

The fact that he hadn't singed off his eyebrows or the fact that he found the drink utterly delicious. It warmed him from the inside out.

A fabulous turn of events in the middle of winter.

"So let's hear it," Glory demanded.

Ugh. There just wasn't enough alcohol in the world for this. "Fine. Yes, I liked Gigi. I liked her a lot actually. But she's a city leopard. She doesn't belong here. She has a life and a business in the city."

"You don't think she can move her business here?" Jenny asked.

"Or enjoy living in the woods?" Karl asked.

"Have you seen the woman?" Adam asked. "She's got high maintenance written all over her. She's color coordinated from the top of her head to the toenails on her feet. More than that. She's coordinated with her dog, for heaven's sake! A dog who hates me, I might add."

"You scared her," Jenny accused. "If you weren't acting

like such a total barbarian, she'd probably love you. JoJo's a sweetheart and you were a bully."

Adam was shocked and by the looks on everyone else's faces, they were too.

Jenny never said anything mean to anyone. She'd said JoJo was a sweetheart, but she might as well have been describing herself, even though right at that moment, Jenny was glaring at Adam like he was some kind of monster.

Great. So not only did Jenny like Gigi an awful lot, but she clearly like JoJo even more.

A dog.

When had his life become so absurd that his wolves were actually siding with a *dog* rather than their alpha?

"What on earth did you *do*, man?" Pete asked.

Adam rolled his eyes. "Nothing. I just told her to get off my land, that's all."

"He showed up, furious, pounding on the door, shouting at Gigi to answer it," Glory said. "JoJo didn't like how aggressive he was and when he took a step toward Gigi, JoJo attacked. Knocked him off the porch into the snow. He's lucky the dog just jumped him. Adam was naked at the time. She could have decided to bite something off." Glory gave Adam an evil grin. "If you know what I mean."

Adam blanched.

This had not even occurred to him.

Now he was going to have nightmares of that pink monstrosity attacking his manhood!

"Thanks a lot, Glory," he muttered.

She grinned. "You're welcome. And on that note, good luck." She stood and walked off to the other side of the bar.

"Were you upset because you'd found out she was pregnant?" Phoenix asked.

"My mom did mention that." Adam decided he wasn't going to say anything beyond that. No point in bringing up that he'd been convinced it wasn't his child.

"So what are you going to do?" Phoenix asked. "If she's pregnant, she's gotta be your mate, right?"

Adam sighed. "Probably."

"But that's great news! You found your mate and she's already pregnant. Why aren't you happy?"

"I don't have time for a mate or cubs," Adam exclaimed.

"Says who?" Max asked. "You're always claiming there's so much work to do, but seriously, there is *not* that much work to do. It's called delegating, dude. Just share the load a little. There are plenty of wolves ready and willing to take on more responsibilities so that you can have a life."

"And a mate," Pete said.

"And cubs," Karl said.

Adam shook his head. "She'll never fit in. She'll hate it here."

"She's already here, man," Max said, "and she hasn't left yet. I'd say that's a pretty good sign."

"You'll never get anywhere if you don't change your attitude," Travis said. "You need to decide that your pack lands and your pack are so amazing they can convince even a city woman like Gigi to stick around. And then you need to convince her that you're the icing on the cake, a mate worth giving up everything for."

"How the hell do I do that?" Adam thought it sounded impossible.

"All you've gotta do is court her," Dan said.

"I don't know anything about courting!" Adam was horrified at the very thought of it.

"It's not that hard," Cole said. "You just have to convince

her that you're the one. Make her feel like she's the center of your universe."

"Exactly," Dan said. "And don't worry. We'll help. Between the lot of us, we have tons of experience!"

"Right," Travis said. "Just ask Harry. He would probably have never won over Lily without our help—well, *my* help anyway."

"Hey! We were helpful," Max said.

"You advised him to chase her tail. She doesn't even have a tail."

"Well, it seemed like a good idea at the time."

"Actually, that's a great idea," Cole said. "Gigi's a snow leopard, which is just another kind of cat. And cats do love to play. So you know, play with her."

"I'm a wolf. We don't play with cats."

"Oh, and you know what else?" Karl exclaimed. "She (admittedly, quite bizarrely) loves dogs. So I'm guessing she'd probably love to meet your wolf."

"Oooh, that's a great idea," Pete said. "You should court her as your wolf, maybe play with her dog. She'd probably melt into a pile of goo."

"Now you want me to play with her dog too? Are you crazy? I'm a wolf!"

"You're never going to win your mate with that attitude," Travis pointed out.

7

ADAM RACED THROUGH the woods, in his wolf form, back toward pack lands. He shook off the snow as he reached the pack house, then lunged up the stairs and inside through the large pet door.

He quickly shifted to human and stalked through the house, heading toward the stairs at the back that led up to the master suite.

"Court her," he muttered as he ran up the stairs. How could they possibly think he would be any good at that? He didn't have a romantic bone in his body. Not to mention, he still wasn't sure he wanted to win Gigi at all.

Right?

The thought of a mate, the demands on his time, the extra responsibility on top of every other responsibility he already had, always made him shudder. Only now, when he replaced the thought of some anonymous mate with the thought of Gigi—

He paused to picture it.

Walking into the pack house and finding it not empty, but filled with Gigi's presence.

Eating dinner with her, rather than alone.

Going to family dinners with her, rather than by himself and having to endure yet another mate-matching attempt by his mother.

Retiring to the master bedroom suite and finding Gigi waiting for him, wrapping herself around him, seducing him.

Suddenly, the thought of a mate, when it was Gigi in that role, didn't seem so horrible after all.

But what if she hated it here? Missed her business? Decided to leave after he'd let her in?

It really did come down to the question Travis had asked him as he was leaving the bar. "Adam," he'd said. "All you have to really decide right now is if she's worth it. Is she worth the risk?"

Remembering the sound of her laughter in the bar when they'd been getting to know each other, the tenderness in her eyes when she'd kissed him at breakfast that Sunday morning, the way their passion had roared all weekend long, Adam knew there could only be one answer to that question.

Of course, Gigi was worth it.

~

The knock on the door the next morning startled Gigi and JoJo, who instantly leapt to her feet and barked at the door.

Great.

JoJo never used to bark when someone knocked. Gigi would kill that mangy wolf if he'd turned JoJo into some crazy barker.

She stalked to the door, JoJo bristling at her side. "It's okay, baby." Gigi stroked a hand down JoJo's back, then opened the door.

Whatever she'd been expecting, it wasn't this.

A wolf sat on her front porch, tail wagging, clearly trying to look as friendly and non-threatening as possible. A quick sniff told Gigi that yes, this wolf, was in fact, her idiot mate.

JoJo growled low in her throat and pressed against Gigi, clearly spooked to be confronted by a wolf at the door.

Gigi dropped a hand onto JoJo's head and stroked it gently, glaring at the wolf. "What do you want, Adam?"

In answer, he dropped to his belly and nudged a bone she hadn't noticed until then toward them.

Gigi raised an eyebrow.

Adam nudged it forward again, clearly intending it as a gift for JoJo.

Gigi glanced down at the poodle, who looked up at her at the same time. Gigi smiled and nodded. If JoJo wanted to accept the offering, Gigi wasn't going to say no.

JoJo studied the wolf and the bone for a long moment, then tilted up her nose, turned her back and walked into the house.

Gigi pressed her lips together to keep from laughing, cleared her throat and said, "I guess JoJo isn't interested. Better luck next time." And with that, she turned and entered the house, closing the door behind her.

Clapping a hand over her mouth, she hurried into the living room where JoJo was sitting in front of the picture window, peeking out at the wolf on the front porch.

The two of them watched Adam lope away, leaving the bone exactly where he'd left it.

"Oh, JoJo, I think you're my hero." Gigi leaned down and

gave her a big hug. "So what do you think? Shall we claim the bone after all?"

JoJo gave her a bright-eyed look and Gigi laughed, then went outside to claim her dog's prize.

The next morning, right around the same time, another knock came at the door.

This time Adam had brought a ball with him. He nudged it toward JoJo, who didn't even hesitate this time to turn her back and walk away.

Gigi just shrugged at Adam, then followed her dog back into the house, closing the door behind her.

The next day, Adam arrived with a tiny basket in his mouth. Inside were three colors of nail polish and a tiny manicure set.

Gigi's eyes widened. She definitely wanted those colors. They were beautiful!

She'd never seen that shade of peach before, and the purple and green shades were so vibrant, she couldn't wait to wear them all. She was already imagining walking through the woods with green toenails and comparing them to the colors of the forest.

Still, if JoJo could turn her back on a couple toys, Gigi could do the same with nail polish. Right?

Dragging in a deep breath, she said, "Sorry, Adam. You gotta win JoJo over first." And she turned and walked into the house, hoping that Adam would leave the offerings on the porch as he'd done with the bone and ball.

Once inside, she and JoJo once again watched through the picture window as Adam left, sending sad puppy-dog looks over his shoulder as he went.

As soon as he was out of sight, of course, Gigi claimed her

prizes and sent a bunch of texts inviting the women over for manicures.

The tiny manicure kit was adorable, but it was nothing like her own professional kits, of course, which she brought out along with her entire collection of nail art and paints for the women to choose from.

Of course, she also encouraged them to try out the three colors Adam had given her and grinned as she imagined the expression on his face when he caught sight of his mother's nails, now painted a rich purple.

And though she tried to resist, she ended up painting her own nails with that peach polish she absolutely adored. While it didn't exactly match her pink hair, it was perfect when paired with one of her favorite skirts. It was a swirl of greens and blues with threads of peach throughout.

"I had no idea that boy had it in him," Agatha said, admiring their nails.

"He's got game all right," Francine said, which made the rest of the women laugh.

It was a pretty awesome afternoon.

~

"I don't think it's working," Adam said glumly that evening at the bar.

"Are you kidding right now?" Cole exclaimed. "Megan came back thrilled at her manicure and pedicure. She went on and on about how romantic it was that you'd given Gigi something you knew she would love."

"Yeah? Then how come she went and shared it with every other woman in the pack, not to mention those outside of it?

Even my *mother's* walking around with nails painted in colors I specially ordered for my mate."

Pete snickered. "Okay, that's pretty funny, but seriously, all the women are happy, and you're the reason why. Just keep it up, man."

"She told me I had to win over her stupid dog first." Adam shuddered at the thought, even as his supposed friends burst into laughter.

This was insane. He couldn't believe he was actually being forced to court a *dog*.

"Guess you're going to have to step up your game." Karl chuckled.

"Oh, come on," Cole said. "It can't be that hard to win over a silly dog."

"Yeah, I thought they were supposed to be man's best friend," Pete said. "You should be making a lot more progress than you are. Jenny's probably right. You really blew it that first time you met the poodle and now she's holding a grudge."

Adam groaned. It was true! She was. Who knew a dog could be so cruel? He couldn't believe his entire mating hinged on being able to win over that stupid dog.

"What else have you got up your sleeve?"

Adam shook his head. "Not enough, clearly. And while I'm busy courting the dog, Gigi's just ignoring me! I've been following Glory's advice to only stop by once a day. She says that'll keep Gigi thinking about me when I'm not there, but I bet as soon as I'm gone, I'm not even a blip on her radar."

"Yeah, Glory's usually right about these things, though," Max said. "If she says to stay away, I'd do it."

"You just don't want to deal with her ranting if I don't follow her advice." Adam knew his beta well and he didn't for a minute believe that Max thought Glory's advice was infallible.

Max let out a bark of laughter. "Okay, true. But still. What we need to do is come up with ways to make sure she's thinking about you, even when you're not around."

"I've got a great idea," Pete exclaimed.

~

The rest of that week was pretty entertaining. Each morning began with a visit from Adam in his wolf form while every afternoon was filled with visits from other members of the pack, most of them male, who apparently felt compelled to share how incredibly wonderful their alpha was.

JoJo, for her part, continued to ignore Adam's best efforts, though after he left each day, she thoroughly enjoyed whatever he left behind, except for those times when the gift was for Gigi. On those occasions, she sulked in the corner and glared at Gigi like it was her fault.

One day Adam brought a squeaky toy that JoJo carried around the house and pounced on for hours, making it squeak incessantly and zeroing out every point Adam had managed to earn thus far from Gigi. There was a reason squeaky toys were not allowed in her house!

That afternoon, Pete and Karl visited. With loud squeaks in the background, they went on and on about how much fun Adam was. When Gigi demanded some examples, they hemmed and hawed, then pulled out stories from when they were all cubs together.

She just rolled her eyes at them and ushered them out of the house. When she returned, it was to a barrage of squeaks.

"You're about to lose that toy. Don't think I won't take it away from you!"

In response, JoJo made the toy squeak even louder.

Gigi let out a huff. The truth was she would never take something JoJo loved so much away from her, but damn, she prayed the next day would bring a different surprise to turn JoJo's attentions elsewhere.

Instead, Adam delivered an e-reader filled with shifter romances, most of them involving a cocky wolf. Some of the stories were so erotic, they made Gigi feel as if her body would burst into flames at any moment.

That afternoon, Pete and Karl returned. This time, they brought an entire photo album with them and spent hours sharing pictures and stories from their childhood. While they didn't manage to convince her that Adam knew how to play as an adult, she was utterly enamored of the pictures of him, Max, Pete, Karl and Sam wrestling and playing as cubs.

They were all truly adorable and for the first time, Gigi felt a real sense of excitement to meet her own cubs.

The next day, Adam showed up with a stuffed wolf. He nudged it toward JoJo, and for the first time, it looked like she might not be able to resist.

Gigi could tell by the quiver in JoJo's backside that she was barely containing herself.

Adam was definitely winning her over.

Eventually though, JoJo turned and pranced into the house.

Gigi was pretty impressed at her willpower. "Sorry, Adam." And she went inside and closed the door.

Fifteen minutes later, when Adam was long gone, she opened the door, and JoJo pounced.

The squeaky toy was abandoned in favor of the stuffed

wolf that JoJo ended up carrying with her everywhere. Gigi let out a huge sigh of relief and as soon as JoJo wasn't looking, she stole that squeaky toy and relocated it into the trash.

Later that afternoon, Sam and Max came by to talk to Gigi about Adam and what a wonderful father and mate he would be.

Gigi could tell by the looks on their faces that they didn't even believe the things they were saying.

"He's always wanted to be a father," Max said.

Gigi just gave him a look. "Are you being serious right now?"

"I mean, you know, deep down inside," Max said.

"Way deep down," Sam muttered.

"Okay, come on. Did he put you guys up to this because it's kind of pathetic?"

"Actually, it was Pete's idea," Max said.

"I told you that listening to Pete is never a good idea," Sam said.

Gigi laughed. "Look, you guys don't have to worry, okay? Adam's doing a pretty good job on his own."

"Really?" Sam asked.

"Does that mean you'll be putting him—and us—out of his misery sometime soon?" Max asked.

Gigi shrugged. "That I don't know. We'll just have to see how it goes."

Both Max and Sam groaned.

"Great," Sam said.

"Well, we'll probably be back tomorrow," Max told her at the end of their visit.

"I figured." Gigi grinned.

The next morning, Adam arrived with a rolled up package around his neck. When Gigi unwrapped it, she found three tiny onesies, each featuring two cubs, one a wolf and the other a pink snow leopard. Gigi's heart melted.

That afternoon, as promised, Sam and Max returned, this time with a gift bag. Inside, she found three stuffed wolf cubs and three stuffed leopard cubs. "Oh, my gosh. They're so cute." She hugged them close. They were so soft and precious.

Max smiled. "We don't have to say anything to convince you today, do we?"

Gigi shook her head.

Sam and Max high fived each other and headed out the door.

"Those are adorable," Jenny said when Gigi showed her the latest gifts.

Though Gigi was used to working long hours at the salon, she wasn't lonely in the cabin because the women of the pack kept stopping by. They came by for manicures, pedicures, haircuts, dye jobs and for the company.

Gigi's little cabin had become a gathering place for all the women of the pack and she loved it.

The main topic of conversation was, of course, Adam and whatever his latest gifts were. The women liked to speculate about what the next day would bring.

One morning, though, Adam didn't arrive.

Instead, Karl showed up in his place and handed Gigi a bag. "For JoJo," he said.

It turned out to be full of dog biscuits, which probably meant that JoJo now had a new best friend in Karl.

An hour later, Pete showed up and handed over a bag of cookies. "For you, Gigi."

An hour after that, Sam showed up with two frilly bows for JoJo and an hour after that, Cole showed up with a fancy barrette for Gigi. Adam had even gotten the cougars involved.

The gifts continued like that, including a dog toy for JoJo, and to Gigi's horror, a sex toy for her, making her blush furiously, which led Max, who had delivered the gift, to raise an eyebrow in question.

Gigi quickly closed the bag, thanked him and darted into the house.

She wanted to be annoyed, but instead, she was just turned on.

Then came the Polaroids.

First one for JoJo. It was a picture of Adam in wolf form sitting in a field of snow, a pink bow around his neck.

Next came one for Gigi of Adam lying on a couch stark naked, with a much larger, strategically placed, pink bow.

And then the invitations arrived.

Beautifully printed, on high-quality paper, they invited JoJo and Gigi to dinner with Adam.

Positively giddy at that point, Gigi leapt into action. She showered and shaved and slathered on lotion, then sat on her bed and gave herself another mani-pedi. Back to pink!

After all that effort she'd gone to that first night in town, Adam hadn't even seen her. So tonight, she was going for pretty in pink once more.

Once her nails dried, she pulled on her pink lingerie, pink skirt and flirty white blouse that dipped low and had bell sleeves. It was just sheer enough to show hints of the bright pink bra beneath it. "All right, JoJo. Time for hair and makeup!"

8

ADAM WAS NERVOUS. He'd walked this path every day for the past week and a half, but this was only the second time he'd walked it on two legs.

Throughout the day, he'd heard back from his friends about Gigi's response to each and every one of his gifts.

"What on earth was in that bag?" Max had demanded, making Adam grin. Apparently, Gigi had blushed furiously when she'd opened it.

The biggest risk, of course, had been the Polaroids. Adam had sealed them in small manila envelopes, but couldn't be sure his friends wouldn't peek anyway. Nor could he be certain that Gigi wouldn't share them.

"I thought she was going to have a stroke there for a minute," Cole reported with a giant grin. "Her face turned beat red and she started fanning herself with the envelope." He raised an eyebrow. "Want to share what was on that Polaroid?"

"Not a chance," Adam said.

Of course, this didn't stop them from speculating and in

fact, led to a few bets. Adam was thinking he might want to retrieve that Polaroid as soon as possible.

And burn it, of course.

He grinned at the memory of Pete telling him that Gigi couldn't quite hide her joy when he delivered her invitation with a box of chocolates.

"She hugged those chocolates to her chest and told me she'd better get ready for dinner," Pete said. "I think you're golden now. That is, as long as you don't screw things up, of course."

Exactly right.

"Don't screw things up," Adam muttered to himself as he walked up the stairs to Gigi's door. He hesitated, drew in a deep breath, then knocked.

A few moments later, the door opened and he about swallowed his tongue. He'd heard all the stories of what she'd looked like the night she'd arrived at Shenanigans 1 and he'd been horribly jealous that everyone had seen his Gigi that night but him.

Now here she was in front of him, dressed the way they'd all described: tiny pink skirt, frilly, see-through blouse, high heels.

"You are a vision, Gigi."

She smiled. "Thanks."

"You ready to go?"

She nodded and stepped out, JoJo at her side.

Adam bent down and held his hand out to JoJo, who sniffed it, then after a moment, stuck out her tongue and licked his hand. Adam couldn't believe how happy he felt in that moment. "Hey, girl." He moved slowly and when she didn't make any aggressive moves, he pet her head, right between her ears that sported two brand new bows.

He looked up at Gigi and grinned. "She liked her gifts then."

"Are you kidding? I had to bribe her with your dog biscuits to get her to leave that wolf behind."

Adam stood and tucked a lock of hair behind Gigi's ears, noting as he did the fancy barrette he'd sent earlier that day nestled in her hair. "And you? Did you enjoy yours?"

Gigi blushed, but then to his surprise, admitted, "Every single one of them."

A flash of heat rolled down Adam's spine at the thought of her enjoying every one of his gifts. "I've missed you." He kissed her on the cheek, then turned and offered her his arm.

~

It was when they reached the top of the stairs and started down them that Gigi noticed the horse-drawn carriage waiting for them in the yard.

She froze and stared. It was like something out of Cinderella. The horse was pitch black while the open carriage was white with red upholstery.

Max sat in the driver's seat, dressed like Adam, in a black suit and tie. He even had on a top hat, which he lifted and waved to her. "Your carriage awaits, my lady."

"Adam," Gigi whispered, stunned speechless.

Adam smiled. "Come along, my love." He led her down the remaining stairs, but when she would have gone to step into the snow, he swept her into his arms.

She let out a squeal, then flung an arm around his shoulders. "What are you doing?"

He grinned at her. "I'd hate for you to ruin those heels in the snow."

Gigi rolled her eyes. "Too late for that. I already gave them a workout the night I arrived. Surprisingly, they held up very well, though the color may be a bit darker than before."

"Well, indulge me. I'm enjoying the moment." He strode toward the carriage, JoJo prancing in joy ahead of them.

When they reached the carriage, JoJo bounded on first and immediately scrambled onto the seat behind the driver. She looked utterly adorable.

Adam handed Gigi into the carriage next and she settled on the seat across from JoJo.

Adam leapt aboard, sat beside Gigi and called, "To dinner, Max!"

It was the most beautiful evening of Gigi's life.

The carriage ride through the snow was an incredible experience. As they traveled through the woods, with snow falling lightly around them, Gigi felt as if she'd fallen into a fairy tale with her prince at her side.

When they finally stopped, she saw they were outside Shenanigans 1. She felt a tiny pang of disappointment to have begun the evening with a magical carriage ride, only to end it at a bar.

And then they went inside.

Shenanigans 1 had been transformed.

Most of the tables and chairs had been shoved to the walls, leaving a huge dance floor and at the center of it, an elegant table set for two.

Adam led her across the floor to their table and Gigi's breath caught when she noticed a lower table to the side of their own with a pillow on the floor in front of it. On the little table was a water bowl, a saucer with a couple dog biscuits and a giant bone.

Gigi's heart about melted when she saw that incredible setup for JoJo. "You're going to spoil her."

"She deserves it." Adam held out her chair, waited until she was seated, then rounded the table to sit down himself. "And so do you."

Phoenix delivered dinner a few moments later, then wished them a happy night and left them alone.

Just as they had the first evening they met, they talked long into the night. Gigi talked about her days with the women of the pack and how kind everyone had been. Adam talked about his work and his mother, who drove him nuts, and his pride in his pack.

Later, when they were finished eating, Adam turned on the music and they danced for hours.

When their energy flagged, they settled in a booth and talked some more.

"I wanted us to have our first dinner here in this bar because I wanted you to know how sorry I am that I missed you the first night you arrived." Adam stroked her cheek and stared into her eyes. "I also wanted you to know that I cherish my memories of our first night together and not just the hours we spent in bed."

Gigi blushed even as her heart raced. She couldn't believe everything she'd ever wanted was finally happening.

"I cherish the memories of the two of us, sitting together in the hotel bar, just getting to know each other, as much as I do the memories of what came after."

Gigi swallowed, then gathered her courage. "So why did you leave me then?"

Adam closed his eyes, almost as if he were in pain.

"I'm sorry. I shouldn't have asked. I—"

"No." He shook his head. "You have every right to ask. I

honestly didn't know we were mates. What I did know was that you have a business in the city and I belonged here with my pack. I didn't think it would be fair to ask you to give up your life to join me here."

"Oh, but I love it here."

"I know. I was an idiot. The thing is I knew if I stuck around, I might offer to give up everything for you. I would, you know. If you need to go back. If you can't be happy here. We'll make it work."

"Oh, Adam. Yes, there are things I have to figure out, like what to do with the salon, but I don't want to go back to the city. My home is here, with you."

Adam's eyes lit up. "You make me so happy," he murmured against her lips, then kissed her.

Heat swept through Gigi as she clutched his shoulders and kissed him back.

"Come on." Adam broke off the kiss, then kissed her twice more before leading her out of the booth and back onto the dance floor.

They danced and talked and dance some more.

Eventually, they decided to leave JoJo sleeping on the pet bed Adam had set up for her in the corner of the bar and go for a run in the snow together.

Gigi had never felt so free as when she raced through the snow in her leopard form, chasing, then later being chased by her mate. The only downside was that she couldn't exactly hide in the snow while pink, which made ambushing her mate a bit difficult. That was okay, though. Getting caught by him was fun, too.

They frolicked and played as the world slowly brightened around them.

The sun was just peeking through the trees when Adam

and Gigi collected JoJo from the bar and the three of them walked home together.

Adam held Gigi's hand all the way to her door, where he kissed her and then handed her a bag. "Today's gifts. For the two princesses in my life."

Gigi peeked inside and found two princess crowns, one perfectly sized for JoJo.

"Here, let me." Adam took the smaller crown first, leaned over and nestled it carefully on JoJo's head.

Gigi giggled. "She's adorable."

Adam straightened and kissed her again. "Now for the other princess in my life." He took the second crown and carefully settled it on Gigi's head, then kissed her breathless.

Long, drugging moments later, he pulled away, kissed each of her hands and sent her and JoJo inside with the promise to return in time for lunch.

The following week was the happiest of Gigi's life.

Adam continued courting her and JoJo, leaving cute little gifts on their porch, joining them for breakfast each morning before heading off to work, then returning each evening for dinner and endless kisses.

When at the end of the week, he asked her to move in with him at the pack house and to officially accept his mate mark, she didn't hesitate to agree.

Which was how, just as she was entering her third month of pregnancy, she ended up traveling back to the city to pack up everything she owned to make her move to Jamesville official.

Of course, many pack members came along to help. With Adam insisting she not lift a finger and instead simply direct the rest of them, it was the most efficient and least stressful move of her life.

The hardest part came, of course, when they visited Furry in Pink so the women could meet Adam and so that Gigi could sign some papers. The women were pooling their resources to buy the salon from Gigi, who was planning to open her own salon in Jamesville, location yet to be determined.

The fairy mall where they'd gone Christmas shopping was a definite option, as was the empty storefront next to the witches' shop. Of course, Agatha and the women of the pack insisted the salon should be on pack lands, which would involve a brand new build.

Wherever it ended up, though, Gigi was thrilled to know that she had a built-in clientele ready to go and that Adam was quite insistent she not give up her dream just to be with him.

For being such a dick in the beginning, he'd turned out to be the perfect mate.

"Ready to go, love?" Adam hooked an arm around her waist and pulled her in for a scorching kiss.

Gigi lost herself in the moment and it was only when he pulled back and she heard all the women sighing around her that she remembered they were in the salon.

It took quite a long time—a flurry of hugs, admonishments not to be a stranger, a thousand pets and tears over JoJo, and of course, many teary goodbyes—before they finally managed to leave Furry in Pink.

Reaching the sidewalk, Gigi screeched to a halt at the sight of the carriage in front of them, Max once more in the driver's spot, this time Glory beside him.

"One last ride, my love?"

As JoJo bounded into the carriage and Adam helped her climb aboard as well, Gigi couldn't help but marvel at how much her life had changed in just a few short months. As Adam settled beside her, she met him with a kiss and a softly murmured, “I love you.”

“And I you, sweet Gigi mine. With all my heart, I love you.”

9

"MERRY CHRISTMAS!" PHOENIX cheered as Gigi and Adam walked into a packed Shenanigans 1.

"It's Merry Christmas *Eve,* my love," Travis called from the bar.

She waved her hand in the air and called back, "Semantics," then flung her arms around Gigi. "Girl, I'm so happy to see you. And you too, Adam."

She dropped to her knees to hug JoJo. "You, though, my darling, I am the happiest of all to see. Such a sweetie!" She popped back up and exclaimed, "You guys got your happily ever after just in time. Look!" She pointed toward the giant Christmas tree standing at the center of the bar, in the exact spot where Adam and Gigi had eaten dinner that glorious, magical night not so long before. "Christmas is here!" She threw up her arms in excitement, then without waiting for a reply, bounded away.

Gigi giggled.

"What a nut," Adam muttered.

"Oh, but look at this place, Adam. It's beautiful!" And it was. Glory, Phoenix and Travis had decorated the bar so that it positively sparkled with good cheer.

The Christmas tree was lit with different colors of lights and bulbs and beneath it were piles of gaily wrapped packages.

The menorah that had been lit in the days of Hanukkah still sat in its place of honor at one end of the bar and the kinara whose candles would be lit in the days of Kwanzaa to come sat at the other end.

Christmas lights were strung along every wall and miniature Christmas trees were scattered on tables everywhere.

A squeal from the bar drew Gigi's attention and she grinned. Travis had dragged Phoenix up onto the bar and was now kissing her beneath the mistletoe that hung there.

Now that Gigi was paying attention, she realized mistletoe was hung strategically throughout the bar and many of the shifters were taking advantage of that fact.

"There you two are." Agatha hurried over, grabbed Gigi's hands and kissed her on both cheeks. "We've been waiting forever for you to arrive. Come on." She dragged Gigi past the giant Christmas tree toward where the women and men of the pack were gathered.

Gigi glanced over her shoulder and saw Adam was following with a smile on his face.

An hour later, Gigi was sitting at a table, discussing plans for the new year with the women of the pack, when Agatha turned to her and said, "You know, this is the first time Adam has ever joined our holiday celebration here in the bar."

"Really?" Gigi glanced over to where Adam stood, laughing and talking with some of his friends.

“It’s true.” Betina joined the conversation. "He’s always been too busy working.”

“He used to say if he wanted to take Christmas Day off, he’d have to work long into the night,” Agatha said.

“But that’s ridiculous,” Gigi exclaimed. “He didn’t say anything about needing to work today. He took the entire day to spend with me.”

“Because you’ve made him happy, my dear. You’ve given him a reason to share the work load and to slow down.” Agatha blinked back tears. “You’re everything I ever hoped and dreamed of for my son. Thank you so much for making him happy, for being willing to give up everything to be here with us.”

“It’s not a sacrifice, Agatha. I love this pack. I love the people. And he makes me happy too.”

“Oh. That just makes it all the more perfect.” Agatha flung her arms around Gigi and hugged her tight.

“I love you too, you know,” Gigi said.

Before Agatha could reply, Phoenix came bouncing up. “Here you go. Drinks for everyone.” She distributed everyone’s orders, including a water for Gigi, but then passed her an extra glass. “And a Snow Kitty Special for my favorite snow leopard.”

The drink she handed Gigi was white as snow, its only other colors a swirl of what appeared to be chocolate and some sprinkles of what might have been cinnamon. It felt ice cold to the touch and looked delicious.

Gigi sighed and went to hand it back. “I’m sorry, but I—”

“Oh, don’t worry, Gigi. There’s no alcohol in it. It’s a special creation I made just for you.” Phoenix leaned over and whispered, “I hear you’re awfully hot these days.”

Gigi grimaced. "An understatement if ever there was one."

Phoenix giggled. "Well, you're gonna love this then. Go on, try it!"

Gigi took a sip and just about died at the explosion of delicious, sweet, soothing, *ice cold* comfort that slid down her throat. "Oh, wow. This is amazing." She took another drink.

"I know, right? I think I'm going to have to add it to the menu. Probably you'll be the only one drinking it in the middle of winter, but I see it becoming a big hit in the summer. I'm trying to create an alcoholic version as well. I haven't quite found the right alcohol yet, but don't worry. I'm sure I'll have it figured out by the time you can drink again." And without waiting for a reply, she darted away.

Adam and the rest of the men joined them a few moments later. Adam took a sip from Gigi's drink and made a face.

"Too sweet?" she asked.

"Too cold. How on earth can you possibly stand it?"

Gigi grinned. "It's your cubs. They're tiny internal furnaces."

"I guess so." He hooked a hand around her neck and pulled her toward him for a steamy kiss.

As the night wore on and the celebration continued, Gigi had never felt so blessed. Surrounded by family and friends, she had so much to celebrate beyond just the holidays: a new mating, three precious cubs nestled inside, and sweet hope for their joyous life ahead.

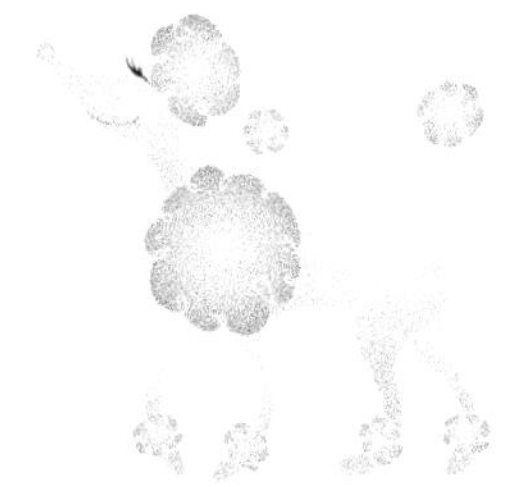

VALENTINE
Shenanegans

Edited by J.L. Troughton
PMG Publishing

1

"OH, COME ON, Val. You can't take a vacation now!"

"I don't see why not." Val continued packing, refusing to slow for even a minute. That was how her last three vacations became working staycations, because she kept slowing down to listen to her brother. Well, no more!

"It's our busiest time of the year! And you're critical to mission success."

"Which is *exactly* why I need a vacation." Val leaned her weight on the suitcase and wrestled the zipper closed. Flush with victory, she dragged the suitcase off the bed, setting it upright on the floor, then grabbed the matching shoulder bag and stalked into the bathroom. She scooped a bunch of cosmetics right off the counter into her bag, collected additional bottles from the shower, tossed in her hairbrush and zipped that bag closed as well.

"It's the most romantic time of the year, Val. You can't just walk away."

Val rolled her eyes and shoved past her brother. "Like you've ever given a damn about romance, Q."

"What are you talking about? It's the family business! Of course, I care."

"Okay, let me rephrase that. You care about romance as long as you don't have to *work* at it."

Q gasped. "How can you say that? I work in the business too, you know!"

Val raised a brow at Q. "Really? Because I'm pretty sure your definition of work is me doing all the work while you're busy flirting your way through the male *and* female populations of all the realms!"

"That's the point, isn't it? Romance. Love. I bring it to the masses!"

Val groaned. "I hate to break it to you, *Cupid,* but an hour banging some hot guy in a bar's bathroom is *not* the definition of love!"

"Hey, that hot guy walked out of that bar and met his true love the very next week."

"And how exactly do you think that happened, huh? That poor guy ended up on the broken hearts list and guess who had to clean up that mess? Me!"

Q let out a huff. "That's because you're good at that kind of thing, Val. You're organized and—"

"Seriously? Do you have any idea how difficult that romance was to manage? I had to hustle and figure out who his true mate was, then arrange for them to accidentally run into each other, which, by the way, wasn't exactly easy considering they were living in different realms at the time. And after all that work, who do you think got the credit for that epic romance?"

"Well, of course, I got the credit. I'm Cupid, the god of fornication!"

"And I'm Valentine, the demoness of romance! *I'm* the one bringing the love to Valentine's Day and all the other days of the year, I might add. But has anyone heard of me? No! They're too busy talking about *Cupid* and his stupid bow and arrow."

"Hey. My bow and arrow are awesome, thank you very much, though I do hate those idiotic pictures of me as a baby with wings. Humans are just ridiculous sometimes. And my arrow is not that small!"

Val snickered. Seriously, that had been the best practical joke *ever*. Who knew it would take off like that, spreading not just through the realms, but across all the timelines as well? Thankfully, Q had never figured out that his sister was the one who had whispered a bit of inspiration to the human who started it all. The next thing she knew, there were Cupids everywhere.

Of course, that had backfired too. Suddenly her brother was getting all the credit for the romances *she* was arranging. While he was slinging his arrows for sexual satisfaction, she was whispering words of love down the many timelines and pathways across the realms, creating romance while he generated chaos.

But who got the credit for all those happily ever afters?

Cupid.

And Disney.

"Seriously, Val, we need you."

"Forget it." Val grabbed her purse, shoulder bag and suitcase and headed for the door.

"Valentine's Day is next week! We'll never survive the holiday without you. Valentine!"

Val paused at the door, then shook her head and walked out.

"Val, please!"

"Sorry, Q. This year, you're on your own." She slung her bags into the trunk of her car and headed for the driver's side.

"But where are you going? How will we get in touch if we need you?" Q demanded.

Val grinned at him over the top of her car. "Hotel Shenanigans, of course."

Q scowled. "That tells me nothing! There are Shenanigans in every realm. Please say you're at least staying on the demon side of the hotel."

"Now why would I do that? This is a vacation, remember?"

"So which realm are you visiting?"

"Not sure yet. Maybe all of them." She winked and climbed into the car.

"All of them!" Q tried the passenger door and when he found it locked, knocked on the window.

At this point, Val had to admit she was rather enjoying torturing her brother, so she rolled down the window. "Yes?"

"You can't possibly be planning to visit all the realms. You don't have enough vacation time!"

"Well, considering I've never taken a *real* vacation, I could conceivably take the year off, if I wanted."

Q let out a gasp of horror.

Val giggled. "Oh, don't worry, Q. I'll be back before you know it."

His face brightened with hope.

"Not before Valentine's Day, of course. Actually, probably not even before St. Patrick's Day, but soon enough."

"At least tell me where you're going so that our parents don't freak out."

Val rolled her eyes. "I told you. I'm not sure. Definitely the Fairy Mall. I need some relaxation. From there?" She shrugged. "Who knows? Maybe earth."

Q looked entirely too relieved at that possibility, which was just ridiculous. Earth was one of the most interesting, not to mention dangerous, realms of them all, but Q never stayed in one place long enough to figure those things out. He was always moving on to the next score.

Still. She couldn't possibly leave him feeling relieved. That wouldn't do at all! With this in mind, she added, "Or maybe the dragon realm," and had the satisfaction of watching her brother's eyes widen with horror before she took off with a screech of tires, heading north toward Hotel Shenanigans.

The demon side, of course.

2

"VALENTINE!" GREGOR, THE demon working the front counter gave her a salacious grin as she walked up to him. "What in all the realms are you doing here? Planning to follow in your brother's footsteps and spread the love in person this year?"

Val grimaced at the thought. "Not even close. Taking a vacation, you know, getting away from it all."

"Wait. What?" Gregor exclaimed, a look of horror crossing his face.

Silence spread through the lobby as demons turned to stare.

Val rolled her eyes. "Vacation. Surely you've heard of it. You run a hotel, after all."

"Yes, but next week is Valentine's Day. You can't go on vacation now!"

"I don't see why not. My brother can surely handle things in my absence."

"Are you joking?" Gregor roared.

Val let out a huff of exasperation. Demons. They could be so damn hysterical sometimes.

"Oh, Val, darling, I-I really don't think that's a very good idea." Serafina slid up to the counter to stand at Val's side. "Really. Let's think about this. Maybe next month you can—"

"Next month?" Val whirled on Serafina. "That's what everyone said last year. Only then it was St. Paddy's Day and I couldn't possibly abandon the leprechauns and the Irish and the Americans and the faeries and the dragons—I don't even know why the dragons celebrate St. Paddy's Day, unless it's because of all the liquor—but regardless, apparently love is necessary to keep that much alcohol from causing endless heartbreak. So I was stuck, wasn't I?

"And everyone said next month again, only then it was spring when everyone was procreating like mad and somehow I was necessary for that as well, which is ridiculous because it's always spring somewhere in the realms. Then it was summer and everybody was taking vacations, which is also ridiculous because people take vacations all the time, but we all know that vacations are when families fall apart—too much togetherness or something like that—so romance is a necessity then as well, so demon knows I couldn't possibly take a vacation when everyone else was.

"And then before I knew it, it was the holidays, first in the dragon realm, then in the fairy realm, then in the troll realm, then in the earth realm, and I couldn't possibly abandon Cupid during the oh-so-important holidays, even though it's holidays somewhere all the time, so I stuck around some more and what do you know, suddenly I'm barreling toward Valentine's Day, *again*, and yet another year has passed without a single vacation day. And before you try to convince me that's not so long, how about twenty-seven *years*?

"That's right! Me! Valentine, the demoness of love and romance, hasn't been on a vacation in almost three decades. I'm so busy spreading the love and romance, there's none left over for me. You know why? Because I don't have a life! I'm too busy helping others find their true mates so they can begin their happy, procreating, indulgent lives, while over here, I haven't had an orgasm that wasn't self-induced in—in—in, frankly, EVER. So stop saying I can take a vacation later, because it's never going to happen, which is why I'm taking one NOW!"

Val panted and gasped for breath.

Damn.

That had been boiling under the surface for a long time.

Felt good to get it out.

Yep.

She felt a lot better now.

Lighter somehow.

With a happy smile, Val turned to Gregor, only to notice he was plastered to the opposite wall, a look of sheer terror on his face. "Whatever is the matter, Gregor?"

He didn't answer.

Val glanced to Serafina, but she wasn't there anymore. Val whirled around, searching for her, only to realize every single demon in the lobby was now clustered around the elevator, Serafina in the lead, stabbing at the elevator's buttons.

"Whatever are you doing over there?" Val called.

Serafina threw a terrified look over her shoulder, let out a tiny squeal, whirled back around and continued stabbing at the button.

"Seriously, Serafina." Val stalked across the lobby toward her.

Every other demon darted away, diving behind couches and chairs and tripping over each other to race down the hall toward the stairs.

Again.

Demons.

So damn hysterical.

Serafina, on the other hand, had frozen, one finger pressed against the elevator door's button, staring over her shoulder at Val with a look of utter terror on her face.

"What in all the realms is the matter with you?"

"Have you really been—um—I mean—um—no sex? Like none? Ever?"

"Okay. That was an exaggeration."

Serafina sagged in apparent relief and the demons fleeing stopped their flight to turn and stare.

"It's been, I don't know—" Val thought about it a moment. Truly. How long had it been? Way too long. "There was that one demon. Craig. But no. We just fooled around, no sex because as it turned out, I found his mate for him. It just didn't feel right. So. He was a good kisser, but no sex. Let's see that was—I don't know—ten, eleven years ago."

"Oh my demonic hell," some unknown demon muttered.

Val rolled her eyes. "Oh, don't be so dramatic. Let's see. So no. No one since Craig. And before that, no, not Jeremy, I found his incredibly hot mate in the dragon realm. Yes. Last I heard, they were so very happy together.

"Let's see, before Jeremy—" Val stopped and tried to remember, but honestly. She didn't think there was anyone before Jeremy. Was there? Oh, yes. "Then there was that idiot, what's his name. Oh. What was his name?"

"F-F-F-Fabiano?" Serafina whispered.

Val snapped her fingers and pointed to Serafina. Out of the corner of her eye, she registered a lot of demons dropping to the floor.

So damn melodramatic.

"You're right. Fabiano."

"But–but–you were–um–really young then."

"Yes. Let's see. Sixteen, seventeen. I suppose I should forgive him. After all, he was young too. We were each other's first. Still. A girl doesn't want to give it all away, only to discover what she got in return really wasn't worth it, now, does she?"

Serafina shook her head quickly. "It wasn't good, then?"

"Eh. That's when I decided I could take care of my own needs much better than fumbling boys. And that was all right *then*. For a time. But I'm the demoness of freaking romance and love! Where's *my* romance, I ask you. Where's *my* love?"

"You're right. You're absolutely right." Serafina dragged in a deep breath, then nodded emphatically. She seemed to be gathering her courage.

So ridiculous.

They were friends, weren't they?

Why on earth was Serafina acting so timid?

"You definitely need a vacation." Serafina hooked her arm in Val's and pulled her around so they were headed back toward the front desk, where Val noticed, Gregor watched their approach with something akin to horror. "Gregor," Serafina called as she dragged Val closer. "Val needs a vacation. Right now. And one that is preferably somewhere not here. You know, just in case, hm." She cleared her throat. "Never mind. Anyway, where would you suggest?" With that last question, she and Val arrived at the front desk.

Gregor swallowed and stepped closer. "Where would you like to go, Valentine?"

"Well, I think I'd like to go to earth actually."

"Earth? Why in all the demon's realms would you want to go there?" Serafina asked.

"Well, honestly, while I do have a lot of romancing I have to do among the humans, the earth shifters are really good at managing their own romances and matings. I really don't have to do anything at all. I think it would be relaxing to vacation with them. At Hotel Shenanigans in the earth realm. I seriously doubt there will be a single romantic issue that I have to manage there. They're all so happy, you know."

"Are you sure?" Gregor asked. "Lately, they've developed a number of ties to the fairy and dragon realms. I'm not sure dragons or fairies are very—"

"Romantic?" Val suggested.

"Right." Gregor nodded.

"Oh, they're not, but that's okay, because I'm pretty sure at this point, all the eligible dragons and fairies have been mated."

Gregor shook his head. "I'm sure that's not right."

"Okay, true. There are a few dragons, but that's perfect. After all, I'm not just looking to relax. I'm looking for a bit of satisfaction and from what I hear, the dragons are all about satisfying their partners, so, you know. Book me. Now."

"Do it," Serafina said. "The quicker the better. She's the demoness of love, for demon's sake. If she doesn't get a bit of love herself sometime soon, even if it's dragon love, you know she's gonna blow."

Gregor nodded and started typing like mad on his computer. "Of all the things the earth humans invented," he muttered, "this one is the most useful."

"Seriously?" Serafina demanded. "What about cars?"

"Forget cars," Val said. "What about vibrators?"

Gregor shuddered and quickly said, "There. You're all booked on the earth side. There's a traveler running that side of the hotel. I hear he's pretty laidback, but he's mated to a fairy, so you know, try not to get on his bad side. Better yet, try not to get on hers."

"Yes," Serafina exclaimed. "No flirting with the traveler."

Val rolled her eyes. "Who in all the realms do you think I am? I'm not the god of flirtation and fornication. That would be my brother, Cupid."

"Fine then," Serafina said. "Just don't fall in love with the traveler."

Val rolled her eyes, spun and walked toward the elevator, dragging her suitcase behind her.

"Or the fairy!" Gregor called after her. "Definitely not the fairy!"

3

THE EARTH LOBBY appeared to be deserted, though Val could hear noise coming from down the hall. It was rather loud actually. Someone must be having quite the party, which would probably explain the empty lobby, though not the man behind the counter. He seemed a little stunned.

"Hello." Val set down her bags and smiled at the man.

He didn't reply. In fact, he seemed incapable of speech at the moment, which really, now that she'd had a closer look at him, she couldn't understand why. He was a traveler, after all. Surely he'd seen a demon before.

"I believe I have a reservation," Val said, more out of curiosity than anything. She wanted to see how long it would take him to recover.

He didn't respond, just stared at her, a look of surprise on his face, which again, didn't make any sense at all. He was a hotelier, after all. And not just of any hotel, mind you, but a Shenanigans. He should be used to unusual guests.

Though now that Val thought about it, fairies could hide

their wings if they wanted and dragons had perfectly normal human forms. Plus if she remembered correctly, this hotel had been dormant for quite some time. Perhaps only fairies and dragons had made it back to the hotel so far. Or perhaps the Traveler was new to the position.

That would make sense, though it *was* kind of awkward. "It's the horns, isn't it?"

At that, the Traveler's eyes widened and he shook his head quickly. "No, no, no, of course not. They're quite lovely."

"Aw, thank you. That's so sweet." He was right, of course. Val had always considered her horns to be her best feature, but it was very kind of him to notice and to mention it.

"Sweet?" A fairy popped out of nowhere right next to the Traveler. "How dare you flirt with my man?"

Valentine chuckled. "Oh, no, I would never. You have me confused with my brother, Q. You see—"

"I don't think so! I doubt seriously your brother would be so obvious about it."

Val grinned. "You don't know my brother."

"And you don't get to flirt with my man!"

"Okay, that's enough, Lily."

"Enough? What's that supposed to mean, Harry? Are you saying that you *want* to flirt with her?"

"Of course not, you crazy fairy." Though his words were rather harsh, Harry had a huge grin on his face and the tone of his voice pretty much said it all. This was a man, Val knew, who absolutely adored his feisty fairy. She knew love and those two practically oozed it from their pores.

"Crazy fairy?" Lily's wings exploded from her back and she lifted off the ground and began to pace mid-air. "I'm crazy because you're flirting?"

"Of course not."

"So you *were* flirting!"

"Of course not. I wasn't flirting and you're crazy because you think I was."

"You were staring at her horns!"

"Well, yeah."

Val grinned and leaned against the counter. This was fun. She was so busy setting up romances and love, then moving on to the next challenge, she never really got a chance to see the aftermath when it was just beautiful and feisty and perfect.

"I can't believe you admit it! You were admiring her horns!"

"Does staring mean admiring in Crazy Town?" Harry asked.

"Of course it does! Everyone knows that. Wait—that's not what I meant. It means admiring in *every* town!"

"So when I was staring at the snot dripping from that troll's nostril the other day, you believed I was admiring his phlegm control?"

Lily made a face. "Ugh, that is so disgusting, Harry."

"I'm just saying. I was staring, not admiring."

"Lies! I heard you call them lovely!"

Harry looked horribly uncomfortable.

Val swallowed a chuckle. What a dilemma. Would Harry admit that he found her horns delightful and thus, anger his fairy-mate, or would he admit he'd been staring at her horns because he was horrified, having never seen a pair on a head like hers before, and thus possibly piss off his paying guest? Normally, in this situation, with most men, Val would bet he'd toss her horns under the demon train in a heartbeat.

This Traveler, however, seemed to be enjoying his mate's ire, so Val honestly wasn't sure what to expect.

"Well. Objectively speaking," Harry said, "I believe they probably are quite lovely. Just as objectively speaking, I find your wings to be exquisite in every way."

The look of fury on Lily's face faltered when Harry mentioned her wings, then disappeared entirely as he continued.

"The difference, my lovely Lily, is that while I can objectively observe the beauty of both her horns *and* your wings, my objectivity is not buried beneath an endless desire to stroke and caress her horns, the way it is when confronted with your wings."

"Oh, Harry." Lily reached out, grabbed his lapels and with an almost audible pop, disappeared them both away.

Val grinned. "I was definitely right about this place," she announced to the empty lobby. "No need for my skills here. These people have it all figured out." And with that, she vaulted over the reception counter and proceeded to check herself in.

Well, she *was* the demoness of romance and love. The ability to navigate hotel reservation systems was kind of a must in her line of work.

In fact, screwing up reservations so that two life mates were accidentally assigned to the same room was kind of her specialty. Hey. When it worked, it worked.

~

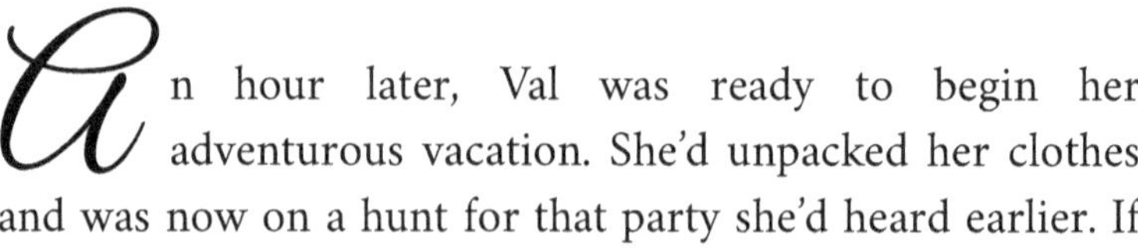

An hour later, Val was ready to begin her adventurous vacation. She'd unpacked her clothes and was now on a hunt for that party she'd heard earlier. If she couldn't find it or found it too dull, she'd make a new plan. Perhaps a visit to the fairy mall. Or to a different realm entirely. Or perhaps she'd explore the pocket of earth this particular hotel inhabited. It didn't really matter for she was quite certain she was about to embark upon the adventure of a lifetime. Considering she'd been planning and postponing this vacation for decades, she was certain it was going to be unforgettable.

That certainty became set in stone when she followed the sounds of revelry to a pair of swinging doors and discovered the hotel's bar. And like all Shenanigans bars, inside was a slew of interesting individuals from any number of realms.

Observing the various tables, she noted a few trolls, some fairies, a number of dragons and even some humans. Witches perhaps. And was that a demon running the bar? It wasn't exactly surprising to find a demon manning a bar. Demons were awfully fond of their alcohol, after all, but it was certainly unusual to see one in the earth realm. Humans here were incredibly superstitious.

It wasn't until Val had reached the bar itself that she realized the woman standing there, chatting with a dragon, wasn't a demon after all. She was something else. Something quite elusive.

The woman paused in her conversation and turned to Val. Her eyes widened slightly (those damn horns) before she pasted a bright smile on her face. "Can I help you?"

Val nodded, but didn't say anything. She was still trying to figure out what the woman was. All of Val's senses told her she was demon, but Val knew that was just a bit of glamour. Camouflage. What was she?

The woman cleared her throat, but before she could say anything, the man she'd been talking to faced Val and exclaimed, “Damn! Haven’t met a demon in a long time. What are you doing this side of the realms?”

“Markos! Be polite,” the woman said.

“Aw, Cassie, my love, don’t be ridiculous. A dragon has no need for polite when he can breathe fire at will.”

Cassie rolled her eyes. “I apologize for my mate. He’s ridiculous.”

Val grinned. “It’s all right. I’m used to that reaction, especially when traveling to earth. So what are you?”

Cassie looked surprised and the dragon, Markos, let out a soft, threatening rumble, which was when Val finally figured it out. Of course.

She waved her hand. “Never mind. I don’t know why I didn’t see it immediately. Earth chameleons are so incredibly good at their camouflage, better than those of the other realms, which is saying an awful lot, actually.”

“I’m surprised you figured it out,” Cassie said. “Most people don’t.”

“She’s a demon, love. They kind of specialize in seeing to the heart of individuals.”

Val let out a bark of laughter. “Yes, especially a demon such as myself.”

“Really? What are you?”

“I’m Valentine, the demoness of love and romance. You can call me Val.”

Cassie’s eyes widened. “No way. I didn’t even know that was a thing!”

Markos groaned.

Val’s eyes narrowed. “What?”

“You’re not here to mate-match, are you?”

“Oh, yes, please, say you are!” Cassie exclaimed.

“Sorry. I’m on vacation.”

"Thank goodness," Markos grumbled. "The women have been plotting for weeks."

"Really?" Val wondered what exactly that meant. The tone of Markos' voice made it sound like plotting was a bad thing, but that couldn't be right. It was always good to be prepared. Right?

"We're not plotting, Markos."

"I don't know what else you would call it. Inviting all those women here, just to parade them in front of Liel, like you're running some sort of mate market."

Cassie scowled. "I haven't invited a single woman here."

"No, you've just served them every time they show up."

"I run a public bar, Markos. It's not like I can refuse service, especially not to friends of people I know."

"So, who exactly is this Liel?" Val interjected.

"My brother," Markos grumbled.

"He's sad and lonely, Val."

Markos let out a grunt. "You're just assuming that."

"I am not! All you have to do is look at him and you can see it. He watches you with me and Zee with Ashlynn and he has such a look on his face. Yearning. Sorrow. I can't believe you don't see it."

Markos sighed. "You can't force a mating, Cassie. It will happen when it happens."

Val rolled her eyes. If *that* were true, she wouldn't have a job.

"I don't believe that at all, Markos."

Of course, it did tend to be true for shifters more often than not. Somehow they always seemed to find their way to their mate without Val's help.

"Just stay out of it, Cassie. I found you, didn't I?"

"Well, yes, but—"

Though there was that one couple. What were they again?

"And Zee found Ashlynn, didn't he?"

Salamanders? No. Dragons?

"That was completely a fluke!"

No. They'd been something unique. Rare.

"If Aiden hadn't—"

They'd been all alone in their world.

"That's how it works, Cassie. The stars align and mates are found."

Oh, yes, that's right. They were—

"Val!" Cassie exclaimed, interrupted Val's musings. "You have to help us!"

"Cassie, things are crazy enough." Markos scowled. "Besides, she told you already. She's on vacation."

"No, no, no. This is too important. Oh, my goodness. Kitty, Jessica! All of you, come quick." She waved to someone, probably multiple someones, over Val's shoulder.

Val didn't turn to look. She figured whoever they were, they'd join them soon enough and even though she was on vacation, there was no harm in appeasing her curiosity. Besides, these two were quite entertaining.

Markos let out a growl, leaned across the bar, caught Cassie by the back of her neck and pulled her into a scorching, hot kiss. He let her loose, grabbed a bottle of what appeared to be Dragon Flame, admonished Cassie to be good and muttered, "Good luck," to Val, before sliding off his bar stool and sauntering away.

4

AS USUAL, LIEL'S friends and family were giving each other shit. The shifters were teasing Logan about mating with one of their kind.

"I'm not really a shifter, you know," Kitty murmured softly.

"Eh, close enough," Dan said.

"Besides, that's not the point," Cole said. "Logan could have mated another fairy, but instead, he chose one of us!"

"Recognizing the superiority of our breed," Dan agreed.

"Not just any shifter, mind you," Cole said.

"But a feline, the best of the best!" Dan said, slinging an arm around Kitty's shoulders.

Logan scowled and knocked the cougar's arm off Kitty, then pulled her right onto his lap.

Despite her blush, Kitty snuggled close and landed a soft kiss on Logan's jaw.

"Please," Jessica muttered.

"You two are ridiculous," Megan snapped at Dan and Cole.

"If you really thought felines were the way to go, what are you doing with us?" Jessica snarled.

Dan's eyes widened. "Uh, you know we're just teasing, sweetheart. Of course, we think witches make the absolute best paranormal mates of them all."

"Exactly," Cole agreed. "No cougar in the world holds a candle to you, my love."

Megan rolled her eyes, then grinned at her mate. "Good save."

As the conversation around him continued, Liel tuned out. It was getting harder and harder to ignore the fact that everyone around him was finding their mates, but him. Well, okay, only two of his five brothers had actually mated so far, but they were the most important two. The two he'd shared a womb with and now a lifelong bond.

Turning his eyes toward where Zee and Ashlynn sat at the end of their table, Liel just felt depressed. Zee was so relaxed and happy, his dragon content in a way Liel had never seen before and that just emphasized his own loneliness.

Zee's laugh rang out through the room and Ashlynn grinned, then leaned into him and landed a kiss on his lips which in seconds turned fiery. Zee dragged Ashlynn onto his lap and the temperature in the room went up about twenty degrees in mere seconds.

Bowen, one of their unmated brothers, pushed away from the table, kicked out a leg and shoved Zee's chair a good foot. That it moved at all, with both Zee and Ashlynn on it, said a lot about a dragon's strength.

Zee ended the kiss and glared at Bowen, who just grinned at him and said, "I'd really rather not have my alcohol boiled.

Just saying." He lifted his now-steaming shot glass and downed it in one gulp.

Zee rolled his eyes, but surged to his feet, set Ashlynn back in her chair and pulled his own back to the table.

A year ago, if Bowen had done something like that, Zee would have taken him to the floor and there would have been a dragon brawl, the likes of which might have seen the bar burning to the ground.

This was what mating did for a dragon and Liel wanted that for himself. The bone-deep joy of a matebond.

At that moment, Cassie called out Kitty and Jessica's names.

Liel glanced toward the bar and his eyes caught on a woman in red sitting there. He could only see her from behind, but what a gorgeous view it was. She had tiny, delicate wings sitting at her shoulder blades. So small, he wondered what they were for as such tiny wings couldn't possibly lift her weight.

And were those horns?

Liel stared.

They were.

Tiny, red horns protruded from the top of her head.

She was utterly exquisite.

At that moment Markos stepped right into his vision, blocking Liel's view of the woman.

Liel scowled, then demanded, "Who is she?"

"Who's who?" Markos walked to the other end of the table, jerked out a chair, sat and poured himself a glass of Dragon Flame. The minute he let go of the bottle, Liel lunged for it and dragged it to his end of the table.

"Who do you think?" Liel demanded as he poured himself a shot.

"She's out of your league, buddy." Markos grinned. "In fact, if you plan on staying single beyond the next month, I'd suggest avoiding her."

"She's looking for a mate?" This was perfect. Not that he'd ever admit it to his brothers, but after watching them find their mates, Liel was more than ready to find his own.

Markos let out a bark of laughter. "Hardly."

Damn. Liel bolted back his shot and reached for the bottle again. "What'd you mean then?"

"She's Valentine."

Liel froze, then carefully set the bottle back on the table.

"Seriously?" Zee exclaimed. "*The* Valentine? The demoness of love and romance? *That* Valentine?"

"Yep."

"What's she doing here?" Liel asked.

"On vacation."

Well, that could work for Liel. Vacation time usually led to sexy times, right? His dragon needed to get closer to see if she called upon his flames. If she did, well, that would be just perfect. He wouldn't have to convince her since the demoness of love and romance should know right away if they were mates or not.

And if it turned out she *wasn't* his mate, well, she could set him on the right path to finding her. After all, it was her job, right?

"Don't even think about it," Markos said. "She's on vacation. Besides, I'm pretty sure the women are procuring her services right now."

Liel scowled as he glanced across the room. Sure enough, all the women were now crowded around the bar, talking with Cassie and the woman in red. Valentine.

"Who are they trying to set up?"

Markos shrugged. "Some poor bastard. Just be glad it's not you, buddy."

Liel wasn't glad at all! He couldn't believe his own sisters-in-law weren't appealing for help on his behalf. He scowled at his empty glass and poured himself another shot.

~

"You're kind of a bastard, you know that?" Cole leaned over to mutter in Markos' ear.

Markos grinned. "It's a bit of a specialty of mine. Besides, he deserves it after bribing Logan to flirt with my mate."

"Wait. You mean when Logan got Cassie to kiss him? Liel was responsible for that?" Zee let out a hoot of laughter.

Markos scowled at him. "Asshole."

~

"You'll help us, won't you, Val?" Ashlynn asked.

"I'm supposed to be on vacation, you know," Val muttered to the universe, but then she sighed. Who was she kidding? She had no idea how to leave the romance behind, despite her best efforts. So fine, she would work her magic one last time, but then, vacation all the way! "Okay," she said to Ashlynn. "Point me to this elusive Liel."

"Awesome," Jessica muttered.

"He's right over there." Cassie pointed across the room.

Val turned and stared at the table full of shifters and fairies. "Which one is he?"

"The one at the end. Dark hair, dark eyes."

That pretty much described a lot of the men at the table, but Val's attention focused on one. The men around him were laughing and chatting, but he was staring into his empty shot glass, an aura of isolation sitting heavily upon him.

"You're right," Val said, deciding then and there this was one match she wouldn't mind making at all. No one should feel that alone while in the middle of a bar surrounded by family and friends.

"About what?" Megan asked.

Val shook her head. "Just give me a minute." She closed her eyes and allowed her gifts to rise. In the dark, brilliant lines came to shining life. A thousand lovelines filled her vision.

She carefully navigated her way through them, seeking the ones belonging to the dragon, Liel. It took her a while to find them, but when she finally did, she could see he had so very many shining lines.

Lines leading to his brothers, his brothers' mates, friends there in the bar, lines leading out the bar and across the realms. Lines of friends, lines of family, but like with the majority of unmated shifters Val had met in the many years of her life, no loveline to follow.

But then—

Val's eyes flew open.

"What is it?" Ashlynn asked.

Val turned and faced the bar. "He's a typical shifter." Though not really. Why could she see only half of his loveline? It made no sense.

"What do you mean?" Cassie asked.

Val sighed. "Here's the way it works. When you connect with someone, you forge a bond. A link that is visible on certain planes. There are many bonds, not just of lovers or mates or true loves, but of siblings and parents and children and friends. It's a mass of bonds, often interwoven and intricate, often very hard to follow. One of those lines, or many of them, as the case may be, will lead to lovers, some of them true loves, some of them simply bonds of a tiny moment in time. Those I can usually follow as well. A true love bond is the hardest to find, the hardest to see and the hardest to follow when it has not yet been activated.

"This is especially true of shifters. It's like the bond hides until it's ready. I can actually see Liel's bond, which is unusual, but not the entirety of it. It's almost transparent and is barely there. It also just ends. I don't mean it's cut. I mean, it ends. I've never seen a bond like his before. It's okay, though. The fact that he has one at all means his mate is out there somewhere. We'll just have to do it the hard way, when it comes to finding her."

Cassie sighed. "We've been doing it the hard way for a month now. I was kind of hoping your help would mean shortcutting us to the easy way."

Val laughed. "If my way was the easy way, darling, then I'd probably be out of a job since everyone could do what I do. Which means there would be no need for a demoness of love and romance at all, which to be honest, could be appealing every once in a while."

Cassie scrunched up her nose. "I hadn't thought of it that way."

"So what do we do now?" Ashlynn asked.

"We search."

"Ugh. We've *been* searching," Megan said.

"Yes, we even cast a spell. It's worked before," Jessica said. "It brought Kitty to Logan and it brought Cole to

Megan, but so far no mates for Liel have walked through that door."

Val smiled. "No worries. My kind of searching isn't the typical kind. Besides, a spell can only go so far, you know."

"Oh, we know," Megan said.

"Well, I really think we should try the goddesses," Kitty said. "None of them have mates. I'd love to see Artemis happy and settled."

Val's eyes widened. These earth-beings were so interesting.

"I thought Artemis was with Orion," Jessica said.

Kitty rolled her eyes. "Propaganda. I assure you Artemis is with no one."

"I'm not sure a match with a goddess is the right way to go for Liel," Ashlynn said nervously.

Val grinned. That was an understatement if she'd ever heard one, but who was she to rain on Kitty's parade?

5

"WELL, KATIE–KITTY, it's quite lovely to see you, but this is a new one. I've been summoned for many reasons before, but never because someone wanted to, what did you call it, oh, yes, mate-match me." The look on Artemis' face was quite hilarious.

So far, this was the easiest job Val had ever had. The women already had a bunch of ideas about who might be a good match for Liel, so all Val really had to do was sit back and watch them work their magic. Of course, they were completely on the wrong track. All of their ideas were absurd, really, but that didn't mean they weren't also entertaining.

"Oh, please, Artemis. He's a really lovely man and he deserves an excellent mate. I was rather hoping it would be you."

"Katie–Kitty, my darling, you were always the sweetest of all my handmaidens," Artemis touched her cheek, "but I assure you, I am not meant for your Liel."

Kitty looked terribly disappointed.

"As for you—" Artemis raised an eyebrow at Val, who smirked back at her. "You're just messing with them, aren't you?

Val chuckled. "I couldn't help myself. Kitty was simply too excited that she might be able to set up the goddess she loves. I couldn't possibly tell her your line was as golden as they come."

"What does that mean?" Kitty asked.

"Not everyone is meant to have a true love or a mate, sweet Kitty," Val said. "And it's not because they're undeserving. It's because they are complete as themselves. A true love bond is only needed when it will bring a greater sense of completion to two individuals. The goddesses, well—"

"They're already complete," Kitty said.

"Exactly."

"Be that as it may," Artemis said. "I find this quite entertaining. I believe we should involve the other goddesses, just for fun."

Val winced. "Oh, I'm not sure that's a great—"

"They do love a good mystery. Besides, I've been contemplating my revenge and I think the time is now." With that, Artemis clapped her hands three times and just like that, three additional goddesses had joined their huddle at the bar.

"Seriously, Artemis?" Athena snapped. "I'm getting rather tired of you yanking us to your side willy-nilly."

"Well, Athena, you'll be quite delighted to know that if you succeed with meeting my demands on this stop, you will be let off the hook and no longer at my beck-and-clap."

"All of us?" Hera asked.

"All of you."

"Excellent," Aphrodite sighed, a look of relief on her face.

"Right, so see that gentleman over there?" Artemis pointed to Liel.

The three goddesses all nodded.

"Your job is to go flirt with him and all the other single dragons at the table."

Hera scowled. "Why?"

"Because we need to know who his mate is and you lot are going to find that out for us."

"How in the world are we going to do that?" Athena snapped. "We're not Valentine!"

"Please," Aphrodite said. "Where do you think she learned the family business, for heaven's sake?"

Val rolled her eyes. Any minute now—

"Valentine!" Aphrodite gasped, having finally caught sight of her daughter. "What are you doing *here*?"

"Didn't Q tell you? I'm on vacation."

"Yes, but here? On earth?"

"Indeed. I've found it to be the perfect vacation spot."

Aphrodite rolled her eyes. "Whatever. She always was the strangest child," she muttered in an aside to Athena and Hera, who both murmured a soft agreement.

Kitty and Ashlynn, who were seated on either side of Val at the bar, inched closer to her, quite surprising her actually.

She glanced at them out of the corner of her eyes and murmured, "Oh, don't worry. She's always like that."

"Well, come on, ladies," Aphrodite said. "Let's get this over with." She led Athena and Hera to the table where the men sat.

"I'm really not sure that's a good idea," Kitty said.

"At all," Cassie agreed. "Dragons aren't known for their patience."

Just as the goddesses seated themselves at the table, Liel grabbed his glass, stood and approached the bar. "Well, that's a wrench in the works," Artemis said, making Val snicker. These goddesses. They were so damn funny.

Just as Liel reached the bar, two other dragons showed up and shoved him out of the way.

"Hello, my lovely. Valentine, is it?" One of the new dragons lifted Val's hand in his and brushed a kiss across the top. "I am Yerel at your service."

"And I am Shepel," the other dragon, an identical version of the first, stole Val's hand from his twin and brush two kisses on top of it.

"We were wondering if you could work some of your romantic magic on our behalf," Yerel said.

A hand gripped both dragons by the nape of their neck and swung them around and shoved them off.

Liel turned and faced Val. "Sorry about that. I heard you were on vacation."

"I am. But I don't mind working a bit of romance on my down-time." What was she saying? Of course she minded! This man, this Liel, was simply too gorgeous to be believed. He scrambled all her thought processes.

"Don't be an ass, Liel." Shepel showed at one side of him.

"Or a cock-blocker," Yerel said as he arrived on his other side. "It's a lovely term, don't you think? Humans have such wonderful vernacular."

Liel rolled his eyes.

"I thought you wanted my assistance," Val said to the twins.

"We do," they said in unison.

"Are you sure? Because it sounded like you just wanted a bit of a hookup."

Yerel and Shepel looked at each other, then back at her.

She waited a moment, but neither said anything. "Okay, let's try this. Are you looking for your true mate or are you just wanting a bit of romance for the holiday?"

"Well," Yerel said, "Is romance really a requirement?"

"Yeah," Shepel agreed. "Can't we just order up some good old-fashioned lust?"

"Who exactly do you think I am?" Val demanded.

"The demoness of flirting and fornication?" Shepel asked.

"That is so annoying! Just because I'm the horny demon—oh, you know what I mean, the demon with horns—everyone always assumes *Cupid's* the one bringing the romance and *I'm* the one bringing the lust. Well, it's the opposite, I'll have you know. *I* am the demoness of romance and love. If you want fornication only, you'll just have to wait for Q."

"Q?" The twins chorused.

Val sighed. "Cupid. The god of lust and fornication."

"Wait, what?" They really had choral speaking down to a science.

"But doesn't Cupid—" Shepel began.

"—shoot people with the arrow of love?" Yerel finished his thought.

"Whatever. It's an arrow of *lust,* people, and he uses it indiscriminately so you might give him a wide berth should you come across him."

"So you can't set us up then," Yerel said.

"Absolutely I can set you up. I can try to find your true mate and bring the two of you together. Or I can just wave a little bit of romance your way and let nature take its course with whomever strikes your fancy next. But it *will* be romantic."

"Yes, but will it be lusty?" Shepel asked.

"Because what's love and romance—" Yerel began.

"—without a bit of passion to go with it?" Shepel said.

Val let out of a huff of exasperation. "Considering passion is usually a by-product of romance, when done right anyway, yes."

"Excellent," The twins chorused. "Set us up."

"For true love or just a bit of romance?"

The twins looked at each other, then back at Val. "Romance."

Val rolled her eyes. "Dragons."

It really wasn't that hard a job. Practically any single person in the room would do. All Val had to do was glance around and she could pick our three fairies, four trolls, seven shifters and two leprechauns who would do the twins in a heartbeat.

She sighed. "Together or separate?"

The twins' eyes got big. "Separate." They spoke so quickly, Val had to swallow a giggle.

"Male or female?"

This caused a bit of a pause as they contemplated their options.

Finally, Shepel said, "Female," at the same time Yerel said, "Male."

Which was quite lovely, actually. Since the possibilities she'd noted were of both genders.

"Any particular species in mind?"

"Surprise us," they said in unison.

Val rolled her eyes, then closed them. She pictured her gifts rising up, the red of romance and of love and yes, though she would never admit it to these two idiots, a tiny bit of lust.

She then set her wings to fluttering so the reds spiraled gently their way, and if they happened to filter through the rest of the room and impact everyone else there, oh well.

Everyone could use a bit of romance in their lives, now couldn't they?

Before things could get too out of hand, she grabbed a couple tendrils of red, fashioned them into romantic spears, hooked one end to each of the twins and sent the other ends spiraling toward their chosen hopefuls.

As if they could almost feel the spears' movements, the twins swung around and sauntered away, headed straight for the ones her spears had pierced.

"Damn."

Val's eyes flew open and she found herself staring into Liel's. Shoot. She'd completely forgotten he was there. Good thing her aim was so true. It would have been disastrous if she'd accidentally hooked him to a brief fling, when what he really needed, according to all his friends, was his true mate.

"That was incredible," Liel said to her. "Did you really just send them off to be romantic with some poor unsuspecting souls?"

Val grinned. "Trust me, those souls were *not* unsuspecting. More like hopeful."

"Okay. Then did you just send them off to break some poor, hopeful souls' hearts?"

"Eh, maybe?" Val shrugged. "But maybe they'll find their true mates along the way. Besides, a little bit of romance never hurt anyone, even if it isn't going anywhere."

"If you say so."

"So what can I do for you?"

"Well, I was wondering—" Before Liel could finish his thought, though, there came a commotion at the door.

"Oh, great," Jessica breathed.

"What is it?" Val asked.

"The Alpha Six," Megan groaned.

6

"DORY!" KITTY EXCLAIMED, bolting from her chair at Val's side to rush across the bar to embrace one of the women there.

Liel took advantage of the moment to slide into the seat at the side of the gorgeous Valentine. His dragon was quite agitated and he was finding it more and more difficult to control the urge to roar. He'd come awfully close to detaching his cousins' heads from their bodies. The only thing saving those idiots was the fact that Val had looked amused at their antics.

Now the Alpha Six were taking his mate's attention away again.

Wait. His mate?

Liel checked in with his dragon and found him fuming and snarling at anyone who got too close to the woman he perceived as his mate.

This was almost too easy.

He decided he was ready and then here she was.

Now all he had to do was get her to recognize him.

And kiss her, of course. Until that happened, he wouldn't know for sure that she could call his flames.

He turned to face her, only to discover in his inattention, she had turned away from him to face Kitty, who was happily introducing her to the Alpha Six.

Groan. This could take forever.

"It didn't even occur to me," Kitty was saying. "But now I think it could be Dory. Don't you think?"

"Dory!" Megan exclaimed. "Isn't she too old?"

"Hey!" Dory snapped. "I don't even know what you're talking about, but I'm not too old for anything, young lady."

Megan winced. "Sorry, Aunt Dory. I didn't mean it like that."

Liel had no idea what they were talking about, but he wasn't happy since it looked like they were settling in for a rather long conversation.

Val waved a hand, as if in dismissal. "Trust me. Age is immaterial when it comes to matters of love."

Liel rolled his eyes. Great. Now he had to sit here and wait while they mate-matched Dory to some idiot he didn't care about, when they should be worrying about mate-matching him!

Not that they needed to do that anymore since he'd found his mate.

Finally!

No thanks to them.

And now they were totally monopolizing his mate's attention, keeping her from realizing his own magnificence.

Liel glared at the women, then turned and rapped the bar to get Cassie's attention.

She smiled at him, grabbed a bottle of Dragon Flame and refilled his glass. "How's it going, Liel?"

He shrugged and bolted back the shot.

"Here's what I think," one of the Alpha Six said. He didn't bother to look, so he had no idea which one it was. "Dory *could* be his mate, but why would she *want* to be?"

"Evie!" Now that was Jessica. Liel recognized her voice.

"Seriously. Dory has always enjoyed a footloose and fancy-free life," another one of the Alpha Six said.

"A very good point," someone said. "I mean, it's not that I've never been with a man, it's just why on earth would I limit myself to just one for all eternity?"

That must be Dory herself. Liel grimaced at the thought. Like he wanted to be sitting here, listening to this.

He contemplated moving away, but was afraid he would lose access to Valentine the minute he gave up his bar stool. He was stuck there. Like a rat on a sinking ship.

"Aunt Dory!" Megan laughed. "You are so my hero!"

"Well, I for one, am thrilled you feel that way, Dory, since your lines are golden as well."

Liel's dragon stretched inside, roaring, reaching toward their mate's voice. He barely kept hold of him.

"Like Artemis?" Kitty asked.

"Exactly like Artemis."

"Really? You go, Aunt Dory!" Megan exclaimed.

Dory chuckled. "Thanks, darling."

"So I guess it can't be one of them, huh?" Kitty asked.

"From what I can see, the rest of you are all mated, right?" Val asked.

"Quite happily," one of the Alpha Six chirped while the rest of the women made sounds of agreement.

"We're running out of candidates!" Ashlynn wailed.

Liel rolled his eyes. Seriously. Who was so damn important to these women that they were desperate to find his mate for him?

Valentine laughed. As the sound rolled over Liel's senses, his dragon lunged to the surface again, and his shot glass burst into flames.

Cassie gasped and quickly smothered it with a dish towel.

None of the other women seemed to notice, but Cassie was now eyeing Liel with a speculative look on her face.

"There are more candidates in the realms than you can possibly imagine," Liel's mate assured the rest of the women. "Now give me a few moments, would you?"

An expectant silence fell.

After a moment, Liel looked up then to his left.

Valentine had turned to face him and was now giving him her full attention.

His heart raced to have her beautiful, dark eyes focused on him.

"What can I do for you, Liel?"

She knew his name!

Liel cleared his throat. "Um." Damn. He'd been sitting here this entire time, waiting for his chance to speak with his mate, and he hadn't used a single moment to figure out what he was going to say!

"Where is she?" A loud voice came from across the room.

Liel glanced over his shoulder, aware that Valentine was doing the same.

A trio of trolls stood in the door to the bar, glaring at a table of four trolls off to the side. One of those trolls pointed to the bar.

The new arrivals shifted their gazes to them and headed their way.

"Are you Valentine?" Their leader demanded, staring straight at Liel.

Liel's brothers and cousins let out shouts of laughter. Bastards!

"I'm Valentine," his mate said at his side.

The leader gave a grimace. "I was sure you'd be taller. Why aren't you taller?"

Valentine smiled. "I guess it's not necessary for my job."

"Hm." The troll let out a loud rumble, then announced, "I am Korana. I need help finding my mate."

Val sighed. "Doesn't anyone understand the concept of vacation?"

Korana looked terribly disappointed.

"Oh, all right." Val motioned to an empty table nearby. "Why don't we go over there to discuss things?"

Liel scowled as his mate hopped down from her stool. She was leaving him. Again!

Would he never get to speak with his mate without interruptions?

He whirled back to the bar, focused on a stack of napkins and let out a stream of fire. The napkins were engulfed in an instant, but his temper wasn't cooled at all.

Cassie dumped a glass of water on the smoldering ashes and raised an eyebrow at Liel.

"Oh, shut up," he muttered, then grimaced when Cassie's giggle had the unfortunate side effect of bringing Markos back to the bar.

Liel tried to ignore his brother and Cassie as they retreated to the far end of the bar and proceeded to make out there.

Damn. He really *was* in hell.

"Oh, now, don't be ridiculous. Hell isn't that bad, after all."

Liel shifted his gaze to the woman sitting next to him. She'd somehow managed to arrive without him noticing, and if he wasn't mistaken, she was—

"Aphrodite. And *you* are quite the man. Dragon. Whatever." She lifted one shoulder with that last word, as if to indicate it mattered not.

Liel gulped. Having the attention of a goddess just couldn't be good.

"Oh, darling, don't be so dramatic. Having the attention of a goddess is *always* good."

7

THIS WASN'T GOING to be quite as easy a job as the one for the twins, but then true love never was as easy as it appeared.

In fact, Val really wasn't sure about this match at all.

It happened that way sometimes, making her question the wisdom of the universe. Some love matches were just destined for sorrow.

Though that wasn't necessarily what she saw in this match.

Just perhaps a bit more enthusiasm than she was used to.

"So?" Korana asked. "Can you find him for me?"

"Oh, I've already found him." Val waved a hand. "That was the easy part."

"You did? That was so fast!"

Val shrugged "Yes, but the next part I'm afraid won't be quite that simple. Lots of arrangements will have to be made to bring you two together. I'll have to think on this."

"Why? What's so complicated about her match?" One of the other trolls demanded.

"Well, you see, Korana's mate isn't exactly in your realm. Or this one. Or any of the known realms, actually."

"How is that possible?" Korana asked.

Val shrugged. "You'd be surprised how many realms there are that are both everywhere and nowhere. I'll have to think on this. How to get you two to find one another."

"Why does that even happen?" the third troll demanded. "Matings across the realms? It's ridiculous! Talk about making a task impossible."

"Eh, it's just life," Val said. "Are you sure you want me to do this? I mean, your mate isn't exactly from one of the civilized realms."

Korana's eyes lit up. "Really? But that's marvelous. I'm always saying we've let civilization steal from us our heritage. We're trolls, not businesswomen and men. And yet, that's all we are anymore. It's quite terrible."

"Right. Well, you definitely haven't been matched with a businessman," Val told her.

Korana rubbed her hands together. "Excellent. Tell me he's the type to storm in here, take one look at me and throw me over his shoulders and cart me away."

Val grinned. She really shouldn't be surprised by now. The powers-that-be really did know what they were doing when they made their matches.

"You'd really like that?" Jessica leaned forward to ask.

"I would adore it!" Korana said. "It would be like a dream come true."

"Well, then, I guess you have nothing to worry about. Let me see what I can do." Val decided the most expedient way to make things happen would be to speak with her mother. Not that she usually went to mommy for help with these things, but she *was* on vacation and Aphrodite was right there. Might as well take advantage, right?

Val had no trouble locating Aphrodite in the crowded bar since she was still where Artemis had sent her and the other goddesses.

"This is not a good idea," Aphrodite informed her a few moments later.

Val rolled her eyes. "True love, Mother. It waits for no one."

"Yes, but, they're so dramatic and male and obnoxious and just, ugh."

Val grinned. "I know. But honestly, I think that's what she wants."

"Can't we just invite her mate? None of the others? Or even better, can't we just send her off to their realm and be done with it?"

"I mean, we could, but you know I'd have to accompany her there, just to be sure they find each other."

Aphrodite's eyes widened. "They're barbarians, Valentine! There's no guarantee they wouldn't claim you for their own."

At that moment, a deep rumbling growl sounded.

Val stared at her mother a moment, then in unison, they looked to Val's left only to find Liel standing there, arms crossed, scowling at Val.

"What's up, Liel?" Val asked.

"You are not going to some barbarian realm, to risk being captured there."

"Of course not," Val soothed him.

"What barbarian realm are we talking about anyway?"

Val just rolled her eyes and looked back at her mother. "What do you think is the best way to get him here?"

"Invitation. Free drinks. He'll come."

Val nodded. "Excellent. Do you want to send that or shall I?"

"Oh, darling, you're on vacation. Allow me." With that, Aphrodite clapped her hands twice and said, "Done."

"Thanks, Mom. You're the best." Val got up, winked at her mother, swung around, caught Liel's arm in hers and dragged him to the bar.

"Mom?" Liel said. "The goddess Aphrodite is your mom? But you're a demon. How is that even possible?"

"Half demon, half goddess, all woman." Val tossed out the same explanation she'd been giving for years before turning to the bar and calling to Cassie, "Do you have any Love Potion #9?"

Cassie giggled. "Is that an actual drink?"

"Of course it is."

"Is it really a love potion?" Megan turned away from her sister and aunt to ask.

Val grinned. "Haven't you heard? Any alcohol has the potential to become a love potion."

Liel let out a bark of laughter. "You've got that right."

"Well, I'm afraid since I've never heard of that drink and I know all the alcohol we have in stock, you're out of luck on that one," Cassie said.

"Okay, how about just a plain bottle of rum?"

"That I can do." Cassie grabbed an unopened bottle and set it in front of Val.

"Are you seriously going to drink some human spirits when you could have any spirit of the realms here?" Ashlynn demanded.

Val raised an eyebrow. "Not any spirits, apparently. But that's all right. Love Potion #9 is easily brought to any party."

"Really?" Cassie asked.

"Well. If you have a demoness of love and romance at the party, that is." Val focused on bringing her gifts to the surface again, then set her wings fluttering.

The bottle was enveloped in a red cloud and when it dissipated, the dark bottle of rum had been replaced with a squat, heart-shaped, red one.

Val twisted the top and removed it.

A puff of red dust exploded from the top, twined together to form a heart, then shattered into tiny dust particles that floated away.

Val leaned in and drew in a deep breath. "Exquisite." She then tipped the bottle and poured out two shots, one of which she passed to Liel.

She waited until he'd lifted his glass, then clinked hers against his and said, "To true love and romance."

She expected he would roll his eyes, but instead he smiled and repeated back to her, "To true *mates* and romance."

Dear demonic possession, that dragon was potent!

Val quickly downed the shot, which tasted as delicious as it smelled.

"Wow," Liel rumbled. "That's incredible. What's in it?"

Val smiled. "Love and romance, of course."

Liel chuckled. "Of course."

They were deep into the bottle of Love Potion #9, flirting outrageously, when the Grenik Horde finally showed.

The door to the bar banged open and seven giant men dressed in leathers and looking fierce poured into the bar.

"Holy wow," Jessica breathed at Val's side.

The men had two giant tusks growing from their lower jaws and were so large, they had to duck their heads and enter single file through the door. Once they were all inside, their leader led the way to the bar where he informed Cassie they were there for their free drinks.

Cassie looked horrified.

Before Val could intervene, or maybe explain, Markos seemed to appear out of nowhere. He vaulted over the counter to stand in front of Cassie and glare at the Greniks.

Ugh.

Shifters.

They could create drama out of nothing.

Val hopped onto the bar and quickly swung over it, dropping down in front of Markos who stood in front of Cassie. "I'll take care of this." She pushed the two of them back a bit, then turned to face the Horde. "Now, then, what can we do for you men?"

"Ale, now."

Liel let out a muted roar, then shoved his way in front of the Greniks so that he stood between the bar and the Horde.

Val rolled her eyes.

Men.

Seriously.

"What kind of ale would you like?"

"Acidic."

Val glanced over her shoulder at Cassie who shook her head. Val faced the Horde and said, "I'm quite afraid we're out of Acidic Ale."

One of the other Greniks let out a loud grunt of annoyance. "What kind of bar doesn't have Acidic Ale?"

The leader shook his head. "A pathetic one. Let's go, men." He started to turn away, causing a lot of the tension in the room to dissipate.

Well, that wouldn't do at all, now would it?

"I'm afraid we've never had a Grenik in here before, you

see," Val said quickly. "Now that we know you might visit us from time to time, we'll certainly stock up, of course."

The Greniks did not acknowledge her, but instead, headed for the door.

"Is there anything else we could get you in the meantime?" Val called after them. "A bit of rum or perhaps some Troll Juice. No? What about a mate? Would you like one of those, perhaps?"

The entire room froze.

The Greniks had almost reached the door, but now they all swung back around to stare at Val.

"What are you doing?" Liel hissed over his shoulder at her.

Val just smiled at him. "Don't worry. This won't take long."

"A mate?" The Grenik leader rumbled as he walked back toward her. "You can find us mates?"

"Well. Perhaps. I am, after all, the demoness of love and romance."

"We shall stay," he announced.

The other six Greniks with him nodded in agreement.

"And what would you like to drink?"

"The strongest ale you've got."

The next few hours passed in a bit of a haze. Lots of alcohol was consumed, to the point that Cassie became quite worried about her stock. "Are they paying for any of this, Val?"

Val grinned. "Of course not, but don't worry, the goddesses have it covered."

When there really was no more ale to be found in the bar at all, not human ale nor ale of any of the realms, Aphrodite came through once more, making a giant keg appear on the bartop from absolutely nowhere.

"What kind of ale is this?" Cassie called to her.

"Acidic Ale, of course. It took me this long to negotiate its purchase."

"Damn. Those Greniks have balls," Liel muttered. "Trying to hustle a goddess."

As far as Val was concerned, this was not good news. The only ones not even a little bit drunk were the Greniks and the trolls. Still, she wanted to give the trolls time to observe the Greniks, just to be sure this was truly the match Korana dreamed of.

"Now, listen up, Greniks," Val called out. "When this keg is gone, that's it. There will be no more ale to be had this side of the realms. Understood?"

The Greniks all let out a rumble, which could have indicated either agreement or dissent, Val wasn't sure. She decided to assume it was agreement.

By the time they were pouring out the very last drops of Acidic Ale, the earth shifters were all passed out, some of them in their shifted forms. Their witchy mates had posed them all in compromising positions, taken photos of them while giggling madly, then had staggered out, headed for home. The fairies had left soon after, Logan leading the way, with a cuddly, sleepy Kitty in his arms.

This left Cassie and Ashlynn, who'd been desperately trying to close down the bar for hours, the Greniks, the trolls and the dragons.

Plus Val and the goddesses, of course.

It should also be noted that most of the dragons were swaying in place, with the exception of Markos and Zee, who stayed close to their mates, determined to defend them if necessary, and Liel, who for some unknown reason, had stationed himself at the bar as Val's apparent champion.

Val took a moment as the last round of Acidic Ale was being poured to check in with the trolls, the mate-seeking three having joined the table of four.

Korana was beside herself with both joy and anxiety. "What if he doesn't like me? He hasn't even noticed me this entire time."

"You've been hiding in a corner, in the shadows," Val said dryly. "Every time he looked like he might be headed your way, you bolted to another part of the bar. While still sticking to the shadows, I might add."

"I know. I just wanted to be sure."

"And are you?"

Korana nodded.

"You're certain?"

"Absolutely, yes."

"All right, then. I'll make sure he visits this corner before they head out, but if you truly want him, you have to stand your ground this time."

Korana nodded. "I will."

"Excellent. Good luck."

Val started to turn away, but one of the other trolls blurted, "Do you think you might be able to find *our* mates too?"

Val rolled her eyes and without turning around, said, "Pay attention, lovelies. Your mates are *all* here tonight."

She smiled at the gasps behind her and started winding her way through the tables back toward the bar.

"You've really gone above and beyond tonight, my dear," Aphrodite said as she appeared at Val's side.

Val shrugged. “It wasn’t that difficult. They’re all in the same Horde after all.”

“You don’t fool me. That whole bit with the bottle of Love Potion #9. You sent a bit of magic the Horde’s way, to ensure the right seven were together when the invitation arrived.”

Val smiled. “I mean, why even bother if I’m not going to give it my all?”

Aphrodite pulled Val to a stop. “That, my dear, is why you are the greatest demoness of love and romance these realms have ever known.”

Val stared at her mother, stunned.

“What, darling? Did you think I never noticed? I am so very proud of you.” She pulled Val into her arms and hugged her tight. “Now, go make those matches stick.”

Val had almost reached the bar when the leader of the Greniks stepped in front of her.

Before the Grenik could say a word, Liel skidded between them, pushing Val back and blocking the Grenik leader’s access to her.

“Move, dragon.”

Val set a hand on Liel’s shoulder and leaned forward. “It’s okay, Liel.”

He didn’t move, so she looked around him to the Grenik and asked, “What’s up?”

“You promised us mates.”

“No,” Val corrected. “I promised *a* mate. One mate for one Grenik. Not one mate for all y’all.” Val was incredibly pleased with herself that she’d finally managed to find an opportunity to use that wonderful human phrase.

The Grenik let out a rumble. “We do not share. Show me this mate of mine.”

"Well, now, if you can't recognize her on your own, that would be quite disappointing for her. Don't you think?"

He glared at Val.

She pushed Liel forward, so that she could get closer to the Grenik.

Liel cast a scowl at her over his shoulder, but she ignored him and said to the Grenik, "Besides, your mate's looking forward to you carting her off in a storm of lusty aggression."

The Grenik's eyes brightened with anticipation. "Excellent," he grunted. "Then I shall go hunting." He spun and surveyed the room.

Val grinned as the Grenik prowled away, but then she noticed the rest of his men weren't following him. She raised an eyebrow at them. "Well? Aren't you going hunting too?"

They all looked surprised.

"You said just one mate," one of the Greniks said.

Val smiled. "Yes, one mate for one Grenik. There are seven Greniks here, so that means—"

"Seven mates?" Another Grenik asked, a look of delight on his face.

"Exactly."

The Greniks immediately swung around and studied the room.

Their leader was sniffing some of the shifters along the back wall.

"Happy hunting," Val said with a smile.

The Greniks each nodded her way, then began to prowl their way through the bar, peering into every corner and sniffing every being they encountered along the way.

Val grinned when she noticed their leader was getting closer and closer to Korana's corner.

With a sudden bellow of triumph, the Grenik lunged for

the shadows and hauled Korana into his arms. "Mine!" he crowed to the room, then tossed her over his shoulder and headed for the doors.

One by one, the rest of his Horde stalked toward the darkened corner where six other trolls waited to be claimed.

By the time the Greniks left the bar, each Grenik had a very happy troll slung over his shoulder and seven matches had been made.

The last Val saw of Korana, she had lifted her head and was sending a happy smile and a wave back into Shenanigans, clearly thrilled to be carted away by her mate.

The dragons, who had looked alarmed when the Greniks started grabbing trolls and had surged forward to intervene, froze when they saw how overjoyed Korana and her friends were, and looked to Val for guidance.

"Don't worry," Val said. "Their trollish dreams have just come true. Those are matches for the record books."

"Yes, quite impressive," Artemis said. "Honestly, most everyone in Olympus bet against you making that match. Quite a difficult arrangement."

"And yet, somehow, she didn't just make one," Hera said. "She made seven of them. How is that even possible?"

Val grinned. "You should all know better than to bet against me."

"True," Artemis agreed. "Which is why I just made a killing. I shall quite enjoy Zeus doing my laundry for the next week."

"You're going to make Zeus wash your clothes?" Liel asked incredulously.

Artemis shrugged. "I'll only make him do one load before I let him off the hook, but I will certainly enjoy torturing him for the entirety of that load."

"You do realize, he'll probably destroy anything you give him to wash," Aphrodite said.

"Of course, he will," Artemis said. "But I'm willing to sacrifice a few of my pretties just to teach him a lesson in humility."

Athena raised an eyebrow. "Do you really think that will work?"

"Of course not, but one must try."

Val didn't catch what the other goddesses said in return because Liel dragged her away at that moment, pulling her to a table off to the side, where he held out a chair for her, then after she sat, settled across from her and said, "So. I know you're on vacation, but I'd really like a bit of assistance."

Val raised an eyebrow. "What's up?"

"I was wondering if you might be able to find my mate. You know, like you did with the trolls."

8

IT WAS THE wee hours of the morning when Val finally made it back to her hotel room.

She should have been ready to crash, but instead she was feeling unsettled. She'd been surprised by Liel's request. She should be gratified by it. It would certainly make the mate-matching easier since he was so cooperative.

The problem was, well, she wasn't exactly sure what the problem was. Except that she'd started to entertain the notion that Liel might be her vacation fling.

But now he wanted her to find him his mate, which really made things rather awkward.

Though she'd already been planning to do that, so it shouldn't make any difference at all that he was now in on that plan.

Except it did.

It did because if she'd had a lovely fling with him and then arranged behind the scenes for him to find his mate afterward, he'd never have been the wiser, and she could go on her merry way.

But now that he'd *asked* her to mate-match him, it just didn't seem right for her to try and seduce him as well.

So now she was out of sorts, annoyed and horny as hell.

"Damn," she muttered. "I'm not going to get me any at this rate."

~

Liel was feeling out of sorts.

That last scene with Valentine hadn't gone as he'd expected. That damn goddess had steered him wrong. And she was Valentine's mother! He just didn't understand it.

It had seemed a good idea at the time. Ask Valentine to find his mate. She'd look for a second or two, then exclaim joyfully, "It's me! I'm your mate!" They'd kiss and she'd call his flames and he and his dragon would never be alone again.

"Ridiculous," he muttered to himself as he paced back and forth in his room. "Nothing is ever that easy when it comes to true mates. You should know that by now."

Still, all was not lost.

Val had agreed to help him find his true mate.

She'd warned him his mating wouldn't be as easy as the trolls' matches were.

"That was easy?" He'd exclaimed incredulously and she'd just grinned.

"Quite," she'd said. "Shifters are harder though. I can't usually see their lovelines at all, well not the matelines anyway. Yours is partially obscured. So it might take a while, to find your mate."

This was both fine and not fine. As long as she was searching for his mate, she wouldn't be abandoning him. But at the same time, as long as she was searching for his mate, she wouldn't be mating him either.

It was a dilemma.

Perhaps he should have just told her.

But what if she didn't believe him? A shifter had to feel it to believe it, but Valentine clearly didn't feel it at all.

He had no idea how demons bonded with one another.

Perhaps they didn't.

She was part-goddess after all.

He let out a huff and kept pacing.

This was a disaster. He had no idea what to do and that damn goddess was nowhere to be found!

~

Val was incredibly grumpy when she woke the next morning.

Too little sleep would definitely do that to you.

This was supposed to be a vacation!

But so far, all she'd done was make matches—nine in one evening, it must have been some sort of record for a non-holiday—and flirt with a dragon who wanted her to find his mate next.

Just the thought made Val exhausted.

She was supposed to be on vacation, damnit!

That's when she had a brilliant idea.

Why should she abandon her vacation plans just because she was mate-matching a dragon? Surely, they could both be done at the same time.

Oh, yes. She loved this idea.

An hour later, she met Liel in the lobby of the hotel as

they'd arranged and informed him they would be going to the fairy mall to begin their search for his mate.

The look on Liel's face was priceless. "Uh, why the mall?"

"It's a gathering place for people from all the realms. Maybe we'll get lucky and encounter your mate right away, but if not, we still might get lucky and someone your mate knows will be there."

"That would help?"

"Any connection at all will help. Magic can only go so far, you know. I'll keep my gifts on the surface and see what they recognize."

Liel looked doubtful, but he didn't protest, and thus began an incredible day at the fairy mall.

Val had been there before, spreading love and romance, of course. Never on vacation and never to shop. Always to work.

And okay, so they were going there for her to work today, as well. The only difference was she didn't really care if they found the dragon's mate. In fact, she'd be quite content if that hussy never came along.

Val made a face, horrified at her thoughts.

"What's wrong?" Liel asked.

She shook her head. "Nothing. Just contemplating all the possibilities. Come along then." And she dragged him into the shoe store she'd always wanted to shop in, but had been too busy for the pleasure.

"Why are we here?" Liel asked as they headed inside.

Val swung around and shushed him. "I'm sure there are potential mates right inside this store, but we're undercover which means we'll have to do some shopping. So here's the plan. I'll shop. You flirt." She spun and hurried to the racks of heels. She had no idea how long Liel's patience would last, so she needed to get in her shopping as quickly as possible.

Four pairs of shoes later, three in bags and one set on her feet—fairy slippers, of course—and she was just hitting her stride.

Liel wasn't in as great a mood as her. Turned out the two workers in the shop were also seeking their mates, something Val had extracted from them quite easily. They'd flirted voraciously with Liel, who wasn't thrilled at the turn of events (they were both male and he was rather traditional in his gender preference) but what upset him the most was that by the time they'd left the shop, Val had mate-matched them both.

"How can you possibly find mates for an incubus and a gnome within moments of meeting them, all while shopping for shoes, but you can't figure out mine? You're not even trying, are you?"

Val stopped in the middle of the walkway.

Liel continued for a moment, then realizing she was no longer at his side, swung around and strode back to her. "What is it?"

"I told you. I don't usually make matches for beings who shift forms. They tend to find their own mates without my assistance and all the tricks I use to find mates never work for them. So we're really flying blind here."

Liel looked like he was about to say something, so Val waited, but he just nodded and looked away. Oh, now she felt bad.

"Look, we'll figure it out. I promise. Dragons are not meant to be alone and when the time is right, your mate will surely show up. I'm not sure you even need me, but I promised, so I'm going to keep trying, okay?"

"Right." Liel nodded. "So what's next?"

"I think we should try a couple clothing stores. It's entirely possible your mate will be working one of those."

Liel let out a huff. "Fine. I'm sure that having a mate who works in retail would be quite wonderful. She could help me pick out my clothes and get me a discount. Bonus." With that, he started off again.

Val followed him, feeling as if she'd been struck.

Was he implying that having a mate who didn't work in retail would be a disappointment? She scowled, then realizing exactly what she was thinking, shook her head.

This dragon was driving her mad.

She just needed to make this match so that she could move on with her life, but instead she found herself trailing Liel by a couple steps, just so she could observe his exceptional ass.

Seriously. The man was hot.

And this was not helping her at all.

She hurried to catch up.

The next several hours, they walked through the mall, shopping and flirting, as much with each other as with the salespeople they met along the way.

Val even helped Liel choose a couple shirts in some brilliant jewel tones that he tried to protest, but she insisted made him look exceptionally hot. He didn't protest after that and as the day wore on, their bags and packages became a little hard to carry.

"We should get a basket," Liel said.

"A what?"

"A basket. For our shopping. It has wheels. Lily was talking about them, that she'd set an entire team creating them as fast as possible and now they're ready, but no one's using them. I thought she was crazy, but now I realize she's a genius."

"So where are these baskets?"

"Down at customer service."

So off they went to customer service, where they rented a basket.

"She *is* a genius," Liel muttered after handing over some cash.

Val had to agree once they dumped all their packages inside and she felt the tremendous relief of not having to carry so many bags anymore. Plus, there was still room in the basket for yet more shopping. It really was a fabulous addition to the mall.

"Come on! There are several stores on this floor I'd love to visit!" And she skipped forward, grinning at the rumble of annoyance Liel let loose.

As they continued their shopping, they were stopped over and over again as people asked about the basket they were using. They directed them all to customer service and before long, there were baskets everywhere.

"Yep," Liel muttered. "Genius."

It happened when they were shopping for dresses. Well, Val was shopping, Liel was looking bored. By this point, he was no longer even pretending to have any interest in flirting with the salespeople or even in finding a mate.

She was starting to wonder if he was really that committed to the process.

Not that she was.

Maybe she was rubbing off on him, which really wouldn't be good. If Val wasn't careful, she'd end up ruining her perfect streak. She'd never before failed to make a match once she'd decided to take it on.

Of course, she'd never tried to mate-match a shifter before either.

Except for that one couple.

But they were unique. And they'd needed each other so badly.

Still they were the only shifters she'd ever tried to match and now she knew why.

No more shifters for her.

Ever.

Well, at least not for mate-matching. For some love of her own, though, she wouldn't mind having this dragon at all.

But he was not for her and she needed to remember that. She eyed him where he was leaning against the wall as she flipped through a rack of dresses.

The man was seriously too hot for words.

Maybe she could borrow him for a while. Just for a short fling. While they were searching. Just until they located his mate.

She liked this idea.

A lot.

Grabbing a dress that was a deep red wine, Val skipped into the dressing room and quickly stripped out of the comfortable clothes she'd worn to go shopping: jeans and a red sweater. She kicked off her new fairy slippers, red, of course. It *was* her signature color.

She then slipped on the dress.

It hugged her form and showed off a hint of cleavage.

Though she'd not asked Liel's opinion to date, she wasn't going to miss this opportunity to set her plan of seduction in action.

She started to put the fairy slippers on, but they weren't quite the right shade of red.

Fine.

Barefoot.

She headed out into the store.

~

Liel was agonizing over his decision not to tell Valentine she was his mate. It was clearly the wrong choice. Maybe if he'd just told her, everything would be perfect right now.

Then again, if she didn't recognize *him* as *her* mate, it could have made things worse.

The problem was he had no idea how to get out of this ridiculous predicament of having hired his own mate to find herself. He'd honestly thought she'd just realize it, but that hadn't happened.

And now she was testing his willpower.

His dragon didn't understand why they weren't kissing their mate.

Frankly, he didn't understand either.

He was an idiot.

He was—damn.

Valentine walked out of the dressing room in a tiny red dress, barefoot, and all he could think was, "Mine." Which led him to remember the Greniks carting off the trolls and he was terribly tempted to follow their example, but he dragged in a deep breath and wrestled back his dragon.

Then Valentine caught sight of him and gave him a beautiful smile.

And that was all it took.

He shoved away from the wall and strode toward her, pushing her back into the dressing room, all the way back until she slammed against the mirror and he was pressing up against her, lifting her in his arms, wrapping her legs around his waist, tugging on her hair to tilt her head back so he could claim her mouth.

Mine.

~

One moment Val was contemplating seducing the dragon and how that might be accomplished when he was clearly determined to find his mate and not dally with some non-mate substitute, and the next she was writhing against the dressing room's mirror, clutching at her dragon's shoulders, kissing him back with every bit of roaring passion she'd been smothering for decades.

He pulled away for a moment and she gasped, "We should take this somewhere else."

"Yes," he growled, but then he was back at her, and long moments of drugging, delicious kisses followed.

"We can get a hotel room," she gasped in his ear.

"Yes," he growled, then dragged her to the floor of the dressing room and all thoughts of hotel rooms were obliterated.

An eon later, when their passion was spent, or at least paused, they clawed their way to standing and dressed.

Val had just slipped her feet back into her fairy slippers when Liel let out a snort.

She glanced up at him, saw he was looking at something over her shoulder, so she turned and couldn't quite contain her own giggle.

The dressing room mirror now boasted a clear, sooty

outline of Val, horns, wings and all. To either side of her head were the clear palm prints of her dragon.

Some women would probably be horrified because the salespeople were going to see that imprint and know exactly what they'd been up to in there, but Val was the demoness of love and romance, and she felt no shame at any expression of either.

Though, truthfully, she was starting to feel a bit more like her brother, Q, with all the flirting and fornicating.

She smirked.

Q would so proud of her right now.

"I'm surprised you didn't burn down the dressing room," she said as Liel led her back out into the store.

"Fireproof room," Liel said. "Fairies aren't stupid. A couple raging dragon fires when they first opened and they renovated the entire mall."

"And the dress?" Val raised an eyebrow as Liel collected their basket and led them to the counter, where he proceeded to pay for the red dress that had started it all.

"Fireproof as well," Liel said.

"Really?"

"Yep."

"Do *all* the shops here in the mall sell fireproof clothing?"

"Oh, no," the salesperson who was folding the dress and placing it into a bag for them answered. "We specialize in it. In fact, there are only a few stores like us in the mall."

"Huh."

Liel grabbed the bag and tossed it into their basket, then pulled Val out of the store. He led her through the mall and across a walkway into a hotel that wasn't quite the same as the one she had checked into on earth, but was definitely similar.

Liel groaned.

She glanced up at him, then followed his gaze to the front desk where Logan was standing, grinning at them.

"You know, I do have a room back on the earth side," Val said.

"Hell, no, all my brothers are on that side of the realms. We'll never get any peace with them butting in." Liel checked them into the hotel, all the while threatening the fairy with mayhem if he told anyone where they were, then dragged Val across the lobby to the elevators.

The next five days were the best of Val's life.

She couldn't understand how she'd fallen so deep for a dragon.

He made her laugh and filled her days with a kind of bright joy and hope, and her nights with a passion that burned into the wee hours of the morning.

They'd discontinued the search for his mate. She hadn't even had to make her pitch about it just being a fling until they found her. He'd just stopped mentioning the search for her and instead had devoted himself to making Val incredibly happy.

Liel had decided that she deserved a real vacation and so he took her on a tour of a new realm every day, then checked them into a fireproof room in that realm's Hotel Shenanigans every night.

Of course, Val had visited all the known realms in the past, and had even stayed in many of their hotel Shenanigans, but never quite like this. Before, she'd always visited with a purpose: to spread love and romance.

This time, however, she was visiting them as a *participant* in the romance, and incredibly, found herself falling in love along the way.

Liel took her flying in the dragon realms, which was the most amazing experience she'd ever had. She had wings that weren't meant for flight and she'd always felt that loss of opportunity.

But now she had a friend and lover who could take her flying, and did so, all the time.

And now she realized. She wasn't falling, but had already fallen. She was in love with a dragon whose mate she would one day have to get back to seeking.

It was total heartbreak and a thing of sheer beauty, the time she spent with him, the time she knew would someday soon be coming to an end.

That end came sooner than expected.

Valentine's Day was approaching and though she'd teased Q that she wouldn't be back until after St. Paddy's Day, she'd never really intended to abandon him on the most romantic day of the year. She might work from the hotel, rather than the offices, but she would still do her part.

This, of course, meant that she would have to prepare Liel for not spending Valentine's Day with her since she would be focused on bringing the romance to everyone else in the realms. Although if she were truly the demoness her mother thought she was, she would do everything she could to find Liel the mate he'd been hoping for.

After all, Valentine's Day was for the mated most of all.

As it turned out, Liel felt the need to return to earth to check in with his brothers, to see if Markos needed any assistance as he prepared for his upcoming mating ceremony.

And so, together, they checked out of their latest hotel, and walked to the elevator that would take them back to the earth realm.

They'd barely stepped off the elevator when Lily came flying across the lobby toward them. "It's about time you showed up!"

"What's wrong?" Val asked.

"What's wrong is you could have warned us. He's wreaking havoc! Flirting with everyone." Lily's wings were going a mile a minute and her arms were waving wildly as she shouted at them. "The shifters are up in arms. It's all I can do to keep them from tearing that god limb from limb. Not to mention Harry! Who knew that man could be so fierce?"

Val had a sinking feeling she knew exactly who Lily was talking about, but surely not.

He wouldn't dare follow her.

Would he?

9

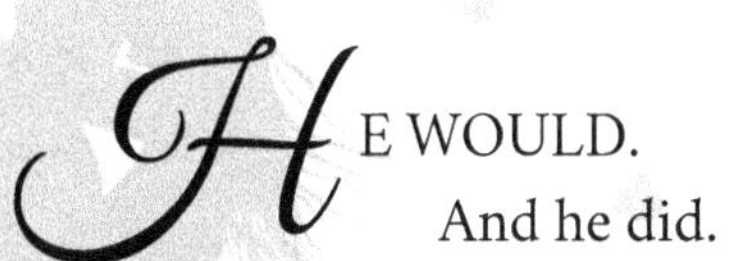

HE WOULD.

And he did.

Q had actually followed her, and upon arrival, had checked into the human hotel and as any god of chaos was wont to do, had driven everyone he met there crazy.

He did that by doing exactly what he was best known for: flirting and fornicating with everyone in sight.

One would think, given that mated pairs would be immune to his power, that he wouldn't bother with them. According to Lily, though, that wasn't the case.

Not that Val was surprised.This *was* her brother after all. Of course, he was going to try to tempt anyone he ran across.

This meant, of course, that he flirted outrageously with everyone, both the men and the women, as well as the mated and unmated.

Which, according to Lily, the women found hilarious. As a result, they flirted back just as outrageously, while their men glowered and growled and threatened Q with dismemberment.

Lily was apparently the only woman not thoroughly entertained. Probably because she was busy trying to protect Hotel Shenanigan's reputation as a neutral location for all the beings of the realms.

Of course, that was an impossible task when Q was around.

Val gave brief consideration to begging Liel to take her to the dragon realm to escape her damn brother, but then she would be abandoning the Shenanigans crew to deal with him. Possibly forever. She could totally see Q deciding to stick around, just in case she might one day return.

Val groaned.

There was no help for it. She was going to have to deal with her idiot brother.

"Where is he now?" she asked Lily.

Five minutes later, she and Liel walked into the bar, where they found Q holding court.

There really was no other way to describe it.

Val could never quite explain how Q managed to charm most everyone he met. There *were* exceptions, of course.

Shifters were less likely to fall for his charms, but on the whole, both men and women found him to be quite mesmerizing.

"Seriously, Q? What are you doing here?" Val stormed toward her brother, who was sitting at a table, surrounded by fairies, witches and even a few shifters. "I can't believe you're interrupting my vacation!"

Q looked up at Val in surprise, then gave her a huge, happy grin, flinging his arms wide. "Val!"

Val scowled at him, desperately trying not to be charmed by his obvious joy at having found her.

"I'm so happy to see you, sister, and I promise I'm not

here to interrupt. Come, join us!" Q waved at the already incredibly full table, then asked, "Could someone make room for my sister and her friend?"

Instantly, several women and men jumped to their feet and got busy increasing the size of their table.

Val sighed and accepted a chair for herself and Liel across from Q.

Once they were seated, Q smiled at them and said, "I decided to join you."

"So you're not interrupting my vacation, you're crashing it instead?" Val demanded.

"Well, if you want to look at it that way—"

"I do," Val snapped. "And what about all the romances? Valentine's Day?"

Q waved a hand. "All taken care of."

"Seriously?"

"Absolutely. I left Luc in charge."

Val gasped, horrified. "You did not! He'll make a mess of everything. There won't be romances. There will be mass murders!"

Q grinned. "That's the brilliance of my plan. I also put Michael in charge."

"You didn't."

"Yep. Made the fallen angel work with the archangel. It's brilliant."

"Don't call them that. You know they hate it when you call them that."

Q shrugged. "Hey. It's not my fault the humans have such distorted views of our kind. And I'm sorry, if I have to live with all those ridiculous cherub images and talks about my tiny slings and arrows, those two can deal with the angel rep."

"Whatever." Val rolled her eyes. "So what you're really saying is that if I want Valentine's Day to go smoothly, I need to clock back in starting in about eight hours."

Q shrugged. "More or less."

"Great." Val huffed. "Well, I'm not ending my vacation just because you're an idiot and can't handle *one* V-Day on your own."

"Whatever." Q waved a dismissive hand. "Introduce me to your friend."

Val sighed. "Liel, this is my brother, Cupid. Cupid, Liel."

Liel, who had started to hold out his hand to shake Q's, froze and turned to stare at Val. "Cupid? Your brother is Cupid? The infamous Cupid who sets up all the romances on Valentine's Day?"

Val scowled at Liel, but before she could set him straight, one of the fairies at the table, squealed, "No way! Q is short for Cupid?"

A man at the table leaned forward and asked, "Where are your wings?" That's when Val realized it was Shepel.

"Yeah, and your bow and arrow?" And that was Yerel!

Val leaned forward and was gratified to see the twins were each with the matches she had made for them the week before. In fact, the fairy who was speaking was the one she'd set Shepel up with.

"Are you going to shoot us with love and romance, Cupid?"

Val rolled her eyes.

"I'm pretty sure my sister took care of that for you, my dear."

The fairy's eyes widened. "She did?" She leaned forward to look down the table at Val. "You did?"

Val smiled. "Well. You are on the arm of a dragon, aren't you?"

"Yes! Yes, I am." She squeezed Shepel's arm and snuggled up to him.

Val tried not to roll her eyes at the indulgent look Shepel sent the silly fairy.

Men.

So damn easy.

"So you don't have a bow and arrow?" Yerel asked.

Dragons. So persistent.

Cupid grinned. "I do. I just don't like to bring it out in mixed company."

Val grimaced.

Liel chuckled, then murmured in her ear, "You should see your face, darling."

"He's my brother and he's an ass," she muttered back.

Val would never admit it to her brother, but she was actually happy to see him as well. They were very close and though she still thought he was an idiot, she always did have fun hanging out with him.

The hours passed in a haze of Love Potion #9 and Dragon Flame, friendship and laughter, and yes, even a bit of romance and love.

10

THE FOLLOWING DAY was Valentine's Day and Val announced she would be working from the hotel bar. She figured if she had to work on her vacation, she might as well do it with plenty of alcohol on hand and friends all around.

Q, of course, immediately announced he would be working there as well.

So they staked out their positions, at two different tables not too far from one another, and got to work.

Things were pretty quiet in the beginning for the bar wasn't set to open for hours yet.

"That couple is in desperate need of some good old-fashioned chemistry and lust," Q announced right before he sent an arrow of lust zinging across the timelines.

The problem was he arrowed it at the same couple Valentine was working.

"Q! They don't need lust. They have plenty of chemistry. Those two burn the sheets up when they go at it. What they need is some romance and love."

"I'm pretty sure they could do with both, sister mine."

Val let out a growl of frustration, but quickly fluttered her wings to usher hearts down the couple's loveline.

And so the hours passed, with Liel keeping Val hydrated with a constant supply of water and the occasional Love Potion #9, usually when he sensed her frustration with her brother was reaching an all-time high. He also ordered them plenty of snacks from the kitchen to keep her from passing out from hunger.

Hey, it had happened at least once before.

And of course, while Val and Q were working their magic, one or the other of them occasionally popping out to problem-solve a particularly difficult romantic entanglement, the bar opened and got busier and busier as word spread through the realms that Valentine and Cupid were working their V-Day magic in public.

As people wandered in, Val or Q, or sometimes even both of them, would take a quick peek and when the recipient was open and hopeful, would usher magic down his or her lovelines.

As the night wore on, Shenanigans became a hotbed of passion and romance, with love and lust leaking out everywhere.

A bunch of earth shifters showed up, apparently abandoning the other Shenanigans in the area, and the bar got even more crowded and louder and happier.

Flirting and romantic gestures skyrocketed, with flowers being delivered, wolves chasing each other and their own tails, shifters making out in darkened corners, sparks flying between mates and among the unmated, and in the midst of it all, a courting was happening that the dragons had just begun to realize was in full swing.

"Is Liel courting Valentine?" Ashlynn whispered to Zee from where they sat at the bar.

"What? No, of course not!" Zee swung around on his barstool and froze.

Liel was sitting next to Valentine, and though it was clear she was concentrating on the romances she was manipulating and that her mind was quite elsewhere, her body was leaning into his and he was gently playing with her hair.

No, not playing with it.

Braiding it. With—

"Is Liel braiding molten lava into Val's hair?" Markos asked incredulously.

Zee just stared in amazement as his brother exhaled an ongoing stream of lava that he manipulated until each portion of the stream hardened into the shapes he wanted.

"That is so romantic," Cassie breathed from behind the bar. "He's making her flowers."

"And leafy vines," Ashlynn added.

"And dragons," Kitty said.

It was true. Liel had manipulated a long trail of his own molten lava into hardened vines and flowers and was now braiding them through Valentine's hair. When he was finished, he affixed a tiny dragon at the end of her braid and another larger dragon on top of her head, its tail wrapping around her braid and its head rearing up just a tiny bit directly between her horns.

"Oh, no, he's not courting her or anything," Markos said dryly. "I can't imagine what you're thinking, Ashlynn."

As if in unspoken agreement, the two dragons abandoned the bar to join Liel and Valentine at their table, where they proceeded to torture and tease their brother endlessly about his clueless mate.

~

Val was aware of Liel's brothers joining them, but she was a bit busy and wasn't really paying attention until she heard Zee say, "So you found your mate and yet, you remain unmated. Explain this to me."

"Yes, please do," Markos said. "I seem to remember you mocking me for taking things slow with Cassie. And yet here you are, on the turtle train."

"Oh, shut up."

Liel had met his mate?

But he'd been playing with her hair, kissing her neck, even caressing her wings on occasion, not to mention taking care of her all day long.

Why wasn't he courting his mate instead of spending all his time with her?

Unless—

Val's attention stuttered and she almost sent agitation and dawning annoyance down the line rather than love and romance.

She wrenched her attention back to the job she was doing and focused on it as closely as she could.

By the time she'd finished manipulating the romance she'd been working and was back to just sending waves of love and romance along the timelines, powered by the movement of her wings, and was no longer targeting any one specific individual or couple, she'd managed to get her emotions under control.

It seemed rather unlikely, but evidence was suggesting that perhaps *she,* Valentine, demoness of love and romance, was mate to a dragon.

Was that even possible?

She'd never heard of a demoness of love and romance getting any of that for herself, but then again, there'd never been one such as she, a blend of her demon father and her goddess mother. Perhaps the rules were different in such a case.

Of course, this meant that Liel had kept this truth from her. But why? She couldn't understand why he wouldn't have just told her.

This called for a bit of revenge.

Val reached out a psychic hand and nipped just a bit of Q's magic.

"Hey!" Q complained.

She ignored him and twined a bit of the love and romance of her magic around the lust and passion of Q's, then flicked the resulting arrow Liel's way.

~

Liel sent his brothers a scathing look, but that just sent the two of them into gales of laughter.

How they could find this so funny, he had no idea!

He was courting his gorgeous mate and he wasn't sure she was even aware he was there!

Honestly, he was starting to think the Greniks had the right of it. Just grab your mate and abscond with her, quick as you can.

As the hours had passed, his courtship rituals had gotten even more elaborate. And she hadn't even noticed!

The lava was a mistake, though.

He just couldn't help himself. His dragon needed to mark

her somehow so the lava vines and dragons seemed the best way to go.

Unfortunately, working with his lava was what caught his brothers' attention in the first place and now they wouldn't go away. He glared at them while nuzzling his mate's neck.

She smelled delicious. Utterly divine.

The more he'd indulged himself with her over the past week, the less control he seemed to have. She managed to call his flames every time they kissed, but they'd gotten wilder and more and more out of control the longer they'd been together.

Then he'd tapped into his lava.

A monumentally stupid decision considering their mating wasn't yet solidified.

If he wasn't careful, she'd call his lava too and that would be a disaster.

He wasn't certain this hotel had lava-proof rooms.

Dear gods of all the dragons, it was hot in this bar, wasn't it?

Liel reached out and trailed a finger down Val's neck, following it with his eyes as it traveled over one shoulder, all the way down to her wings, then gently stroked along their fluttering edges.

Her wings stuttered for a moment, then sped up, fast enough that he withdrew his finger and settled it back on her shoulder.

A flush had gathered in Val's cheeks, but still she continued working.

With a sigh, Liel slowly trailed his finger down her arm all the way across her hand to the tip of one finger. He settled his palm against hers and linked their fingers together.

~

Damn.

It was heating up in the bar and Val was finding it more and more difficult to ignore Liel's scorching-hot touches.

He'd been caressing her off and on all day long, light touches, a gentle kiss to the top of her head or a quick nuzzle at her neck, but suddenly his caresses were firmer, hotter, more demanding.

The latest was when he'd settled something on top of her head and in the process had stroked gently at the base of both horns.

Dear gods and demons, he should have been a demon of lust himself, the way he was heating her up.

A firm stroke across her left wing and she almost lost her connection to all the timelines.

Her wings actually stuttered.

She did a quick check.

Everything looked good.

The soft pinks of romance mingled with the deeper reds of love and passion.

Well, perhaps there was a bit more passion this year than in previous years. Q would be so proud of her.

"How's it looking?" Liel rumbled in her ear.

She opened her eyes and glanced his way.

He arched an eyebrow in expectation.

"Pretty good."

"Good enough? Or lots more work to do?"

Val studied him a moment, noting the tension in his entire frame, the way he almost seemed to be vibrating with expectation. It was the look on his face, though, that sent a shiver down her spine and sent her body temperature skyrocketing.

She glanced over at Q's table to see him leaning into one of his groupies and whispering in her ear.

She grinned.

Yep. He was planning to abandon her all right, just like he did every Valentine's Day, when things started to really heat up after an entire day of spinning magic.

Well, for once, Val was going to be the one taking off early.

She grinned at Liel and said, "Definitely good enough."

Liel let out a whoop of joy, pulled her into his arms and kissed her. He then surged to his feet, without breaking the kiss at all, and strode toward the door, Val in his arms.

The last thing she heard was Cupid yelping, "Wait a minute. Val, you can't leave *now*!"

Too consumed by Liel's kiss to respond, Val simply waved a hand toward the room and enjoyed the unusually romantic moment of being carted away by her very own mate.

It was in the wee hours of the morning, after their passion and Liel's flames had blazed out of control for the fourth time that night, when Val was sprawled at Liel's side, feeling pretty good about life, that he finally decided it was time to talk.

"So," he said. "About finding me my mate."

Val scowled at the ceiling and waited, but that was all he said.

So she waited some more, but *still* that was all he said!

Seriously?

"Val?"

"Yes?"

"Oh." He cleared his throat. "I thought you might have fallen asleep."

"I was just waiting for you to continue your thought."

"Right. So." Long pause, then finally, "My mate."

Good demonic hells. Was he never going to get to the point?

After several additional long moments of silence, Val decided that no, he was not. So fine. *She* would start this ridiculous conversation.

"I'm afraid I haven't found your mate yet." Wait. That wasn't what she'd meant to say, was it? Ugh. She was as bad as him!

"Oh, of course not. I wasn't really expecting—"

"You weren't? I mean, you *did* ask me to find her."

"Well, yes, but—"

"But what?"

"Well."

Val rolled her eyes. "Okay, fine, I'll get back on the hunt tomorrow."

At that, Liel hauled her into his arms and admitted, "I don't need you to find her. I've already found her."

"What? And you didn't tell me right away?" Val said in her most dramatic voice, then pushed herself up from Liel's chest to stare into his eyes. "I can't believe you're cheating on your mate with me!"

Liel looked horrified, then spoke hurriedly. "No, no, that's not what I'm doing. I mean—" His eyes narrowed at Val's grin. "You're just messing with me, aren't you?"

"Of course I am. I'm your mate, aren't I?"

The look of relief on Liel's face was indescribable. "Yes, my darling, you definitely are. How long have you known?"

"I figured it out today when your brothers were teasing you."

"Oh." Liel's eyes widened.

Oh, yeah. He'd known a lot longer than her. "When did *you* figure it out?"

"Oh, you know. A while back."

Val studied his face and thought about what she knew of dragons. Supposedly, a dragon's mate could call its flames and that was how they knew they were destined to be. "You've known since our first kiss, haven't you?"

Liel winced. "I mean, I was absolutely certain then, but I honestly suspected from the moment we met."

"Argh. That is so annoying! Why didn't you just tell me?"

"Your mother told me not to."

"*What?*"

"Well, okay, she didn't say exactly that, but she *did* tell me I should ask you to find my mate. I figured she meant you'd figure it out when I asked, but then you didn't and I didn't know what to do."

"My mother told you to ask for my help."

"Well, I didn't know she was your mother at the time, but yeah."

"So you thought I'd figure it out right away, and that would be that."

"Yep. Only you didn't, so then I had to go to Plan B."

"What was Plan B?"

"I didn't have one."

Val burst into laughter.

"I've pretty much been winging it ever since."

"Well, even though I think you're kind of an idiot, I wouldn't change a thing."

"Well, I would."

"You would?"

"Absolutely. Valentine's Day is supposed to be the ultimate day of romance, but you, my darling mate, were sending the romance to everyone but me!"

"Oh, please," Val laughed. "You kept bringing me flowers, kissing my neck, rubbing my feet, and you think I wasn't sending any romance your way?"

Liel surged up and dumped her flat on the bed, then leaned over her. "Wait, are you serious?"

"Plus I kept leaning into you, kissing your cheek, rubbing mine against your shoulder. Did you really think we weren't caught in the midst of our own romance all day long?"

"I just figured that was a by-product of your work, not that it was intentional or anything."

"Do you really think I can't control my powers? Q might be an idiot, but did you see his powers of lust and passion leaking all over the place? Of course not."

"Uh, the shifters were all over each other by the end of the night."

Val grinned. "Are you serious right now? I've not been around very long, but even I've noticed that's not unusual behavior for earth shifters."

Liel thought about it, then shrugged. "Okay, valid point. So all the craziness at the bar tonight was just *normal*?"

"Well, plus it's a full moon. Also, I love you and that *may* have made my romantic conjurings a bit more potent than usual."

"Wait. What?"

"Did you really think I wouldn't fall in love with you after so many wonderful days wandering the realms with you? I love you, Liel."

"Hold on. You loved me even before you knew we were mates?"

"Love doesn't happen because of some predestined bond, Liel. It happens because we are worthy. And you are definitely worthy. So it's a pretty good thing it turns out I *am* your mate because if there was some other mate out there for you, well, she probably wouldn't survive an encounter with the demoness of romance and love."

Liel let out a chuckle. "Yes. Lucky indeed. So, on another note, don't you think it's interesting that of all the shifters in all the realms, my loveline is the only one you can actually *see*?"

Val's eyes widened. "That is interesting. What do you think it means?"

"Well, since mates can see through any glamour to their mate's true self…" Liel trailed off.

Val rolled her eyes. "It's so obvious. I can't believe I never figured that out."

"The only thing I haven't been able to solve is why you can't see the other half connecting to *your* loveline."

"Ugh. I'm such an idiot."

"What?"

"I can't *see* my own loveline. I've never been able to see any of my lines." Val surged up, dumping Liel to the side. "And my mother knew that! She set us up."

Liel chuckled and pulled her back down into his arms. "And what a setup it was. I, for one, am grateful." He rolled them over and kissed her. "And just so you know, my love, *you* are worthy too. Indeed, I fell in love with you right from the very start." He kissed her again and the world slid away in a brilliant blaze of fierce passion and love.

11

When Liel and Val walked into Shenanigans the next evening, the entire room erupted into applause.

Val stumbled to a stop, but Liel pulled her forward through the crowd of friends and family.

Along the way, they were stopped many times to hear congratulations on their mating and gratitude for a fabulously romantic Valentine's Day.

They also heard an awful lot of teasing.

Apparently Liel had left footprints of lava as he carried her out of the bar the night before. Those prints led all the way down the hall, into the elevator and onward from there to the fireproof room he'd gotten them checked into earlier that day. They'd discovered these prints on their way back to Shenanigans, so weren't exactly unprepared for the teasing, though they were both a little in awe of the lava stone prints that were completely embedded in the carpeting.

They were actually quite cool, in Val's opinion, though Liel seemed a bit embarrassed.

Personally, Val found that to be very sexy, both the lava itself and the hint of a blush in his cheeks.

They were laughing with his brothers and their mates when Cupid stumbled into the bar and was treated to the same cheers and gratitude, though of course, no congratulations for him.

Val expected Q would not be accepting those for many decades to come.

"Val, I kind of need your help again. I hope you don't mind." Cassie set a bottle of Love Potion #9 in front of her. "This is on the house if you'll just help me with a wee problem."

"What's up, Cassie?"

"It's my brother, Darren." Before she could go on, someone called for her attention and she hurried to the other end of the bar, extracting their promise not to go anywhere before she left.

It took a good while for Cassie to make it back to them and she had to explain her request in short intervals as she worked the bar.

"He's all work, work, work and no play ever since he took over the Coalition," she explained as she poured out shots and mixed drinks for Ashlynn to deliver.

"He's still coming to your mating ceremony, isn't he?" Ashlynn asked.

"Well, of course, he wouldn't miss that, but he's just so serious all the time. You can help, can't you, Val?"

Val sighed. "I don't know, Cassie. I mean, of course I can try, but people like Darren, well, they don't always want to meet their true love, if you know what I mean. It could be a disaster. Do you have a picture of him?"

Cassie pulled out her phone, found a picture and handed

the phone to Val, saying, "I'll be right back," before hurrying down the bar again.

Val studied it a moment, then closed her eyes and focused.

She sifted through the lovelines of the people standing nearby, until she could separate out those belonging to Cassie.

She then plucked them gently until she found the one that led away from Jamesville, stretching across space toward her brother.

By the time Val had followed the line all the way to Darren, all of the lovelines she found there were so incredibly faint, she could barely see them.

Taking a deep breath, she began the careful process of sifting friendship and family lines away from the one true mateline that belonged to the Luckiest Chameleon of them all.

Long moments later, she followed that mateline somewhere she never expected to go.

"Oh, dear," she murmured.

"What? What?"

Val's eyes flew open to see Cassie standing anxiously across from her, waiting impatiently. "Are you sure you want to do this?"

"Of course, why?"

"Well, you know, not every match is made in heaven."

"Huh?"

"Or maybe they are, but I'm pretty sure a number of them are made for the amusement of the gods, rather than the joy of the actual mate-matched."

"Oh, please." Cassie rolled her eyes. "Just because we've

met some goddesses and now a demon doesn't mean I believe they're really that invested in our trivial lives."

Val grinned. "Not buying into all the propaganda, eh? That's probably good. Still. It bears repeating. Not every match—"

"Yeah, yeah, but what does that *mean*?"

"It means your brother's lucky streak is about to take him on one hell of a wild ride."

~

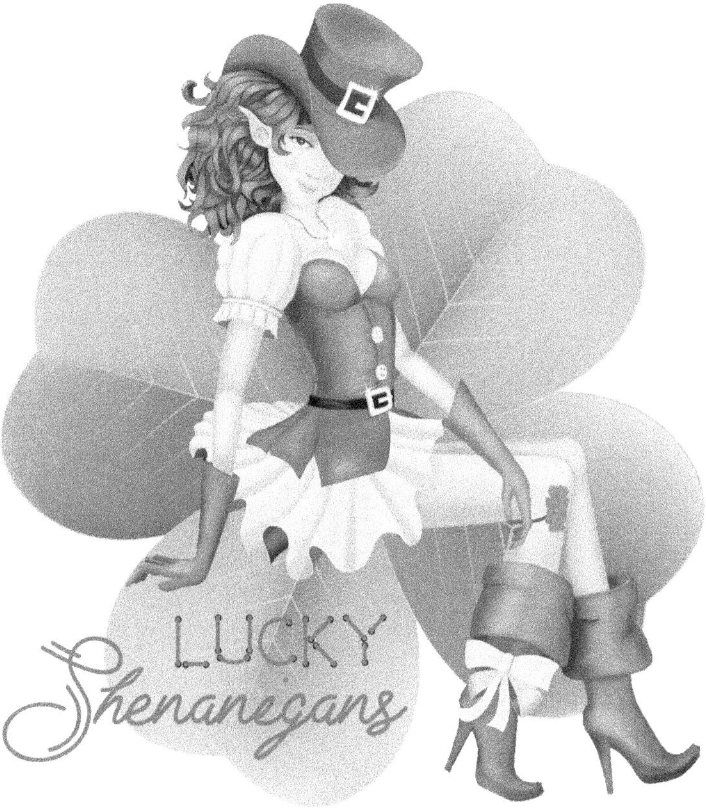
LUCKY
Shenanigans

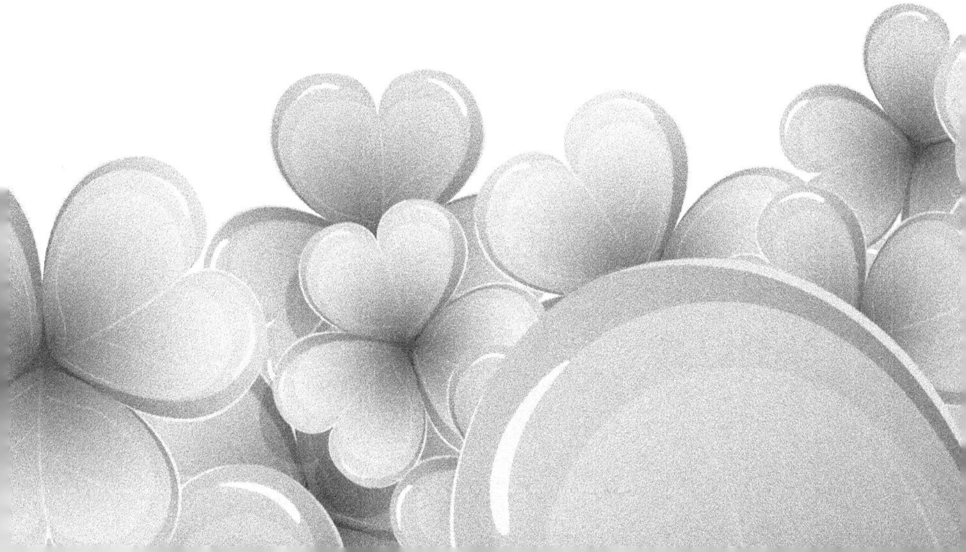

Edited by J.L. Troughton
PMG Publishing

1

"ALL YOU HAVE to do is convince the dragons," Lucky's mother said. "Should be easy enough."

Lucky groaned. "*Easy?* Have you *seen* the dragons? They're huge! And unlikely to be open-minded."

"Well, then try the fairies first," her father advised.

"The fairies?" Lucky exclaimed. "Are you insane? What if I get caught? They're vengeful and mean!"

"You're a leprechaun," her brother, Charming said. "We don't get caught!"

"Besides, we leprechauns have always gotten along with the fairies," her mother said.

"Yes," Lucky said dryly. "And that's why we've been banned from the fairy mall for almost three hundred years."

"Eh, semantics." Her mother waved a hand in the air as if to dismiss even the thought of their banishment, though it was the reason for this whole mission in the first place.

"The fairies were just making a point," her father said. "I'm sure they've forgiven us by now."

Yes, because fairies were known for being so forgiving.

"It really can't be that difficult, Lucky," her mother said. "The other leprechauns have already paved the way. All you have to do is show up, get the attention of the dragons and the fairies by tapping into your trickster instincts and everything will turn out just fine."

"My trickster instincts won't save me if the fairies catch me wreaking havoc."

"I told you," Charming said. "Leprechauns don't get caught."

"And certainly not by fairies or dragons," her mother said. "We're far superior to pretty much any other being of the realms. Besides, we're not just your *average* leprechauns. We're royalty!"

Lucky grimaced. Again with the royalty nonsense. "We haven't been royals in a century, Mother. No one uses our titles anymore. We *are* average leprechauns now."

"Don't be ridiculous. You're *still* a princess and nothing will ever change that reality, my dear. Now chin up and go trick those dragons and fairies into giving us everything we've ever wanted!"

"*Everything?*" Lucky exclaimed incredulously.

"Oh, just go already!"

Lucky smirked, flicked the space in front of her and zipped into the tiny fold she created there. A quick flick behind her and the fold slammed shut right in her brother's face.

She grinned as his angry shout followed her into the next realm.

Earth.

Why the fairies and dragons had chosen *this* realm, Lucky had no idea.

Well, okay, it probably had something to do with their mates.

In fact, it was because of these mates the leprechaun mission was a go in the first place. As it turned out, one of the dragons was mated to the manager of a Shenanigans bar. Even better, this particular bar was located inside a *Hotel* Shenanigans managed by the mate of a *fairy*.

Two incredibly lucky developments for the leprechauns since all Shenanigans were neutral territories, which meant the leprechauns finally had access to not just the dragons, but the fairies themselves.

This, of course, meant they now had a tiny pocket of opportunity to potentially reverse their banishment.

Or not.

Lucky was certain this mission the Leprechaun Nation had united to embark upon was doomed for failure. Still, despite her dire predictions and her enjoyment of torturing her family with her protests, Lucky was very much looking forward to this adventure.

She was absolutely certain things were going to get out of hand fast. Which in her world, equaled a whole lot of *fun*!

"Do you have any idea how unusual it is to see one leprechaun, let alone several at a time?" Markos demanded.

Cassie rolled her eyes. "Um, yes, I do have a bit of an inkling."

"You do?"

Cassie had no idea why Markos was so surprised to hear this. She ran a Shenanigans, for heaven's sake. "You know I worked at a variety of Shenanigans before settling here. And in all those Shenanigans, not once did I meet a leprechaun."

Markos huffed. "Those were earth-bound Shenanigans and they weren't even in Ireland. Of course, you weren't going to see any leprechauns there. That's not the point."

"He's right," Zee said.

"Then what is the point?" Ashlynn asked. "Because I'm as confused as Cassie."

"The point is it's rare to see a leprechaun at all, and never in groups."

"Exactly." Markos pointed to his brother. "They're up to something."

"Okay, did you ever stop to think that it might be connected to the fact that *this* Shenanigans is inside a *hotel* Shenanigans where all the realms converge?" Cassie asked.

"Plus it's a bar," Ashlynn said. "Don't leprechauns love to drink?"

Zee groaned. "You just don't get it."

"You're right. I don't," Ashlynn said.

"What does it matter anyway?" Cassie asked.

Zee and Markos looked at each, then back at their mates, incredulous looks on their faces.

"What?" Cassie exclaimed. Before they could respond, she held up a finger. "Hold that thought." She headed for the opposite end of the bar where she took a couple orders, handed out drinks, then headed back to her mate and their friends. "Okay, explain."

"Leprechauns," Zee said, "visiting *this* bar."

When Cassie just shook her head at him and Ashlynn cast him a confused look, he repeated, "*This* Shenanigans."

"Right. Where all the realms converge," Cassie said again.

"Cassie," Markos sighed. "*This* Shenanigans. A known dragon hangout."

Ashlynn and Cassie looked at each other, then back at their mates.

"So what?" Ashlynn asked. "Are they supposed to be scared of you or something?"

Cassie grinned. "Tell me you guys don't eat the leprechauns."

"What a horrible development that would be," Ashlynn said with a giggle.

"Is that a joke?" Markos demanded, a look of horror and disgust on his face.

"Of course, it was, darling." Cassie bit her lip to keep from laughing out loud.

He stared at her suspiciously.

"We're getting off track," Zee said. "Think about it a minute."

"I *am* thinking about it," Ashlynn said. "Dragons and leprechauns. Still don't get it."

Cassie shrugged. "I'm with Ashlynn on this one."

"Okay, let's try this," Zee said. "What do you know about leprechauns?"

"They wear green," Ashlynn said.

"They're probably Irish or maybe fairies," Cassie said.

"Or Irish fairies," the women said together, then grinned at each other and exclaimed, "Jinx!"

Markos stared at them a moment, then shook his head in exasperation. "What else?"

"Shoes," Ashlynn said.

"Shoes?" Cassie asked.

"They have those weird, curved shoes. And maybe they like to make them? Or eat them? I can't remember."

Zee let out a growl.

Ashlynn scowled at him. "Hey, don't growl at me!"

"Seriously? That's all you two know about leprechauns?" Markos demanded.

"Oh!" Cassie exclaimed. "Rainbows!"

"Oooh, and pots of —" Ashlynn broke off, stared at Cassie and they both said at once, "Ohhh."

"Tell me you're not planning to steal the leprechauns' gold." Cassie said.

Markos shrugged. "Hey. It's their responsibility to make sure their hordes are safe."

"Yeah," Zee agreed. "Especially from dragons."

"I don't think leprechauns have hordes," Cassie said.

"Probably because dragons keep stealing them." Markos grinned.

"Stealing is wrong!" Ashlynn admonished him.

"Plus they're leprechauns. They're like tiny, baby fairies. And you're dragons! It's a little unfair, don't you think?" Cassie asked.

"Unfair?" Zee and Markos exclaimed. They looked at each other, then burst into laughter.

"What?" Ashlynn and Cassie demanded together.

"That's hilarious," Zee said.

Markos nodded. "Next thing you know they'll be telling us not to be mean to the poor, innocent leprechauns."

Zee let out a snort of laughter.

"You know." A new voice intruded on their conversation. "Speaking from experience here: it's never a good idea to mess with the leprechauns *or* their pots of gold."

"Darren!" Cassie exclaimed, then darted around the bar and flung herself into her brother's arms.

~

Though Darren had seen Cassie several months before when he'd maneuvered the Council into visiting to make sure she was safe and happy, it had been an extremely short visit—their first one in years, in fact—and had been awkward at best. So when Cassie lit up at seeing him again and threw herself into his arms, for one long moment, he froze in surprise.

Then, muscle memory kicked in and his arms closed tight around her and for one too-short moment in time, Cassie was once more his baby sister and he was the center of her world.

"Ah, Cassie, it's good to see you, love."

She pulled back. "I've missed you so much, Darren. I'm so happy you're here and *early*!"

He smiled at her. "I thought it'd be nice to spend some time with my sister before her mating ceremony. You don't mind, I hope."

Cassie beamed at him. "Are you kidding? This is the best surprise ever!"

Darren chuckled. "I'm happy to hear it. So what's all this about leprechauns?"

Cassie waved a hand in the air. "The better question is what's with the dragons?" She turned and stared at her mate. "They're all wound up because we've had leprechauns drinking in the bar every night for the past month."

"The same leprechauns?" Darren asked. If it was the same group, that would probably be—

"Not at all," Markos said, motioning Darren to grab a bar stool and join them. "Different leprechauns every night."

"Okay, that's not true," Cassie said as she walked back around the bar. "They like to mix it up, so it's not the same group every night, but it is the same leprechauns week after week."

"How many are we talking about?" Darren asked.

"Hundreds," Zee grumbled.

"Are you serious?" Darren asked.

"He's exaggerating!" Ashlynn giggled. "It's probably no more than fifty total."

"*Fifty* leprechauns?" Darren exclaimed incredulously. "In one place at the same time?"

"See? That's what we're talking about!" Zee exclaimed.

"It's not fifty leprechauns!" Cassie said. "Stop exaggerating. It's maybe five or six a night. And okay, maybe over the course of a week it could be thirty or forty different leprechauns, but still."

"Six in one night?" Darren said. "That's not good."

"I told you, Cassie!" Markos exclaimed. "Even your brother agrees."

"They're definitely up to something," Darren said.

"Exactly!" Zee said. "And that's why we're going to steal their pot of gold. Serves them right."

"You don't even know what they're up to," Ashlynn said. "Could be something completely innocent."

Darren shook his head. "Not possible. Leprechauns aren't innocent by any stretch of the imagination."

"And how would you know that?" Cassie asked.

"Remember the Dublin con?"

"The one in Ireland that didn't go so well?"

That was one way of putting it."Yes. The only con I ever led that *failed*."

She nodded. "I remember."

"Well, I blame that failure on the leprechauns."

Cassie grinned. "Are you serious right now?"

"Completely. We didn't know it at the time, but we were targeting a family the leprechauns claimed as their own. Some weird connection from back in the 1300s. Ridiculous, really. But the leprechauns were quite put out."

"How did they figure out you were chameleons?"

"Oh, they didn't. They figured we were a rival band of leprechauns."

"Oh, dear."

"Yep. All I have to say is, it's a really good idea to avoid crossing the wee folk."

"Isn't that the con where Jackson came back with a broken leg?"

Darren grinned at the memory. "Yep. Like I said. Best not to cross them. Honestly, though, I rather enjoyed that development. Couldn't have happened to a nicer guy."

Cassie giggled. "You're terrible. Jackson's not that bad."

Markos let out a growl and Darren smirked. If there was one chameleon Darren knew that Markos hated, it was Jackson.

"Markos, don't be mean. Jackson's just... gullible."

Well, that was one word for it. The chameleon had been determined to mate with Cassie all because the Council had claimed they were destined to do so. The man never even questioned why if they were mates, he didn't miss Cassie when she was gone.

Actually, gullible was probably the right word for it. It was why the Council wanted him to mate with Cassie in the first place. He was too gullible to be a successful chameleon and Cassie had too much of a conscience. So the Council figured they'd pair the two of them together and minimize the damage so to speak.

Luckily for Cassie, she'd found her mate among the dragons.

Too bad Jackson hadn't found his.

If one of his chameleons had to leave the Coalition, Darren would have preferred it be Jackson and not his sister. But looking at Cassie now, as she leaned across the bar to kiss the grumpiness from her mate's expression, Darren knew this was the best possible result for her. He missed her, and always would, but that was okay as long as she was happy, which was all he'd ever wanted for his baby sister.

"Well, there aren't any leprechauns in here right now, so I guess maybe you were wrong about them being up to something, Zee," Ashlynn said.

That was when a bunch of leprechauns started popping into the bar out of thin air, one after the other. And they didn't stop at five or six.

Zee raised an eyebrow. "You were saying?"

2

MISCHIEF LEAPT TO his feet the instant Lucky appeared. “It’s about time.”

“Hurray!” The rest of the leprechauns cheered. “We get to go to earth now. We get to go to earth now!”

“Okay, calm down.” Lucky grinned at her fellow leprechauns. They got so excited about the silliest of things. “Haven’t you been to earth every night for the past several weeks?”

“Well, sure, but now you’re here and the fun can really begin!” Peppy exclaimed.

Lucky giggled. “Also, aren’t we already on earth?”

“Well, sure, but no one can see us, so it doesn’t really count,” Nosy said. “Look!” He pointed at the shimmering barrier that gave them the ability to see anything they needed to see without anyone knowing they were there.

Lucky stepped forward to stare across the barrier. “Is that Shenanigans?”

“It sure is. Look, there are already a couple dragons sitting at the bar with a phoenix, but don’t be fooled by the bartender. She's not a leprechaun," Brainy said.

"She's tricky," Loopy agreed. "We thought she was one of us for a while, and we were quite impressed."

"Yes," Nosy agreed. "We couldn't believe we'd gotten a leprechaun undercover at a Shenanigans."

"But then we heard one of the dragons call her Cassie," Mischief said sadly, "and that's when we knew."

"Knew what?"

"That she's the chameleon."

"Ah, the mate of one of the dragons." The woman was quite infamous throughout the realms. A chameleon who had managed to hide her true nature from the dragons themselves. Only her mate could see her true nature. The rest of the dragons, all of them, had believed she was one of them. A most unusual, most talented chameleon.

Oh, the tricks they could play with a chameleon such as she on their team.

At that moment, Charming popped in beside Lucky and whacked her on the back of her head.

"Hey!" Lucky smoothed her hair down and scowled at her brother.

"Don't hey me. It took me a while to track you down. I can't believe you left me like that."

Lucky rolled her eyes. Seriously. Her brother could get lost walking from one end of a four-foot tunnel to another.

"Prince Charming!" The rest of the leprechauns cheered, then immediately burst into laughter.

Ugh. Lucky almost gave herself an aneurysm, she rolled her eyes so hard. The Leprechaun Nation had ditched the titles more than a century before, but that didn't stop the leprechauns from using them around Charming.

They thought it was hilarious, as was quite evident from

the way they were all chortling and muttering, "Prince Charming," over and over again.

"Okay, that's enough," Lucky snapped. "Let's get this over with, shall we?" She started to step forward, but Charming caught her by the arm and hauled her back from the shimmering veil.

"Oh no, sister. We're doing this in style. Mischief, would you start us off please?"

Mischief beamed in joy, straightened his green vest, puffed out his chest and solemnly strode his way through the barrier.

~

As the leprechauns arrived, they swiveled to face each other, creating a line of leprechauns down the middle of the bar and then right in front of the doors a pair of leprechauns appeared.

One of the leprechauns was unlike any Darren had ever seen before.

"Is that—?" Markos began

"A lady leprechaun," Zee said. "I thought they were just a myth."

"Princess Lucky," one of the leprechauns shouted.

Darren could swear he saw the woman roll her eyes at that proclamation.

Surely not.

"And Prince Charming," another leprechaun bellowed.

This time, Darren was positive the lady rolled her eyes. He also thought she sneered a bit.

That was when the leprechauns began to chortle and giggle.

Though not, Darren noticed, the Princess Lucky or Prince Charming.

Instead, arm in arm, the two progressed solemnly down the line of snickering leprechauns, nodding regally to each one as they passed him by.

"I thought all the leprechauns were men," Ashlynn said.

"That's what I heard," Cassie said. "No females allowed."

Darren was too busy staring at the only female leprechaun he'd ever seen to respond.

She was exquisite!

Dressed all in green with a matching hat set at a jaunty angle atop a riot of red curls, she had a mischievous grin on her face and her eyes danced with delight.

Delight that is, until she heard Markos say rather loudly, "What kind of trickery is this? There's no such thing as a lady leprechaun!"

Her smile disappeared, her eyes narrowed and she said in a rather exasperated voice, "Tell me that ridiculous rumor isn't still going around."

"It's just a rumor?" Ashlynn asked.

"Of course, it is. How exactly do you think leprechauns are born if there aren't any females?"

Markos shrugged. "Eh, I just figured they were always one gender."

"I never really thought about it," Zee said.

"Asexual reproduction?" Ashlynn offered.

Princess Lucky rolled her eyes. "Whatever. Lady leprechauns *do* exist, thank you very much."

"We just don't let them out very often," Prince Charming said, slinging an arm around her shoulders.

Darren's eyes narrowed, annoyed at the thought that

these two might be a couple. He couldn't possibly be that unlucky, could he?

"Ugh. Get off me." Princess Lucky shoved Charming away from her. "More like we're better at hiding than our idiot male relatives."

"Hey!"

Darren grinned. This was promising. "So you're not—"

"We're not what?" The princess asked a split second before her eyes widened. "Oh, dear goddess of tricksters, no. He's my idiot brother."

"Hey!"

The leprechauns, who had all dispersed to tables around the room, snickered.

The princess smiled at Darren. "You want to grab a table?"

Darren leapt from his seat. "Definitely." He couldn't believe of all the paranormals in the room, she had singled him out. He led her to a table in a shadowed corner of the bar, thanking his lucky stars for his sister's mating.

~

Cassie grinned as she watched her brother lead the princess to a table. "I can't believe it," she whispered.

"What?" Ashlynn asked.

"Remember when I asked Val for help? I think it worked."

Ashlynn swung around and stared at Darren and the princess as they settled at a table in the corner. "Wow. That was really fast."

"No kidding!"

"Well, fine," Charming shouted, making Cassie jump. He

was glaring in his sister's direction. "I'll be over here. Drinking. Alone."

At that moment, one of the leprechauns shouted across the room, "Charming, drinks!"

Charming lit up and swung toward Cassie. "We need—" He glanced over his shoulder and took in the number of leprechauns in the room. "We'll say ten bottles, no, better make that twenty, of Tricky Charms."

Tricky Charms was one of those potentially dangerous drinks every waitress and bartender had to learn about in order to work at a Shenanigans, but Cassie hadn't had a chance to serve it until very recently when leprechauns started showing up night after night.

Now she had it delivered every week, along with all the other alcohols being consumed on a regular basis. She kept having to increase her order though because the leprechauns could put away some serious amounts of alcohol.

She'd also learned it was much easier to just leave the bottles in their boxes.

She stepped to the side of the bar and grabbed one of the boxes stacked against the wall there. She carried it back and set it on the bar. "There's ten bottles in there. I'll get you another box and start you a tab."

Charming grinned, grabbed the box and wandered off, distributing the bottles as he went. A few moments later, he returned for the second box, winked at Cassie and wandered away again.

"Don't you want any glasses?" Cassie called after him.

He just laughed and kept walking.

Cassie shook her head. "They never want glasses. I keep asking, but they apparently prefer drinking straight from the bottle."

"Leprechauns," Markos said, disgust in his voice. "There's no explaining them."

"I'm curious about Tricky Charms," Ashlynn said. "Have you tried it, Cassie?"

"No way. I've heard the stories. You can't have worked at a Shenanigans and not have heard them."

"What stories?" Kitty showed up, Logan at her side, and hopped onto a bar stool.

"Hey, guys!" Ashlynn exclaimed. "I was just about to try the leprechaun drink, Tricky Charms. Want to join me?"

"I'm not sure that's a good idea," Zee said. "After all, it's a drink made by tricksters."

"Oh, don't be ridiculous," Ashlynn said.

"I have to agree with Zee on this one," Logan said.

"You cannot trust the leprechauns," Markos said.

"*They're* drinking it and nothing's happened to *them*," Kitty said.

"Exactly," Ashlynn said. "Who's joining us?"

"Not I," Markos said.

"Nor me," Zee said.

"I'm out," Logan said.

"I guess it's just two Tricky Charms, for the only ones courageous enough to try it," Ashlynn said.

"Will you join us, Cassie?" Kitty asked.

"Not a chance." Cassie grabbed two wine glasses and poured their drinks. As the liquid sloshed into the first glass, a tiny charm appeared around its stem. A moment later, the same thing happened with the second glass.

"Look!" Kitty exclaimed, reaching for her glass. "It's a tiny shamrock!"

"Mine too," Ashlynn said, lifting her glass to stare at the charm.

Cassie rolled her eyes. "Yes, well, feel free to keep the charm. Just know that Shenanigans is not responsible in any way for those tricky charms. You should direct all complaints to the Leprechaun Nation."

Cassie had been required to memorize that warning when hired at her very first Shenanigans years before, yet even though this was the first time she'd ever had to deliver it, the words flowed off her tongue as if no time had passed at all.

To be honest, she wasn't exactly thrilled that the first people she had to deliver the warning to were friends of hers, especially since she had no idea what the repercussions might be, and neither of her friends seemed be taking it seriously.

Ashlynn was already unhooking the charm from around the stem of her glass and slipping it onto the corded necklace she wore while Kitty was adding her charm to a bracelet.

"I'm so glad I wore my charm bracelet today. It fits perfectly right here. See?" Kitty lifted her arm and shook it gently so that all the charms jingled merrily. "The shamrock's so cute!"

Cassie wanted to agree, but truthfully, she was afraid. And she could tell by the looks on the dragons' and fairy's faces that they were worried too.

3

LUCKY COULDN'T TAKE her eyes off the gorgeous man seated at the bar. He had dark skin and gorgeous brown eyes she could drown in.

She was supposed to be mingling with the dragons and the fairies, but it wouldn't hurt to add chameleons to that list. Right?

It was interesting that she knew he was a chameleon. The bartender, she would have thought was a leprechaun if her friends hadn't warned her otherwise.

This man, though, must not be a very good chameleon if Lucky could see through his disguise to his true self so quickly.

She couldn't resist inviting him to a private table, in the hopes of getting to know him better.

As he led her away from the bar, she could hear her brother being an idiot in the background, but she just ignored him. Something she was very good at doing.

"So you're a princess," the chameleon said as he pulled out

a chair for her—so charming—then settled in the one across from her.

"No," Lucky said. "The leprechauns sometimes cling to tradition, plus it makes them laugh every time they say 'Prince Charming,' and leprechauns do love their laughter."

The chameleon grinned. "I noticed. I'm Darren Prescott, by the way."

What a wonderful name. "And I'm Lucky, though not really. Or at least no luckier than any other leprechaun."

"And are leprechauns naturally lucky?"

Lucky shrugged. "Your guess is as good as mine. Is it lucky that we're so good at tricks or is it natural talent? I mean, we *are* leprechauns."

Darren laughed. "So, Lucky, tell me all about yourself."

That was how Lucky ended up spending her first evening at the Shenanigans in the earth realm flirting with a chameleon rather than making friends with the dragons and fairies.

~

"That's it," Markos said, slamming down his drink. "I'm going in."

"Wait, what?" Cassie turned from where she was serving a couple trolls to stare at her mate.

"Those leprechauns are up to something and I'm going to figure out what it is."

"I'll join you," Zee said.

Logan grinned, leaned over and kissed Kitty's cheek. "I should probably go with them. It's highly likely they'll offend the leprechauns and then where will we be?"

Kitty giggled. "Well, have fun, darling."

"You two need to be nice to those leprechauns," Ashlynn admonished as her mate downed the last of his drink and hopped off his stool.

Zee gave her an innocent look. "What are you talking about? We'd never hurt the wee folk."

"Never," Markos agreed. "It's their gold they should be worried about." With that, the three men sauntered off, crossing the bar to where Charming and a group of rowdy leprechauns were laughing hysterically.

Cassie shook her head. "This cannot be good."

~

Logan followed the dragon brothers, thinking they probably had no plan and were headed for disaster. Zee must have thought the same because at that moment he muttered to Markos, "So, what's the plan?"

"Get them drunk, then follow them back to their gold."

That was their plan? "You two are delusional." Logan darted in front of them and faced the dragons, forcing them to halt. "You do realize leprechauns are master tricksters. They'll see you coming a mile away. Not to mention, they may get drunk—all the time, mind you—but they never lose their wits. And frankly, attempting to follow a leprechaun is an exercise in futility."

"You've never seen us in action," Zee said.

"Exactly!" Markos agreed. "Just watch and learn, fairy. Watch and learn."

The dragons diverged, moving around Logan and making a beeline for the closest table of leprechauns.

Logan closed his eyes, shook his head, then spun and followed the idiots to their doom.

~

As far as Markos was concerned, he and Zee were quite smart in their approach. They offered to buy the leprechauns a drink and were instantly invited to join them. Their mistake was offering to share a bottle of Dragon Flame, which meant in order to be polite, they had to accept the offer of Tricky Charms in return.

Markos was rather relieved when Charming produced a couple glasses for the dragons, which was very nice of him. Markos had worried for a moment that he'd be expected to swig from one of the communal bottles. So he happily accepted his glass of Tricky Charms and discovered to his surprise that he quite liked it.

Of course, he ignored the tiny charm that appeared on his glass. After all, he *was* a dragon. Too smart for trickery, even though the thought of adding the charm to his horde was rather tempting, especially since it was in the shape of a tiny flame. Still, he wasn't going to fall for temptation like the women did. He was actually feeling quite superior about it when he noticed his brother carefully extracting the charm from his own glass.

"Zee!" Markos exclaimed.

"For Ashlynn," Zee said as he shoved the charm into the pocket of his jeans.

Markos worried at first that something might happen, but as the hours passed and Zee's jeans didn't burst into flames (which honestly would have been quite hilarious considering Zee was a dragon wearing fireproof clothing), Markos decided he was just being paranoid. That didn't make him change his mind about his own charm, though.

Better safe than sorry, he figured.

As the hours passed, Markos decided that Charming was aptly named, for all the leprechauns had a fair bit of charm, not to mention they were entirely hilarious. They told endless jokes and ridiculous stories and generally kept everyone in their vicinity laughing all night long.

Laughing and drinking, that is.

In other words, they were all becoming increasingly drunk.

Tricky Charms turned out to be quite the potent drink and much to the dragons' chagrin, the leprechauns kept pace with their drinking all night long.

Kitty and Logan retired for the night several hours before closing, Logan leaving the dragons with one final admonishment. "Don't get too drunk and whatever you do, don't let the leprechauns take you with them."

Markos and Zee just laughed.

"Take us with them?" Markos exclaimed. "Isn't that what we want them to do?" He looked at Zee, who grinned drunkenly and shrugged.

Logan just shook his head and walked out with his arm slung around Kitty's shoulders, his head bent to murmur who-knew-what in her ear.

Markos figured it was probably sexy talk to get his mate in the mood or trash talk about the dragons' probability of success.

Possibly both.

That was okay though. The fairy would learn eventually that dragons never gave up.

Even when their mates demanded it.

Ashlynn had tried to convince Zee to leave when Logan and Kitty did, but he just dragged her into his lap and kissed her until she curled up quite happily and fell asleep in his arms.

Of course, she was supposed to be waitressing, but Cassie just grinned and announced that everyone would need to come to the bar for any future drinks.

Finally, last call arrived and it was time for the dragons to implement their plan.

Markos found himself a little conflicted, though, when it came time to actually follow the leprechauns. Usually he stuck around while Cassie closed down the bar, but that night, they had a mission. As the bar crowd began to thin out, he made a beeline for Cassie.

"You're going the wrong way, Markos." Zee hurried after him, dragging a sluggish Ashlynn in his wake. "The leprechauns are crazy fast. We don't have time for romance!"

"Hey!" Ashlynn exclaimed.

"It's true," Zee said. "Look around you."

Markos groaned. Zee was right. Half the leprechauns were already gone, even though Markos hadn't seen a single one actually leave.

At that moment, a commotion caught their attention, as Charming and a group of leprechauns snagged Princess Lucky from a table across the room, surrounded her and headed for the door, leaving Darren behind.

"Huh," Markos said. "Didn't know Darren was still here."

"Those are the last of the leprechauns," Zee hissed. "If we're going to follow them, we have to go now."

"Right," Markos said. "Hey, Darren, help Cassie shut down the bar, would you?" He then spun to face the door, staggering a bit as he did so.

Not because he was drunk or anything.

He'd just moved too fast, that was all. "Come on!"

Zee grinned. “Excellent.”

“Love you, Cassie,” Markos called over his shoulder, almost stumbling over his own feet in his haste to follow the leprechauns. “Back soon.”

Cassie was busy counting money and just waved him on.

Markos stumbled out of the bar and screeched to a halt. Zee slammed into him from behind, then shoved him forward as Ashlynn slammed into both of them.

“Where’d they go?” Markos spun in a circle, stumbled into a wall, then righted himself.

The leprechauns had literally exited a split second before them and yet, the hall outside the bar was completely deserted. Not a single leprechaun in sight.

“I told you we didn’t have time for romance,” Zee growled.

“Whatever,” Markos said. “I’m going to go help Cassie. We’ll try again tomorrow.” He headed back into the bar, fuming that the leprechauns had managed to escape him after all. Tricky bastards.

Darren couldn’t help but snicker when Markos stormed back into the bar.

Totally predictable.

“Back so soon?” Cassie asked with a big smile.

Markos let out a snarl that made Darren tense up, especially as the dragon stormed toward the bar, headed for his mate.

Darren got ready to intervene, but saw he didn’t have to when Markos just kissed Cassie’s cheek and muttered, “I’ll catch ’em tomorrow.”

These dragons were something all right. Stubborn, if nothing else.

With Darren and Markos helping (though Markos was so drunk, he was more of a hindrance than a help) they closed the bar fairly quickly and headed out.

They were passing the lobby when Darren caught sight of Lucky.

"You coming, Darren?" Cassie called from the elevator. How she and Markos had managed to walk right by where Lucky was perched without seeing her, Darren had *no* idea.

"You guys go on ahead. I'll see you tomorrow," he called.

Cassie called out something in reply as Markos pulled her into the elevator, but Darren wasn't really paying attention. He was too worried Lucky was going to fall and kill herself.

What on earth was she doing?

He walked toward Lucky, incredulous at what he was seeing.

Somehow Lucky had managed to stack two tables upside down, one on top of the other. Even more bizarrely, atop one of the legs of the second table was a chair, also upside down.

And Lucky herself was standing on two of those chair legs, delicately balanced, stretching toward a chandelier high above her.

Was she—she was! She was changing the lightbulbs in the chandelier. By standing on two upside down tables and a chair. It made no sense!

She was clearly insane.

The question was whether Darren could get her attention without causing her to fall.

He needed her down from there.

Right about that moment, Lucky noticed him for the first time.

They stared at each other for a long moment, Darren trying to ignore the fact that a single step forward would give him an exceptional view straight up her sassy, green skirt.

Finally, she said, "Darren?"

At that, he exploded. "What are you doing up there? Are you crazy?"

Lucky looked incredibly surprised, then shrugged, gave a tiny giggle and hopped down.

Literally.

She hopped from the chair's legs to one of the legs of the second upside down table, balancing there in what appeared to be a ballerina pose, one foot resting on the other. She made the landing without difficulty, but swayed in place, causing Darren to leap forward, arms stretched out as if to catch her.

"Aren't you sweet?" She winked at him, then leapt forward, landing in his arms, almost as if they'd planned it.

Stunned at his sudden armful of lush leprechaun, Darren stared into her eyes, then gently swung her legs down and set her on the ground.

Lucky smiled up at him. "I can't believe I messed up this trick!"

"What do you mean?" he asked.

"No one's supposed to catch us. That's the whole point. Yet here you are, staring right at me, catching me in your arms."

"You leapt at me like you *wanted* me to catch you."

"Well, who wouldn't? I mean, okay. Maybe a straight guy wouldn't, but otherwise, I'm pretty sure anyone would." She winked at him.

Darren was utterly speechless. He couldn't believe this

gorgeous leprechaun was flirting with him. Sure, they'd flirted in the bar, but when her friends had swept her away at the end of the night, he'd figured that was that. A beautiful night, but it had ended with her walking away from him.

Yet, now, here she was, flirting again.

He was by far, the luckiest damn chameleon that had ever walked the earth. "You're enchanting." Wait. He hadn't meant to say that. But honestly, it was true, so why bother to deny it? "Utterly enchanting," he repeated.

Lucky blushed a little, peeked up at him from beneath her jaunty hat, then offered to walk him to his room. "But just a walk," she insisted, winking at him again.

Of course, Darren accepted, so off they went, Lucky skipping at his side, chatting a mile a minute.

As they walked, Darren began to notice the lights dimming as they passed them by, then brightening once they were past.

It wasn't until they reached his room that he realized all the light bulbs in the hallway were glowing green. "That's odd," he muttered.

Lucky looked around innocently. "What's odd?"

"The lightbulbs. They're all green."

"I like it," she said brightly.

Darren grinned. "Well, the lighting does complement your coloring very nicely."

She smiled. "You're so sweet, Darren." She hopped up and kissed him on his cheek. "I hope to see you tomorrow."

And then she disappeared.

Just like that.

One second there.

The next, poof.

She was gone.

4

THE NEXT DAY when Darren ventured downstairs, planning to meet his sister and her mate for lunch, he found a rather hectic scene in the hotel lobby. Guests were complaining that their furniture had been turned upside down in the middle of the night, *while they were sleeping.*

Harry, the hotel manager, looked overwhelmed and Darren felt quite sorry for him.

"Darren!" Cassie hurried to him. "Can you believe this?"

Considering what he'd seen the night before, yes. He really could.

Interestingly, though, the lobby furniture appeared to be in its proper place, no upside-down tables in sight.

"The lobby looks fine," he said to Cassie.

"According to Lily, that's only because she and Harry spent an hour this morning setting it all to rights. When I saw her, she was cursing the leprechauns. Do you think they did this?"

"Probably." What he really meant was definitely, but he

wasn't going to admit that he'd caught one of the leprechauns in action the night before. He wasn't sure if he was protecting Lucky or himself. Based on how aggravated Harry looked, he was thinking it was probably self-preservation.

"All the lights in my room are green!" An angry troll bellowed.

"Poor Harry," Cassie murmured. "Come on. Let's get out of here." She grabbed her brother's arm and led him outside to where Markos, Zee and Ashlynn were waiting.

"About time. I was afraid I was going to have to go in to save you from the masses," Markos said, pulling Cassie into his arms with a grin.

They spent the rest of the day in downtown Jamesville, having lunch out and wandering through the shops.

Well, the women shopped.

Darren and the dragons just stood around and chatted.

Eventually they ended up at a shop called The House of Light, where they met up with three witches and their shifter mates.

The women were apparently close friends, which is why Ashlynn and Cassie insisted the witches join them at the bar later that night.

"I thought we were going to Shenanigans 1 tonight and 2 tomorrow night," one of the cougar mates protested.

"Yeah," said the wolf. Karl, Darren thought his name was. "After we have dinner with your aunt Dory tomorrow."

"Well, I guess we're going to Shenanigans 2 two nights in a row," Megan said.

"Exactly," one of her sisters said, either Jessica or Lara, Darren wasn't sure.

"Just like we've been to Shenanigans 1 the last four nights in a row," the final sister said.

The rest of their day was uneventful, at least until they arrived at Shenanigans to set up the bar later that day.

All the tables were upside down, with bar stools on top of them, also upside down.

"Seriously?" Cassie did a fair imitation of a dragon's growl.

Markos chuckled. "Don't worry, darling. You go get the bar ready. Darren and I'll deal with the furniture."

Darren couldn't even imagine the point of this. Was it just to be funny? Did leprechauns think turning people's beds upside down, while they were sleeping in them, was funny? Did they think it would be funny to eat and drink while perched on the leg of an upside down stool?

It was really quite the mystery.

They'd only managed to right about half the tables when patrons started arriving.

The leprechauns were first and they chortled and chuckled their way to the tables Markos and Darren had set back up, spreading out so that when non-leprechauns arrived, they either had to stand or help with righting the furniture they wanted to sit on.

Meanwhile, the leprechauns were drinking and laughing while watching patrons and employees bustle about, setting the bar to rights.

"You lot are a menace," Cassie called to them, which sent them into giggling fits. "I should cut you off."

This threat sobered the leprechauns immediately.

"You can't cut us off," Charming protested. "This is neutral territory."

Cassie scowled. "I have to let you in, but that doesn't mean I have to keep Tricky Charms in stock. Or any alcohol for that matter. Maybe this will become a dry bar, did you ever think about that?"

This made the leprechauns fall all over each other, they laughed so hard.

"A dry bar! A *dry* bar, a dry *bar*, a *dry bar*," they chanted, giggling all the while.

Cassie just rolled her eyes, but Darren could tell she was charmed by the leprechauns' antics and wasn't really annoyed at all.

"So." Markos plopped into a seat at one of the leprechaun tables. "Let's drink!"

Unbelievable. The dragon wasn't giving up anytime soon.

Darren was about to join them when Lucky showed up.

He immediately abandoned the dragons in favor of spending the evening with his lady leprechaun.

As he walked away, Lucky on his arm, he heard one of the leprechauns say, "Haven't you heard, laddie? You've got to follow the rainbow if you want to find a pot of gold."

~

Cassie was hard at work, filling drink orders and wondering where Ashlynn was—the phoenix hadn't shown up for her shift yet—when Kitty arrived, absolutely filled with joy, dragging a disgruntled looking Logan behind her.

"Look, Cassie!" Kitty exclaimed, showing off her arms.

Cassie froze and leaned over the bar to stare. "Are those—
"

"Tiny baby shamrocks! My freckles are turning Irish. Isn't that so cute?"

Before Cassie could really decide how she should respond to that question, Kitty exclaimed, "I have to go show the leprechauns. I'll be back!" And off she darted toward the leprechaun tables, Logan following in her wake, still looking rather put out.

If Cassie had to guess, she'd say the fairy wasn't too happy with the leprechaun magic that was clearly changing his mate's appearance.

At that moment, Ashlynn came sweeping into the bar, clearly in a rage. "Look at what those leprechauns did to me!"

Cassie's jaw dropped. She'd heard the phrase before, but this was really the only time it had ever happened to her. She couldn't even speak, she was so incredibly…

Dismayed?

Horrified?

She gulped.

Entertained.

Must not laugh. Must not laugh.

Now that Ashlynn was in front of her, Cassie realized she probably should have expected this result. After all, Ashlynn had a lot more freckles than Kitty and many of them were in tight clusters.

Still, she didn't think she could ever have predicted these results.

Though Cassie was looking closely, she couldn't really pick out any shamrocks. Well, maybe that giant cluster there. If she squinted her eyes and tilted her head just so, maybe that was a giant shamrock on Ashlynn's—

"My arms are completely green!" Ashlynn shrieked. "And my boobs—Ooooh, I'm so mad. They look like I've got patches of grass all over them. Or a disease. I look diseased, Cassie!"

Cassie was trying so hard not to laugh.

They were friends and Ashlynn was clearly upset, but this was just hilarious.

"What am I supposed to do?" Ashlynn wailed.

Cassie was pretty impressed she wasn't screaming at the leprechauns, who were really completely out of control at this point.

"Well, first, I'd suggest taking off the charm," Cassie said, raising her voice to be heard over the din of leprechaun giggles and, well, it had to be said, the guffaws of the dragons.

Ashlynn glared at Zee, who had followed her into the bar, a huge grin on his face, and who was now laughing with his brother. "I can't believe you find this funny!" She whirled back to Cassie. "And I can't get the necklace off. It's almost like it's been welded shut."

Cassie swallowed a giggle, cleared her throat and called across the bar again, "A total menace!"

This, of course, just set off the leprechauns again, some of them going so far as to fall to the floor where they rolled back and forth and laughed and laughed.

Cassie shook her head, hurried around the bar and gestured for Ashlynn to turn around.

Ashlynn swept her hair out of the way and Cassie tried to get the necklace unlatched.

"Damn," she muttered. "You're right. This is really hard to —I can't quite see where the latch is. It's like it's—I don't know."

"I told you! It's been welded shut!" Ashlynn wailed.

Thus began a round of all of the patrons (except the

leprechauns) trying to get the necklace's latch to open.

The dragons tried melting the metal clasp.

The trolls tried brute strength.

The witches tried magic.

Nothing worked.

~

"Your friends are certainly having fun tonight," Darren observed.

Lucky giggled. "They're always happy when a trick comes out even better than planned."

"They didn't plan that?"

"Well, the thing about a good trick is that you *can't* plan it perfectly, no matter what you do because people are unpredictable. You have to send your trick out into the world and then wait for the results. Sometimes they're nowhere near as funny as expected and sometimes they're way funnier."

"Interesting." Especially because the theory behind what she was saying very closely mirrored what they taught chameleons about their cons.

People were unpredictable.

Expect the unexpected.

"Take Kitty and Ashlynn, for example. It was the exact same trick, using the exact same charm, and yet the results were entirely different and their reactions were completely opposite from one another. There was no way for my frolic to know how either one of them would react, so they just set up the trick and waited for the results."

"Your frolic?"

"It's what we call a group of leprechauns. Family, friends, a clan, really."

“I like it. It’s especially appropriate for your particular friends.”

“Oh?”

“I mean, they’re fun and irreverent and always laughing, so yeah. I bet it’s a frolic a minute in your realm.”

Lucky laughed. “Or at least a trick a minute.”

5

ASHLYNN COULDN'T BELIEVE the trouble one small charm had caused and it was all for the enjoyment of those silly leprechauns.

She really wanted to be mad, but their general hilarity was so amusing, it was impossible not to want to laugh along with them.

She didn't, of course, because hello—green skin! Plus her mate was laughing enough for both of them.

When Kitty offered to ask Artemis for help, though, Ashlynn finally decided she'd had enough.

The fact that she actually considered saying yes to involving the goddess of the hunt meant that it was clearly past time to seek a solution from the source of the problem.

Ashlynn waved away the dragons and fairies and witches and trolls, not to mention the former handmaiden of a goddess, and headed for the table where the leprechauns had been thoroughly enjoying the show.

She settled in a chair and said, "This was quite the ingenious trick, but I'd really like to have my normal skin color back please."

"Ah, are you sure, lass? You look mighty pretty in that shade of green," one of the leprechauns said.

"I'm positive. Please?"

"All righty then." He reached out and touched a finger to the shamrock sitting in the hollow of her neck.

A slight tingle ran through her and she was utterly relieved to see the green appeared to be fading. Just a little.

"It'll take about twelve hours for the full effects to subside," the leprechaun told her.

"But they will go away?"

"They will."

"Thank you! What's your name again?"

"Jolly."

"Thank you so much, Jolly." Ashlynn leaned over and kissed his cheek, causing him to blush a brilliant red and Zee to roar in annoyance from where he was watching from across the room. "It really was a good trick." She stood and headed back toward the bar.

When Zee would have grabbed her as she walked by, she darted out of his reach and shook her finger at him. "Don't even think about it. I'm mad at you."

"Me? I'm not the one who turned your skin green!"

"No, you're just the one who laughed about it."

Zee scowled. "And who was that laughing like a loon last night?"

Ashlynn blushed. "Well, I'm sorry, but that was hilarious!"

"And this isn't? Personally, I think if anyone has the right to hold a grudge, it's me!"

"Hey, I deleted those photos." Something she'd regretted immediately after.

"Are you sure? Did you get every last one, even the ones in the cloud?"

Ashlynn bit her lip. "Maybe." Hopefully not though.

Zee growled.

"Hold on a minute," Markos interrupted. "I'm finding this conversation a little hard to follow. I got the whole Ashlynn's boobs are green bit, but I seem to be missing something. What photos are we talking about now? And are they recoverable because I sense an opportunity I would hate to miss."

Ashlynn giggled. "Well, see—"

Zee lunged for her and slapped a hand across her mouth. "Not a word, babe. Not one single word," he muttered in her ear.

Ashlynn giggled hysterically as he carried her out of the bar, Markos' voice following them into the hallway. "No problem, guys. I'll just bribe you later, Ashlynn!"

~

"What about your Coalition?" Lucky asked. "Is it a con a minute?"

Darren laughed. "Not even close. We could spend months setting up a con, years even if it's an especially complicated one."

"Really?" That seemed like it would require a lot of patience, something leprechauns weren't exactly known for.

"Definitely. Though we do always have different cons in motion. Some chameleons prefer to work alone, some in pairs, some in groups. The cons they choose reflect that."

"And you? Do you prefer to work alone or in a group?"

"I've always been really good at leading teams into some of our more complicated cons. Recently, though, I stepped into a leadership role, so now I'm responsible for helping the team leaders coordinate all the cons of the coalition, rather than leading my own."

"Wow." That sounded like a lot of responsibility, also something leprechauns weren't exactly known for. "Don't you get bored? Or impatient? Or bored?"

Darren laughed. "Sometimes. But I still love it and when I need a break, I take it. Like this week, hanging out with my sister, getting to know her mate, attending her mating celebration. Also, I do tend to jump into cons sometimes, you know, just to keep my skills up-to-date."

"And to escape the boredom, right?"

Darren laughed again. "Exactly right."

~

The rest of the night was fairly uneventful to Cassie's way of thinking.

Zee and Ashlynn eventually returned and Zee joined his brother in their continuing quest to drink the leprechauns under the table.

"You'd think they'd have learned their lesson from last night," Ashlynn said. "Zee was a bear when he woke this morning."

Kitty giggled. "A bear-dragon."

"Exactly," Ashlynn said. "He was so hungover. He didn't appreciate it when I made him get up."

"Markos was annoyed as well," Cassie said. "Serves them both right."

"That's what I said."

Kitty giggled. "I thought Logan was going to insist on

staying last night, but then he decided your mates were on their own."

"Smart fairy," Cassie said.

Kitty giggled. "I think it had more to do with the fact that fairies aren't that fond of leprechauns and vice versa."

"Really? But aren't leprechauns a type of fairy?"

"Yes, but they're trickster fairies, and I guess they have no problem playing tricks on their own kind, which the fairies don't appreciate." She grabbed her drink and stood. "And on that note, I'm off to join my mate. See you guys later."

"Later," Cassie and Ashlynn chorused as Kitty walked away, headed for the table where Logan had joined the witches and their mates.

And so the hours passed, with the many paranormals in the bar drinking and laughing, and in the dragons' case, trying to get the leprechauns to reveal where their gold was hidden.

When Cassie announced last call, a flurry of orders came in as usual, then slowly, the bar began to empty out.

Surprisingly, the leprechauns weren't stealthily disappearing the way they had the night before.

"Great," Ashlynn said.

"What is it?" Cassie asked.

"They're just toying with them now. You know that, right?"

Cassie grinned. "Again, I feel very strongly that they'll be getting what they deserve."

"We're terrible," Ashlynn said. "We should be trying to protect our mates from the leprechauns' trickery."

Cassie stared at her incredulously.

Ashlynn burst into laughter. "I'm just kidding. Zee

freaking laughed at my green skin, although to be fair, I did laugh at his misfortune last night."

Cassie leaned forward. "Let me in on the secret? Please."

"Okay, but you can't tell Markos. He'd never let Zee live it down and Zee, well, he'd never forgive me for telling."

"My lips are sealed."

"Okay, so, basically, Zee had one of the charms in his jeans pocket. It was a tiny flame, so last night when he got undressed, well, let's just say certain things were fire-engine red, and as the night progressed, they got redder *and* hotter."

"You don't mean—"

"Yep. Zee kept sending me to the ice machine down the hall. He was *not* a happy camper."

Cassie snickered. "Well, at least it wasn't a shamrock charm."

"I think he might have actually preferred that. At least shamrocks aren't flaming hot."

They were both laughing when the lights went out in the bar.

A split second later, they came back, though darker—and greener—than before.

"Are you kidding me right now?" Markos bellowed from across the room.

Cassie glanced his way to see that he and Zee were sitting all alone at tables that only moments before had been filled with leprechauns.

"They did it again," Zee growled.

Ashlynn giggled and Cassie couldn't help but join her when Markos snarled, "Tricky bastards."

6

AS THE NIGHT progressed, Darren found Lucky to be increasingly charming and enchanting, and she seemed as interested as he was. He was gearing up to ask her out on a real date when suddenly the lights went out.

They came back on a split second later, but when they did, Lucky was gone.

All it took was a quick glance around the room to realize *all* the leprechauns were gone.

Darren sighed, then picked up his drink and joined the dragons at their now-deserted table.

"Not having much luck following the leprechauns, are you?"

"Oh, shut up," Markos growled.

"We'll figure it out," Zee said. "It can't be that difficult. We just need a plan."

Darren snorted. Like a plan was going to help these two. "You should leave it alone. The leprechauns are never going to let you get your hands on their gold, but you might just find yourselves without your hands if you're not careful."

"Don't be ridiculous," Zee said. "We're dragons!"

Darren shook his head, marveling at their stubbornness.

It didn't take too long to close down the bar and they all left together.

When they passed the lobby without a sign of Lucky, Darren was rather disappointed and entered the elevator feeling quite let down.

Cassie and Markos got off on the second floor while Ashlynn and Zee got off on the third.

Darren rode the elevator all the way to the fourth floor and had just turned the corner, heading toward his room, when he ran into Lucky.

She was standing in front of a portrait, appearing to examine it very closely.

"Now what are you up to?" Darren asked.

Lucky jumped and whirled around, looking startled.

And guilty.

Darren looked around, but he couldn't see anything amiss.

No stacked furniture.

No green light bulbs.

"Oh, hi, Darren." Cassie smiled at him innocently.

Yep.

She was definitely up to something.

"So what trickery are you up to tonight?"

"Oh, nothing. I was just out for a leisurely stroll." For a moment, she looked cross. "Though I can't understand how I'm getting worse at the tricks rather than better."

"Why do you think you're getting worse at them?"

"Because you keep catching me! You're not even supposed to be able to see me. Although I suppose it's only fair seeing as you're not exactly very good at the chameleon thing, are you?"

Darren jolted. "What do you mean?"

"Well, come on. Aren't I supposed to think you're a leprechaun or something?"

Darren hadn't really thought about it until that very moment, but of course, there'd be no reason for Lucky not to share what she was up to if she believed he was a leprechaun like her. Yet she hadn't invited him to join in the trickery. "Weird."

"I know, right? You can see me, even when I'm at my trickiest, and I know beyond a shadow of a doubt that you're a chameleon. Something's weird about this hotel I think."

"Or maybe—"

Before he could finish that thought, Lucky said cheerfully, "Well, gotta go. See you tomorrow, Darren!" She hopped up and kissed his cheek, then disappeared.

It was a repeat of the night before and it made him growl in frustration. "Great," he muttered. "Now I'm sounding like a dragon."

He'd been standing there for a full minute before he realized the painting Lucky had been examining now sported giant googly eyes springing from the bosom of the woman in the portrait.

~

The next several days were a pretty close repeat of the previous ones.

Cassie was getting nervous as her mating day approached and Markos wanted her distracted as much as possible so they went on several excursions. A day trip into the woods to visit the local wolf pack and another day spent wandering the fairy mall. Both days, Darren tried to focus on his sister and her mate to enjoy his time with them, but he was a bit distracted constantly thinking about Lucky and wondering what she was up to.

The evenings were spent at Shenanigans, flirting with Lucky and observing the leprechauns in all their goofiness, which ratcheted up every time a trick of theirs was revealed in all its glory.

A perfect example was when Kitty showed up thrilled with her bright green nails one night.

"I'm not sure about this, Kitty," Ashlynn said worriedly.

"Tell me about it," Logan grumbled. "You should see her when she shifts. She's green from the tip of her whiskers to the tip of her tail."

"Green whiskers?" Cassie asked.

"Green everything."

The leprechauns all giggled.

Logan glared at them while Kitty skipped over to them to show them her nails, all of which had tiny shamrocks in the center.

"Very pretty, lass." The leprechauns all complimented her on her green accessories and Kitty skipped back to Logan, looking incandescent with joy.

Darren shook his head.

Folly. This was utter folly.

More than his concern about Kitty's progressive greenery, though, Darren found Markos' obsession with finding the leprechaun's stash of gold utterly worrisome. Normally, he wouldn't care what a dragon was up to, but this was his sister's mate. He tried repeatedly to talk sense into the dragon, but every time he thought Markos might be about to come around, his brother Zee chimed in with another ridiculous idea.

When Darren wasn't trying to talk sense into the dragons, he was spending time with Lucky, flirting and falling in love.

Unfortunately, Markos and Zee eventually realized that Darren was seriously courting Lucky, and began to make a nuisance of themselves as a result, often joining them at the worst possible times.

Darren would send them pointed looks, but just like the stubborn dragons they were, they would simply settle in to torture him. Of course, invariably, much of Lucky's frolic would follow. And so Darren had not yet managed to ask her out on an official date.

It was almost as if Markos and Zee could predict the very moment Darren was about to bring up the subject for that was always when they descended upon them, leprechauns typically in tow.

With members of her frolic around her, Lucky was as sassy as ever. She would tease the dragons and the fairies when they joined them, riling both groups up as much as possible.

The dragons continued to try to trick the leprechauns into revealing the location of their gold while the fairies began a campaign to figure out a way to extend the banishment of the leprechauns from the mall to the bar and to the hotel itself.

It wasn't possible, of course, what with Shenanigans being neutral territory, but the fairies were certain there had to be a loophole somewhere and recruited the witches to help.

Unsurprisingly, the witches said the same thing, but with

a lot of magical mumbo-jumbo to accompany it. The magic protecting neutral territory would always nullify any spells cast upon it. Nothing they could do magically. Blah-blah-blah.

And so the fairies pouted and the dragons fumed while Lucky and her leprechaun friends taunted and teased and laughed the nights away.

As expected, the dragons never managed to follow the leprechauns. "Tricky bastards," Markos would mutter each night when somehow they managed to disappear yet again from under their noses.

Darren was beginning to find it all terribly amusing.

Except for the part where they kept interfering with his attempts to court Lucky.

Happily, he still managed to catch her alone after leaving the bar each night.

One night, he followed the sound of tapping to find Lucky knocking a tiny hammer against a wall in the west wing of the hotel.

Innocently answering, "Nothing," when asked what she was up to, she accompanied him back to his room, holding his hand and chatting all the while. As they walked, she swung her free hand, the one holding the hammer, back and forth, tap-tap-tapping it against the walls.

That was the first night she gifted him with a kiss when they arrived back at his room. Well, she kissed him on his cheek every time she saw him, both coming and going, but this was their first real kiss.

One Darren hadn't even initiated.

Not that he minded. In fact, the minute she touched her lips to his, he was lost.

They dueled for control of the kiss, his tongue tangling

with hers and vice versa, until they ran out of breath and would break for a moment, then one or the other would lunge forward and they'd be at it again.

Those long minutes spent in the hallway right outside his door, learning what made the other shiver in delight, were lost in a haze of passion, to the extent that Darren was always surprised to see how much time had passed when they finally parted and he staggered into his room, drunk on Lucky's kisses.

He'd almost forgotten about Lucky's tiny hammer until he left his room the next morning and saw shamrocks growing from the walls in great trailing vines.

He found Lucky's trickery to be enchanting, and even though he knew it wasn't hers specifically, he couldn't help but be amused at the charm trick that just kept growing and growing, as it did that very night.

"Oh my gosh, Kitty! Tell me you dyed your hair for St. Paddy's Day and that it's not a result of that stupid charm," Cassie asked.

"Nope. I just woke up to green hair."

Ashlynn shook her head. "Well, it may be gorgeous, but I wouldn't like not having control of my own body like that."

"You know," Darren interjected. "It might be a good idea to ask the leprechauns to turn off your charm before it gets really out of hand."

"Oh no," Kitty exclaimed. "I *like* it. I didn't even have to bleach my hair to get it this color. It's just naturally green."

Logan, on the other hand, didn't look quite as happy as Kitty. In fact, he spent most of the night glaring at the leprechauns. "This trick is getting out of hand."

"Oh, leave it be, Logan. I'm sure everything will be fine," Kitty said.

"You don't understand how tricky those leprechauns are. They can't be trusted."

"He's right," Darren said. "You never know what might happen next."

"I'm sure whatever it is will be simply wonderful," Kitty said.

Ashlynn snorted.

When the leprechauns disappeared literally into thin air —again—at the end of the evening, Markos was not happy.

Darren couldn't believe the dragons hadn't given up their quest yet. Talk about stubborn.

"How do they keep doing that?" Zee demanded.

Lily rolled her eyes. "You do realize leprechauns are fairies, right?"

"Yes, but they don't have wings," Markos protested. "How are they moving so quickly on those little legs?"

Lily giggled. "Not all fairies have wings, you know. And they're not a requirement for moving quickly. Leprechauns are trickster fairies. You can't trust them at all. And like all fairies, they can pop between the realms just like this." She snapped her fingers and with an almost audible pop, disappeared.

Harry growled. "I hate it when she does that. I never know if she's lurking or really gone."

"Lurking!" Lily reappeared from thin air. "How dare you? I'll show you lurking!" She reached out, grabbed the traveler by his lapels and this time, disappeared them both, all at once.

"This place is a nut house," Darren said to Cassie.

"I know. Isn't it great?" Without waiting for an answer, Cassie walked back to the bar, probably to begin closing it down.

"You know, I've been thinking," Zee said. "We've been trying to follow a bunch of leprechauns all at once. Maybe we should focus on just *one* instead."

"I like this idea," Markos said. "The question is, which one?"

They both turned and stared at Darren.

Darren narrowed his eyes at them. "Not a chance. I'm not joining your foolish games."

"But you've clearly managed to strike up a friendship with Lucky," Markos said.

"I bet she'd be happy to go for a walk with you. As soon as you get her outside, we'll grab her!" Zee said.

Darren scowled. "You two need to stay away from my Lucky."

"*Your* Lucky?" Markos grinned.

"So it's like that, eh?" Zee slapped Darren on the back. "Good for you, man. Having a mate is the most amazing thing."

Darren froze. He hadn't really considered that Lucky might be his mate. He'd had the thought briefly a couple nights before, but then it had evaporated in a haze of passion.

It made sense though.

Except for the part where she was from an entirely different realm. That didn't make a whole lot of sense. Why would he be matched to someone he might never meet?

Then again, his sister's mate was from a different realm.

In fact, it seemed a bit of an epidemic around Shenanigans.

Mates from different realms finding each other at the bar.

Perhaps they were being drawn together by forces none of them expected.

The dragons were still chatting and laughing, but Darren was distracted thinking about all the possibilities.

Suddenly, he felt extremely motivated to get on with his night. He hurried over to his sister. "Hey, Cassie. You need my help closing down?"

"Nah. You go on. I'll see you tomorrow for lunch, yeah?"

"Yeah." Darren leaned across the bar, kissed her cheek, gave the dragons a nod, then headed out.

As he walked to the elevator, he practiced what he was going to say.

First, he'd mention the possibility of them being mates, then—no, wait. That might make it sound like he only wanted to date her because they might be mates.

Okay.

First, he would ask her out on a date, then if the date went well, he'd bring up the possibility of them being mates.

Yes.

This was a good plan.

Now if only the elevator would arrive.

He was contemplating taking the stairs when the doors finally opened to reveal Lucky leaning against the back wall, eating marshmallows.

Darren stepped inside the elevator and raised an eyebrow at her.

"What are you up to now?"

"Nothing," Lucky said innocently (the same thing she said every night), then offered him a marshmallow.

Darren accepted it, but didn't take a bite. Instead, he could only stare as Lucky slowly devoured her own marshmallow, licking her lips and tempting him greatly.

When she was finished eating, she reached for his hand,

the one holding the marshmallow he had yet to eat, and lifted it to her lips.

He gently fed the marshmallow to her, breath hitching when her lips closed around his fingers and licked them clean.

The elevator arrived and they slowly exited, lost in a haze of attraction.

They walked slowly to his room, eating marshmallows along the way, feeding them to each other and stealing long, drugging kisses.

When they finally reached his door, Lucky said, "Will you meet me for lunch tomorrow? Maybe around two?"

Even though he had just confirmed lunch with his sister, Darren didn't even hesitate. "Absolutely. Where?"

"How about in the lobby? We can have lunch in my realm."

Darren grinned. "I'd love that."

"Awesome! It's a date then." And with a quick hop and a kiss, she was gone.

It didn't even occur to Darren until he was relaxing in bed that he'd never actually managed to ask her out on a date. Instead, she'd asked him.

He fell asleep with a smile on his face.

7

THE NEXT DAY, Darren met his sister in the lobby around noon as they'd already planned, but after explaining his lunch plans with Lucky, swore her to secrecy.

"What's the big deal?" Cassie asked.

Darren just raised an eyebrow, which made her giggle.

"Okay, fine. I guess it's probably a good idea if Markos doesn't realize you're hanging out with a leprechaun this afternoon."

"Where is Markos anyway?"

"He's so hungover, I couldn't get him out of bed this morning."

Darren grinned. "Okay, color me not surprised at all. Those leprechauns have been getting the dragons drunk night after night."

"I know!" Cassie exclaimed. "You know what the most hilarious part about that is?"

"That the dragons believe *they're* the ones getting the *leprechauns* drunk?"

"Exactly!"

As Darren laughed with his sister, he was so incredibly grateful he'd decided to come out a full ten days early, just to see her. He'd missed her and it was so nice being able to laugh with her and get to know her mate.

Even better, he was starting to think the dragons were right, and he'd gained something even more valuable than time with his sister this trip.

"So, is she really your mate?" Cassie asked.

She must have been reading his mind. "Markos told you, huh?"

"Yep."

"I'm not sure. Maybe. Probably."

"What makes you think so?"

"In addition to the incredible chemistry?"

"Ew, I don't want to hear about that!"

Darren laughed. "She knew I was a chameleon right from the start, never once thought I was a leprechaun. Plus I keep catching her playing tricks in the hotel."

"You've been catching her? She hasn't been hiding while doing them?"

"She seems to think she's hiding, which could mean—"

"That you're seeing through the veil to your true mate!"

"Exactly."

"Darren, I'm so happy for you!" Cassie flung herself into his arms and hugged him tight.

"Yeah, well. There are a lot of unknowns. I mean, I'm head of the Coalition. She lives in a whole different realm and is a leprechaun princess."

Cassie waved a hand in dismissal. "Lucky told me the title's a relic of the past. They don't really have royalty anymore."

“I know. But still. Am I really going to take her away from her people?”

“Darren. She’s a leprechaun. They’re fairies. She can pop between the realms on a whim. And she can probably take you with her. Lily’s always dragging Harry along when she pops in and out of the realms.”

“Huh. I never even thought of that.”

“I say go for it. You like her, right?”

Darren grinned at the memory of the mischievous look on Lucky’s face as she switched out the lightbulbs while balanced on the leg of a chair, and of the innocent smile she greeted him with right after attaching googly eyes to a painting, and of walking hand in hand with her while feeding each other marshmallows. “I think I love her.”

“Oh, Darren. That’s just so lovely.”

Darren was thinking about how happy Cassie was for him a couple hours later when he met up with Lucky in the lobby of the hotel.

One moment he was standing on his own, the next the elevator doors opened and an adorable leprechaun popped her head out and waved him to her. “Darren!”

He smiled and jogged to the elevator, backing her into it and stealing a quick kiss. “Where to, sweet Lucky?”

She spun to face the elevator buttons and pushed the 2nd and 3rd floor buttons at the same time.

The doors closed, the elevator gave a small lurch, then slowly climbed from the first floor to the second, and began to inch its way to the third. It stopped right in between the two floors and the doors opened to reveal a giant field of clover.

As they exited the elevator, Darren exclaimed, “How exactly did that happen?” He turned to stare at the elevator and watched as it winked out of existence. "The other day, Cassie pushed the same two floors, but we ended up in the fairy mall."

Lucky laughed. "Oh, Darren. You should know the answer to that question."

"I should?"

"Of course. The elevator's in a Hotel Shenanigans and *that's* how that happened."

That non-answer hurt Darren's brain, though from all the stories Cassie had told, it was clear Hotel Shenanigans was a rather spooky place.

"Right. Well. As long as we can get back." He paused. "We *can* get back, right?"

Lucky giggled. "Of course we can. Come on!" She grabbed his hand and led him deeper into the field until they reached the edge of a light green blanket spread across the clover.

The blanket had a dark green shamrock in the center and each corner was pinned down by shamrock-shaped stones.

Off to the side of the blanket was a huge picnic basket.

"Wow, Lucky. This is amazing."

Lucky beamed at him. "I hope you're hungry."

"Famished."

Lunch was delicious and they talked for hours, about everything and nothing, pausing every once in a while to punctuate their conversation with long kisses as they rolled across the blanket and fed their passion.

Eventually, they wore each other out and fell asleep in each other's arms, Lucky's head pillowed on Darren's chest.

He played with her hair until he eventually fell asleep and it was the most restful sleep of his life.

When he woke, Lucky was sitting at his side, smiling at him.

He leaned up on his elbows and she leaned down to kiss him.

"You know what?" she whispered against his lips.

"What?"

She lifted up to stare in his eyes. "I think we might be mates."

Darren surged up and swept her into his lap. He kissed her, pouring all of his joy at finding his mate into the kiss.

When they finally pulled away, he said, "You know what?"

"What?"

"I do believe you're right, sweet mate of mine."

Lucky squealed in joy and hugged him tight, then kissed him again.

As the day's light started to wane, they packed up the picnic supplies and trash, folded the blanket and began to walk, hand-in-hand, back toward where the elevator had dropped them off.

"It's my lucky day," Darren said.

"It is?" Lucky asked.

"I found my mate and look!" He leaned over and plucked a clover from the ground. "I also found a four-leaf clover."

Lucky giggled.

He handed the four-leaf clover to her, then leaned over and picked another one. "Hey. Are they *all* four-leaf clovers?"

"Maybe." She gave him a sassy smile and tucked into her hair the clover he'd handed her so that it sat at a jaunty angle over her ear. "Well, I suppose I should get going. My frolic will be wondering where I am."

"More tricks to play, I take it?"

She shrugged. "Maybe."

At that moment, the elevator reappeared right in front of them.

"How does it do that?" Darren demanded.

Lucky shrugged. "I told you. It's a Shenanigans elevator." She pulled him in behind her and pushed the lobby button.

They kissed all the way back to the earth realm.

When the elevator doors began to open, she pulled away and said, "I'll see you tonight," and then she was gone.

~

That night at Shenanigans was about as predictable as it could be, Darren thought.

It all began with Kitty's arrival.

"Look, my eyelashes and eyebrows turned green! They match my hair and my eyes now. I mean, my eyes have always been green, but now it's like my whole body is an accessory for my eyes!"

"Um, I'm not sure this is a good thing, Kitty," Cassie said.

"Why not? It's just a bit of fun."

"Well, do you want to stay green for the rest of your life?" Ashlynn asked.

"Who said anything about the rest of my life? I'm sure it'll wear off eventually. In the meantime, I'm going to enjoy it!"

"I just don't understand it!" A commotion at the door had everyone looking that way. Megan, Jessica and Lara were storming into the bar, accompanied by their mates.

"All of Dory's plants are blooming marshmallows," Megan exclaimed. "What's up with that?"

"I kind of like it," Karl said.

"You would!" Lara scowled. "How many of those things did you eat anyway?"

Karl grinned. “Not enough. We should stop at your aunt’s on the way home for another snack.”

“How can we cast spells with our herbs if they’re all sticky and marshmallowy?” Jessica demanded.

The leprechauns all started giggling again.

“Marshmallows are yummy,” Mischief exclaimed.

“Tasty,” Bossy agreed.

“Someone did you a tricky favor,” Joker said.

“They’re right,” Charming said. “You should be grateful.”

The witches just glared at them and grumbled some more before eventually deciding they needed to buy more herbs and stormed out again.

~

Lucky was sitting at a table, flirting with Darren, when the dragons finally stumbled in. They looked somewhat ragged, what with the bloodshot eyes and hair standing on end.

Darren shook his head. “I think maybe your frolic should give the dragons a break tonight. Don’t you think?”

Lucky grinned. “Oh, come on. When your cons are going well, do you just give them up?”

Darren scowled. “I suppose not. So tell me about your favorite trick.”

Over the next several hours, Lucky shared the stories of her favorite tricks and listened to the stories of Darren’s favorite cons.

The more they talked, the more Lucky realized he was quite the trickster himself.

As she listened to his story of the con in Ireland where her brethren bested his, she couldn’t help but grin as he explained how some poor chameleon named Jackson managed to get stuck in a fairy mound.

"We had to pull him out. It really wasn't easy and well, his leg got a little mangled in the process."

Lucky hated to giggle at someone's misfortune, but really, they deserved it. Targeting a family protected by leprechauns was quite the misstep. When she pointed that out, Darren just nodded.

"True that. We haven't stepped foot in Ireland since."

"Probably a good idea. Do you like leading your Coalition?"

"It's a pretty good deal. We have a lot of fun. You should join us on a con sometime. Between we chameleons and you leprechauns, the cons we could manage would be glorious."

Lucky loved that idea. "Oh, and just imagine the mischief we could cause!"

They grinned at each other.

~

"Is Zee feeling as horrid as Markos?" Cassie asked Ashlynn.

Ashlynn giggled. "Oh, I'm not sure there's a being anywhere who feels worse than Zee right now. I told him he shouldn't come out tonight. Seriously, I'm starting to worry about alcohol poisoning."

Cassie laughed. "Okay, I shouldn't laugh, but they're dragons. Can you imagine the amount of alcohol they'd have to consume to poison themselves?"

"Well, I'm pretty sure they've made a good start."

The women stared at where Zee and Markos were once more hanging out with the leprechauns and like the idiots they were, desperately attempting to get them to share their secrets.

Of course, they were doing this by drinking heavily.

Again.

Cassie shook her head. "I doubt they'll make it the night."

Ashlynn grinned. "Agreed. Unconsciousness has to be imminent."

Cassie laughed.

As it turned out, Ashlynn was right.

The night wasn't half done before the constant overindulging finally caught up with the dragons.

Too much alcohol combined with not enough sleep night after night meant one minute they were laughing uproariously and the next they were both passed out under the tables while the leprechauns giggled and drank toasts to the foolish dragons.

Ashlynn and Cassie did their duty, of course, by taking a plethora of pictures and immediately texting them to everyone they knew.

Then Cassie went a step further and posted them to the Shenanigans boards, the comments on which entertained both women for the rest of their shifts and made it worth having to shut down the bar without the assistance of their mates.

For once, the leprechauns managed to slip away without causing the dragons endless frustration, if only because they were still unconscious.

8

THE NEXT DAY, Cassie and Ashlynn were quite entertained by their extremely grumpy dragon mates.

Uncertain whether to blame the leprechauns or the women more, both Zee and Markos spent the day glaring and grumbling.

They'd woken on the floor of the bar, under a couple tables, covered in crumbled nachos, bits of pretzels, peanut shells and popcorn kernels.

Crawling out from under there at close to ten in the morning, they were extremely disgruntled to realize they'd been abandoned by their mates, and they made this known to both Ashlynn and Cassie all day long.

They were still grumbling when they arrived to open the bar later that evening.

"You should look at this as a sign," Cassie told them.

"Exactly," Ashlynn said. "You do know stealing is wrong, right?"

"Please," Zee said. "It's not exactly stealing if they can't protect what's theirs."

"Yes, it is," Ashlynn said. "It's totally stealing."

"Yeah, that's the very definition of stealing," Cassie agreed.

"Eh. Maybe by earth standards," Markos said. "But I'm pretty sure their pots of gold aren't on earth."

"Exactly," Zee said. "It's just that following the leprechauns to their realm has been a bit trickier than we expected."

"Right," Ashlynn said, drawling the word out. "Because if you managed to somehow make it to the leprechaun realm, I'm sure they'd be just fine with you stealing their gold and wouldn't do anything to keep you from leaving with it."

"Eh, we're dragons," Markos said. "What could they possibly do?"

"Dragons," Darren groaned as he walked up to join the conversation. "So arrogant."

"Hey. That's what makes us so good at what we do," Markos said. "You do know that all we really need is to catch one."

"Exactly," Zee said. "If we manage that, we can demand to know where their gold is and they'll have to tell us."

"Plus we know someone who can catch one for us." Markos grinned at Darren, who scowled back at him.

"I already told you no."

"Leave Darren alone," Cassie said. "Besides, if that's all there is to it, then why haven't you caught one yet?"

"Yeah," Ashlynn said. "You've been drinking with them every night."

Zee looked horrified. "Shenanigans is neutral territory. We can't just snatch a leprechaun from the bar."

"Or the hotel," Markos said.

"And that's why we have to follow them *out* of the hotel," Zee said. "Then we can grab them and make them take us to their gold."

"I had no idea you were so morally bankrupt," Ashlynn said to her mate.

"Hey, all's fair in hoarding and war," Zee protested.

"Exactly," Markos said. "Why do you think dragons have hordes? Because we're the best hoarders in all the realms."

"And the best thieves," Zee said.

"Beg to differ," Darren said.

"Oh no," Cassie said. "Do *not* encourage them."

"What? I'm just saying. No one is better than a coalition of chameleons."

Cassie snorted. "Unless you're going up against a frolic of leprechauns."

"Come on, Zee. We're not going to get any sympathy here." The two dragons wandered off.

Darren winked at his sister, then followed them to a table full of leprechauns.

No Lucky yet, Cassie saw, but she figured it wouldn't be long.

Kitty wandered up to the bar at that moment, looking rather glum.

Cassie examined her closely, but couldn't see any new green on her, which could be good if it meant the charm's magic was finally wearing off or it could be very bad if its effects were now being felt where they weren't easily seen.

"What's the matter, Kitty?" Ashlynn asked.

Kitty gave a big dramatic sigh. "I don't think anything turned green today."

Cassie bit her lip to keep from laughing.

Because Kitty was very wrong.

Cassie glanced at Ashlynn who gave her wide eyes in return.

"So, Kitty," Cassie said. "Did you happen to brush your teeth this morning?"

"Gross. Of course I did."

"And you didn't notice anything new?"

"Nooo. Logan was still sleeping when I got up so I brushed in the dark." Her eyes widened. "Are my teeth green?"

"Here." Ashlynn pulled a compact mirror out of her purse and passed it to Kitty.

Kitty took one look and let out a shriek of horror. "My tongue is green! It looks like a slab of moldy meat!"

"Well. At least it's not your teeth," Cassie said.

"Not yet anyway." Ashlynn smirked.

Kitty stared in the mirror. "I'm really not liking this development." Her eyes narrowed. "And I do *not* believe that Logan didn't notice. He's kissed me like a thousand times already today." Her eyes widened. "This is why everyone at the hotel was looking at me so strangely! I bet they thought I did it on purpose!"

She whirled around and yelled at Logan across the room, who was keeping his distance, for obvious reasons. "You're in so much trouble! No more kisses for you!"

Logan grinned. It was obvious he knew he had nothing to fear in that regard.

"Dang it." Kitty swung back around to face the bar. "He's so sexy, I'll never be able to follow through on that one."

"And why would you want to?" Ashlynn asked, making Kitty giggle.

"Okay. I don't. But still. He should have told me!"

"Agreed," Cassie said. "But you know, I think maybe you should consider asking the leprechauns to put an end to their tricky charm."

Kitty sighed. "I suppose. But I really liked the green hair and the nails and even the tiny shamrocks."

"Fear not," Ashlynn said. "We can totally get all of that done at the fairy mall. The fairies are quite talented with nails and hair and I bet we could even get them to apply some temporary tattoos for you."

"Or even a real one," Cassie said. "I hear the trolls have a tattoo parlor in the mall."

"Oooh, good idea." Kitty hopped off the stool. "Well, I'm off to throw myself upon the mercy of the leprechauns. Wish me luck."

As Kitty walked off, Cassie said to Ashlynn, "My plan worked."

"What plan?"

"Look." Cassie nodded toward the leprechaun table, where Lucky was now sitting in Darren's lap.

"Oh my goodness!"

"I know. Val really came through for me. He looks so happy."

"This deserves a toast!" Ashlynn said.

"Incognito?"

"Dragon flame."

"Gotcha."

Cassie pulled out two bottles, one of Incognito for her and one of Dragon Flame for Ashlynn. She poured out their shots and stared in amazement as the alcohol turned green the minute it landed inside the glass.

"That's weird," Ashlynn said.

"I know." Cassie picked up her glass, but nothing happened.

No change of colors, no mixing rainbow.

"Hey! Where did all my colors go?" She glared across the room at the leprechauns, who apparently always knew when one of their tricks was about to come to fruition because they were all staring at her, huge grins on their faces.

"Aw, it's just a wee bit of green," Topsy called out.

"A wee bit? It should be a rainbow of colors!" Cassie exclaimed.

"Eh. Green is so much better, don't you think?" Impy asked.

"But I thought you guys liked rainbows," Cassie protested.

The leprechauns all glanced at each other, then chorused, "Propaganda."

"Wait a minute. Does that mean your pots of gold *aren't* under a rainbow after all?" Markos demanded.

Charming grinned. "That's for we leprechauns to know and you dragons to never find out."

The dragons growled in frustration.

Cassie sniffed at her glass. "Well, still smells like Incognito." She clinked her glass against Ashlynn's. "To Darren and Lucky."

"To true mates."

They bolted back their shots and grinned at each other.

"This is ridiculous!" The doors burst open and Megan, Jessica and Lara trooped inside, their mates directly behind them.

"What now?" Cassie asked when they reached the bar.

"All the water in Dory's room has turned green!" Lara exclaimed.

"Really?"

"Yes! And none of our spells are turning it back." Megan scowled.

"Even the toilet bowl water's green," Jessica said.

Her words set off the leprechauns who started up a storm of chortling and giggling and laughing.

"That's a good trick," Silly said between laughs.

"Who thought that one up?" Caper asked.

"Me." Tricky sent a mischievous grin their way. "Thought it'd be funny to pee in green water."

If the leprechauns thought green toilet bowl water was funny before, the thought of actually peeing in said water was so hilarious they almost fell to floor, they laughed so hard.

"This is getting out of hand," Markos said.

That's when the fairies arrived.

9

DARREN WAS ENJOYING playing with Lucky's hair when Lily stormed into the bar, clearly furious, with a number of unknown fairies at her back.

"Uh-oh," Logan said.

"What is it?" Kitty asked.

"Looks like Lily ran out of patience. Those are all very high-ranking fairies from our realm."

"This is completely out of hand," Lily raged at the leprechauns. "There are green shamrocks all over the floors, googly eyes and shamrocks on the walls, our reservation computer has turned into a giant shamrock, all the hotel rooms and the keys for those rooms are no longer labeled with numbers, but instead with shamrocks. *Shamrocks!"* She shrieked. "Everywhere I go, it's shamrocks, shamrocks, shamrocks.

"How am I supposed to know what key to give our guests, not to mention how are they supposed to find their rooms if they're all labeled with shamrocks?" She paced back and forth in front of the giggling leprechauns, flinging her arms this way and that, wings fluttering in fury.

"Every single floor is labeled with arrows indicating this way for these numbers or that way for those numbers, but guess what those signs say now? Shamrock to shamrock this way!" She flung one arm to the left. "Shamrock to shamrock that way!" She flung her other arm in the opposite direction.

She whirled to face the leprechauns who were clearly having the time of their lives, chortling and chuckling as the fairy ranted and raged at them. "How are we supposed to have a functioning hotel if you leprechauns keep messing things up?"

Silence.

"Well?" Lily shrieked.

"Were you wanting an answer?" Charming asked.

"Of course I want an answer," she shouted.

"I just want to be clear," Charming said, a ridiculously innocent look on his face. "Are you accusing the Leprechaun Nation of being responsible for these terrible occurrences?"

"Terrible occurrences? You mean tricks, don't you? Tricks you people specialize in!"

"Oh, now, that's harsh," Lucky said.

Darren had a hard time containing his chuckle and he knew Lucky could feel his chest shaking in amusement.

"It really is," Charming agreed.

This was just getting better and better. The sibling leprechauns were hilarious when they got going.

"After all," Lucky said. "We're just sitting here, innocently minding our own business, having a wee drink with friends." She glanced over her shoulder at Darren. "And mates." She gave him a quick kiss, then turned back to the fairies. "Then, out of nowhere, we're suddenly being accused of *terrible* misdeeds."

"Oh, go sell that troll manure somewhere else!" Lily snapped, making Darren snort with laughter. He'd never seen the fairy quite so riled up before. "Just tell us! What exactly do you want?"

Lucky shook her head. "I don't understand."

"Nor I," Charming agreed. "Whatever gave you the idea we want something?"

"Because leprechauns are never *this* annoying! You want something and I know it. So just tell us what it is and maybe we can negotiate."

At that word, Markos and Zee appeared to perk up.

"Fine," Lucky said. "We'd like our banishment lifted."

"Seriously?" Lily exclaimed. "You cause all this mischief and think it will convince us to *lift* your banishment?"

"Hold on a minute. What banishment?" Markos asked.

"The fairies banned the leprechauns from ever setting foot in the fairy realm, which just so happens to include the fairy mall, a good three hundred years ago."

"Why would you banish paying customers?" Zee exclaimed.

"Because they never paid," Lily snarled.

"What are you talking about?" Charming protested. "We always paid."

"Yes, with your magic coins," Logan said.

"Magic coins that are no good in here, by the way," Cassie called from the bar.

The leprechauns all gasped.

"Cassie, we would never try to use our magic coins in neutral territory," Lucky said. "Why, that might actually get us banned from all Shenanigans everywhere!"

"Like you were banned from the fairy mall?" Lily asked.

"Oh, come on. That was just a few bad actors and you banished our entire species! Plus we're fairies like you," Lucky said.

"She's right," Charming said. "I honestly can't believe you would banish your own kind like that."

"But you're not like us," Lily exclaimed. "You're tricky, tricky fairies and we don't like being tricked. "

"Well, that's not very kind of you, judging us just because we like a good trick now and then," Mischief said.

"Yes, and let's be clear," Lucky said. "Our banishment had nothing to do with our magic coins. It was that ill-fated love affair."

"Ugh. Not that stupid story again," Logan groaned.

"Those two *were* stupid," Lily agreed.

"What are you talking about?" Zee asked.

"Well," Lucky began. "Legend has it that once upon a time a fairy princess fell in love with a leprechaun prince."

Darren grinned. Lucky had told him this story just the night before. He was interested to see if the fairies agreed with the leprechauns' version of it.

"The only problem was," Charming said, "their parents hated each other with a passion."

"Something about a trick one leprechaun played on a fairy about a hundred years before these two were even born," Lucky said.

"Seriously?" Zee exclaimed.

"Oh, yes," Logan said. "Fairies can hold quite the grudge."

"And it was a horrible trick," Lily exclaimed.

"It was brilliant!" Charming protested.

"*Anyway,*" Lucky said. "These two fell in love, but their

parents were determined they would *not* spend their lives together."

"Even though legend has it they were mates," Charming said.

"So, the fairy family, desperate to end the match, got all the fairies riled up about magic coins in the mall and got the leprechauns banished. This meant, of course, that the leprechaun could no longer venture into the fairy realm to visit his lover. This didn't stop the fairy from visiting him, of course. Unfortunately, the leprechaun prince blamed the fairy princess and her family for his people's banishment and they had a terrible fight. She ran away in tears and got caught in a storm. He caught up with her just in time for the two of them to be swept away in a flood."

"Of course, both families blamed the other," Charming said, "and there was no forgiveness to be found. The banishment became permanent and leprechauns have not been welcome in the fairy realm ever since."

"That's a terrible story," Ashlynn exclaimed.

"I know!" Lucky said. "Can you imagine? Never being able to shop at the fairy mall? Now *that* was a cruel and unusual punishment."

"I was talking about the prince and princess."

"Oh, yes. That was sad too."

"But not as sad as our banishment," Charming said.

"Especially since we weren't even using those magic coins on the fairies," Lucky said. "They punished us when we weren't even targeting them."

"Oh please, you know that fairies don't run every shop in the mall," Lily said. "Management was getting constant complaints from the trolls, the dragons, the gryphons, the gargoyles, the mermaids, the—"

"Yes, yes, we get it," Charming said. "But they didn't even try to negotiate."

"Negotiate?" Markos leaned forward. "We dragons love to negotiate."

"No, no." Lily said. "There will be no negotiating with leprechauns. They cannot be trusted."

"How rude!" Lucky exclaimed. "I cannot believe you would tarnish every leprechaun with the same brush."

"Disappointing," Charming agreed, "and such a shame the fairies are so bigoted."

Lily gasped. "We're not bigoted!"

"Really?" Lucky asked. "Because I'll have you know that leprechauns are very trustworthy. You can trust us to keep our word."

"And strictly your word," Logan said.

Lucky grinned. "Exactly."

"Look. We can't help you with your banishment from the fairy realm," Markos said. "That's up to the fancy-schmancy fairies to decide. But we *can* help you with the fairy mall."

The leprechauns all smiled.

"We know," they chorused.

"Wait! You can't do that," Lily exclaimed.

"I don't understand," Ashlynn said. "How are you going to help them again?"

"Well, the fairy mall may be *called* the fairy mall, but about half of it happens to cross over into the dragon realm," Markos said.

"And that half," Zee said, "belongs to the dragons."

Darren grinned. Suddenly all the leprechaun tricks in the hotel and at the bar were making a whole lot more sense.

"So," Markos said to the leprechauns, "What are you offering?"

"Commerce, of course," Lucky said. "We leprechauns love to shop, so you can pretty much be guaranteed a lot of sales if we're given access to the dragon side of the mall." She glared at Lily and the fairies standing behind her. "Though the fairies certainly won't benefit."

"Also," Charming said, "Shoes."

"Shoes?"

"Yes. We would like a store in the mall to sell our most excellent shoes. It would be a boon for all the beings of the realms, to have access to the leprechauns' greatest inventions."

"Are they as awesome as our fairy slippers?" Ashlynn asked.

Charming frowned. "Fairy slippers?"

Lily spun and frantically shook her head at Ashlynn, who look confused.

"What's this about fairy slippers?" Lucky asked.

"Oh, nothing, I'm sure," Lily said.

Lucky narrowed her eyes, leaned forward and glared at Lily. "She wouldn't happen to be talking about our very popular, very expensive *leprechaun* slippers, now would she?"

"Oh, where would you get that idea?" Lily looked rather nervous.

And guilty.

Darren feared quite suddenly that these negotiations might end in war.

And all because of something called fairy slippers, or leprechaun slippers, as the case might be.

"She is!" Mischief leapt to his feet. "How did an earth being get her hands on our slippers?"

Everyone stared at Ashlynn, who said in a hesitant voice, "I bought them at the mall?"

"The fairy mall?" A roar echoed through the room as the leprechauns, though full of mischief usually, proved they were also most definitely fairy when they got mad.

"Our slippers are being sold in a mall we've been banished from?" Charming snarled.

"And you're calling them fairy slippers?" Lucky screeched.

Darren thought she might have leapt across the table and strangled Lily if it weren't for the fact that he had an arm around her waist and was busy stroking a soothing hand down her back.

"Okay. Let's all calm down," Zee said. "It's clear there's been a bit of confusion around these slippers so perhaps we should open negotiations with that issue. Here's the thing. Lily doesn't own the mall or sell the slippers. So, we need to get the right fairies to the table."

Lily looked over her shoulder at the five fairies who had followed her in, but up to that point had remained silent.

The one at the center nodded and stepped forward. "*We* are the right fairies." With that pronouncement, all moved forward to sit across the table from the leprechauns, and negotiations began in earnest.

It took hours, even with the dragons acting as mediators.

Darren was quite impressed.

He would never have thought the dragons had it in them for such diplomacy, but they were truly skilled at working through the centuries of bad blood and anger on both sides.

The fairies eventually admitted they had spies who would slip into the leprechaun realm and purchase leprechaun slippers that they then turned around and sold at the fairy mall at a very high upcharge.

Darren worried that Lucky might explode, she was fairly vibrating in rage at that point, but she managed to contain her fury and channeled it into negotiating furiously for a percentage of the profits from the last three hundred years.

The fairies protested this might bankrupt them, but apparently they were quite rich, something that seemed to be public knowledge, so no one really believed them. As a result, the fairies eventually conceded, though they negotiated fiercely for as small a percentage as possible.

The leprechauns were also granted a shop inside the mall on the dragon side, of which the dragons would reap a percentage of sales.

At this point, the fairies demanded to know where the benefit was for them.

"You've given them everything they wanted and we've gained nothing," Lily protested.

Markos just raised an eyebrow. "You banished them for centuries, yet still profited off their ingenuity. And you call *them* the tricksters? Perhaps you should be grateful we've managed to broker peace and try negotiating some good will to go with it."

"Well," Lucky said. "If you lift the banishment from the *fairy* side of the mall, the fairies might enjoy quite a bit of profits from leprechaun commerce."

"Likewise," Charming said, "if you lift the ban from the fairy hotel, you might find a lot of leprechauns are spending their hard-earned money to stay there."

The fairy who had taken the lead in all the negotiations glared at the leprechauns, then said, "Only if the leprechauns agree to *never* use their magic coins on *any* fairy property *ever again.*"

"Agreed!" Every leprechaun in the room chorused in unison and negotiations were finally concluded.

Lucky rewarded Darren with a passionate kiss, and the celebration, both in the bar and later in Darren's hotel room, lasted all night long.

10

IT WAS FINALLY time for Cassie's mating ceremony, which was taking place at Starlight, a night club in the fairy mall.

This meant that since the leprechauns' banishment had been lifted, they expected an invite as well.

As a result, her ceremony wasn't quite as elegant as Ashlynn and Zee's had been.

Instead, it was raucous and loud and full of hilarity and mischief.

Every drink served was green and shamrocks were everywhere, but Cassie didn't mind. She spent the evening dancing with her mate, mostly lost in a haze of joy and lust, though Darren did steal her away for a brother-sister dance.

"Are you happy?" he asked her.

"So happy. All my dreams have come true. How about you and Lucky?"

He grinned. "She's met the members of the Coalition who are here for your ceremony and she's planning to go back with me when everyone leaves tomorrow. We'll figure it out.

A bit of time in her realm, a bit in ours, a lot of cons, a lot of tricks."

Cassie grinned up at him. "It's going to be a beautiful life, Darren."

"It really is."

"I'll claim my mate back now." Markos executed some complicated dance move, somehow pulling Cassie into his arms while passing Lucky, with whom he'd been dancing, into Darren's.

The last Cassie saw of her brother, he was swaying in place, staring into his mate's eyes, clearly enchanted by what he saw there.

~

"I love you, Lucky mine."

Lucky's heart clenched at those words. "I love you too, Darren. I can't believe how lucky we are. We found each other, even though we were living in different realms."

"And I can't imagine a more perfect mate–match," Darren said. "The trickster and the conman."

"It sounds like some cheesy romance novel."

Darren grinned. "Well, we are experiencing our own happily ever after."

"We are."

They dance for hours, only breaking apart once more, this time to allow Lucky a dance with her brother.

"Only one," she warned.

Charming grinned and swung her out across the dance floor, then pulled her back in. "We did it, Lucky."

"I know. I can't believe it."

"The greatest trick our Nation has ever attempted and we made it happen."

"Was it really a trick though? I mean, we got what we wanted, sure, but in the end, they agreed."

Charming laughed. "Of course, they did, darling. Those fairies weren't going to risk the sheer volume of trickery the entire Nation was willing to bring their way."

"You don't think they might have just abandoned the hotel? I mean, it's happened before."

"Not a chance. Did you see that fairy with her mate? That hotel is his legacy. She would never make him give it up."

Lucky smiled. "You're right. So we won."

"We did."

~

Kitty danced in Logan's arms for hours on end. She loved the feel of his arms around her and the way he slid his fingers through her hair.

She especially loved how he liked to play with the one green streak that hadn't yet faded.

"Dance, my lady?" Jolly approached with a grin on his face.

Logan scowled, but Kitty just patted his hand and murmured, "Let it be, Logan." She stepped away from her mate into the leprechaun's arms. "So what kind of mischief have you caused this evening?"

"Me? Cause mischief? I don't know what would give you that idea."

"So you're not responsible for the toilet bowl water that's green or the fact that the wedding cake has shamrocks for a bride and groom or the green strobe lights or—"

"Oh no, not at all. This is Cassie's mating celebration. We would never play tricks, though we might leave her a few gifts."

"Ohhh. Gifts, are they?"

"Indeed. You know that earth saying, 'Something old, something new, something borrowed, something blue?'"

"Yes."

"Well we decided it should be 'Something lucky, something mean, something Irish, something green.'"

"Oh dear."

~

When Darren finally managed to reclaim Lucky from her brother, he told her, "You're mine for the rest of the night. No more dances with anyone else but me."

Lucky smiled and stepped into his arms. "That sounds perfectly lovely."

And so they danced the night away in each other's arms, enveloped in a cocoon of love and joy and wonder.

~

"Oh no," Megan groaned.

"What is it?" Jessica asked.

"What are *they* doing here?"

"Who?" Lara asked.

"The Covingtons."

"No!" Jessica exclaimed. "Where?"

"There." Megan nodded across the room and her sisters swung around to stare.

Their twin cousins stood across the room, almost identical in appearance, but so very opposite in personality.

"They're friends of Cassie," their aunt Dory explained. "The three of them worked together at a Shenanigans a number of years ago and have kept in touch ever since. I'm going to go say hello."

Lara waited until Dory was out of earshot before she spoke again. "This place is doomed."

"We should evacuate," Jessica said, "and not just the club. The entire mall."

Megan burst into laughter. "Oh come on. They're not that bad!"

"Their out-of-control casting almost burned down their high school," Jessica said.

"Not to mention when they turned their cat blue," Lara exclaimed.

"And that car accident on highway nine," Jessica said. "It's a miracle no one was hurt."

"Also, that mini hurricane. If you hadn't been there, Megan, to spin it out to sea, I have no idea what would have happened," Lara said.

"They were young then," Megan said. "Surely they have better control by now."

"Control? You have met Serena, haven't you? I mean, look at her. Here a few minutes and already surrounded by leprechauns. That is not a good combination," Lara said.

"Not at all," Jessica said. "So I repeat, we should definitely evacuate."

Megan sighed. "Well, at least Samantha has some control."

The three of them switched their attention to Serena's twin, who was standing at rigid attention, listening and nodding solemnly to something a leprechaun was saying to her.

The leprechaun was giggling and gesturing, but Samantha wasn't even smiling.

"Too much control, if you ask me," Lara muttered.

Megan groaned. "And here I was hoping she'd have learned to loosen up, even if just a little, by now. That control combined with her sister's lack of it—" She shook her head.

"Terrifying," the three sisters said in unison.

~

~

Read on to meet the Covington twins in an excerpt from *No Rest for the Wicked.*

EXCERPT

There was something about Jack cuddling sweet Lexi in his arms and looking so natural doing it, that made Samantha's heart rate pick up.

Handing the little girl off to her older brother, Jack turned to Samantha and winked.

A wave of heat rushed down her spine and she spun on her heels, intending to hurry away.

Except somehow her body overrode her mind and she swung back around, grabbed him by the hand and dragged him out of the main room and down the hall to the walk-in linen closet.

She jerked open the door and pushed him inside, followed him in and closed the door behind her. All the while, her brain was shrieking, "Abort, abort!" Hands on hips, she advanced on him. "What exactly are you doing?"

Jack looked a bit stunned. He glanced around at the shelves of towels and cleaning supplies, then back at Samantha. "Uh. I think that should be my question. What are *you* doing, Samantha? Not that I mind being dragged into a linen closet." He waggled his brows at her.

Samantha's heart gave a little leap and then began to race. Damn the man. He was messing with her equilibrium and taking total advantage. "My mother put you up to this, didn't she?"

Jack looked confused. "What are you talking about?"

"Oh stop acting so innocent. You're taking advantage of the reckless curse."

"The reckless—"

"You need to stop being—" She waved her arms in the air.

"Being what?"

"So very much you!"

Jack grinned at her.

That freaking sexy grin again. She just couldn't take it.

"And who exactly am I supposed to be if not me?"

Samantha growled low in her throat, then lunged at him.

She caught him by the lapels, dragged him down and kissed him.

Heat spiraled through her and then Jack took over the kiss.

He backed her against the door, leaned into her and utterly ravaged her mouth.

Only the door and his hands on her hips kept her from sinking to the floor in a puddle of goo.

Long, wicked moments later, he pulled away from her mouth to trail a line of kisses across her check and down her neck, then back up again.

"Damn," he muttered in her ear, bringing her back to her senses.

She pushed against his chest, trying to get a bit of space between them, trying desperately to catch her breath and to think for a moment. Dear goddess, everything was spiraling out of control, most especially her own emotions and actions. What had she been thinking, dragging this utterly scrumptious man into a linen closet with her? She was supposed to be avoiding him, not attacking him.

"I have to go." She pushed him back and reached for the doorknob behind her. "I have to get back out there, but—" She caught a breath at the thought of everyone seeing her in this state of agitation. "Do I look okay?" She reached up and patted at her hair, then smoothed down her shirt. She looked down at herself, but couldn't tell if she was put together enough to fool the press and anyone else who saw her.

And what if someone saw her exiting the closet? What if someone had seen her dragging Jack *into* it? This was a nightmare.

Jack chuckled. "You look beautiful, as always." He reached out a hand and tucked a lock behind her ear.

Samantha's breath hitched in her throat as she stared up at him. God. He was just so— "No. This, this right here is what I'm talking about." She waved an arm through the space between them. "You need to stop it. Stop acting so damn sexy." And she stormed out of the closet.

It wasn't until she'd reached the main room that she realized she hadn't even looked first to be sure no one was in the hall to see her exiting the linen closet.

She was utterly doomed.

Jack stared at the linen closet door as it slammed behind Samantha's retreating form, then grinned.

"Damn."

He just hadn't seen that coming at all.

But now that he had Samantha's taste on his tongue and seared into his memory banks, now that he'd experienced her passion, there was nothing that would keep him from claiming her as his own.

He was fully invested now.

Samantha Covington's days as a single witch were numbered.

Start reading *No Rest for the Wicked* today.

THANK YOU FOR READING

Please consider leaving a review on

your favorite book site.

If you would like to be notified of Pepper's new releases, please sign up here: www.peppermcgraw.com/newsletter

Join Pepper's reader groups on Facebook:

Matchmaking Cats of the Goddesses

The Shenanigans Crew

OTHER BOOKS BY PEPPER

BLACKTHORN ACADEMY

Monster's Reward

Monster's Madness

MATCHMAKING CATS OF THE GODDESSES

Catnapped

The Real McCat

Unbearably Cute

A Catmas to Remember

This Cat's for You

Santa Kitty

Hocus Purrcus

Abra-CAT-Abra

Tridents & Tails

Her Purrfect Familiar

Chocolate Furnanigans

Satan's Kitty

Valen-Cats

Catanic Rituals

A Beautiful Catship

Going Catty

Grave Cattitude

MURRYSVILLE COALITION

The Crazy Cheetah Lady

One Sad Kitty

SHENANIGANS

Shifter Shenanigans

Witchy Shenanigans

Full Moon Shenanigans

Hotel Shenanigans

Dragon Shenanigans

Undercover Shenanigans

Spooky Shenanigans

Holiday Shenanigans

Valentine Shenanigans

Lucky Shenanigans

STORIES OF THE VEIL

Guardians of the Veil

Astra

Glory

Luna

Zara

Guardians of the Realms

WICKED

No Rest for the Wicked

Wicked Is As Wicked Does

ANTHOLOGIES & COLLECTIONS

MATCHMAKING CATS OF THE GODDESSES BUNDLES

The Cat's Meow

Holly Jolly Pawliday

Familiar Meowgic

The Devil's in the Cattails

SHENANIGANS ANTHOLOGIES

Crazed

Amazed

Holidazed

STORIES OF THE VEIL

The Unveiled

The Veiled

COMPLETE SERIES COLLECTIONS

Shenanigans

The Veil

Wicked

ABOUT THE AUTHOR

WWW.PEPPERMCGRAW.COM

PEPPER MCGRAW is a USA Today Bestselling Author of paranormal romance. Her life to date has sadly been paranormal-free, but she expects that will change in time. Until then, she keeps herself busy writing (and reading) paranormal romances.

Pepper loves animals, especially cats, and spends her free time volunteering at local shelters and for Trap-Neuter-Release programs. She's had the supreme honor of winning occasional head butts and meows from the community cats in her neighborhood and has even convinced a few to come inside and adopt her as their own.

amazon.com/author/peppermcgraw
bookbub.com/authors/pepper-mcgraw
facebook.com/ShenanigansSeries
goodreads.com/peppermcgraw
instagram.com/peppermcgraw_author
tiktok.com/@peppermcgraw
x.com/peppermcgraw

www.ingramcontent.com/pod-product-compliance
Lightning Source LLC
LaVergne TN
LVHW010049110826
845155LV00028B/263